He walks the trail of Revenge...He taunts with subtle Threats...He Lures Innocence to Death...

A revenge-seeking psychopathic killer suddenly invades the small, private world of a congressman's daughter who is intent on reconciling her faith with her desire for love and family.

A Congressman's Daughter...A Deceptive Trail of Murder...A Secret Concealed Far Too Long...

A young woman of faith, whose principal desire is to love and be loved, is propelled into the arms of a man she has long considered an enemy, when a homicidal, scripture-quoting stalker viciously pursues her.

SMALL WHISPERS

ANNETTA P. LEE

Genesis Press, Inc.

Mount Blue

An imprint of Genesis Press, Inc.
Publishing Company

Genesis Press, Inc.
P.O. Box 101
Columbus, MS 39703

ISBN-13: 978-1-58571-251-9
ISBN-10: 1-58571-251-5
Manufactured in the United States of America

First Edition

Visit us at www.genesis-press.com
or call at 1-888-Indigo-1

DEDICATION

I dedicate this book to my Lord and Savior, Jesus Christ, who placed a desire in me to express His way through fiction.

I can do all things through Christ who strengthens me.

ACKNOWLEDGMENTS

Thanks to my dear friend, Kathy Shelley, for your support, advice, wisdom, laughter, and friendship; and to my sister, Beverly Carter, owner of *Greenleaf Flowers and Gifts,* which I used to design *Small Whispers;* to Dr. Rodney Sandberg, who advised me on several aspects of the political arena; and finally to my cousin, Ronald Reese Davis, who advised me in procedures of the pharmaceutical industry. Many thanks and may God richly bless each of you.

SMALL WHISPERS

How faint the whisper we hear of him! Who then can understand the thunder of his power?
—Job 26:14

PROLOGUE

Rose Creek, Washington
June 1983

The afternoon was warm and sticky despite the gentle wind wafting through the leaves of the large shade trees. Ten-year-old Kendal spotted her best friend, Sheila, behind an evergreen and raced towards the back steps to touch home base. Although quite chubby, Sheila shot across the yard with lightning speed, beating her by a blink of the eye.

Kendal looked around the backyard again, and it appeared free of any other hide-and-seekers. In actuality, five other children were hiding behind Nana's numerous shrubs and trees.

Then she saw her brother, Eric, who was two years younger, rushing towards her from behind a rose bush. She rolled her eyes in annoyance. Normally, Nana would have let him go to the schoolyard and play with some of his own friends, but they had been instructed to stay in the back yard, as Nana was expecting a reporter from the local newspaper. Both she and Eric had been excited to hear that the paper wanted to run a story about their dad, Master Sergeant Stan Boyd, who was now stationed in Germany.

Kendal missed her daddy. The Air Force had sent him overseas three years ago. He was all alone and had been home only once, but she got to talk to him every other Saturday night. Sometimes she would cry herself to sleep afterwards, but she never told Nana about that.

"Out!" she shrieked, touching home base. "Ollie, ollie oxen free!" Four other children appeared from behind various garden shields. "Eric is *it* this time."

At the squeaky sound of the screen door, they all looked towards the porch in anticipation of Nana's homemade cookies and milk. But she didn't have any this time.

"It's time to come in, children," Nana said. "Our guest is here." Raising her hand to shield her eyes from the sunlight, she peered down at the upturned faces. "The rest of you go on home. You can play again tomorrow."

Though eager to talk about her daddy, Kendal was nonetheless disappointed when they had to stop playing. Once inside, she forgot all about play after being introduced to the reporter, Jack Sumner. The tall, thin man had a sad smile and large blotches on his pale face. He reminded Kendal of her daddy before he shaved in the mornings. She recalled how scratchy his face was when he would kiss her cheek.

"Hey, kids," the man said. "I'm here from the *Rose Creek Clarion* to write a story about your father."

Kendal wrinkled her nose and stepped back, repulsed by the man's smelly breath. For reasons she did not quite understand, she felt sorry for Sumner.

After a brief tour of the house and lots of pictures, they all returned to the living room to talk. Kendal sat close to her grandmother, while her brother disassembled an old radio on the floor in front of the fireplace.

Nana began by telling Sumner about her only son's childhood. Kendal thought it was funny how much her grandmother sounded like her teacher when company was around.

"Can I go back outside now, Nana?" Eric pleaded, looking up from the floor.

Nana nodded her reluctant consent and Kendal used the brief interruption to study the reporter. He didn't smile much, and he looked around as if he were afraid of something. Sweat beaded on his brow and his hands shook. He turned suddenly and took a quick shot of her and Nana on the sofa.

Kendal had noticed that one of Sumner's shoestrings was frayed. She wondered if he was alone like her daddy, or maybe he just didn't have time to buy new ones. "Mr. Sumner?"

"Yes, Kendal?" he replied.

"Do you have any children?"

"Kendal Diane," Nana snapped, a disapproving frown on her face. "That is none of your business. We don't ask personal questions like that."

"Aw, it's all right, Mrs. Boyd. I don't mind. As a matter of fact, I have one son. He's away with his mother right now."

Nana leaned forward and cleared her throat. "I appreciate your lenience, but my grandchildren are taught to stay within set bounds."

Kendal swallowed a lump of embarrassment and slunk back on the couch behind Nana. Mr. Sumner probably thought she was rude and nosy. Nana casually placed an arm around her shoulders, gently urging her forward again.

"Of course, ma'am," he said, winking at Kendal when Nana looked away. "You have a very unusual first name, Mrs. Boyd. Would you give me the correct spelling?"

"E-u-l-a."

"Do you have any idea when your son will return from Germany?"

"He'll be back in about a year. It's an unaccompanied tour, so the children couldn't go." She looked down at Kendal and squeezed her shoulders. "It's hard on them, too. But everything will be fine again when he comes home."

"Did you know the Democratic Party was eyeing him to represent a district in Spokane?"

"I've heard talk," she said. "I don't know if anything will come of it. If it does, he will probably sell his company. He has a small textile company, you know."

"Yes, ma'am. Who runs it while he's in the military?"

"He's got a general manager."

The man made several notes in the pad he held. "I understand Tessa Boyd died giving birth to little Eric."

Nana abruptly turned a cutting glare on the man. "If you're finished with your pictures and questions, my granddaughter and I have a few things to attend to."

Just then Eric's frantic scream came from the backyard, and Nana bolted to her feet. Kendal stood to follow, but her grandmother held up her hand. "Sit here with Mr. Sumner."

Kendal turned silently towards the reporter, who was now hurriedly collecting his camera equipment and notebooks. "Great. You can help carry my equipment, Kendal."

"Eric's probably climbed that old tree again," Nana said, rushing towards the kitchen.

5

In a matter of moments, Sumner had snapped his camera case shut. "Kendal, I'm sorry you were scolded. Would you mind helping me to my car?"

"Sure," she said, as he handed the smallest of his bags to her.

As they walked towards the door, he pulled out a red lollipop and handed it to her. "This is for being a good girl today."

"No, thank you," she said. "We're not suppose—"

"I won't take no for an answer," he interrupted, bending to kiss her cheek. "Your grandmother won't mind. She knew I would bring you a treat." She took the candy and stepped back, touching the spot where his scruffy chin had brushed against her face. "Did you know you were born in Baltimore, Maryland?"

Her eyes widened and her mouth dropped open. "How did you know?"

They moved outside and through the front gate. He placed the large case on the backseat of the car and turned back to her. "Do you know what adoption means, sweetheart?"

She was pleased that she indeed knew what the word meant. "Yes, sir. I have a friend in school that's adopted."

Sumner frowned and squeezed his chin as if he had forgotten something. Kendal was about to offer to go back and check the living room when he spoke up. "I wonder if he was stolen from his real parents. Things like that happen sometimes."

She cocked her head to the side. "Stolen?"

"Yeah, sometimes babies are stolen right out of the hospital. But that just means they're special babies. Everybody loves special babies. You're special, Kendal. Did you know that?"

Kendal beamed, her eyes shining. "Yes, sir. Nana says God loves me more than anybody else could. Even her and Daddy and Eric."

Kendal held the camera bag underneath her arm and removed the wrapper from the lollipop. "Can I have a lollipop for Eric, too?"

He reached for her hand. "Maybe later. Right now, I want to tell you something nobody else can know about. Eric and your grandmother are busy, so we can go and talk."

As the sweetness of the candy melted in her mouth, Kendal's stomach danced with excitement. "A real secret?"

"A real secret," he assured her, leading her around to the other side of the car.

Though young, Kendal thought it strange that Sumner had parked on the street rather than in the driveway. When he opened the door, she handed him the camera case, but he grabbed her arm and thrust her into the seat. Alarmed, she pulled away and scrambled halfway out of the car.

"No, I'll get in trouble." Her heart was beginning to pound.

"No, you won't," he said, shoving her further into the car. "Nana knows." He bent down and buckled her seatbelt, then gently stroked her face with his fingers. "You're such a pretty little girl, and your skin is so smooth and brown."

Distressed, Kendal shrank back and began to unbuckle the seatbelt. "I need to get back."

"No," he said, his voice edged with something she sensed but didn't recognize. "Besides, I need to tell you the secret. Remember?"

Her innocent love of secrets overcame her growing alarm. She settled back against the seat, curious to hear something nobody else knew. "What is it?"

He glanced around guardedly, then hurried to the other side and hopped in. "Let's go where nobody can hear."

Kendal's stomach felt the way it did when Sheila pushed her too high on the swing. "Can't you tell me here?" she asked, fidgeting with the seatbelt.

Sumner grasped her hand firmly and started the engine. Then he sneered, displaying crooked, stained teeth. "The secret is that I'm your real daddy, Kendal. You were adopted by the Boyds, you really belong to me. Nobody loves you like I do. Not even God."

As the car pulled away from the curb, she glanced back at the house. Now terrified and screaming, she managed to unbuckle her seatbelt and began wildly flailing the man with her fists. "You can't be my daddy! My daddy's brown like me, and he's in Germany."

He smirked and struck her in the face with the back of his hand. "Sit back and shut up, kid. I'm your daddy now. Don't ever forget that." He laughed and stared into the rearview mirror to see if anyone was watching. "And if you know what's good for you, you'll do everything I tell you."

-ONE-

"Frank? Missing?"

An eerie sensation crept down Kendal's spine and settled in her gut. It took all her powers of concentration to fully grasp what the man was saying. He had introduced himself as an agent with the Office of Criminal Investigations, a division of the Food and Drug Administration. She stared at him.

"Yes," Agent Mike Sanner said. "Dr. Frank Peck went missing several days ago. Just after learning of his possible arrest."

Kendal pressed her back into the conference-room chair and set a perplexed gaze on her manager, Jed Mason, and three company executives. Having worked at Howard-Hadley Laboratories for five years as a pharmaceutical rep, she knew that the FDA summoning her to a meeting with all three executives meant something serious was up. It obviously had much to do with one of her clients—a client who just happened to have proposed to her.

She felt like a lone rabbit in the midst of ravenous wolves. "Arrest? For what?" Jed evaded her eyes and focused on dabbing his brow with a paper towel he had grabbed from the wet bar.

Agent Sanner cleared his throat. "Miss Boyd, Howard-Hadley Laboratories has been under investigation for several months, and so has Dr. Peck. The FBI was just about to arrest him for diagnosing and treating nonexistent conditions, as well as for purchasing and selling drugs this company manufactures. I understand you have been the doctor's rep for almost as long as you've been here."

Fear and anger knotted inside her. "Me? You think I gave him drugs?"

"It's logical. I understand the two of you are…involved. I was hoping you would want to avoid possible prosecution and tell us where we can find him."

She withered a bit under the intense scrutiny of everyone in the room, but she bravely met each gaze in turn. Olivia Howard, the company's largest shareholder, looked almost amused as she stared back. Walter Hadley Sr., looked pale and annoyed, keeping his eyes fixed on the papers in front of him. But Walt Jr. maintained a sympathetic expression throughout the interview, smiling and nodding encouragingly as she answered the agent's questions.

It suddenly dawned on her that she was being set up as a scapegoat. Based on Jed's earlier innuendoes and subtle finger-pointing, she was sure of it. Her face grew hot with indignation as she glared at Jed, who was still mopping his brow. Despite her plan to leave the company soon, she couldn't allow her name to be dragged through the mud.

Suddenly, aware she would probably need legal advice, she thought of Jackson North, the attorney assisting her and her roommate, Sheila Dodd, with a personal business acquisition. While he wasn't a criminal attorney, he could perhaps advise her. She pushed her chair back from the table. "If you don't mind, I want to phone my attorney before answering any more of your questions."

Agent Sanner straightened and cleared his throat. "This is an informal inquiry that is part of an ongoing investigation into the affiliation between this company and Dr. Peck, Miss Boyd. Since you seem to be the only common denominator between these two subjects, the investigation also includes you."

"All the more reason to phone my attorney and let him know what's going on," she said, sounding braver than she felt. "And contrary to what Mr. Mason here might have told you, Dr. Peck and I were not involved in any way other than professionally."

Although she felt guilty for failing to mention Frank's persistent attempts to move their relationship to another level, she had no intention of giving them more ammunition to use against her.

Having mustered a sufficient amount of anger to boost her daring, Kendal pulled her employee badge from her jacket and tossed it onto the table in front of Jed Mason. Then she hurried from the room to phone Jackson.

Like lightning flashing across a stormy sky, flashbulbs exploded in Kendal's face the instant she and Jackson moved through the company's main doors. She flinched and recoiled at the very idea of storms. She didn't like them. She didn't like reporters, either. She cringed when one of them shoved a microphone into her face. "Do you think Dr. Peck is guilty of this scam, Miss Boyd?"

"No comment," snapped Jackson, as he guided her down the steps.

"C'mon, Miss Boyd, were you a party to this con? Will the feds arrest you?"

She heard a giggle to her left, but refused to turn her head in either direction. "She'll get off. Nothing like being the congressman's daughter."

"Does Congressman Boyd know what his little girl has been up to?" shouted another reporter.

Her heart pounded as she thought how much they hated her—almost as much as she hated them. She continued staring straight ahead, aware of Jackson's hand holding her arm firmly and pulling her towards his car. "I'm parked towards the back," he whispered. "Keep walking. We'll pick up your car later."

"What will the ice princess do if she's locked up in a cell?" someone shouted.

Reporters thought they were so clever, she mused. She had been the notorious ice princess ever since she was nineteen and had attacked a reporter, smashing his camera against a park railing. It was during an uncommon visit to see her father in Washington. She had lost her temper when two cutthroat reporters rushed her father regarding a vote and began flashing pictures of them despite his protests. She had never lived down her explosive temper, which of course was exaggerated by her refusal to speak with any of them.

"Congressman Boyd will get her off," a woman shouted. "Even before she has a chance to thaw."

She felt Jackson tightening his grip on her arm, and was grateful she didn't have to face these vultures alone. He shoved a reporter aside as he opened the passenger door and pushed her inside. She watched him make his way around the car, open the driver's side door and slide in behind the wheel.

Another flash went off in her face, then another and another. She lowered her head, but there was no escaping the blinding lights until they drove off.

As Jackson drove, her thoughts struggled with the tangled situation and how it would affect her father in the upcoming election. She closed her eyes, willing her thoughts away from him and onto Walt Hadley Jr.'s bizarre and untimely interest. Until today, she had no idea that he had such notions about her.

Walt was a tall, sullen man with intense brown eyes and fiery red hair. Though a bit too long and thin, his face was both expressive and intelligent. He generally strutted around the company wielding his influence. Until recently, she had seen him as a man who rarely dirtied his hands with the small stuff. Other females had willingly fallen under his domineering spell simply because he was single and imposing. Perceiving him as arrogant and unpleasant, Kendal had determined early in her tenure at Howard-Hadley to avoid contact with him at all cost.

However, twenty minutes after she'd quit her job, Walt Jr. had escorted her to his office. While they were still talking, his assistant, Jace, warned him that a throng of reporters was lying in wait outside. She closed her eyes, remembering how she had flinched when the buzzer had gone off on his desk. Jace's voice came over the speaker. "Jackson North has arrived for Kendal, sir."

Her knees still wobbled dreadfully, but she quickly gathered her things. Walt had stood to help her to her feet. He had reached the door ahead of her. But instead of opening it, he turned and tucked stray curls behind her left ear. "Frank Peck was a fool to give up so easily."

She wasn't certain why—maybe the fear of going to prison, maybe the fact that he seemed to know about Frank's unwelcome advances, or maybe she just needed to be held—but when Walt reached for her, Kendal moved into his arms and let him kiss her.

She had tried to relax when his arms tightened around her. But she tensed and pulled away, feeling foolish and disappointed. "I'm sorry. I shouldn't have let that happen."

A car horn jolted her back to reality and she shook her head regretfully, pondering her lax behavior, as well as her lack of response to his kiss. It did nothing for her except make her want to run away as fast as she could. She had been right in refusing to get involved with Frank Peck, but now, in a weak moment, she had made the mistake of letting Walt kiss her. Thankfully, he realized that it meant nothing.

Jackson pulled into her gravel driveway behind Sheila's car and parked. "Your phone will probably ring off the hook for a few days and your picture will be in the paper. I'll make some phone calls. But you make sure the only thing you and Sheila say to reporters is 'no comment.' Understand?"

Kendal swallowed hard and nodded.

"I'll go back by my office and get my assistant to drive your car home." Jackson hopped out and moved around to open her door.

She gave him the key to her brand new maroon Sable and summoned the energy to slide out. "Thanks for coming to my rescue, Jackson."

He nodded. "Tell Sheila I'll see her later."

Kendal numbly climbed the steps to the home she had inherited from her grandmother. The old brick colonial was two stories high with a basement and a huge back yard. The instant she opened the front door, Sheila's five-year-old daughter, Marcy, rushed her, nearly knocking her over.

"Hi, Aunt Kem," she yelped, flashing a smile, her tongue protruding a little. Though her motor skills were sluggish, her eyes shone with the life of a million fireflies. In contrast to her mother's blond curls, Marcy's dark brown hair was straight and often disorderly. "You on TV."

"Hello, my pretty," Kendal said, gazing into the child's sweet flat face and slanting eyes. Then she bent to embrace her, relief and love touching something deep inside.

Marcy's eager embrace once again sparked the hunger for a child of her own, so much so Kendal had to fight to keep her emotions in check. She still wasn't sure artificial insemination was right for her. But she desperately wanted a baby, and it looked as if that would be her only available option.

Of course, she would love to get pregnant the traditional way—with love, marriage, the works. But she didn't have a husband and wasn't sure she trusted men enough to identify a prospect within the next few weeks.

"There you are," Sheila said, strolling into the room. Her chipper friend was the picture of perfection after struggling through the end of a difficult marriage. Having a Down syndrome child and a husband unwilling to take on the responsibility such a child requires had been heartrending.

Sheila's hardship, though unfortunate, had come at an incredibly opportune time for Kendal. Nana had needed constant care, and Sheila had eagerly agreed to provide it while Kendal continued working. She and Marcy had moved in two years ago. Although Nana had passed on, Sheila and Marcy were still a part of her home and family.

"Hey," Kendal said, gazing into her friend's sapphire blue eyes. Her blond hair was pulled back into a ponytail and her tall, slender frame settled in a challenging stance.

"You all right?" she asked. "We saw you and Jackson on television."

Although her usual positive self, Kendal sensed the intensity of Sheila's concern. She straightened as rising dread headed for the pit of her stomach. Marcy wrapped her arms around Kendal's legs as she shrugged out of her jacket. "Yeah, I'm fine. Thanks."

"Let go, Marcy," Sheila scolded, reaching to pull her away.

But Kendal placed a restraining hand on Marcy's shoulder. "Leave her be. I need all the affection I can get right now."

With Marcy in tow, Kendal moved into the living room, while Sheila's brow formed a worried peak. "I've been a nervous wreck. The news said Frank Peck disappeared and you were possibly being charged as a co-conspirator."

Kendal dropped down into a chair and closed her eyes, restraining anguished tears behind her lids. Marcy squeezed in beside her. "I'm so scared, Sheila."

"Did that creepy Jed Mason have anything to do with your invented involvement?"

Her friend's informed expression of her and Jed's volatile association made Kendal chuckle in spite of herself. But before long, tears began to trickle down her cheeks. Marcy reached up and brushed them away. "I'll tell you about it later," she said, forcing herself to push aside the distress and panic.

Sheila sat down, her eyes suddenly bright with excitement. "Maybe *my* news will cheer you up a little. We are now the new owners of *Blazing Blossoms.*"

Elation having instantly replaced anguish, Kendal jumped up and rushed to embrace Sheila. Prompting the three of them into a dance around the living room, Kendal said, "Thank you, God. This is so right on time."

"I've already got Jackson moving on changing the name to the one we decided on," Sheila said.

The reference to Jackson made Kendal appreciate just how considerate he had been. He had seen her through an unnerving experience, and could have been quick on the draw with the news, but he had respectfully left it for Sheila. They had used portions of her inheritance and Sheila's divorce settlement to buy an established floral shop.

After returning several phone calls and putting Marcy to bed with a story, Kendal joined Sheila in the living room and described the events of her day. "I just wasn't expecting anything like this. Even though Jed took every opportunity to point an accusing finger, Walt Jr. stood up for me."

"I would think so…after that big raise he gave you on Friday. Now you won't even be able to enjoy it." Sheila suddenly stopped and frowned. "Did he know about all this?"

Kendal squirmed. "Agent Sanner said the company has been under investigation for several months. I suppose it wouldn't have been very professional for him to warn me."

"Hmph. And it wasn't very professional for him to make a pass at your annual evaluation either, but he did."

Kendal averted her eyes. She had thought very little of the pass Walt made on Friday because he treated almost all the women that way. But today…she wasn't about to admit to Sheila that just hours earlier she had let Walt kiss her. "It doesn't matter, Sheila. I know I've done nothing wrong. Jackson said they were just trying to scare me into telling them where Frank is."

"How would you know?"

"They think I'm romantically involved with him."

"I can only imagine where they got that idea," Sheila said, rolling her eyes. "I know how you feel about your dad getting involved, but you've got to call him. This is serious."

Kendal shook her head. "His press secretary will probably advise him against involving himself in this scandal. I don't really need to call him."

"Are you crazy! Stop trying to be the martyr and get some help. Those newspaper reporters will probably surprise attack him just to get a reaction they can play up to the hilt. You know how sneaky they are! If you don't call him, I'll do it myself."

Kendal saw the determination on Sheila's face and felt ashamed. Of course, she was concerned about what this would do to her father. But she had played the detached role so long she didn't quite know how to turn it off. Nana's funeral had been the last time she had seen her father or brother. She looked at Sheila again, knowing her friend would make good on her warning if she thought it necessary.

"I'll call him later. I just don't want this interfering with his reelection chances this year."

Sheila rolled her eyes upward. "Yeah, like you're really concerned about that."

"Just because I don't agree with his choices doesn't mean I don't want him to be happy, Sheila."

"Well, reporters will be predatory at the first wind of this, especially with your history of evading them. Not to mention if you proceed with this idea of having a baby."

Kendal slipped her feet out of the too-tight pumps and drew them up into the chair. "We won't have to worry about that if I go to jail." She set her eyes on the picture of her grandmother on the mantle. "I sure wish Nana were here to celebrate the shop with us."

Sheila smiled and reached for a magazine. "How do you think Miss Eula would feel about your decision to have a baby this way?"

Kendal flashed a smile. "She was the one who gave me the courage to check into it."

"Being artificially inseminated?"

Kendal shook her head. "I have to admit she wouldn't like that part. She wanted to see me married." She leaned back and closed her eyes. "But I don't even think I've ever been in love, Sheila."

"What about Josh Huggins in our tenth grade history class? You hung around him all through high school."

"He was just a nice boy, that's all."

"Well, there was Wayne Jefferson and Keith Dixon in college."

Kendal shook her head wearily and returned to thoughts of her grandmother. She strained to remember the words the old woman had uttered—words that inspired the naming of their new business. *The Lord speaks needed balm to ailing hearts. It comes in small whispers.*

The sound of the telephone jarred her back to the present. Sheila closed the magazine she had been browsing and picked up the phone. Almost immediately, she handed it over. "It's for you," she whispered. "I'll just run upstairs and check on Marcy. Don't forget Jackson's warning."

Kendal took a deep breath and placed the receiver to her ear, prepared to utter a simple *no comment.* "Hello."

"Death crouches at your door, Kendal Diane Boyd," the voice droned. "And I aim to see that it gains entrance."

Fear, stark and tangible, raced through her. "Who is this?"

Bloodcurdling laughter erupted, and then, "Someone who's watching."

By the time Kendal thought to slam down the phone, the caller had already broken the connection. She stared at the receiver, his words echoing in her mind. They were as icy as death, but there was something odd about the voice. She couldn't shake the feeling that she had heard it before.

Eric Boyd stalked into Bill Andersen's office with a determination that almost frightened him. It was one of those rare occasions when his supervisor wasn't on the phone or chewing out some rookie behind a door that might as well have been made of air.

"Come on in and have a seat, boy."

The word *boy* made him cringe. Bill was certainly older—by more than twenty years—but the usage had always made Eric think that the speaker felt superior. And that was especially distasteful in today's racial climate. As if that wasn't enough, his father's call had provoked a decision that could very well backfire. He knew he had to keep a lid on his personal feelings and tread lightly if he was to accomplish anything at all.

"Sir, I know you've already made your decision about my request for temporary assignment to Seattle, and I don't mean to harp on the issue. But something else has happened I think you should know about."

"Yes, I have made my decision, Agent, and I've already had a little pressure from your father, which does not change my mind. So if you don't mind, I'm very busy."

"Bill. I really need you to push this through for me. I know you don't take kindly to politicians who try to manipulate the system. Dad doesn't usually do that unless he finds it absolutely necessary. I would really appreciate it if you would look past his ploy and hear me out. I need to be near my sister now, and I wouldn't even have to be on a case that involved any of this."

Probably sensing Eric's anxiety, Bill softened a bit. He leaned back in his chair, absently twirling a pen between his plump fingers. After a few awkward seconds, he put down the pen with a sigh. "Look, I talked to Cashion in Seattle yesterday. They're working closely with an FDA agent and are busy as all get out. If anything turns up, I'll let you know."

Eric stood and moved to the window in an effort to hide his irritation. "I've made a few phone calls, sir. I know about the joint investigation. I won't lie to you. I want in, but I'm not pushing for that. I just need to be near Kendal right now."

Eric took a deep breath and turned back to face his supervisor.

"I admire your devotion to family," Bill began. "That's exactly why I think it best you stay out of the way for now. In addition to the Howard-Hadley case, they're also in the middle of serial killings. You and I know serial killers aren't as rare as people think." Bill drew his chair closer to his desk. "I want you to know I'm not under the impression you'll interfere with some lofty theory about your sister's situation. But...."

Eric felt his chest tighten as his temper flared. "Then why are you sitting there with that full-of-yourself look on your face? I need to go take care of my sister. You said yourself that they're investigating the company. What about the allegations against her? She didn't receive a threat until the FDA accused her of some wrongdoing."

"Agent, I know everybody's wired differently. But I can't just let you dictate my job every time something comes up with the congressman or Kendal. Now, I've tried to be patient with you on this."

"I know, Bill, and I appreciate your tolerance. But...."

"Didn't I let your unauthorized access to classified information slide?" Bill continued, pointing his pen at Eric. "And that was a personal matter concerning a twenty-year-old case."

Eric swallowed, feeling guilty. At the time, he had been looking into Sumner's death. "It was just a theory I was looking at, Bill. Something that happened when I was a kid." He forced a smile. "And I *am* grateful you didn't clobber me."

Bill's lips formed a straight line. "Eric, calm down and let Seattle do its job. I promise to keep you posted. Cashion and his team are pretty good."

"Sir…"

The first sign of emotion from the man was a careful swallow. "I know you've been under a lot of stress lately, especially since Linda announced her engagement. I'll give Cashion another call. But don't push me any further than that."

"I appreciate anything you can do," Eric said, desperately trying to settle down. "Knowing my sister, she's probably hiding her terror after getting a threatening telephone call. My dad is still trying to keep the media hounds off her."

A spasm of irritation crossed Bill's face. Mentioning his father had been a mistake. "And how do you suppose the mighty congressman can accomplish a thing like that?" Bill asked, standing. "I wouldn't care if Stan Boyd were president. I run this slice of the bureau the way I see fit. And if you think coming into my office in the grips of a tantrum will sway me into jumping through hoops, you have another thought coming. Now I suggest you get back to work. The only thing I can do is give you information Cashion cares to share."

The tone in Bill's voice made every other enthusiastic remark on the tip of Eric's tongue fall flat. "I can't do that, Bill. I need to find out who is threatening Kendal."

Eric knew he had crossed the line the moment he had spoken. Tension forced out every word Bill spoke. "You are out of line, Agent. Seattle is not even close to our jurisdiction." He sat back down and picked up his pen. "You're very capable as an agent, but you're too close to this situation. And the bureau can't afford any more negative attention."

"So? I'm capable."

Bill looked up over his glasses. "This crusade of yours isn't helping your argument. Now back off and let Seattle—who are, incidentally more in tune with the situation—do their job."

Eric cleared his throat and moved towards the door, pausing only after he grasped the doorknob. "I'm requesting a leave of absence, Bill. Family emergency."

-TWO-

Precisely at 10:30, Quincy Morgan arrived at the offices of *The Hill Watcher*, the small newspaper he had been a part of for a year. He felt slightly out of sorts, having just put his Aunt Barbara on a plane back to Atlanta. She had come to attend last night's banquet. The White House Correspondents' Association had presented him an award. The recognition was certainly appreciated, but he was shocked that he had even been nominated, especially after all that had happened.

The award was nice, but it did little to comfort him after the losses he had suffered. He rolled his shoulders remembering the tears in his aunt's eyes. It had been the story that forever changed his life—the story that had landed a senator behind bars and driven a decent young woman to take her own life.

As he moved towards his desk, Quincy stopped mid-step when several co-workers standing around his desk began applauding. He was surprised to see Clay Willis, the very reporter who had taken his desk at the *Sun*.

He had always liked Clay during the years they worked together. Despite the awkwardness between them now, he still did. He was a good reporter and an honest man. After Quincy had accepted slaps on the back and congratulatory greetings, Clay sauntered over to him. His resemblance to a much younger Jimmy Carter was uncanny and always made him chuckle.

"I knew I would make you smile," he said, offering a hand. "Congratulations, Quincy. You certainly deserve the honor. The recognition will boost your resume, too."

"Thanks, Clay. I appreciate your coming over."

He placed a half-empty cup of punch on Quincy's desk and started toward the elevator. Compelled to follow, Quincy caught up with him just as he turned the corner.

"You didn't hear it from me, but I think Max will probably ask you to consider coming back over."

A strange ripple looped through Quincy's gut. Part of him wanted to laugh, part wanted to retaliate in anger. He swallowed to ease the tightness in his throat and silently chided himself. He had to maintain his ability to detach facts from fantasy, and faith from emotions. "Why would he do that? I'm still the guy who embarrassed him in front of his cronies."

"You know the story, Quince. It wasn't personal. Max is big on smoozing the big boys, but he still thinks highly of you. It was all about power and politics. Now that the buzz is down and you're once again viewed as an asset, he probably wants your name restored to the *Sun's* masthead. This is just a big, crazy game. You know?"

Quincy relaxed a bit and nodded as if he understood. "So are you out here running interference for Max?"

Clay chuckled. "Not really. I like your old desk too much. Anyway, I had better make myself scarce. Your colleagues see me as the enemy. I almost had to beg to be let off the elevator."

Quincy offered another firm handshake. "Thanks again for coming." He stood there until the doors closed.

"They courting your favor now?"

He turned around. Joe Amory was standing with both hands sunk into his trouser pockets and an uncertain smile on his face. He rocked back a little on his heels and gazed at Quincy as if waiting for an answer.

"Nothing like that, Joe. I understand you have an assignment for me…in the state of Washington. The only news out there is still in session on the Hill in D.C."

"Come to my office," he said, waggling his thick eyebrows up and down.

Resisting the urge to laugh at the spectacle they probably made, Quincy followed Joe through the lobby, down the hall and past the cubicles on the open floor. His six-five frame towered over Joe's five. Joe, confidently strutting ahead of him, made him feel like a balloon bouncing over his head. He peered down at the editor, and noted that he had combed the long strands of his hair over a balding crown.

Joe slammed the door shut behind them. He was keyed up about something because he was talking before he even reached his chair and before Quincy could take his.

"I finally think I got her, Quince. The congressman has shielded her for years, but I finally got her."

The man was overcome with excitement. Quincy leaned forward in his chair. "Who are we talking about?"

"Kendal Boyd," he said. "Congressman Boyd's daughter."

Quincy lifted an eyebrow. "The ice princess?"

Obviously pleased with himself, Joe clapped his hands loudly. Despite seeing him do this, the popping sound still startled Quincy. He could swear the man's eyes actually shone iridescently.

"I got an anonymous call last night."

"What?"

Joe's laughter was grating and sounded devious. "Apparently, the pharmaceutical company Miss Boyd works for is being investigated by the feds. And she's right in the middle of the dirt."

Quincy tensed a little when his mind went to Eric, Kendal's younger brother. Although a little fiery, Eric was accommodating, as was their father. But he could only imagine how off-putting Kendal's reputedly snooty ways might be. From what he had picked up, she was indeed an ice princess with fire in her midst. He recalled a file photo of her. Despite being intrigued by those gorgeous brown eyes, he couldn't think of any reason he would want to be around her. He wondered how she could be so different from her brother.

"I have no interest in flying clear across the country to have some prima donna slam her door in my face. Besides, I need to take a few days off."

Joe frowned. "I really needed you to fly out tomorrow. How long are you needing?"

Quincy yawned and stretched. "Maybe you should send Ron Reese, or get what you can off the wire."

"Ron Reese is busy with another assignment. How long?"

He shrugged. "I don't know. Maybe a week...maybe I need an indefinite leave of absence."

Joe bolted up-right. "No!"

Quincy straightened and glanced through the glass wall of Joe's office. Sure enough, his reaction had prompted several heads to turn. His eyes were wild. The vein in his neck bulged dangerously as he quickly moved around the desk and drew the blinds.

"I've waited too long for a break like this. And you're not messing it up for me. You're my ace in the hole."

"How do you figure that? I'm a reporter. She hates reporters."

"You're a friend of Eric Boyd's. I figured he would be your 'in'."

Quincy held up his hands in protest. "Calm down, Joe. I never said specifically that I was Eric's friend. All I said was that I had gotten along well with him at a reception a couple years ago."

Joe dropped back down into his chair, making a swooshing sound. "Ron can be on hand when you call in, but I want you on that plane to Seattle tomorrow afternoon. I'll give you as much time as you want when you get back."

"With pay?"

"With pay."

Quincy chuckled and shook his head. "My, my. You're certainly bloodthirsty for this one."

"The congressman built a fort around her years ago. This is my chance to get in. They're not as squeaky clean as people think. I can feel it. And I want you to get the dirt and break the story. It'll put you back on the map more than that award last evening." He paused. "Or for that matter, Max Clayton."

Quincy's lips curled. "Is it me you're concerned about putting back on the map, Joe, or is it *The Hill Watcher*? Besides, you know I don't dig for dirt. I dig for facts. And the whole thing sounds too flimsy to bust your budget flying me out there."

"This is what I want, Morgan. You owe me this. I gave you a chance when no other paper would touch you."

When Joe called him by his last name, Quincy knew the editor was getting close to blowing any restraint he might have managed up to now. He decided it wouldn't hurt to do him this one last favor before handing in his resignation, especially with the lure of an indefinite vacation upon his return. "I guess I can, Joe. But we need to have a long talk when I get back."

Joe grabbed a cold cigar from an overflowing ashtray and leaned back in his chair and lit it. "And while you're out there, get a line on Olivia Howard. She owns the biggest part of Howard-Hadley Labs. She's also the sister of Senator William Howard. Congressman Boyd was close to Howard several years ago. I'd like to know if he and Olivia are friends."

Quincy stood up to leave. "So you think Olivia Howard is involved with Congressman Boyd because his daughter happens to work for her?"

His laughter had an ugly edge to it. "You're a newshound. What do you think?"

Using the calf of his leg to push the chair back, Quincy stood and strolled towards the door. Feeling a bit impish, he paused and turned back just before opening it. Joe's feet were up on the desk.

"By the way, Joe."

The man flinched, drawing his legs back. The chair snapped forward with a loud clamping sound. "Yeah?"

"I don't owe you anything. I look forward to our talk when I return."

That said, Quincy strode out, quietly closing the door behind him.

The next afternoon, Quincy ambled through the doors of the small church he had attended for years. James Timmons, his pastor and friend, must have been delayed by something else. Maybe it was a mistake to come, but he had been so intrigued by James's teaching on the end times and felt a need to talk personally with the pastor.

Leaving, Quincy paused on the steps and glanced down at his worn sweats. He had come straight from the gym and had waited in the church office for twenty minutes before deciding it was time to go. He had used the time to once again think about what he wanted to do with the rest of his life.

He loved newsgathering, but didn't like the ruthlessness the industry sanctioned to get a story. He thought of the history he had learned back in college and shrugged. Perhaps the callous disregard for principle had been there all along. But he hadn't come face to face with it until his own ethics had been challenged. It had been easy to ignore because he was kept so busy. He couldn't help wondering if in some ways he had become as insensitive as what he now saw as the norm in the business.

He continued down the wide concrete steps headed for the side parking lot where he had parked his jeep. The wide lawn had a peaceful appearance with a few sparse trees and newly planted flowers. Still, the sound of noonday traffic was especially unsettling today. He checked the time. He had just over three hours to pack and get to the airport.

"Quincy!" James hurried towards him with a wide grin and an extended hand. "Sorry I'm late for our talk. Stella's in her second trimester and finding it a little more taxing to get things done."

Quincy smiled and slowed his pace. "No problem. It wasn't really important."

A sudden gust of wind propelled an empty soda can from beneath his jeep. The racket made them both turn. James picked up the can and then returned to Quincy's side, giving him a friendly slap on the back. "Does it have anything to do with the award the other night? I'm real proud of you."

Quincy stood silent for a moment, tracing the lines in his left palm with the tip of his key. "I've been doing some thinking lately…about my place in life. I just wanted to run something by you."

"Why don't we step back inside?"

Quincy shook his head and opened the door to the jeep. "Don't really have the time."

"Then how 'bout coming over for dinner tonight? I'm giving Stella a break and making lasagna. I think."

"Thanks, but I'll be on a plane to Seattle in a few hours."

James squeezed his shoulder. "How long this time?"

Quincy climbed in behind the wheel and shut the door. "Hopefully, just a few days."

"What's going on, Quince?"

Quincy sighed and scanned the busy street. A horn honked at a stray canine trying to cross. He returned to James' concerned eyes and shrugged. "I'm thinking of leaving the news after this assignment. I don't have any real peace about the industry anymore. I guess I just need to know I'm making the right move."

James lifted an eyebrow in surprise. "Leave the news? The news is your life."

Quincy laughed and started the engine. "You're the last person I expected to say that."

James shrugged. "You just took me by surprise…that's all. I guess I just assumed you were a lifetime newsman."

"I know. And I love the challenge my jobs have given me. But it feels so repulsive of late, James. I need order and direction. I've got to close some doors and move on." Once again, he moved his gaze to the landscaped lawn. "I'm trying not to conjure up any notions of my own, but the series you've been conducting has triggered a new hunger to be in God's perfect will." He looked straight ahead, sensing his friend's surprised gaze on his face. "I believe that's the only way I'll truly have peace."

James leaned against the door. "I think you've already made your decision. How does your gut feel?"

"A little scared, but eager for the change. How will I know it's the right one?"

James placed a hand on his friend's shoulder and smiled. "I pray God will give you clarity and direction. Try not to spend a lot of time worrying about it. He generally guides us with his peace."

Three hours later, Quincy settled into a seat by the window at the airport. He looked around soberly. He used to enjoy traveling, but lately waiting in airports had become wearying.

He closed his eyes and let his mind wander back to yesterday morning before taking his Aunt Barbara to the airport. "It still feels strange celebrating without her," he had said, remembering his mother.

She had smiled and patted his forearm. "I know, but I choose to believe your mama was right there with us in spirit. Noticed you weren't very excited when you went to the podium."

"Something's stirring in me, Auntie. I've lost my passion. What do you think the Lord is trying to tell me?"

"That you need a good woman in your life."

Her words had surprised him. Even so, he had been thinking a lot lately about his lack of companionship. He had even prayed the Lord would send him another wife, a real wife—one who wanted a man, not a puppet. He chuckled aloud as he remembered his aunt's mischievous gaze. "These days I seem to repel women rather than attract them."

Wrinkling her nose, she had snorted. "You talked to that wife of *yours* lately?"

He had felt instant revulsion. Quincy knew it wasn't healthy to feel the way he did about Sherry, but she was a different breed. What had he ever seen in her? Why had he fallen so in love with her? They'd had nothing in common.

She had grown up in a wealthy family and held to the notion that it was perfectly normal to let her father keep them in cars and houses. She found it unthinkable to do anything that might break a nail or smear her makeup. And despite the brevity of his incarceration, Sherry had refused to wait and work on their troubled marriage. The citation he had received for contempt of court was not only unacceptable to her, it was humiliating. Two weeks into his sentence, he was served with divorce papers.

"Sherry's not my wife, Auntie. She's an ancient mistake."

"Then you need to get on with it, baby. I've been here a week, and if a female called your house, somebody knocked me over the head. You all just weren't meant to be together, that's all. But it's been long enough. You're too young to just sit and stew in your own regrets."

He had looked at her and smirked. "Thirty-three isn't all that young."

Quincy was jolted from his musing when a child on the other side of the gate waiting area began to laugh. The sound was musical and infectious, conveying an impression of happiness, and even a degree of comfort. He chuckled and silently reaffirmed the validity of his desire for a family.

His aunt had reminded him of that dream before she left. She had stood back on her heels and peered up at him, her hands on her hips.

"Grab for the stars, Quince. What do you see yourself doing in two years?"

It was the faith exercise she had taught him when he was a boy. He had closed his eyes. "I have a job I'm proud of. I'm married to a beautiful Christian woman like you, and I'm bouncing a chubby son on my knee."

Patting him on the back, she had said, "I said grab for the stars, not the sun and moon, too. That would take a miracle, but miracles are possible."

"Like you always said, there's no harm in reaching."

"No, son. You'll face things that will try and pull your eyes from that dream. But remember, not one word to the Lord falls on a deaf ear."

I trust even now, Lord, that it is you who is guiding me. Make your will clear to me.

Curious about the subject of his assignment, Quincy pulled out the dossier on Kendal Boyd. Maybe some level of interest will be ignited and, at the very least, he could formulate a plan of approach. Despite the fact that Kendal Boyd had built a reputation for avoiding the press, he tried not to consider the probability that she wouldn't see him.

What was Joe thinking sending him on this wild-goose chase? Still, in light of such a major scandal, she should fully expect reporters to seek comments from her. Even so, unless by some miraculous occurrence Joe had found favor with Howard-Hadley Laboratories, it was unlikely he would even get to see her. Perhaps with the company in such a negative light right now, he would at least be able to talk with someone else of significance.

Taking a long breath, he opened the file. For the sake of her father's campaign, a smart next move would be to make a public statement—even an apology. Congressman Boyd had always been cooperative and openhanded with interviews—except when it came to his daughter.

He looked down at the top sheet and was surprised to see that Baltimore was her place of birth. Could he possibly use that fact as an angle of approach? The photograph stapled to the inside of the folder was labeled *Kendal Diane Boyd*. Somehow Joe had gotten a more current likeness of her. This image made her look softer than the one in the paper's archives. He stared at the picture, oddly moved by her bashful smile and pleasing figure. She was a striking woman with shoulder-length curls piled around an appealing face. Her eyes glistened with determination, but quiet agony was also there.

He wondered how involved she was with the accused doctor and the mounting allegations against him. His mind flashed to his ex-wife and on impulse he lifted the photograph from the inside cover and shoved it towards the back of the file. She was probably just as selfish and shallow as Sherry.

He scanned the accompanying pages and saw snapshots of her parents, Stan Boyd and his late wife, Tessa. When he spotted one of Eric, one side of Quincy's mouth lifted. He liked Eric. Despite his youth, he was friendly and obliging. His smile widened when he recalled the fiasco on the Hill two years ago at a banquet honoring ambassadors from several countries.

He had simply walked into the men's room and found Eric and an inebriated young woman handcuffed to the door of a stall. This was startling by itself, but the two of them had been stripped down to their underwear. In addition to feeling physically ill, Eric had been horror-struck, worried about how the reports would affect his father.

After questioning him thoroughly, Quincy was finally able to figure out that a group of unscrupulous journalism students were the culprits. They had apparently slipped something into Eric's water glass at the banquet that evening. Feeling disoriented and nauseated, he had excused himself and gone to the men's room, where he was ambushed and photographed with the young woman in a compromising position.

Eric had been worried that the incident would not only embarrass the congressman but would also land him in deeper water with his supervisor at the bureau. Although he chose not to press charges, he was infuriated. Quincy located the perpetrators and even visited their school and talked with the dean. The students were all expelled.

He glanced at the file again. Despite his aversion to prima donnas, he vowed to do his best to be lenient with Miss Boyd for Eric's sake. He decided, however, that she was probably involved in the alleged pharmaceutical fraud. After all, she was the doctor's drug rep and was likely his mistress. He turned another page. She would finally have to face her own music.

He flipped through a few more clippings. There were newspaper articles stretching all the way back to Stan Boyd's military life, the sale of his business and his early days in the political arena. A party candidate, Congressman Boyd had eagerly left a lucrative textile business and entered the world of politics eighteen years ago. When hard-pressed by questions about his daughter, he explains her desire for privacy and with practiced diplomacy sidesteps further inquiries.

Quincy frowned, realizing that the congressman's attempt to shield her had unwittingly incited much of the industry against his media-phobic adopted daughter. He leafed through more clippings and came to one of Stan Boyd and Senator William Howard just prior to Howard's death. According to the accompanying article, Boyd had first befriended Howard while in the military.

He and his family lived in Spokane where he was stationed at Fairchild Air Force Base. He had taken over his father's textile business, also in Spokane, but had let someone else run it until he had finished his tour of duty. He regularly flew to Washington on military business and while there, during his off-duty time conducted business in regard to the textile industry. Stan Boyd's mother, Eula Boyd, had returned to her hometown of Rose Creek following the death of her husband.

Quincy wondered why Joe thought there was such a mystery. Based on what he just read, the connection was obvious. He leafed through the clippings again, thinking he had missed something. He hadn't.

The next article had a photograph of Eula Boyd and her only two grandchildren. The article was from the *Rose Creek Clarion*. Apparently back then it wasn't widely known that Kendal was the adopted daughter of Stan and Tessa Boyd, but the paper had tinted it as a cover up of some kind. The grandmother was seated with one arm casually around Kendal's waist and the other around Eric. Kendal was all smiles, both arms wrapped around her grandmother's neck. It was clear the two were very close. Seeing it made Quincy think of his own mother and their closeness.

His cellphone rang just as the gate attendant announced pre-boarding. He noted Joe's number on the caller ID and answered.

"Morgan."

"Quince! I'm glad I caught you. I just got word that Kendal Boyd's employment at Howard-Hadley was terminated day before yesterday. Right after the FDA cornered her. Congressman Boyd is sitting tight on the Hill, but making a lot of calls."

"To whom?"

"Nobody knows. Ron Reese says he's very agitated and everyone is tiptoeing around him."

Quincy shoved the file back into his briefcase. "Considering the gravity of the situation, I would say his reaction is normal. This scandal has focused all eyes on the ice princess and may ultimately engulf her father. Do you know anything about…um…Dr. Frank Peck? Have formal charges been filed against him?"

"Yeah," Joe said, panting with excitement. "But as far as I know, none against her. By the way, according to one of our sources, Eric Boyd is leaving Denver to fly to Seattle." Joe emitted a gravelly guffaw. "This could be the story of the century."

Quincy snapped his briefcase shut and went to stand in line. "I still think you're giving this more attention than it merits."

"Nah. If Eric Boyd is flying to her rescue instead of 'daddy', something strange is underway. He's with the FBI out of Denver."

Quincy handed the attendant his boarding pass. "Kendal is his sister. I wouldn't expect him to be anywhere else. I'm telling you, you're getting yourself all worked up for nothing."

"It's my call, Morgan."

"That it is," Quincy said, smiling though still unconvinced. "But I can't say how long I'll be able to gratify *your calls*. Got to go."

After forty-five minutes of navigating SeaTac Airport, Quincy finally retrieved his bag and headed for the car rental. He was tired and could hardly wait to get to the lone hotel in Rose Creek, thirty-five miles east of Seattle. He still had a little drive ahead of him.

He had just gotten the keys to a black Ford Explorer when he heard his name and swung around to see Eric Boyd hurrying towards him.

"Hey, Quincy, I thought that was you," he said, slightly out of breath. "I saw you at the rental counter and rushed after you, but your strides are a lot longer than mine."

Eric's friendly grin was contagious. Dressed casually in denims and a pullover under a sport jacket, the younger man was about six feet, lean build with clean-cut features. Quincy smiled back and offered a firm handshake.

"It's good to see you again, Eric. How's it going?"

Eric grinned shyly, resembling an eight-year-old who had just scored his first dare. "Just regular routine, I guess, Quincy." He gestured towards the doors he had just come through. "You should hear what those women are saying back there at the counter. I think they suspect you're a professional body builder."

Quincy threw back his head and laughed. "Don't think I would quite make the cut."

Eric grinned and gave him the once-over. "I think you could. I wanted to thank you again for that piece you did two years ago, Quincy. *Shoddy Teachers and their Renegade Progeny* kept those pictures out of the nation's tabloids."

Pleased, Quincy asked, "You read the article, huh?"

"Sure did. Your outrage got me the roll of film in the mail, as well as an apology from the school. A lot of reporters would have taken advantage of the situation, but God sent you to that restroom that night."

Somewhat surprised by Eric's reference to God, he slowed his stride. "You a believer?"

"Sure am. So is my sister. You haven't met her, have you?"

"No, I haven't." Falling back into step, Quincy tried to prepare himself for what he would ask of Eric. "I knew your dad was a believer, but I didn't know about the two of you."

"How are you, Quincy? I mean, you were in the news quite a bit last year. I can't imagine what it's been like for you."

Quincy winced. The memory of being escorted by prison guards to his mother's funeral came crashing into his mind. Uneasy with the sensation, he looked away. "I'm doing well. I suppose it was just another one of life's surprises, but I got through it. I appreciate the card you sent after my mother passed. It was very thoughtful."

Eric nodded slightly and shifted his luggage from one hand to the other. "I only wish I could've done something to get you out. Sometimes justice just doesn't seem to work in favor of right."

Quincy came to an abrupt stop. "I have to admit...I have a new appreciation for people imprisoned wrongly. But thank God it was only three months. I take it your car is down this way?"

"Oh, I didn't...I'm sorry." He slapped his forehead with his free hand. "I'm not thinking. Actually, the Seattle field office didn't send anyone to pick me up. I hate to rent a car and have to take the time to return it tomorrow when they drop one by my sister's."

Quincy resumed walking. "So you need a lift?"

"If you don't mind. I would sure appreciate it, Quincy."

Quincy laughed, not believing his good fortune. "Of course not."

"Thanks, man. I guess I got so caught up in catching up I forgot to ask. It will give me a chance to introduce you to Kendal."

Quincy tried hard to keep his smile from broadening. Joe would probably dance a jig if he knew about this. Eric was an impressive young man, but clearly not quite the shield his father was when it came to Kendal. "You sure...."

"I know what you're thinking," Eric interrupted. "But Kendal doesn't have to know you're a reporter."

"But...."

"I hope I'm not being presumptuous, Quincy, but I consider you a friend. Since our first encounter, I've checked you out. I know you're a believer—you're tough and you're discreet. You took some pretty heavy hits and stayed with the game."

"Thanks," he said, touching his shoulder as a sudden phantom ache arose. Although Quincy by nature wasn't hypersensitive, memories of being shot were often activated by the slightest of things—a word, scent, even a certain time of the day could set his psyche on a downward spiral. He would start to brood and feel sorry for himself. But he couldn't remain there.

Joe, who had been in the business for twenty-five years, suggested it was burnout. But Quincy felt it had more to do with an awakening of sorts—a chance to get back on the right path. Not that journalism was an unseemly vocation per se. This particular brand was just no longer appealing to him. At thirty-three, he seemed to have hit an undefined brick wall, and he didn't have a clue what to do next.

"I believe this is our coach," Quincy said, pressing the key remote. The lights flashed, signaling that the doors were unlocked. He motioned for Eric to follow.

When they were headed east on I-90, Quincy noticed that Eric had finally relaxed. "You know, I really appreciate this."

"I might as well tell you I'm here to try and interview your sister. You think she'll tolerate me?"

Eric's eyes narrowed. "I knew you were headed out here, but I thought it was to look into the company. This *is* about the trouble at Howard-Hadley, right?"

Quincy nodded.

"As you already know, she generally doesn't have anything to do with the press. But Dad is adamant about her giving a statement regarding this whole mess."

"How is the congressman?"

"A caged lion," Eric said. "He's been advised to stay away from Kendal for now. It's killing him. Actually, I'm here on another matter."

Quincy gave him a sidelong glance. "To offer your support in your dad's absence, right?"

Eric turned towards him, but said nothing.

"My editor caught me just as I was boarding the plane. He said your sister had been fired from Howard-Hadley."

Looking straight ahead, Eric said, "I suppose I *am* here to offer my support. In a way." He went silent, and Quincy wondered if his comment had offended him. He turned back suddenly, a grin on his face. "Is it true several journalists have a bet going over Kendal?"

"A bet?"

"Yeah, on who'll get the first interview with her?"

Quincy grinned. "This is the first I've heard about it."

Eric chuckled, but after a moment his light mood turned serious again. "Um, Quincy, I might as well tell you. She didn't get fired; she quit. I'm here because somebody threatened her life."

-THREE-

Sheila did a double take when she strode into the kitchen and saw Kendal sipping a hot cup of tea at the table. "I thought you were in the dining room working on the computer. You're already in your pajamas and robe?"

Kendal nodded and watched as her doting friend since childhood made herself a cup of tea. Nana had once referred to them as salt and pepper because of their obvious racial differences. As a child, Sheila had been chatty, chubby and as pale as a cloud drifting across a blue sky. Nana never imagined Sheila would grow into a real-life Barbie doll.

Kendal, on the other hand, was brown and introverted, and she frequently used jokes to hide her shame or alienation. "I was about to fold some of this laundry," Kendal said, kicking the basket at her feet. "I read Cinderella to Marcy again tonight. She really likes that story." She smiled absently, wishing she could borrow Cinderella's prince to pluck her out of the mess she was in with the feds. And the telephone threat hadn't helped to quiet her jitters, either.

Sheila sat across from her and pulled a pair of Marcy's pajamas from the basket to fold. She glanced up and made a feeble attempt at stifling a giggle. "I can't seem to visualize you actually letting Walt Hadley Jr. kiss you on the lips. I was shocked, considering you don't trust men."

Kendal rubbed her forehead and looked out the window into the backyard. She couldn't believe she had let the one thing she had intended to keep secret slip out during their banter last night. She cringed as she noticed her reflection in the window. She was the picture of utter homeliness, dressed in a pink terrycloth robe over outsized satin pajamas. Her eyes were weary, her hair disheveled. She certainly didn't look the part of a new business owner. "I hadn't planned on telling you that," Kendal said, glaring across the table. "You're not going to let me forget that one, are you?"

"Nope. I suppose you were too distraught to think about the fact that you were letting a genuine toad touch your mouth. Yuck. Walt Hadley Jr.?"

"I know it was a stupid thing to let happen, but part of me was gripped with fear and part of me wanted to see if I could feel anything."

Sheila's eyes flashed. "Well?"

"Well what?"

"Stop hedging, Kendal," she said, tilting her head to the side. "Is he a good kisser?"

She sighed and pulled another article of clothing from the basket. "Maybe you're asking the wrong person. I don't think my judgment counts for much."

"Maybe if you weren't so fickle, you would learn to relax and even trust men," Sheila said. "You *know* what the Bible says about the double-minded."

"I'll have you know I have trusted plenty of men. They just all turned out to be deceitful frauds. Anyway, if I were double-minded, I wouldn't have gone through with this acquisition. There were plenty of times when—"

"I'm not talking about the flower shop, and you know it," Sheila interrupted. "I'm talking about all that stuff you have locked inside that keeps you from committing to a relationship."

Kendal sniffed haughtily as she started a stack of folded laundry in the middle of the table. "I can commit. I just haven't found the right man."

"Yeah, right. What about Dr. Peck? He seemed pretty nice, and you wouldn't give him the time of day. By the way, did *he* ever try to kiss you?"

"Sheila, as you know, I was never interested in Frank that way. He's been trying to turn things romantic for over a year. It was getting really awkward trying to conduct business with him." She glared defiantly at her interfering friend. "And, yes, I finally let him kiss me." Her chest tightened as she recalled the moment. "It was the last week…the time I had dinner with him…the last time I saw him."

Sheila wrinkled her nose. "I guess that answers that. They're both lousy kissers," she said with finality as she continued to fold laundry. "But I liked Dr. Peck. He was kind and really seemed to be fond of you." Sheila playfully nudged Kendal's shoulder. "I guess it's a good thing you quit. Walt Hadley would be guilty of employee sexual harassment."

"I know it sounds weird, Sheila, but even though Walt considers himself some kind of irresistible Lothario, I'm really sort of flattered he finds me attractive."

Sheila looked at her friend and sneered. "Of course he does. You're a knock-out."

Kendal chuckled. "Thanks for the compliment, but I think I could stand to shave a few pounds and have one of those total makeovers done."

The allure of Walt's kiss was probably due to her underlying yen for true love—one she had ignored for much too long. Kendal felt somewhat validated by his attention. Still, she found the situation just as amusing as her friend.

"Your looks aren't your problem, my friend. If you weren't so wacky about men, you wouldn't have to be thinking about having a baby through a test tube. Are you at least going to go out with Walt Jr.?"

Kendal wrinkled her nose. "Of course not. I don't really like him. I just like it that he likes me. All of us enjoy feeling wanted."

"Anyway, when are you going to get started on the pregnancy bit?"

"Dr. Matthews, that's the specialist I've consulted, gave me documents to fill out before I can get started. For that, I need medical history. I've already been searching for information about my biological parents online. It's hard when I don't even have names to start with."

"Why didn't you tell me? I could've helped," Sheila scolded. "You wouldn't have to be doing all this if you had fallen for Dr. Peck."

"Hmph. Clearly, Frank Peck isn't as nice as we thought. Besides, my decision has nothing to do with other people."

Sheila rolled her eyes. "Obviously."

"Oh, be quiet."

"You sure you want to do this?"

Kendal paused as she put the final fold on a shirt. "I really want a baby before I get too much older, Sheila. I have to admit, I've never wanted to be a single mom. I just believe I should be in love to get married. Considering, the time span for courtship, I don't have time to meet Mr. Perfect, marry and hope to conceive. Even if I met him tomorrow, I could be thirty-five before anything happened. My goal is to have a baby before my thirty-second birthday."

"Let's see," Sheila said, biting her lower lip. "You'll be thirty in December. That means you have less than three years."

Kendal nodded. "I've been on the Internet every day, hoping my birth mother might be searching for me, too. It's exasperating."

"You really should think about asking your father's office to help locate medical history. Surely they'll be able to pull some strings."

"I don't want Dad to know about this yet. After seeing my face splashed over the newspaper, it's the last thing he needs."

Sheila grinned and held her friend's eyes. "You sure it's Stan's feelings you're worried about? You pretty much leave him out of everything, including the flower shop deal."

"I've already got some stuff in the mail from the hospital where I was born," Kendal continued, ignoring Sheila's jab. "But it doesn't help much. They only sent non-identifying information."

Perhaps Sheila was right. Kendal had a lot of issues stuffed inside her that distorted her perception, which from time to time made her feel that her notions were unreliable. Things hadn't been right with her and her father in a long time. She loved him, of course, and imagined the hurt he would feel if he knew about her search for her birth family. She wished she felt comfortable enough to talk with him about the matter, but she didn't.

"You think he'll be at the grand opening?" Sheila no longer sounded saucy; she was genuinely concerned.

"I doubt it. A lot of people-pleasing between now and November, you know."

"You still don't think much of politics."

"Dad is insisting I make a brief statement about my resignation. His press secretary is supposed to call to set up everything. The very thought of talking into a microphone or standing in front of a camera scares me silly. I guess it's necessary, but my nerves are frayed."

She suddenly felt a chill as murky images crowded her mind. She gasped, aware that they were fragmented memories from her childhood abduction. Panic gripped her throat as the dreadful words entered her consciousness.

I'm your real daddy. Nobody loves you like I do. Not even God.

Obviously, the current stress was unleashing things hidden deep in her subconscious. She had managed for years to keep them at bay, but now they pierced the surface of her thoughts like shards of glass. Another chill raced up her spine, and she turned and saw a troubled look on Sheila's face.

"Kendal, you all right?"

"I'm fine," she lied.

"Maybe you should go on to bed," Sheila said. "I'll put this laundry away. You haven't gotten much sleep. You were up roaming around the house way past midnight last night."

Her stomach lurched once again, and she reached out and covered her friend's hand. "Stop worrying so, Sheila. That man hasn't called back, and it's already been two days. I'm just stressing over this federal investigation."

"But Jackson said all they have is circumstantial evidence against you. Nothing concrete at all. They just need to find Frank Peck. His absence is what's implicating you."

"Do you really think he would deliberately incriminate me?"

Sheila's eyes widened. "Don't you?"

"I'm honestly not sure," Kendal admitted, swallowing hard. "He must have been pretty desperate for money to get mixed up in something like this. If Jed Mason is really involved, I wonder what he got out of the deal."

"Frank Peck's not desperate for money. He's got plenty, and Jed obviously wants some of it. Why else would he take such a foolish risk?"

"I don't know, Sheila," Kendal said, feeling uncertain. "Jed is ornery and unpleasant, but he doesn't strike me as the greedy type."

"Oh, right," Sheila said, grasping the basket to pile in the folded laundry. "And you're doing such a fine job of judging character these days. People like that don't think they'll get caught."

"I'll just breathe a whole lot easier when this is all over," Kendal said. "Anyway, that prank call is the least of my worries."

"I don't know. The police seem to think it's serious enough to patrol the neighborhood every fifteen minutes. And those reporters calling don't help matters. We could unplug the phone after eight o'clock, you know. Jackson said he probably wouldn't call you any later than that. Maybe you should have taken your dad up on his offer to hire a personal bodyguard."

Kendal looked up into her friend's frightened eyes, amazed that she had voiced the very thing she had been thinking. She forced a giggle. "We can leave the phones connected. I really don't want a few calls to force us to change the way we live our lives, Sheila. And Dad is overreacting, as usual. I'm just glad Eric convinced him to stay in D.C. All I need is a melodramatic father underfoot." She smiled, making an attempt to calm the sudden alarm she saw on Sheila's face. "Maybe it would be a good idea for you and Marcy to move to a hotel...just until all this is over."

"Leave you here alone?" Her voice was shrill. "Are you out of your mind? With this nut out killing women...."

"What nut? What women?"

"Didn't you hear? The FBI issued a warning for the entire Seattle area about a serial killer. He's already killed three women."

Kendal shuddered. "Three! That gives me the creeps. I guess I've been so wrapped up in work, the acquisition and now the investigation that I haven't paid much attention to the news."

"We have to make sure all our windows and doors are locked." Sheila's eyes flashed as if a brilliant idea had just come to her. "Hey, let's call Eric and see what he knows about this one."

Kendal smiled. "Just because he's an agent doesn't mean he knows what's going on with all FBI cases. Besides, he's in Denver."

The doorbell rang, startling both women. They froze for several seconds and then moved down the hallway, faces etched with panic.

Sheila grabbed the baseball bat from beside the coat rack near the front door.

"Who is it?"

"It's Eric. Open up."

"Eric?" Limp with relief, Kendal quickly unbolted the door and rushed out onto the porch, throwing herself into her brother's arms. After several moments, he held her back a little. His coffee brown complexion was flawless and his short haircut made his ears look bigger, but he still had the same mischievous sparkle in his brown eyes.

"Hey, Sis. What's all this? You're shaking like a leaf. You all right?"

"I'm fine," she said, stepping back to take a look at him. "What are you doing here?"

Before he could answer, she caught sight of a gorgeous, six foot-plus man standing behind her brother, muscular arms folded across his chest. He was built like an ancient sculpture of a Greek god—broad chest and wide shoulders. His dark eyes were alive with amusement as he studied them. Although she felt a little exposed being observed by a stranger, she couldn't seem to take her eyes off of the absurdly handsome man. The porch light was on, making his bronze complexion shine under the five o'clock shadow.

Eric motioned with his head. "Sis, this is Quincy Morgan, a friend of mine. Quincy, my sister, Kendal."

Rarely at a loss for words, Kendal was momentarily speechless as she offered the stranger her hand. "Hello."

"Pleased to meet you, Miss Boyd," Quincy said. His smile broadened as he looked past her. "I didn't bring a ball, but for a hot cup of coffee, I might be able to come up with something."

Puzzled, Kendal followed his gaze. Sheila was still blocking the doorway with the bat still in her grasp. She was relieved that the laughter she had seen in his eyes had nothing to do with her appearance. Feeling a bit more poised, she turned back to face him. "This is Sheila Dodd, my roommate and business partner."

"Best friend and guardian thumper, too," Sheila added, lifting the bat to her shoulder for effect.

Quincy nodded towards Sheila, his grin revealing straight white teeth. Then he turned his eyes back to her, causing her to warm. She looked away nervously, bewildered by her reaction to Eric's friend.

"It's good to meet both of you," he said.

This man had a smile that made you feel as if you had just been scooped from an overflowing river. She braved glancing back at him, fully intending to look detached. Yet in the brief instant their eyes met again, she felt anything but detached and was oddly drawn in by his penetrating gaze. "Same here, Quincy. And please call me Kendal."

The faint scent of aftershave and deodorant—and man—tickled her nostrils. "Thanks, Kendal."

Sheila gave Eric a lively hug and held out her hand to Quincy. "Why don't we all come inside? I'll put my bat away and get us some refreshments."

Quincy flashed another smile that made Kendal's heart tremble. Flustered, she abruptly turned away.

"I'll go put on a fresh pot of coffee and make some sandwiches," Kendal said, hurrying past Sheila.

"I was going to do that. You should stay and visit with your brother."

Kendal wanted to shove a sock in her friend's mouth. "Why don't you check on Marcy? I need to work off this nervous energy."

"What nervous energy?" Eric called after her. "By the way, is the suite ready for me?"

"Always," she answered, without looking back.

-FOUR-

Although houses lined both sides of the narrow street, there was plenty of room between each. The small town of Rose Creek was splendidly comprised of suburban qualities, as well as rural. This particular street was pleasantly quiet. Most of the cars were parked in driveways, but a few were on the street.

Intense eyes peered from the shadows of Kendal Boyd's two-story colonial. The man inhaled the moist air that hovered over a stand of budding roses in the front yard. Then he turned and glowered at the black SUV in the driveway.

Who was her visitor, he wondered. He didn't recognize the vehicle. He scowled as a wave of agitation washed over him. He didn't particularly like seeing her with other men. He wanted her all to himself. And he could hardly wait for his chance. Despite her futile resistance, he knew in the long run she would be sensible.

He bent down lower, closed his eyes and envisioned her loveliness. She was the perfect sacrificial lamb. He smiled and moaned softly as he thought of her kindness—her wholesomeness. He loved the way the light glimmered against her creamy brown skin. Her dark curls shone with highlights and was styled so that they fell across her face when she moved her head a certain way. Her melodic laughter was the first thing he had noticed about her.

She had looked superb in the purple pantsuit she had worn on Monday. Though modest, it accentuated her pleasing figure. He chuckled softly. It was strange how he both loved and hated her at the same time. Whatever the reason, he enjoyed watching her—almost as much as he enjoyed dreaming of her death. For months, he had been consumed by the vision of her eyes resting on him the moment she slipped into oblivion. Other men chased her for the wrong reasons. He wouldn't—he couldn't chase after her like that. He didn't have to. He knew her origin and her destiny, and was convinced she would come to him willingly.

He dropped to the ground when headlights from a passing car swept the yard. A police cruiser slowed at the drive and shone a spotlight on the SUV. After several long moments, it pulled away. His heart pounded as eager anticipation surged through him.

"Wonder not at your sudden magnetism, my darling," he whispered, crushing the petals of a rosebud between his fingers. "You're in bloom and the fragrance of your season calls to every man near and far."

He flinched as the late April breeze thrust a thorny branch against his face. He trembled, tempted to climb the sturdy lattice to her bedroom just to peer inside again. Instead, he slipped out of the shadows and made his way back down the street to his car.

-FIVE-

The foyer of the old house opened onto a hallway that led past the staircase and out into a spacious kitchen. The living room was positioned to the left and was in full view of anyone standing in the foyer. The dining room, which stood to the right of the hall, also had a kitchen entrance. Halfway to the second floor, the stairs turned at a landing that also led back down into the kitchen. Eric smiled as he recalled the many times he had bumped his head sliding down the banister.

"Come into the living room, Quincy," Eric said. "Make yourself comfortable."

While Sheila went upstairs to look in on Marcy, Kendal disappeared down the hallway toward the kitchen. He then followed Quincy into the living room and smiled appreciatively as he looked around. He hadn't visited since Nana passed away almost six months ago. Kendal had done quite a bit of remodeling, but it was still the inviting space he remembered from his childhood. The cream-colored couch and two matching chairs were new. They were overstuffed, with several pillows, and looked very comfortable.

Quincy had just settled on the couch, and Eric in one of the chairs, when they heard a noise behind them. They both laughed when they turned to see Sheila in the hallway, placing her bat behind the coat rack.

"We have to keep alert around here, Quincy," she said with a smile. "Especially since a serial killer is on the loose."

Eric leaned forward in the chair, uncommonly edgy all of a sudden. Perhaps Kendal's nervousness had set off his own. Still, he felt a lot better being here. Maybe he could get Sheila to give him a clue about his sister's frame of mind.

Sheila sat on the opposite end of the couch. "This is such a nice surprise, Eric. And I know Kendal is relieved you're here."

"It's great to be here," he said, smiling. "How's Marcy?"

"She's great, thanks."

"She get a chance to see much of Lance?"

"Every other weekend. Funny you should ask. He's meeting me for breakfast tomorrow morning." She giggled. "I'm a little curious about what he wants to talk about. I guess you know Jackson and I have been seeing quite a bit of each other."

"I think my sister e-mailed me that bit of news."

"It's so funny. We were just talking about you. It's been months since we have seen hide or hair of you."

Hoping he could get a straight answer out of the forever-chatty Sheila before she went off on some tangent, Eric cleared his throat. "Sheila, how's Kendal doing? Really?"

Her face took on a serious look as she glanced toward the kitchen and whispered, "I guess your dad pulled some strings to get the two of you out here, huh?"

"Actually, no," he said, briefly looking at Quincy. "He didn't get very far this time using his influence."

"There's been only one call," she said quietly. "Kendal is pretending not to be scared, but by the time the police left the other day, she was trembling like crazy. She hasn't gotten much sleep, either." She glanced over her shoulder again. "To be honest, Eric, I'm a little scared, too. Those reporters have been trying all sorts of tricks when they call. I think it's all stirring up a lot of memories for her. But you know how she is. She won't admit it."

Eric indeed knew how his sister was. Obviously, she was still pretending certain things didn't bother her, and even now was holding her feelings inside. As a child, he had been awakened many nights by her crying. But he always got an irritated glare whenever he questioned her about it. "Try not to worry," he said, gazing into Sheila's fearful eyes. "What's the scoop on this doctor who scammed the drugs?"

Happy to oblige, Sheila's manner took on even more of a confidential note as she proceeded to tell what she knew. "Frank Peck was one of her clients, you know. I just can't believe it. He actually asked her to marry him a week ago. He's been after her for a while—buying her gifts and flowers. She returned most of his gifts, but he kept trying. There was one that she even tried to hand off to me." She lowered her voice. "I guess it was a little inappropriate. But he refused to take it back. She had even discussed her concerns with her manager. That was around the time Miss Eula died. But he still refused to remove him from her client load as she wanted."

"Marry!" Eric repeated, shocked by the disclosure. "When did this happen? I didn't know Kendal was serious about anyone."

"She's not. But he was very persistent—obsessed, if you ask me."

Gawking in disbelief, Eric took out a notepad and started scribbling furiously. "What else can you tell me about him?"

"Before all this happened, I honestly thought he was a good catch for her. I even tried to change her mind about keeping him at arm's length. Needless to say, I'm glad I failed."

Eric jotted down a couple of things to check into and then raised another sensitive issue. "She still thinking about the baby thing?"

Sheila rolled her eyes and nodded. "Yeah, for some strange reason, she really wants this. She's been searching for medical history on her birth parents."

Despite feeling a stab of anxiety, Eric plunged ahead. "Has she talked to Dad yet?"

"She's chicken."

"I don't know how he'll take her wanting to get pregnant," he said, more to himself than to Sheila. "Much less wanting to dig up information on her birth parents."

"I'm worried about her, Eric. She's holding too much inside. And she still clams up when we happen on the subject of Jack Sumner."

Eric's lips twitched as he shot a worried glance at Quincy. He hadn't expected the conversation to turn so abruptly, and was now painfully aware that it was a mistake to start Sheila talking.

Quincy felt ill at ease listening to personal information about a woman he had come to interview. He slowly studied his surroundings, hoping to block out anything that made him feel too sympathetic or less than completely objective. He did, after all, have a job to do.

The house was comfortable. Though much larger, it reminded him of the house in which he had grown up with his mother and aunt. He was twelve when his father died. Aunt Barbara, having never married, moved in with them to help out. She and his mother were present at as many football or wrestling events as they could manage. He had fond memories of how they both celebrated in the stands whether he scored or not.

He looked toward the foyer, noticing the half-closed sliding door across the hall. Having gotten a glimpse as he walked past, he knew it was a formal dining room.

Curiously, the sounds coming from the kitchen made him relax a little more. He never expected their meeting to impact him the way it had. She seemed warm and gracious—nothing like he had imagined. He had almost thought this the wrong address when she flung open the door and rushed out onto the porch in a robe and fluffy pink slippers.

Despite her relaxed appearance, her loveliness was breathtaking. Bright eyes, creamy honey-brown complexion, long soft hair that hung wild around a beautiful face and a smile filled with mystery. Her simple movements were feminine and graceful, but not the least provocative. Physically, she was perfect. But behind the shell and in contrast to that open-handed hospitality, he had seen the remoteness—sadness, really. The same quiet agony he had noticed in her picture from the dossier.

He inwardly chided himself. If he got too attached, he could sabotage his story. Her trusting manner could very well be an act. After all, she had been exposed to politics for a number of years.

Still, she seemed a far cry from the woman journalists had labeled 'the ice princess.' And the photos he had seen hadn't done her justice. He mentally shook himself. He had to stop this. Perhaps his aunt's remarks about him needing a good woman were influencing his thoughts.

He strained to refocus his thinking. But despite his best effort, his mind immediately bounced back to the image of Kendal Boyd's face. He fidgeted, feeling like a fly ensnared by a spider's web. What was it about her that had captivated him so instantly? Surely, it wasn't just a physical attraction. He worked with gorgeous women every day. It took more than that to catch his eye. Maybe it was her unexpected charm. Though he suspected she was quite capable of deception, she couldn't so skillfully portray such depth if a trace of it wasn't there.

The reporter in him knew that an interesting story lay behind her detached elegance. However, he was, in spite of himself, more than a little intrigued by her. He cocked his head and glanced at Eric, who seemed intensely edgy.

As he had alluded to earlier, the young agent had deliberately side-stepped mentioning Quincy's profession to the women. Perhaps they wouldn't have been so cordial if it had been made clear. Looking down, he spotted a child's doll beneath the heavy oak coffee table. He assumed it belonged to the Marcy Eric had asked Sheila about. He was about to comment, but Eric started speaking again.

"I spoke with Jackson this morning. He briefed me on the legal matters. Have they said anything else about arresting her?"

Quincy cleared his throat and looked at Eric. "I think I'll wander into the kitchen and see if I can lend a hand. You think she'll mind?"

"No," Eric said. "Go on back through the hallway, past the stair-case."

Quincy nodded and walked through the narrow corridor toward the kitchen light and the sound of clinking dishes. He stepped into a bright, old-fashioned kitchen with several added conveniences. The floor had large black and white ceramic tiles that underscored the stain-less steel fridge and an oversized stove with a microwave above it. There were two large windows; the table sat next to one, and the other was over the sink on the adjacent wall. Oak cabinetry lined the walls over the sink and counter. Kendal was standing at the sink, her back to him. He noticed she had brushed and pulled her hair back into a ponytail.

"Thought I'd offer a hand."

She swung around, her eyes wide with panic. The plate she was holding slipped from her fingers onto the tiled floor and shattered. Quincy quickly moved to pick up the pieces.

"I'm sorry," she said, hurrying towards what he assumed was a broom closet near the entrance. She sighed and shook her head when she returned. "I've been a nervous wreck all day. Be careful. Those pieces are sharp."

He dumped the larger pieces into the trashcan. Then he reached for the brush and dustpan she was holding and swept up the smaller fragments.

"I shouldn't have walked up on you like that," he said, aware that her eyes were evading his. "My mother told me to always make a little noise when I approach somebody on the pool bank, especially if his back is turned."

She giggled a little. The sound was almost musical. "What does *that* mean?"

"I think it has something to do with broken dishes."

They both relaxed as the mood turned light. The strain in the air dissipated, and they made small talk about metaphors and riddles. After rinsing his hands over the sink, he felt surprisingly comfortable helping arrange sandwiches on a large platter. Cookies and coffee mugs were added.

"You pretty good with riddles, aren't you?" she asked. At that exact moment, a child's cry was heard and Kendal turned too abruptly and tripped over the hem of her pajamas, falling into his arms.

Unsure how to manage the resulting awkwardness, Quincy steadied her and, without missing a beat, answered the question she had asked before stumbling. "I'm not really all that good with riddles. I just make a lot of analogies in my work. I've always enjoyed brainteasers, though."

Clearly flustered, Kendal pulled away. "I'm sorry. Guess I'm just a little clumsy tonight. How 'bout we take these on in before something else happens."

He bent down, looking back up at her doubtful expression. "It would probably help if you rolled up your pajamas a little. Do you mind?"

Before she could respond, he grasped the hem of one pajama leg and rolled it up to the ankle. Then he did the other. When he stood and took the large platter from the counter, she grabbed the coffee carafe and went ahead of him.

"Okay, you two," she said, walking into the living room. "I've managed to complete the task without break…." She stopped and looked around, realizing that Sheila had probably gone to check on Marcy.

Eric, seemingly half asleep, became fully alert when he saw the platter Quincy was carrying. He eagerly rubbed his hands together and, for an instant, the gesture reminded Quincy of his boss. "Looks great, Sis. I'm hungry."

Kendal placed the carafe on an end table and set the coffee table with napkins, cups and sandwich plates.

"Here we are," she said, carefully placing the food on the table. Once they were all seated, Eric grabbed a sandwich and chomped down as if he hadn't eaten in days. Kendal served the coffee, asking Quincy, "Cream and sugar?"

"Just black, thanks."

She shot a disapproving look at her brother, who had already eaten half his sandwich. "Don't you think you ought to bless the food before you choke on it?"

Eric stopped chewing immediately. His embarrassed facial expression and bulging cheeks prompted an eruption of laughter. Warmed by the lighthearted moment, Quincy, without reservation, took their hands and uttered a blessing. It was only after they had started to eat that he became concerned that his well-intentioned gesture might have been presumptuous. After all, he was a guest. But since he had not observed any negative reaction from either of the siblings, he decided not to dwell on the matter.

After a few quiet moments, Eric returned his plate to the table and cleared his throat. Kendal's eyes shone with a hint of mischief as she peered over her mug at her brother. "So how are things faring in Denver?"

"Just fine, thanks. How are you dealing with the investigation and recent threat?" Eric asked.

Kendal's jaw dropped. She clearly hadn't been expecting her brother to broach the subject, particularly with an outsider looking on. What was Eric doing? This was a family matter, after all. Glancing nervously at Quincy, she looked into the distance and said nothing.

As for Quincy, he deliberately turned his attention to the photographs on the mantle. The largest was one of the congressman and his mother. Several others in smaller frames surrounded it.

"I need to know if you recognized the voice on the phone," Eric pressed. "Was there anything familiar about it?"

Kendal laughed nervously. "Eric, do we have to discuss this? You just got here."

"Yes, and the sooner the better. Did you hear anything in the background? Cars, voices, any sounds at all?"

Her mouth tightened into a stubborn line. "I've already talked to the police. We called them just after I got the call."

"Kendal, please."

"Dad called you," she said, glaring at him accusingly.

"He told me about the threat," Eric said. "He's worried, Sis. We both are."

She returned her cup to the table, folded her arms across her chest and gazed at the darkened fireplace. "I don't remember any other sounds, Eric. Just his voice."

Quincy's attention was suddenly drawn to Eric's gaze, which was so intense that for a moment he hardly looked like himself. "I spoke with the Rose Creek police yesterday. We thought you would be able to remember things more clearly if you talk to me. Tell me what kind of feeling you got while he was on the phone with you?"

She shuddered visibly. "What difference could that make?"

"Stop fighting me, Sis, and answer my question."

She closed her eyes and tightened her arms around herself. Quincy could tell by the deep breaths she was taking that she was trying to remain calm. "His voice was husky and whiny at the same time, if you can imagine that."

"And what were his exact words?"

"'Death crouches at your door, Kendal Diane Boyd. And I aim to see that it gains entrance.' It was really creepy. I'm hoping it was just a prankster. You know, since I was on the evening news."

She began to rub her arms, and Quincy suppressed an impulse to offer her comfort.

Eric's smile was genuine and tender. "I can only imagine how terrifying it must've been. I'm sorry."

Her eyes anxiously moved from Eric's face to Quincy's. "It's not like *that* so much as it is painful, Eric. I guess it just hurts to think somebody really hates me so much. And the things the reporters were yelling at me...."

Eric frowned and glanced down at his pad. "Did you notice that is words sounded almost poetic? Even Biblical."

"I thought so, too," she whispered. "I remember feeling like I had heard the voice before. It was just a flash of an impression. But after thinking about it...um...I suspect it wasn't familiar after all. Just shock."

"Sis, what about Dr. Peck? Could he have something to do with the call?"

She ventured a response. "I guess at this point, I really don't know. Anything's possible. But I can't imagine he would do something like this just because I declined an unexpected marriage proposal."

Eric's face stiffened. "So it's true. He *did* propose?"

Kendal smiled and leaned back. "I can see you've been talking to my talkative blond conscience."

"I'm glad Sheila's here," Eric said, smiling.

"I am, too."

"Let's look at all this realistically, Kendal. You got this call after you declined Dr. Peck's marriage proposal. Then he mysteriously disappears after learning about the FDA investigation. Then you gave notice at Howard-Hadley. That sound about right?"

"I suppose."

"Was Peck aware of your plans to conceive?"

Quincy watched as embarrassment spread across her face. She squirmed a little and picked up her cup, refusing to look directly at her brother. "I may have mentioned it once."

"Have you had any luck getting information about your birth parents?"

Quincy thought he saw a hint of irritation in her eyes. Perhaps the real Kendal Boyd was about to surface. Now she stared at her brother as if he had just asked her to explain a complex surgical procedure.

"What does that have to do with some stupid prank call, Eric?"

"Maybe nothing. But I suspect the call either has something to do with Peck, the company, or you digging into the past. Is there something else going on you haven't told me about?"

"Well, it probably doesn't mean anything, but Walt Hadley Jr. offered me my manager's position the day I quit."

Eric turned the page on his pad. "The same manager you spoke to about Peck's advances?"

"Yes."

"What's his name?"

"Jed—Jed Mason. He's a real jerk, but I can't see him doing something so…so juvenile."

"What don't you like about him?"

"He never lets up on me—he's never forgiven me for being Stan Boyd's daughter."

"I can relate," Eric said. "One more thing. Besides this doctor you went to see, does anyone else know you're delving into your adoption records?"

"Just Sheila. But what does that have to do with anything?"

"I'm just trying to rule out as much as I can. You sure Dad doesn't know?"

Kendal clasped her hands and kept her gaze on Eric's face. "Of course not," she said, frowning. "Can we talk about all this tomorrow? I've been a bundle of nerves since Sheila told me about this serial killer. And your interrogation isn't helping right now."

Quincy noticed her strained voice, her uncertain movements, and trembling she tried so hard to hide. She was agitated. Despite feeling like an eavesdropper, he found the conversation incredibly fascinating. And now he was wondering what Sheila had meant when she mentioned memories of somebody named Jack Sumner.

Complexities, he thought. Everybody had complexities. He rolled his shoulders in an effort to work out the tension. Eric fell back against the chair and closed his eyes. "I suppose it can wait 'til morning. I'll be meeting with Jackson for lunch tomorrow. You want to come along?"

"No," she said. "I have plans of my own."

Quincy put his empty mug on the table and stood. "I'll be happy to help with clean up, Kendal."

"No," she said, leaping to her feet. "I've already got this under control. But thanks. I'm sure you're tired after your flight from Denver. Sit down and relax while I go make sure the beds have fresh linen."

As she strolled away, Quincy looked at Eric. Did he really intend to continue this pretense with his sister? In the airport parking garage, Eric mentioned he had checked him out. When had he done that? And he hadn't missed the comment about his knowing he would be in Seattle, either. It was strange how conveniently Eric needed a ride to his sister's home. It slowly dawned on him that the agent had played him.

He was stunned. Why hadn't he picked up on this earlier? What exactly was Eric working? While Quincy wasn't sure what he was up to, he knew it could sabotage his chances for an interview later. He managed to stifle a yawn. "I think I'd better go to my hotel. I've already got reservations."

"Why don't you stay here?" Eric said, getting to his feet. "I have my own suite downstairs. There's a private bath, a small kitchenette and two bedrooms. There's plenty of room. Kendal doesn't mind."

"No, I couldn't impose…."

"Don't be silly," Kendal interrupted, coming back into the room. "Of course you'll stay. The beds are clean and ready."

Quincy gave Eric a blank stare and headed for the front door. He didn't want to openly decline and possibly expose her brother's game plan, but he didn't like deception.

"I'll give you a hand," Eric said, lightly whacking him on the shoulder.

Outside, the mild fragrance of roses and junipers teased Quincy's nostrils as he made his way down the walkway and through the chain link gate. Even in the dimness, he had noticed the roses on their arrival. She had a vast array in the front and side yards, which was enclosed by a four-foot chain-link fence. Although most of the roses hadn't yet opened, he could tell they would be beautiful.

The sound of a dog barking in the distance cut through the quiet of the neighborhood, making him feel even more uneasy. He took a deep breath and plunged his hands into his pockets as he moved toward the SUV. The night air had grown dense and damp. A swarm of gnats danced drunkenly in the muted glow of the street lamp must at the end of her gravel drive.

Eric moved up beside him. "Kendal and I grew up in this ole' house. It was our grandmother's. She's done a lot with it, but I'm sure it's a challenge to keep up."

Quincy turned narrowed eyes on his young companion. "It's very nice. Now would you mind telling me what's going on?"

"I'm sorry, Quincy, but as you know, it would upset her if I told her you were a reporter. I told you I didn't plan…."

"You set me up, didn't you?"

Averting his eyes, Eric began. "Well…."

"Regardless of my personal feelings about this matter, I won't be party to deceiving her, Eric."

"You actually believe she's involved in this scam?"

"You can see yourself that it doesn't look good. But after meeting her, I-I just don't know."

"Quincy, I know you have a lot of questions. But it's like I said, with this nut scaring her like this, my dad and I don't want her harassed by media."

Quincy steadied himself, his pulse pumping wildly. "Are you forgetting I'm with the press? And why are you going to such great lengths to shield her from the inevitable? Why has your dad done it all these years?"

Eric shifted his weight and leaned against the vehicle. "My dad and I don't agree about a lot of things, but we agreed on this. We talked a long time before deciding on a plan of action. We trust you, Quincy. Some newsperson is going to get to her sooner or later. We would much rather it be you."

Quincy folded his arms across his chest, trying not to be annoyed. "I assume the anonymous call my boss got…."

Eric nodded even before Quincy finished his question. "I hope you'll forgive the pretense. But we just needed to get you in place before things got out of hand."

Quincy took several steps toward the street. "If you trusted me so much, why didn't you just ask?"

"We were afraid you would refuse."

"What exactly am I in place for?

"Your interview." Eric grabbed his bag from the back. "You saw how nervous she was in there. She still doesn't have a clue about the ramifications of all this. Not to mention this threat on her life."

Quincy had seen a lot more than nervousness in Kendal's posture. She was terrified. And he couldn't help wondering if her decision to reject Peck had backfired, exposing her own cunning. Joe might have been right in his assumptions about the Boyds. Perhaps they weren't squeaky clean. This could turn out to be an incredible finale to his journalistic career.

He cleared his throat. "I suggest your father's office set up a press conference for her. She needs to make a statement as soon as possible."

"She's aware of that. But we were hoping...."

Quincy turned back. "Quitting her job makes it look worse, Eric. Are you sure she has nothing to do with Peck's scam?"

Eric stiffened. "Of course I'm sure. Besides, she and Sheila just closed a deal on a gift and flower shop. Why would she want to jeopardize that?"

"Where would she get the money for such a timely investment?"

Eric was silent for several moments. Quincy was sure the question had rubbed him the wrong way. "Perhaps Dad and I were wrong about you. I apologize."

Quincy placed his hands behind his head and flexed. It felt good to stretch. Suddenly, he remembered Kendal's words when she introduced Sheila. "That's what she meant by *business partner*. I should've realized," he said, trying to untangle his thoughts. "And the child I heard upstairs?"

"Sheila's little girl, Marcy. Please, Quincy. Do this favor for us. You know how ruthless some reporters can be. Kendal couldn't handle it."

"I can see she's scared. But I think she's a lot stronger than you're giving her credit for," Quincy said. "I don't know about all this, especially this notion of my staying in her house. Joe can have someone else out here by morning."

"No," Eric said. "We trust *you*, not Joe Amory. You went through a lot to protect a source that didn't really need it. We didn't necessarily want *The Hill Watcher*, but that was all a part of getting you. So we staged that call to rush the game. Joe Amory knew about this situation before most other national newspapers. We thought we had more time, but as you know, news like this travels fast."

Having decided to accept the sleeping arrangements, Quincy's mind was speeding towards a resolution. "You do realize anything I get or do will be cleared and owned by the paper I work for?"

"We don't care about that. We just want Kendal handled delicately and with respect. I'm prepared to offer you an exclusive—after I get her to understand its necessity, of course."

His heart lurched. "An actual unscripted, exclusive interview?"

"For sure. But I would prefer you let me arrange that one."

"Eric, I'll agree under one condition. It's not negotiable." He paused for effect. "She's got to know who I am and what you and your dad are proposing before this goes any further. I already feel awkward having heard so much personal information."

"I trust you'll keep all that under your hat until it's cleared?"

"You haven't agreed to my condition."

Eric took a deep breath, shoving his hands into his pockets. "All right, I promise."

Quincy stepped closer to the vehicle. "I'll call Joe when I get settled in. He'll be able to get everything set up for us. I trust you'll eventually tell me why she avoids reporters like the plague."

"I'll let *her* do that."

Quincy increasingly recognized that he had underestimated Eric Boyd. The agent and devoted brother was just as shrewd as his father in shielding his sister.

-SIX-

Kendal slept fitfully and awakened with a dull sense of loss. Dreams of Nana always made her feel that way. Nana had been the most stable guiding post in her life. Her childhood ordeal with Sumner had left her intensely disenchanted with her father. Disenchantment turned to anger, which became so unmanageable that it eventually expanded to include God.

Nana had tried to soften her fury by constantly reminding her that she was still alive. She had convinced her that despite bad experiences, God was a loving father who had protected her and that her opinion of his method did not matter. Kendal eventually realized the poisonous effects of her rage and surrendered. To a degree.

While she still distrusted men, the entire abduction was a near-blank in her mind—an old dream that had faded into little more than occasional wisps of memory. It was absurd to blame God for something she couldn't even remember. With Nana looking on, she had rededicated her life to Christ during a church ceremony honoring its high school graduates. But her devotion had since regressed to the point that she felt hypocritical in her faith.

Kendal stretched and placed her hands behind her head, gazing up at the ceiling. She let her mind travel back to her last moments with Nana at the hospital. The bleeping sounds the monitors made barely registered anymore. For years Nana had suffered from congestive heart failure, causing her brown skin to turn almost as black as soot. Her voice was weak and unsteady. Yet there was a warm glow about her, and her eyes still sparkled with unabashed affection for her granddaughter.

"Kendal?"

"Don't talk, Nana. You need to save your strength."

But she had continued talking anyway. "I've got to go, you know. Just hate leaving you alone."

Kendal had suppressed the urge to cry, even managing a smile. "Don't talk like that. You've always beaten these attacks."

"Don't ignore my meaning, sugar. I'm a tired old woman, and I know you know that."

Kendal had looked away, her eyes stinging. "I know, but you shouldn't be worrying about me. I'm grown now."

Nana turned her eyes towards the window, which was next to her bed and began twisting the edge of the sheet. "Grown and empty," she murmured. "You ought to be married with children by now."

"You know I'm not the marrying kind, Nana."

She stilled her fingers and turned back to her granddaughter. "I know no such nonsense, Kendal Diane. You hide your real feelings behind pretense. But God sees your heart, and he has somebody special for you."

Kendal was surprised that her grandmother had broached the very subject she had avoided for years. She chuckled mirthlessly and leaned closer to Nana's ear. "I'm not even sure I can fall in love. I can't seem to feel. Maybe something's wrong with me."

Eula Boyd gazed at her, a quiet smile on her face. "Too many questions," she whispered.

Initially, Kendal thought she was referring to the comment she had just made and was about to apologize. "I'm...."

"You've had them locked inside you since that sly devil stepped into our home." Tears trickled from the corners of the old woman's eyes, forming a trail to her ears. Kendal leaned in and brushed them away. "Things were never the same. Your daddy never stopped blaming himself. Feels he should've been here."

"He should have," Kendal said, instantly regretting her impulsive remark. "I guess there's a reason we never talk about that time. Even though I can't remember everything, I don't really like thinking about it."

"You're a smart and capable young woman, Kendal. You just need to relax a little and pray wide open...no more make-believe."

Kendal nuzzled her cheek next to her grandmother's. "Sometimes it's still hard to believe God even hears me, Nana. And I'm not sure what I'm supposed to do afterwards."

"That's what faith is all about. He hears and you believe. Just tell him all about it and wait for his instructions."

"I will, Nana," Kendal said, wanting to change the subject.

But Nana was not finished. "I 'magine you'll do well to warm in the fire of family. A child of your own would do that. But you never been still long enough for God to guide you."

"What d'ya mean, *be still?*"

Nana coughed and cleared her throat several times before she could continue. "Be still and listen, sugar."

Kendal resisted the impulse to question her grandmother further. Nana stopped suddenly, her face distorted by pain. Clutching her hand anxiously, Kendal asked, "Nana, you all right? You want me to call for the nurse?"

She shook her head, her mouth slowly relaxing as the pain subsided. "Make me a promise," she whispered.

Kendal held her breath. "Anything."

"I think I put back enough to help buy that flower shop you been wanting. If it ain't, sell the house. When everything is settled, you'll find your answers. Maybe then you'll settle down and marry."

"I will, Nana."

"Things ain't been right between you and your daddy for a long time, sugar. I want you to fix that. Then you grow on up and marry...have your own children."

"Nana, I'm already grown up."

Her grandmother chortled, the effort triggering a succession of hacking coughs that made Kendal feel guilty for letting her ramble on so. "Twenty-nine might be grown up, but most of the time you stuck at ten. Even so, the Lord speaks the needed balm to ailing hearts. Comes in small whispers."

The odd saying baffled Kendal. Before Nana could continue, the coughing spasms became so persistent she could scarcely breathe. Monitors went off just as Kendal called for the nurse. There was nothing they could do to save her.

Kendal sat on the side of the bed and watched the curtains gently sway in the breeze coming through a partially opened window. Sheila would badger her if she knew Kendal had modified the setting on the security system to allow her to leave it open last night.

She stretched again, noting that it was eight-thirty, later than her usual rising but still early. Despite her present melancholy mood, she had slept well for the first time in three days. Having two federal agents in the house had clearly restored her sense of security.

On her way downstairs to prepare breakfast for her guests, she passed Sheila and Marcy's rooms and remembered that Sheila had a breakfast date with her ex-husband. She had probably left early to take Marcy to school. Today was physical therapy day, which the child hated, and Sheila usually had to bribe her with some treat to coax her out of bed.

She would meet Sheila at the shop later to help finish cleaning before the new display stands arrived. They planned to open the Saturday before Mother's Day, hoping this tactic would boost their first week's sales. The opening was just over a week away, and she was finally feeling a touch of excitement.

She was thankful that Sheila and Jackson had taken care of all the legal details, even handling the advertising. They had moved rather fast, as they had less than two weeks to set up.

Kendal plodded down to the midway landing and turned left rather than right. This would cause her to come out onto the kitchen stairway entrance. Her eye caught sudden movement and she screamed, stopping the instant she recognized Eric sitting at the kitchen table.

Eric bolted up and hurried to her. "I didn't mean to scare you, Sis," he said, putting an arm around her shoulders.

Feeling silly, she pulled away and fanned her chest, trying to calm her nerves. "I was so deep in thought, I forgot you were here."

Eric led her to the table. "It's May Day, and you only have nine more days before your big day. You probably have a right to be distracted."

"I guess so."

"Sit down," he said. "I'll pour you a cup of coffee."

She gladly sat, feeling a bit self-conscious. "I suppose with everything happening at the same time, I'm also a bit more jittery than I want to admit."

He smiled sympathetically. "And you're hardly used to having guests roaming around, are you? What's on *your* agenda today?"

"We have a few things to button down at the shop. I ordered fountain from a place over in Bellevue. I'll pick it up next week. Are you still going to be here?"

"Maybe."

"I'll need some help. You want to go with me?"

He moved across the kitchen to the counter and picked up the coffeepot. "We'll see how it works out," he said. "I'm sorry I haven't been much help around here. You've been through a lot in the last year. First, Nana's illness and death, and now all this."

Kendal watched him pour coffee into her mug. The soft trickling reminded her of the sound the rain made when it coursed through the drain from her roof. Eric then placed the mug and a bottle of hazelnut creamer in front of her.

"There was nothing else you could've done. You have a life of your own to live."

She could see her rose garden through the kitchen window, and this had a calming effect on her frayed nerves. The array of colorful buds and open blooms made her think of Nana and her final riddle, which led her to think of Quincy and his knack for old sayings.

Determined to hide any sign of interest in their guest, Kendal decided not to ask her brother any of the questions darting through her mind. She absently stirred the creamer into her coffee, inhaling the robust aroma. The coffee was stronger than she liked, so she stirred in extra creamer.

Like one of Marcy's kisses, the steam twirled upwards and touched her nose with a misty splash. "Thanks. I wasn't aware you knew your way around the kitchen."

"I'll have you know I'm a wonderful cook. And to prove it, I'll prepare you a morning feast. How 'bout bacon, eggs, pancakes and...."

"Just eggs and toast will be fine," she interrupted, taking a sip of the strong brew. "So how's Linda? Any upcoming plans I can buy a new dress for?"

His shoulders slumped. "Linda is getting married in a couple of weeks, Sis. To someone else."

Totally surprised, she looked up open-mouthed. "I thought…."

She caught herself as soon as she saw the hurt in her brother's face. He was the sensitive one in the family. He had always put too much of himself out there, seeming to get pricked by cupid's arrow too readily. Despite having envied him for his ability to fall in love, she was suddenly doubtful about her desire to experience it.

Eric focused on whisking eggs in a bowl. She sensed his grief, and decided to let the subject drop until he was ready to talk.

A few minutes later, she was crunching on a slice of bacon and cutting into her eggs with a fork. "Mmm. I'm either hungrier than I thought or these are pretty good."

"That's not such a compliment, considering you're the worst cook on the West Coast," he retorted. "I hope Sheila does most of the cooking around here, because poor Marcy would starve if she had to depend on her Aunt Kendal."

"Actually, I do pretty well. I have the microwave, and plenty of instant box dinners and precooked meals in the freezer. And Marcy loves them all."

He chuckled, prompting her to look up quizzically. "Remember that time you fixed Nana breakfast in bed?"

Kendal smiled faintly and bit into her toast.

"We caught her dumping it into the toilet when she thought you had gone downstairs. Remember?"

She rolled her eyes as the memory unfolded in her mind. Then she began laughing so hard she grew concerned she might choke on a piece of toast.

Eric fixed a plate for himself, and sat down to eat. "It's good to hear you laugh."

She reached for his hand. "I'm glad you're here. How did Dad manage to get the bureau to send two agents?"

Chuckling, Eric said, "He called my supervisor and explained the situation. He didn't get very far though. Bill Andersen doesn't take kindly to Dad's manipulation. But Dad thought since I was your brother…."

"Ah," she said, "exploiting the Justice Department. And just a representative, too."

"Representatives spend just as much time trying to throw their weight around as senators," Eric said facetiously. "By the way, I need to borrow your car. I'm supposed to meet Jackson and then go over to the Seattle field office in a little while."

"Why don't you use the car you brought?"

"Quincy has some snooping to do at your former employers. I need to try and butter up the special agent in charge here. They're working with some guy from FDA."

She smiled slightly, but her heart was thumping. "Probably Agent Sanner. He's nice enough, I guess, but he sure put the fear of prison in me."

Eric stopped chewing. "How?"

"It doesn't matter. I'm just glad he finally realized I had no access to the drugs in question. I hope they can find Frank, though…so he can clear me completely."

"Aren't you being just a little naïve, Sis?"

"What do you mean?"

"Think about it, Kendal. If Frank is found, he's facing a barrage of charges. What makes you think he'll be inclined to rescue you?"

After a shave and shower, Quincy felt alive again. Starting his day with the Lord had been his custom for years, but due to his schedule, he had been negligent the last couple of weeks. The solitude given him after Eric had gone upstairs was right on time. He had taken out his Bible and resumed his practice of spending time in the Word of God.

Then it dawned on him that his doubts and uncertainties about his future had intensified after being distracted—too busy to start the day off right. The ease and stealth with which complacency had moved in troubled him more than he wanted to admit.

But he had gotten a hardy dose of encouragement from the book of Philippians—the very passage James had alluded to the day he left Baltimore. *And the peace of God, which transcends all understanding, will guard your hearts and your minds in Christ Jesus.*

Quincy dressed, made his bed and headed for the stairs. Passing through Eric's bedroom, he caught sight of two firearms in the open drawer of the agent's nightstand. He froze.

An unsettling memory flashed into his mind. A dull ache that he knew wasn't real pulsed in his thoughts, and he instinctively touched his left shoulder where the round had penetrated. He swallowed, trying to suppress the conjured emotions. Squeezing his eyes shut, Quincy tried to blot out the memory of the blast and screams of bystanders.

Lord, I need to let go. Help me accept my past and move on. Renew my mind so I can sense your leading.

He refocused his thoughts on his phone conversation with Joe the night before. His boss had been in a deep sleep when he called. But the instant he recognized Quincy's voice, he sprang to attention. Joe had practically salivated over the phone when he heard Eric's proposal, especially the part about getting an exclusive interview with Kendal.

Like a dog getting a whiff of a meaty bone, Joe was quick to emphasize his connections with television. He was apparently related by marriage to one of the owners of WLSV News in Seattle, a CBS affiliate. He agreed to arrange a restricted press conference, where only invited reporters, namely Quincy, would be allowed to question Kendal.

Quincy laughed. Even with hundreds of miles and a phone line between them, he could sense the little man's rush of adrenaline. But Quincy was noticeably less eager to exploit the situation.

All the same, meeting Kendal had suddenly turned an unwelcome assignment into an exhilarating challenge. Up to now, he had not sought an interview with her—never had a reason to. To be honest, until Eric bummed a ride, he had dreaded even the idea of meeting her.

But all his preconceptions disappeared the moment her eyes held him hostage.

That had never happened to him before. It was almost scary. After getting a good night's sleep he had a much clearer perspective. He now realized the degree of his vulnerability and wouldn't allow himself to get too personal.

He paused on the stairs and smiled, listening to brother and sister in the kitchen. Their laughter was deep and true. Perhaps more than anything else, they needed to be with each other. The aroma of bacon drifted past his nostrils, overtaking the dank smell most basements held. He was hungry.

Quincy slowly resumed his climb. It was apparent that Eric had not yet informed Kendal of his profession. He was certain she wouldn't be laughing so unreservedly if he had. He walked into the kitchen and was instantly drawn into the conversation. "Good morning. Uh…I hope I'm not interrupting."

"No," Eric said, jumping up from the table. "Come on in. I'm the morning chef. What would you like?"

Quincy took a seat in a chair on Kendal's right. "Whatever the two of you are having is fine."

"Eric and I were talking about the time Nana caught him smoking in the back yard," Kendal recapped. "She sneaked up behind him and slapped the cigarette from his hands with a flyswatter."

"Yeah," Eric chimed in. "Quick Draw McNana."

They all laughed, and Quincy's misgivings melted away. He followed Kendal's eyes when he noticed them constantly turning to the window. The backyard roses were even more lush and abundant than those in the front.

"Wow," he said earnestly. "Those are nice. You must be pretty good with flowers."

She smiled gently, her teeth sparkling like stars at midnight. "I have more climbing up a lattice beneath my bedroom window," she said. "I let them go a little wild on the side." Turning back towards her brother, she added, "The lattice has come loose from the house, Eric. I'll need your help securing it later."

"Sis, I think we should maybe cut back some of the growth in the side yard?"

"No!" Kendal said. "Besides, I plan to harvest some for the shop."

"They're pretty and everything," Eric said, cautiously, "but they just hide so much of the house. Those you have in the front and back should be enough."

"No, Eric."

"Your wishes are my command, madam."

Listening to the good-natured bantering, Quincy grinned. Just then the sizzling sound of eggs in hot butter triggered a succession of belly growls. Embarrassed, he grabbed his stomach as if he could silence the sound.

Kendal chuckled softly. "I guess you must be hungry, too."

"Just a little."

"I hope you slept well last night."

"Oh, yeah," Eric put in. "I could hear him snoring through the wall."

They all laughed. "So how do you like working with my very intense brother? Are you teaching him how to lighten up?"

At a loss for a response, Quincy stole a quick glance at Eric just as he put a plate in front of him, saving him from having to respond. "Sis, I really need to get going. I can drop you by the shop and you can ride back with Sheila. Do you have everything you need before we head out?"

"No," she said, leaping up. "Let me run upstairs. It'll only take a few minutes."

An unsettling awareness gripped Quincy as he wordlessly watched Eric evade his gaze.

-SEVEN-

Kendal hurriedly gathered cleaning supplies from under the upstairs bathroom sink and stuffed them into a large tote. They had packed Sheila's car last night with things they had purchased for this project, but she decided to take extra just in case.

Feeling a nagging unease, she pondered Eric's sudden change of mood. Although pleasant enough, he seemed more agitated after Quincy came up from the basement—almost as if he were intimidated. Maybe Quincy was his supervisor. But hadn't Eric introduced him as a friend?

She was very much aware of Quincy's presence in her home. Chewing on a hangnail, she puttered about upstairs, making sure everything was in order. She would hate for him to wander around and think them a messy lot. After a few moments, she relaxed, her smile deepening as she recalled the night before. He seemed decent. And based on the way he had asserted himself in offering the blessing, he was probably a believer.

She shook herself. No, she couldn't let herself become too attracted to Eric's friend. Then again, there was no real danger of that since she had never been able to connect with men. And there were probably a thousand reasons she shouldn't think twice about this one in particular.

Sheila's words echoed in her mind. *I'm talking about all that stuff you have locked inside that keeps you from committing to men.*

True, she thought most men were pretenders. Men had been disappointing her since she discovered not a one was the prince charming she had read about in books. If her meager dating experiences hadn't been enough to convince her of her ineptness in romance, the recent disasters with Frank and Walt made it very clear. Still, she didn't want her past to forever block her chances at having the love and family she craved.

Perhaps her problems lie in the fact that she needed so much more reassurance in her early teens than her grandmother could give. She had simply wanted someone to coddle her a little—reassure her. Later, she craved someone to connect with—someone that recognized, despite her need to hide it, how lonely and scared she really was.

She smiled inwardly. Maybe that's why she and Sheila had remained friends. An aunt with four kids of her own and very little time to mend emotional wounds had reared Sheila. Her parents had abandoned her at age six and moved to Canada.

You'll do well to warm in the fire of family. A child of your own would do that.

It was now 10:40. She should have been at the shop forty minutes ago. Sheila had probably decided that she was dawdling. When she turned right at the landing, and descended the steps into the front hallway, she saw that her keys weren't in the tray on the table behind the sofa. She checked her purse. Not there, either.

She caught a faint whiff of Quincy's aftershave. He had looked so nice at the table in his gray business suit. Oddly, she was pleased he was still there. Her mind had gone back to the burly visitor hundreds of times since last night. His brawny build, easy laughter and confidence had instantly turned her insides topsy-turvy.

Cut it out, Kendal. You met this man less than twenty-four hours ago. He's here to do a job, nothing more. If he's looking for romance, no doubt he had plenty of beautiful women to choose from. You certainly can't compete with any of them.

This upheaval, this sensation was new to her. It had to stop. If Quincy was to do his job and return to Denver, she had to put any unrealistic notions aside. Besides, with him in such close proximity, it was wise to repress such stirrings, even if Quincy also felt it, and she glumly suspected he did not.

"Eric, did you find my keys?" she asked, entering the kitchen.

She stopped short at the sight of Quincy pouring himself another cup of coffee. He smiled at her, openly assessing her appearance. She shrank inwardly, feeling drab in faded jeans, white canvas sneakers and an old paint-covered shirt.

His smile broadened into a grin. "You really *do* plan to work today, huh?"

"Sure do. Where's Eric?"

"He left. Wanted me to drop you off at the shop on my way to Howard-Hadley."

"I see. So you guys really think the threat came from someone there? Eric seems to suspect my former manager."

"I'm just going to talk to Mr. Hadley," he said, keeping his tone light. "I've already made an appointment. You need any help with anything?"

"No, all I have is this tote."

He pulled it from her shoulder, lightly brushing against her. "I'm ready when you are."

Pushing her nervousness aside, Kendal grinned up at him. "You *are* a safe driver, right?" She felt like an idiot for asking such an inane question, but she couldn't think of anything else to say.

"Hmm?"

She was flustered by her silliness, but Quincy hadn't even heard her; his mind seemed to be elsewhere. "Quincy?" Her knees nearly buckled when his gaze suddenly met her eyes.

"Oh, uh…sorry. I was just thinking about how best to tackle my interview with Mr. Hadley."

"Straight on," she said, heading toward the front door. "I think he can be pretty guarded, but you're a cop. He'll be straight with you. If you want a broader perspective, though, I would try to talk with Olivia Howard. She's the engine of the operation. Mr. Hadley Sr. has been ill and is seldom around."

Quincy smiled. "Thanks. I appreciate the advice."

They stepped out into Seattle's notorious rainfall. Though there was no longer any hint of winter, the air was still cool. The patter of rain plopped in perfect tempo against the windshield of Quincy's SUV. Like the quiet pulse of a love ballad, the rhythmic hum of the wipers soothed her anxiety—to some extent, anyway.

Kendal opened the vent on the passenger side and breathed in the fragrance of damp earth and evergreens. Despite her pleasant surroundings, the anonymous threat and the FDA investigation had her twisted in knots.

But she once again pushed aside her anxiety and was enjoying Quincy's amusing comments when he neared their turn-off. The thirty-eight mile drive had been much too short.

"Turn right at the next stop sign," she said.

He pulled into the parking lot and let out a long whistle when he saw the green and white sign on front of the red brick building. The shop's dark-green delivery van was parked directly in front, beside Sheila's white Chevy.

The area was pleasant and quaint, resembling a scene from a Norman Rockwell painting. Both sides of a red-bricked median held several parking spots. The median itself was decorated with a black iron bench, large potted plants and an ornamental shade tree.

"Small Whispers Flowers and Gifts?"

She nodded, her eyes bright with pride. "You like it?"

"Interesting," he said. "What does it mean?"

"I'm really not sure. It's one of my grandmother's riddles—something she said just before she passed."

He took her hand, a gesture that first startled and then disturbed her. His strong fingers gently enclosed hers. "I'm sorry. I hope I didn't…."

"Don't be," she said, realizing he assumed his question had triggered sorrow. "I love thinking of Nana. Besides, I'm sure a lot of our customers will ask the same thing."

He released her hand. "You should probably be prepared to give them a better answer."

"You seem to be good with riddles, Quincy. Maybe you can help me figure Nana's meaning."

He took a deep breath, his dark eyebrows furrowing. The SUV suddenly seemed much smaller, and Kendal deliberately tried to shut out the intense awareness of him. "I have to admit, I like puzzles, but I'm not particularly good with interpretation when I don't know the source. My mother and aunt used to quote a lot of proverbs, too. I don't mind giving it a try."

"I think Nana enjoyed challenging us with her old sayings."

"My Aunt Barbara is like that," he said, smiling. "She used to tell me when the sun shines during a shower, the devil is fighting his wife."

"What does that mean?"

Laughing, he said, "I'm not sure, but it got my attention. So…what exactly did your grandmother say?"

Kendal hesitated, and then whispered, "The Lord speaks the needed balm to ailing hearts. It comes in small whispers."

He frowned pensively. "Hmm. What was the context? I mean…what was she talking about when she said it?"

Closing her eyes, Kendal envisioned the mischief twinkling in her grandmother's eyes.

"Kendal?"

"I'm sorry. What did you say?"

"I asked if you knew the context of her proverb."

"Sorry," she said, embarrassed. "We were discussing my past, my future and my desire for children. She said something about being still for God."

"Sounds like something my mother used to say," he said, looking around again. "This is real nice, Kendal. This section of Seattle reminds me a little of Kansas City."

"I've never been there," she said. "Do you travel a lot?"

"I do."

"That must be very exciting."

He checked his watch. "It used to be. The offices of Howard-Hadley are right off South Lake Union, right?"

"Yeah," she said, grabbing the tote. "Just off I-5. You can't miss it."

"And where is the lab and plant?"

"That's north on I-5 in Everett. You wouldn't be allowed past security without proper authorization, even with your badge."

He smiled, and her stomach fluttered. "Well, maybe I'll just stick with interviewing the executives. How 'bout I stop back by after my meeting? Maybe we can all grab a bite to eat."

"Sure, but you really don't have to. I can ride home with Sheila."

"But I really want to see the inside of Small Whispers. In the meantime, I'll give your Nana's proverb some thought."

Kendal hopped out of the vehicle with a lightness she hadn't felt in a long time, and practically skipped to the shop's front door. Chimes announced her arrival when she entered. Sheila was nowhere in sight, but she could smell the scent of her friend's efforts. "I see they delivered our plant stands," she called out.

Sheila stumbled from the back, her face and clothing smudged with dirt. "Hey, it's about time you showed up. Where are the guys?"

"Eric is at the field office. Quincy's on his way to a meeting." Kendal walked across the wide-open front and stopped to lean against the counter. She stared curiously at her grimy partner. "I didn't think we had *that* much cleaning to do."

Sheila waved her hand dismissively, oddly avoiding eye contact. "I spilled some soapy water on the floor in the back and slipped on it. Why are Quincy and Eric going separate ways?"

"I don't know. Maybe they have a strategy of striking at both ends and meeting in the middle."

Despite the smile Sheila managed, Kendal did not miss her somber demeanor. "You're beginning to sound like Miss Eula."

"You okay, Sheila? Did you hurt yourself when you fell?"

"I'm just dandy," she said, moving back through the heavy green curtain. Certain now that something was troubling her friend, Kendal followed. She hoped it had nothing to do with her tardiness.

She passed the desk on her immediate left just as a book on floral design tumbled onto the floor. Sheila must have brushed against it when she passed. Kendal noticed that the computer had already been turned on. Because it took up more space on the desk than expected, they had installed the phone on the wall just above it.

The shop had two distinct sections. The front would have a running fountain, display cases, shelves and two coolers. The back was already equipped with a walk-in cooler on the far right wall. Next to it were two large sinks and a long L-shaped worktable with drawers for tools and supplies that almost reached the back door in the far right corner. The back door opened out into the alley between the shop and a small antique bookstore. The restroom was in the far left corner of the back, behind other shelving units temporarily stored there. Unfortunately, they were able to salvage only a couple of the former owner's units. But purchasing new ones was as exciting for Sheila as shopping for Marcy at Christmas time.

"You've been busy," Kendal said, looking around at the sparkling surfaces. "What else do we need to do?"

"The bathroom still needs a good going over. Did you bring any more cleaning supplies? I knocked over some when I fell."

A hint of unease gripped Kendal. Something *was* wrong. She set the tote on the table and began unloading its contents. "I'm sorry I got here so late, Sheila. I really didn't want you to do so much by yourself."

She moved the tall rolling stool closer to the table and sat down. "No problem. I understand that we have guests. Besides, after a busy morning I was almost enjoying the quiet."

Kendal glanced around and grinned. "I'm excited. I can't believe it's all ours. Feels so good not to have to deal with Jed Mason."

"Speaking of which, did you let Walt Jr. know you wouldn't be interested in that job?"

Kendal put her hand to her mouth. "I forgot. I should've turned him down the instant he offered it, but I was in shock. Maybe he has seen some of our advertisements and figured it out. At any rate, I'll call him tomorrow. When are the other supplies coming in?"

"There's one more stand coming today. Plants will arrive Monday. I found a good deal from a place down in Tucson."

Kendal took the scrub brush set from the tote and headed for the bathroom.

"You want a snack?" Sheila called after her. "I packed some food this morning."

"Nah, I'm not hungry. Eric made breakfast." Kendal poured liquid cleaner into the toilet bowl and let it stand. Then she sprinkled scouring powder onto the sink and began scrubbing it vigorously.

"Jackson stopped by earlier," Sheila said, leaning against the door-jamb. "Lance was still here."

Kendal's eyebrows shot up in surprise, and she tossed the sponge into the sink and turned to face her friend. "At the same time?"

Sheila nodded, looking distressed.

"What happened?"

"Nothing," she said, retrieving the sponge from the sink. "Jackson is very sweet."

"What about Lance?"

She swallowed hard. "He's getting married in August."

Kendal gazed into her friend's pooling eyes. "What?"

Sheila ran her tongue over her bottom lip and continued scrubbing the sink. "By the way, he wants to do an unfolding photo shoot of Small Whispers as we set up. During the grand opening, too. I told him I would check with you."

Too stunned to think clearly, Kendal closed the toilet lid and sat down limply. "A photo shoot?"

"I think it would give us some much needed-publicity," she said, her voice cracking.

Kendal's eyes narrowed. "Is that why Lance took you to breakfast?"

She nodded, blinking rapidly. "He wanted my permission for Marcy to meet her."

Sheila's eyes began to brim over. Kendal's face grew warm with anger. She felt as if she could whip Lance silly for hurting Sheila again. "Why didn't you tell me?"

"You've got enough going on. My situation is no big deal. After all, we've been divorced for over two years."

"It is a big deal," Kendal countered. "I'd like to tell that Lance Dodd a thing or two."

"No, Kendal. Both of us should be moving on with our lives." She dabbed at her eyes. "By the way, Eric really seems to be worried about this investigation thing. We saw him this morning before we left. Naturally, Marcy was her usual morning-standoffish mood. Wouldn't even let him touch her."

"Are you really okay with this wedding, Sheila?"

All at once, tears trailed an already damp path. Kendal rose and embraced her friend. "Let's get out of here."

She sniffled. "We can't. There's another delivery coming."

Kendal led her out of the small bathroom and over to the L-shaped worktable. "Then how about we have a soda. Where is it?"

Sheila slumped down onto the seat. "There's a liter of ginger ale in the cooler. A bag of ice, too. The cups are on the sink counter."

Kendal took the refreshments from the cooler, grabbed a couple of cups and sat next to Sheila. "Do you still love him?"

After a long silence, Sheila answered. "No, but I guess the announcement just blindsided me. I didn't even know he was serious about anyone."

"Then why are you carrying on so? Like you said, it's been over two years."

"I hate to admit it, but I wanted to be the first to move on." She smiled and lowered her eyes. "I know it's silly."

Kendal placed her elbows on the table and cradled her face between her palms. "Maybe so, but I think I can understand it. It's funny how likely we are to take the things we have for granted during times of disappointment."

"What do you mean?"

"You really *have* gone on with your life, Sheila. You and Jackson have been seeing each other for a couple of months."

"I guess you're right."

"I think Eric is going through something similar."

Sheila's eyes widened in surprise. "Eric? I thought he and Linda were pretty close to getting hitched."

"Me, too. But he told me this morning she's getting married in a couple of weeks."

"Wow, must be something in the air. Poor guy."

"He's all right. Tell me about today. What happened?"

"Lance came inside to snap a few pictures when he dropped me back off; Jackson walked in five minutes later. I guess I was still in shock over Lance's announcement. I just lost it. Couldn't stop crying. They both probably think I'm nuts."

"I'm sure they understand. But if you plan to continue seeing Jackson, you had better explain what happened. Men tend to think the worst in situations like this."

"You should know," she said teasingly. "So what's with you and Quincy? You two sat out there for quite a while. And it's not raining all that hard."

Kendal pursed her lips. "We were just chatting about proverbs and riddles. He's really nice for a fed."

"Nice looking, too," Sheila said, pouring her soda over the ice. "I asked Eric if he knew anything about the serial killer, but he didn't."

"What about Jackson?" Kendal asked, returning to the previous subject. "How do you feel about him?"

Sheila smiled. "I like him a lot, and he adores Marcy. He's good with her, too."

"I've noticed," Kendal said, recalling the time Marcy knocked over a vase of silks in his office. It hadn't broken, but Sheila had been so embarrassed she scolded the child. Jackson had patiently taken Marcy by the hand and helped her pick up the vase and return the arrangement to its original state, by making a game of it. Marcy was so engrossed in the game that she soon forgot her distress. He later revealed that he had a niece with Down syndrome.

After their break, Kendal noticed the blinking red message light on the phone across the room. "Somebody call?"

"Not while I've been here," Sheila said, crunching on an ice chip. "Probably came in last night. Our phone number is on the front window, as well as the advertisements. Maybe this is our first order."

Kendal quickly went to the phone and hit the play button without picking up the receiver. The caller's voice came over the speaker.

Hello, Kendal.

She instantly recognized the low, whining voice of the man who had phoned her the day she quit her job. Alarmed, she covered her mouth with trembling hands and stepped back, bumping into Sheila.

Before we start on our journey together, my rose blossom, I wanted you to know that I will not tolerate unfaithfulness. You must get rid of the SUV driver, or someone might get hurt. Nobody can love you like I do, Kendal. I'll say bye for now, but you must pay for your sins. Perhaps you're familiar with the passage: "Eye for an eye, foot for foot, burning for burning, wound for wound."

At that moment, the phone rang and the two women screamed in unison, frantically clinging to each other. When the machine answered and Eric's voice came over the speaker, Kendal quickly picked up.

"Hello," she said in an unsteady voice.

"Hey, Sis, I'm glad you're there. I have good news. They've dropped any notions of arresting you. The FDA has apparently been watching

Frank for months. Jackson and I just left a meeting with Agent Sanner."

Kendal breathed a sigh of relief. On the verge of tears, she tightened her grip on the phone. "Thanks, Eric," she managed. "That *is* good news."

Looking as pale as a ghost, Sheila moved closer and placed an ear next to Kendal's. Kendal then switched Eric back to the speaker.

"You okay?" he asked. "I was just about to bring your car over."

"Uh…yes, but I can ride home with Sheila. After our last delivery arrives, we'll be finished here."

"You sure? I need to stay and visit with the agent in charge. They *are* kind of hesitant about giving me one of their cars. It would really help if I could keep yours."

"Sure. Fine."

"Sis, you sound funny. Anything wrong?"

"Eric, when you're done, will you stop by anyway? Please?"

-EIGHT-

Eric was still pondering his sister's odd tone when he entered the office of Special Agent Kent Cashion, who hung up the phone and motioned him to the leather visitor's chair. The smell of damp soil hung in the air. Eric looked around curiously and noticed several withered leaves on the carpet beneath a large potted plant.

Cashion was tall and stocky. He had thinning hair and looked to be in his late fifties. He had a stern face but a generous smile that somehow reminded him of the kindly image on an oatmeal box. Eric shifted in the chair and cleared his throat. "I appreciate your seeing me on such short notice, sir. I know you're very busy."

Cashion smiled again, and Eric's eyes were immediately drawn to the photograph on his desk with a similar contented beam. The portrait was of a very comfortable Cashion and a woman Eric assumed was his wife. Two younger adults and three animated children in various poses surrounded them. He felt a sickening ache crawl through his gut as Linda flashed in his mind.

"There's no need to thank me, Agent Boyd," Cashion said, breaking into Eric's musing. "I see you and your attorney have already met with Sanner. Bill warned me you were a go-getter." He laced his stubby fingers and leaned forward. "What can I do for you?"

"I assume since Bill expected me to show up, he explained my concerns. My sister's life was threatened the same day Sanner questioned her. I believe she needs to be protected. I've already asked for your help, but...."

"It's unfortunate that things like this get so tangled," he said matter-of-factly. "She is presumed innocent, so I don't see any real need for placing her under surveillance." Cashion leaned back in his chair and hardened his gaze. "Unless, of course, there's something else going on."

"No, sir, I just have a gut feeling that this wasn't just a prank. In fact, it may have nothing at all to do with the FDA investigation."

"As a favor to Bill, I will let you have a desk and work on a few minor cases while you're here. I've already cleared it with him. But the FDA investigation is off-limits for obvious reasons."

"Thank you, sir. I appreciate that."

"And, Boyd, please don't tramp all over my field without first clearing it with me. I know you're concerned for your sister, but as long as you're in Seattle, I expect you to observe protocol."

"With all due respect, sir, what makes you think I wouldn't?"

"Bill also told me you could be very stubborn when you sunk your teeth into something. I understand you were caught doing some unauthorized digging into a twenty-year-old case out of Auburn. Anything to do with this one?"

Eric held his breath. "Bill *told* you about that?"

Cashion nodded. "If you have reason to believe...."

"At this point, my main concern is Kendal's safety, especially since she's no longer a suspect."

Cashion looked at him skeptically and scratched his chin. "I don't know, son. I think I have to agree with Bill. You're overreacting. Are you sure you aren't holding something back on us—something that would justify your concern?"

"No, sir," Eric answered. "I simply want to make sure this threat is really a prank before I head back to Denver."

"I see. Well, in that case, I'll have Agent Vera Mackey show you to the desk you'll be using. Unless, of course, there is something else I can help you with."

Eric watched Cashion straighten the curves out of a large paperclip. "I've been thinking that the call Kendal got might shed some light on Dr. Peck's whereabouts."

Cashion abruptly stopped fiddling with the clip and asked, "You think the caller may have been Peck?"

Eric nodded. "I'm leaning that way. Perhaps, if we monitored the phones...."

Cashion shook his head before Eric finished his comment. "The circumstances don't merit that much equipment and manpower. I know this is your sister, but you should know by now things don't work like that."

Eric managed a smile. He knew he was probably being paranoid and overly sensitive. "Just thought I'd ask."

"Don't hesitate to come back in here if you come up with something more substantial. In the meantime, Bill wants me to keep you busy in a corner with a laptop. Some of the other agents would probably jump at any assistance along the line of research."

Thankful that he was at least accepted, Eric nodded. "Thanks again."

"Then I have your word you won't interfere with Mackey and Sanner's investigation?"

"Yes, sir. Would it be a problem for me to check with the locals in Rose Creek?"

Cashion shook his head. "Not with me. But please don't go flashing your big federal badge at them. They tend to get a little touchy about jurisdiction."

Quincy sat in the outer office waiting on Hadley Jr. to get off the phone. His assistant's unfriendly attitude had surprised him. He had gotten him a cup of coffee, but had seemed irritated and unhelpful. He had been friendly and accommodating when he phoned earlier to confirm the appointment. What had happened in the last couple of hours to sour his mood?

A door across the lobby opened, and a tall redheaded gentleman wearing glasses appeared. "Mr. Morgan," he said, striding across the room. "I'm Walt Hadley Jr. Sorry to keep you waiting."

Quincy stood and accepted a hearty handshake. "That's quite all right," he said, smiling. "I'm sure you're a very busy man."

"Come on into my office, and we can chat." Seeing the empty cup in Quincy's hand, he asked, "May I offer you another cup of coffee?"

"No thanks." Quincy grabbed his briefcase and followed him. "I promise not to take up much of your time. Do you mind if I record our conversation?"

"Not at all," he said, closing the door behind them.

Quincy pulled out the small recorder and flicked it on. "I'm sure you've heard these questions a few times in the last week."

Hadley smiled broadly. "I'm used to it. In fact, I've instructed my assistant to distribute our written statement to reporters and journalists. Of course, we'll have a formal press conference tomorrow afternoon."

"I know. And I plan to be here. But I want to ask you about the involvement of one of your former employees."

"Mr. Mason?"

Quincy frowned. "No, I wasn't referring to Mr. Mason."

"Ah, yes, Miss Boyd," he said. "My mistake. We've been getting a lot of inquiries about her from the press. But I assure you she is in no way connected to this con. She's just an innocent victim of circumstances…like the rest of us."

"Is it true that she was romantically involved with Dr. Peck?"

"That would be a question you should ask Miss Boyd. But the company has a policy against that type of thing."

"I'm sure you do," Quincy said. "I suppose by your earlier assumption, Mr. Mason is somehow connected to Dr. Peck's activities?"

His face stiffened ever so slightly. "I'm sorry, but I can't answer that either. I *will* say, however, that we've terminated Jed's employment and are conducting an internal investigation. And of course, the situation is still under federal investigation. I'm hoping Miss Boyd will consider returning when all this has blown over."

Quincy gave the man a slow, appraising gaze. Obviously, he wasn't aware that Kendal had moved on to something better. "Would Miss Boyd actually be interested in returning? I mean, after all that's happened."

Hadley flashed a confident smile. "Miss Boyd and I are special friends, Mr. Morgan. I'm quite certain she'll agree to a sound offer."

Despite Hadley's assertion of the company's policy on such things, his hint that he had a relationship with Kendal was not lost on Quincy.

From the sound of it, she burned her candles at both ends. He felt as if he was getting nowhere. "Since you would welcome Miss Boyd's return, you obviously don't think she had anything to do with this. Do you have any idea where Dr. Peck obtained unapproved drugs?"

The overconfidence Hadley had been exuding faded fast. "No, I don't. But as I stated, we're still investigating."

After several other routine questions, Quincy decided to change directions. "Miss Boyd is the daughter of Congressman Stan Boyd. Could you tell me if that had anything to do with her employment here?"

Hadley's face paled to the point of looking physically ill. "I don't believe so. And if you knew Miss Boyd as well as I do you would know she would never accept a job her father arranged. No, she got her job based on acceptable qualifications and pure determination."

There it was again, Quincy thought. "But isn't Congressman Boyd a personal friend of Olivia Howard's?"

"I'm not aware of any such association," he said, the vein in his neck bulging. "Obviously, that's a question she is better equipped to answer."

He had hit a nerve. Quincy clicked off his tape recorder. "Shall I set up an appointment with Ms. Howard through you or your assistant?"

"Olivia has her own personal assistant. She regularly works from her home, and Suzanne is there with her. However, I'll be happy to contact Suzanne about Olivia's availability." He picked up a pen. "When is convenient for you?"

"I would need to talk with her within the next few days, if at all possible. I'll be flying back to Baltimore soon after."

"It's Thursday. Let's try for tomorrow or Saturday."

"Yes."

"Where may we reach you?"

Quincy gave Hadley his cell number and then stood and extended his hand. "Thank you, Mr. Hadley. I appreciate your time."

Hadley stood awkwardly. "Not at all. I'll have my assistant phone Suzanne this afternoon. She'll give you a call."

On his way back to Small Whispers, Quincy felt as if he had been hoodwinked. The man had deliberately implied that he and Kendal had more than an employer-employee relationship. Just when he decided they were all wrong about the ice princess, Hadley casually drops that unsettling bit of information. Perhaps that was a part of her appeal to these men. Kendal obviously had a more active social life than he had imagined. Still, after meeting her, he couldn't quite picture her that way. And how could Hadley be so close to her when he wasn't even aware of Small Whispers?

He swung the black Explorer onto Bennington Road and into the parking lot at the flower shop. The building was hidden just off a main thoroughfare near Lake Washington. He pulled in and parked in front of an attractive tree with leaves so glossy they looked as though they had been spit-shined.

He sat for several moments, trying to gather his thoughts and calm himself. Why should he be so disturbed? He had no qualms about interracial relationships, and Kendal wasn't anything to him. He had to push Hadley's implication from his mind and remember the sweet lady he had dropped off three hours ago.

Lord, help me remain impartial, even as I try to help Kendal unravel her grandmother's proverb. Show me what her Nana's saying means, and let it bring her peace and comfort.

He finally hopped out, just as Kendal's maroon Sable turned in on the other side of the median.

"Hey," Eric called. "Get your interview?"

"Yeah. How did your meetings go?"

"She's no longer a suspect," Eric said. "Come on inside. I have more news. And I think now is the best time to tell Kendal who you are. You ready?"

"I'd better be," Quincy said, lagging behind a couple of steps.

The instant they entered the building, Sheila rushed towards them, her eyes wide with apprehension.

"Where do you think you're going?" Eric asked playfully.

She clutched his arm. "I've gotta go pick up Marcy at school. I didn't want to leave Kendal alone. That creep phoned again."

The smile faded from Eric's face. "What?"

"We called the officer who came to the house the first time, but he said something about jurisdiction and suggested we wait for you."

Eric squeezed her hands. "Where is she?"

She pointed toward the back. "Trying to keep busy."

"Go on and pick up Marcy. We'll meet you at the house later and fill you in."

Sheila nodded, pausing briefly to peer up at Quincy. "She's so scared. This guy is crazy. You should hear his voice. Can't y'all do something more to protect her?"

She was clearly worried. Quincy smiled, impressed by the two friends' devotion to each other. "I'm sure Eric will come up with something, Sheila. Try not to worry. It'll be all right."

Quincy closed and locked the door behind her, but wasn't sure whether to follow Eric to the back or wait out front.

He paced around the large room for several minutes and then wandered to the back.

-NINE-

Kendal squeezed her eyes shut, trying to block out the words snaking through her memory. *I'm your real daddy, Kendal. Nobody loves you like I do. Not even God. You belong to me.*

Her chest tightened and the shakes came with a vengeance. She raised trembling hands to her face, fighting the images that beckoned her. Her heart hammered, and she fought to catch her breath.

She gripped the rim of the bathroom sink to steady her hands. The porcelain felt solid and soothing, somehow imparting an impression of stability. Despite her uncertainties about her future, she had to find a way to keep the flashbacks at bay. The patchy images flashing before her were frightening. They pulled at her like a gaping black hole about to swallow her alive. They forced her to relive things that terrified her.

She was clearly having a panic attack. She couldn't let Sheila know, because she knew her friend would nag her nonstop to go into therapy. Besides, she didn't want to upset her any more than she already had.

"Sis."

Her eyes sprang open. Her brother's six-foot frame was like a ray of sunshine. He rested against the door, his face frozen with concern.

"Come sit down," he said, wrapping his arm around her shoulders and leading her out of the bathroom.

"Sheila told you?" Though spoken in a soft, timid voice, her question somehow sounded high-pitched, almost shrill, in the room of empty shelves.

He nodded. "I'll listen to the recording and call it in. Then there are some things I need to talk with you about."

Kendal moved to the table and sat down, thankful he was there. Moments later, Quincy came through the curtain. For an instant, the vise-like dread lessened. She smiled slightly, but didn't have the energy to speak.

"Quincy, you mind getting Kendal a glass of water or something. I need to make a call."

Eric activated the only message in memory, and Quincy scrounged around for a glass.

"Cups are on the counter by the sink," she said, avoiding his eyes. "The water is in the cooler."

He handed her a red disposable cup and then straddled a nearby stool. Motioning toward Eric, he asked, "He checking out that call?"

She nodded, placing the cup on the table without drinking. "It must've come in last night. We didn't check until a little while ago." She shuddered and wrapped her arms around herself.

"I can only imagine how frightening all this is for you, Kendal," he said, touching her hand. "I'm very sorry."

The contact was tender, and given that he was new to her small world, she was surprised by the calm it produced. Perhaps it had something to do with the fact that he was a federal agent. His presence made her feel safe.

"Thank you for your kindness, Quincy. I appreciate it."

"You're welcome," he said, looking over at Eric, who was talking on the phone with his back to them. They couldn't hear what he was saying, but it was apparent he was annoyed. He hung up and placed another call. Kendal could tell it was long distance by the number of digits he punched. Was he reporting to their father? She wanted to stop him, but decided to suppress the impulse when she felt Quincy's gaze.

Eric had news, she thought, feeling her stomach tighten. Was it good news? Should she pray? But she had no real desire to. Why, after all, was God allowing this nightmare in her life? Especially now? Had she done something—ill-treated some soul without realizing it?

Despite having walked a tight line in her faith for many years, she felt further away from God than she ever thought possible. She had learned from Nana that it was important to take her concerns to Him, but she never quite sensed a connection. And yet she had continued to pray simply because she was supposed to. But that wasn't good enough anymore. She obviously hadn't done enough.

"How was your interview?" she asked, attempting to refocus her thoughts.

"Unexciting," he said, pushing her cup closer to her. "I'm waiting for an interview with Ms. Howard."

She looked at him, feeling numb. "You didn't talk with her?"

"Hadley Jr. told me he would contact her secretary. I can only hope she'll get back with me soon."

"I see."

"May I ask you a question?" Quincy asked.

"Sure."

"Why did you quit your job?"

"I just got mad." She folded her arms loosely across her midsection. "Sanner's questions were scaring me, but Jed Mason was willfully accusing me of wrongdoing."

"I'm surprised he didn't choose to support you. After all, since he was your supervisor anything you might have been accused of would also fall on him."

"I don't know. I just assumed he was too busy trying to keep himself out of hot water. Anyway, I was his favorite scapegoat. He was a sore spot from day one of my employment. It felt good to throw that badge in his face."

"And you've put up with that type of behavior for five years? Why?"

She looked up and held his eyes. "It doesn't matter now. It's over."

"Kendal."

She turned at the sound of her brother's voice. He was off the phone. "Yes?"

"Will you be up to talking with my superior later this evening…after he talks to the special agent in charge here in Seattle?"

She tensed up. Quincy engaged her eyes and blinked slowly. She didn't know why she was so confused and indecisive, or why she was allowing herself to meekly depend on Quincy at this moment. But she'd done it so instinctively it somehow seemed right. She looked up towards her brother. "Of course."

A short time later, Eric came up to them, looking determined. "I might as well get this over with."

Kendal could feel his tension.

He stood at the head of the table and looked down at her. "Dad and I have asked Quincy to help you with a public statement. He's actually from a newspaper back east."

The breath caught in Kendal's throat. Her chest tightened and her face burned. "What?"

"I'm sorry, Kendal."

She leaped up and slapped Eric hard across the face. He caught her wrist before she could strike him again. "A reporter! You actually brought a reporter into my home?"

"We…I mean, Dad and I decided…." Exasperated, he sighed heavily. "You've got to give a statement, Kendal. Dad thought it would be easier on you if we arranged for Quincy to be the only reporter questioning you. You've met him. Is he such a monster?"

She reluctantly turned to look at Quincy, but quickly turned back to Eric and involuntarily started to shake.

"Quincy talked to his editor last night," Eric continued. "He's supposed to set things up with a local television station and call us back. Everything's already arranged. All you've got to do is work with Quincy and get it over with."

Quincy turned to Eric and held up his hands. "I'm sorry, buddy. I understand what you and your dad are trying to do here, but I can't force myself on Kendal. I refuse to work with anyone who doesn't trust me. I'll move into a room at the hotel. If y'all decide to move forward, I'll be there until after I interview Olivia Howard. If not, that's fine, too."

A mix of alarm and irritation swirled inside her, but she was silently grateful for Quincy's position in the matter. She began pacing in circles, hoping to hide her trembling.

Eric grabbed her arm. "Sis, wait."

"How could you?" she whispered, tears welling up in her eyes. "I thought he was an agent…like you. You let me run off at the mouth in front of him. My whole life is going to be in the headlines. How could you do this to me?"

He took a hold of her shoulders and shook her a little. "Be quiet. Nobody is that interested in *your* life, Kendal. It's time to stop running."

His words stung, but they somehow broke through the thick fog that surrounded her. She had been running for years for no reason. Eric was right. She was a twenty-nine-year old fake. She tried to pull away, but Eric tightened his hold.

"Sis. I know you're upset, but there's something else you need to know."

She stood rigid between her brother's hands, only a few feet away from Quincy. Mist blurred her vision, but she refused to cry.

"We found Frank Peck's body this afternoon in the wooded area off Thatcher Park."

Kendal screamed, but the sound stuck in her throat.

Her breathing grew fast and shallow and she started to back away from Eric—away from everything. Her freshly acquired knowledge of Quincy's profession slipped into the far reaches of her mind. She saw Eric's mouth moving, but she couldn't make out what he was saying. He reached for her again. She shrank back, frightened by something lurking in her subconscious. She turned toward the back door, but it was latched. She wanted to run. But to where?

"Kendal, snap out of it!"

Eric's sharp tone brought her back. His hands were on her shoulders again, shaking her hard.

"Let go," she said, pushing him away. "I'm all right."

He ignored her resistance and gruffly pulled her into his arms. "No, you're not."

Once again, she tried to pull away, but Eric's arms tightened around her shoulders. She didn't want to cry. She wouldn't.

Frustrated, she glanced over at Quincy. His eyes were filled with anxiety. Why, she wondered, why would a reporter care about her? She stopped struggling, alternately imagining Frank's dead body and an insidious voice on her telephone.

"How?"

"We won't know until after the autopsy."

"If Frank's dead, Eric, who's calling me? Is it the person who killed him? Is it someone I could know?"

"I don't know," he answered, squeezing her ice-cold hands. "But it's a real possibility. They're now considering putting you under protective surveillance."

She stepped back. "No! I don't want a bunch of strangers underfoot. I have too much…." She stopped mid-sentence, uncertain exactly what she was about to say. "Who found him?"

"Some teenagers. They're a little shaken up, but they'll be all right." He began pacing in a semi-circle. "The head agent here is clearing some things with my boss so I can head up your surveillance."

Kendal blinked in surprise. "I thought that's why you were here."

Eric looked away briefly. "I took a leave of absence, Sis. They wouldn't let me in on this until now. This last call, as well as Peck's death, opened the door."

Kendal bit her lower lip and grasped her brother's shirtsleeve. She wanted desperately to crawl into a hole and bury her head until this entire mess was over. "I'm scared."

"The bureau suspects the calls have something to do with the Howard-Hadley scandal. Based on the tone and nature of his comments, the caller seems to be seeking vengeance for something."

She frowned and released his shirt. "You said the bureau thinks that. Don't you?"

"Kendal, I'm just not sure."

"But if he killed Frank…." She gazed hard into her brother's face. "A murderer is after me? Did he also threaten Frank? Is that why he was acting so funny?"

"I honestly don't know. You have to remember he was involved in some pretty heavy stuff, and he knew the FDA was on to him."

Quincy cleared his throat. "Eric, what makes you so certain this is the same guy?"

"I'm not. But right now it's the only thing the bureau has that makes sense. Kendal got the first call the day she was questioned. That was four days after she last saw Peck."

"What about you? Do you have any specific suspects?" Quincy asked, his face showing both concern and a newsman's curiosity.

"I want to check out Jed Mason. By the way, you might need to watch yourself. This nut seems to be the jealous type, and he somehow knows you're around." He turned back to his sister. "We've got a lot of searching to do. I need you to make a list of everyone you and Frank might have in common. Other clients, his receptionist, whatever."

Kendal shivered, feeling dazed and barely there.

Eric stayed behind at the shop to wait for Cashion. His nerves buzzed with a vague sense of foreboding. What in the world was going on? He shoved his hands into his pockets and watched through the window as Quincy helped Kendal into the SUV.

He hoped he hadn't made a mistake trusting Quincy Morgan. He was risking Kendal's life, as well as his own career, on this man's integrity. But he needed Quincy, not only because he could help Kendal with her statement, but also because he had the resources to obtain information he couldn't get without raising flags with his superiors. He just hoped Quincy would go along with him, and prayed his plan wouldn't backfire.

He knew he was much too zealous when it came to Kendal's safety. He'd almost had a coronary when his dad phoned him with news of the threat. To an outsider, his reaction might seem obsessive, but he had to protect her.

He realized that if he was to keep Kendal safe now, he had to put aside his fixation on the old case. For years, his mind had been preoccupied with learning more about Jack Sumner's reasons for snatching her. Answers had only created more questions.

He had checked the newspaper and police records from Auburn, where Kendal had been found wandering down a back road. After graduating high school, he had finally gotten the nerve to question his dad about Sumner's motives. Eric never quite accepted his dad's nebulous answers. It had to be something more.

He had even looked through case files and police reports on Sumner's death. Nothing came together right. He had known this even before he joined the bureau. When this present danger was over, he planned to take some time and settle the case in his mind. There were simply too many haunting possibilities about Sumner's death for his satisfaction.

Eric had already concluded that Kendal's digging into adoption records wasn't spawning the threat, but it had intensified his curiosity about Sumner. And he still couldn't help but wonder if the present menace was somehow related to the old—even indirectly. He knew it sounded wild, and he dared not tell his superiors for fear they might send him to the bureau's shrink. That would follow him throughout his career, if, in fact, he still had one. He would be labeled, and advancement would become an elusive dream never to be attained.

He started pacing the large room, and he let his mind drift back twenty years, to a telephone conversation with his dad. *I'm counting on you to be the man of the house while I'm away, Son. Take care of your sister and Nana.* It was the week before Kendal was taken. His dad obviously hadn't expected the worst, but he had been an eight-year-old kid. He had blamed himself, and had never been able to shake the guilt.

He forced his mind back to the current threat against his sister. He had to come up with a way to force this guy out into the open. But how?

He thought of Vera Mackey then, and smiled. She was an attractive agent who had readily accepted him, despite the reluctance of some of the others. Vera had treated him as an equal and had willingly conveyed pertinent information about the case against Howard-Hadley.

If he was going to succeed in keeping Kendal safe, as well as getting to the bottom of a twenty-year-old case, he needed both Vera and Quincy.

Under the circumstances, Quincy was surprised that Kendal accepted a ride home from him. He looked at her out of the corner of his eye. She was either a very skilled actress or a very frightened young woman.

He wondered what Eric meant when he told his sister she had been running too long. Running from what? Could it have something to do with this Jack Sumner that Sheila had mentioned.

"I apologize if I made you uncomfortable, Quincy," Kendal said. "You must think I'm awful. I didn't mean for you to see me act that way. I just got a little mad. And I don't trust reporters."

Forthcoming, he thought. He liked that. "I know you don't, but don't assume I'll print anything you didn't first approve. Right now my main objective is to get you ready for your public statement. That is, if you'll agree to it."

She turned her head to face the window. "I didn't know…I don't want you to be a reporter. I never…."

Puzzled, he reached across the console and took her hand. His stomach tightened when he realized she was still trembling. "It'll be all right. I promise."

He could see she was struggling to contain her emotions. Suddenly, she turned back. "May I ask you something personal?"

"I guess so."

"What do *you* get out of doing us this favor?"

He answered her without the slightest hesitation. "An exclusive, unscripted interview with you. Eric assured me last night he would tell you about his and your dad's proposal. Knowing how you feel about reporters, I didn't really want to be present when he did."

Her eyebrows shot up. "They sold me out!"

He was still holding her hand. "Not really, Kendal. They're protecting you from what they know a live press conference can be like. The only reason reporters are anxious to get at you is because of your dad, the mystery surrounding you. Some reporters are always digging to expose some dirt on an elected official. Your dad seems very intent on protecting you from all that. And that, as well as the incident ten years ago with a reporter's camera, has bred a ravenous suspicion in the industry."

"That's why you're here?"

"In a manner of speaking."

"I have no concept of what reporters want from me." Her voice cracked. "I wish you hadn't agreed to this."

"You're going to have to do this—either in a controlled way, like your dad and brother are planning, or in an ambush. I admit nothing Eric offered was any different from what I had hoped to accomplish in the first place. The icing on his proposal is that I was promised an exclusive."

She pushed back against the headrest, looking distraught. Her anguish bothered him.

He continued to talk, hoping it would somehow make her feel safe with him. "I'm sorry if this disillusioned you. You should've known before now. I didn't know about the plan myself until last night. I thought I was just giving your brother a lift from the airport."

"It's all right," she said. "What will you write...in the exclusive?"

He turned to look at her. "What would you like me to write?"

"I don't know," she said with a shrug. "Maybe you could write about a woman's desire for a real life prince charming, or a real dad."

Quincy heard the sadness and anger in her voice. But he said nothing.

She turned slightly toward him. "May I ask you something else?"

"You sure you want to?"

His slightly teasing tone made her smile. "I noticed when we ate last night...I mean...." She paused and tried again. "Are you a believer?"

"Yes, indeed. Since childhood."

She smiled again, but this time Quincy got the feeling it was heartfelt. "Thanks for being open with me. About everything."

"You're very welcome," he said. "What did Eric mean about this guy being jealous?"

At first, she looked puzzled. "Oh, the message. He said somebody would get hurt if I didn't get rid of the SUV driver."

Quincy's facial muscles twitched. "I'll just get my things when we get to the house and move to the hotel."

"Why should you? You're just doing your job. Besides, as Eric so tactfully pointed out, I'm not as newsworthy as I think, so you might as well hang around."

"What about the threat? I *am* the SUV driver."

"Eric didn't say anything about your leaving."

"Kendal, are you sure? I don't mind…I mean, I already had a room at the hotel."

She nodded and gazed out the window. They drove the rest of the way in silence. At the front door, he took the key from her limp hand and inserted it into the keyhole.

"Thank you," she murmured, stepping past him.

He moved in behind her and stiffened as a little girl rushed at them. "Aunt Kem!" The child stumbled and fell when she realized an outsider had come in. Though he had already spent a night in her home, she had yet to be introduced to him. She looked up at him, not sure what to make of the tall smiling stranger.

He leaned down. "Well, this must be Marcy."

She drew back instinctively and struggled to her feet. "Hello, my pretty," Kendal said, stooping to lift the child. "There's nothing to be afraid of, sweetheart. This is Quincy. He's a friend." Kendal made a point of looking directly at him when she said it.

The child looked at him briefly, but her gaze got no higher than his tie. She sat heavily on Kendal's arm, tugging anxiously at her own hands.

"Hello there, Marcy," he said, trying again. "It's good to meet you."

She turned her face into the side of Kendal's head and refused to look at him again.

"Surely, my sweet little Marcy can greet our guest," Kendal urged. "You're a big girl now."

"Hi," the child managed without coming out of hiding.

"I'm sorry, Quincy. She's shy around people she doesn't know."

"I understand," he said, smiling. "She certainly loves her Aunt Kendal, though."

Kendal grinned, squeezing the child closer to her. "And I love her."

Without revealing her face, Marcy locked chubby arms around Kendal's neck and murmured something. Kendal chuckled and drew back and kissed her cheek, her eyes suddenly glistening with tears. He wasn't sure if she was responding to Marcy's comment or to the goings-on of her day.

His silent questions concerning Kendal's unconventional decision to be artificially inseminated was partially answered as he witnessed her affectionate interaction with Marcy. She headed for the stairs, still holding Marcy in her arms. "You're tired, Kendal. Why don't you go get some rest?"

She shook her head while sniffing the air. "Sheila has dinner started. I need to help Marcy get cleaned up. You go on down and freshen up. I'll see you later."

He watched her move up the stairs without looking back. Marcy's face peered from around her head. She smiled timidly and wiggled stubby fingers at him in a coy wave.

He waved back and started for the basement steps, struggling to swallow past the lump in his throat. Why, he wondered, was interacting with this family affecting him so intensely?

-TEN-

Quincy got very little sleep that night. He couldn't get his mind off what Hadley had implied about Kendal, or her reaction when she learned he was a reporter. He knew she didn't like reporters, but he hadn't expected her response to be so vehement. He had seen actual terror in her eyes.

He also pondered Eric's use of shock and the order in which he had delivered two blows. The young agent was intense, but he was also very clever. Clearly, news of Peck's death had taken some of the sting out of the fact that she was housing a reporter.

Wondering what to expect next, he dressed and went upstairs to the kitchen, where Eric was anxiously pacing the floor.

"Hey, no breakfast this morning?"

Eric stopped pacing and spun around, worry plain on his face. "Quincy."

"You all right, buddy? You look like you just saw a ghost."

Eric's mouth was drawn and his face shone with perspiration. "I'm fine…just worried about how Kendal is going to take what I just did."

"What do you mean?"

He reached inside his pants pocket and pulled out a sheet of paper. "This."

Quincy looked down at what appeared to be a photocopied picture. "What is it?"

"It's a threat, Quincy. And I'm asking you to remember our agreement about my sister's privacy."

Irritation shot through Quincy. "What else can I tell you, Eric? I've given my word that I have no intention of printing anything without her permission."

"I'm sorry," Eric said, tossing the sheet onto the counter. "I'm just agitated and tangled up worried about her."

Quincy got a mug from the dish rack and poured himself a cup of coffee. Then he propped an elbow on the counter and took a closer look at the sheet. It was a picture of a doll with a rope around its neck. The caption read, "Judas Threw the Money Into the Temple and Left. Then He Went Away and Hanged Himself. You Do the Honors—Or I Will."

"My God," Quincy said, picking up the paper. "Where did you get this?"

"Kendal has a small office set up in the dining room. It was on her fax machine this morning."

"When did it come?"

"Last night. After Sheila got a good look at it this morning, it was all I could do to get her and Marcy to the car. I checked with a couple of the neighbors this morning, too. Ms. Miller across the street thinks she saw a black Mercedes drive by and slow down a couple of times this week. But she can't really see anything past the front yard. I think I've talked Agent Cashion into letting me place a movement-activated camera out front, along with telephone line and computer monitoring equipment. She's already got a security alarm system."

Quincy sat down at the table, curiously eyeing Eric, who had resumed pacing the floor. "I take it Miss Miller didn't get a license plate."

"Nah, she didn't. And a black Mercedes could be just about anyone. But I'll check out my suspects."

"The Howard-Hadley group?"

He nodded. "I sent the agent assigned to Kendal with Sheila this morning. Cashion couldn't spare another right now, but he's working on it. With these threats intensifying, I can't take any chances. I need you to help me get Kendal out of this city. She needs to be somewhere else, and quick. I'll contact the FBI in Spokane to help us out."

"I agree."

Just then Kendal entered the kitchen from the stairs. Eric grabbed the fax from the counter and stuffed it back into his trouser pocket. "Hey, what are you two whispering about?"

Quincy had learned that once Eric's mind was made up about something, he jumped right into it without second guessing himself.

"I've asked Sheila to take Marcy and move to a hotel."

Kendal froze in her tracks. "Why? Has something else happened?"

"You've received another threat, Sis. I want you to pack and go to Spokane to stay at Dad's. I've asked Quincy to drive you."

She folded her arms across her chest and slowly shook her head. "No, Eric. I've got too much to do before next Saturday. Can't you protect me here?"

"Kendal, I don't need your stubbornness right now. This man may have already killed."

"I won't go," she said. "I've waited too long for this dream, Eric. You know I have. And even if you *do* think he's the same guy that killed Frank, I just can't let his tactics paralyze my life. You said yourself I had to stop running from things."

"I didn't mean for you to deliberately set yourself up as a target. I'm trying to protect you."

"I'm not setting myself up. You're here. I don't know how to explain how much I need to get on with my life."

Eric threw up his hands in obvious exasperation. "What else do you expect me to do?"

Her nostrils flared. "Just do your job and let me do mine."

She was just about to reemphasize her plans when Eric pulled the faxed threat from his pocket and smoothed out the wrinkles on the counter.

Kendal suddenly gripped the counter edge to steady herself, and her face became a mask of terror. Eric led her to the table, and she dropped into the chair next to Quincy's. He felt foreign and powerless, and wondered why on earth he was even here becoming so involved in the Boyds' lives.

"Eric, what am I supposed to do?" she asked, resigned.

"Go to Spokane. Dad's in Washington, so you won't be disturbed."

She shook her head. "I just can't. Please don't ask me to leave my home. Besides, I have responsibilities here."

"To be honest, Sis, I don't know if there'll even be an opening."

Her head snapped around. "Yes," she said, rallying to meet his eyes. "I'll do whatever you ask, including sitting in front of a camera with a reporter. But I will not let this bring Sheila's and my life to a halt. We plan to open next Saturday."

Her tone and posture left nothing to be misconstrued. Eric shifted. "Then I want you out of here. No shop today. Agent Sullivan is on Sheila while she waits for deliveries. Once that's done, they'll come back here and pack some things for their move. Your surveillance starts at your return. An agent will be with you at all times during the day. Since I'm at the house at night, there's no problem."

"And where am I supposed to go now?"

"Quincy will take you for a long drive. I don't want you back here until evening."

"Why?"

"Because, Kendal, I'm trying to keep you safe. Now please stop fighting me."

By the time they were headed east on I-90, it was early afternoon. Kendal had been quiet all morning. They had already driven around the city, Quincy trying to make sure no one was following them. "Where are we going now?"

"Where would you like to go?"

"Did you know there is a city called Quincy here in Washington?"

"How far?"

"Maybe a hundred fifty miles."

"You want to go that far?" he asked, admiring her stamina.

"Might as well. Since I'm supposed to stay gone all day," she sighed. "I guess he's bugging my house or something, huh?"

Quincy smiled. "Yeah."

"I'm sorry my family pulled you into all this, Quincy. I know you came to do a job." Suddenly, she gasped and covered her mouth. "You're missing the press conference."

"I don't mind," he said. "Really I don't. I don't think Hadley has anything more to say than he already has."

"I'm so sorry. Will you get in trouble with your editor?"

He gave her sidelong glance and chuckled aloud. "Probably. But it won't be the first time."

After a long silence, she looked at him and smiled. "Mr. Morgan, I just don't know what to make of you. You seem too human to be a reporter."

"What do you mean?"

"Why does my brother trust you so much?"

"Probably has something to do with a situation I was involved in over a year ago. As well as a little snag I helped him with a while back. Why?"

"You're so accommodating," she said, staring at him. "I don't know whether you're lying in wait to pounce, or just willing to be controlled by my family."

"I assure you, Miss Boyd," he said, trying to keep his composure, "that I'm not controlled by anyone. And I'm obliging to people because that's who I am. It always seems to come back."

"I apologize. I didn't mean that the way it sounded."

He changed lanes and accelerated to pass the sluggish traffic. "No problem."

Kendal tucked a stray curl behind her ear and zipped the jacket she was wearing. Despite the overcast days and light mist, it was supposed to get up to 60° today. Even with more overcast than sunny days, she loved the Seattle area.

She loved the moisture and crisp chill in the air, too. That's why she slept with her window up. The breeze was generally chilly to her, but it was refreshing and made her feel free. She was glad she had remembered to let it down and lock it before she left. Last night, however, had been spent tossing and warding off memories that threatened to erupt. Totally caught up in her thoughts, Kendal jumped nervously when Quincy's cellphone rang. He quickly flipped it open.

"Morgan."

She liked the timbre of his voice, she thought, turning to look out the window. She savored the memory of him catching her in those strong arms that first night. She pondered what it would be like to actually be wrapped in them.

She shook herself. Why was she thinking like this? Her whole life was spinning out of control, and here she was behaving like a school-girl. Maybe she was just vulnerable—understandable considering all the threats, calls from the press, and the stress of opening a new business.

She fidgeted a little. Stress mingled with loneliness created an atmosphere she felt awkward trying to navigate. She was more jumpy now than she had been since it all began. Part of her needed Quincy's powerful presence, but she felt guilty about that. Eric's presence was just as important. After all, he was the trained federal agent. But she couldn't seem to get past the fact that he was first and foremost her younger brother.

She smiled, recalling the moment Quincy declined to take part in Eric's plan if she wasn't in agreement. Her mind had shouted a silent hooray. She stole another sideways glance at him. Should she so willingly trust this man? Oddly enough, in her heart, she already had. And despite her skeptical view of men, and especially reporters, she felt safe with him.

Apart from the controlled fury she sensed, he seemed so right, so perfect. Or course, she didn't really know much about him. She listened as he spoke into his cellphone. He had an easygoing manner, and yet there was a strange intensity about him that she found appealing.

"We got it," he said, closing down the phone and returning it to the pocket of his pullover.

She stared at him. "We got what?"

"Olivia Howard has agreed to meet us at the television station for the interview. After that, I'll hang with you until the day after your grand opening. I can write my article from what I glean from your daily routine and any personal stories you might share."

Her stomach suddenly tightened. "You're leaving on Mother's Day?"

He nodded. "Yes, I want to spend it with my aunt. You have eight more days of me shadowing you. With this morning's turn of events, I forgot to mention it. I didn't even have a chance to tell Eric."

"When…."

He answered before she could finish the question. "My editor called last night. We'll film a private interview Monday morning. I thought including Ms. Howard would ease the pressure on you, as well as let the public see your parting wasn't unfriendly."

Kendal buried her hands in her lap. "I guess I'm a little nervous, Quincy. Are you sure you won't ask anything that'll embarrass or piss me off?"

"I wouldn't want to piss *you* off, Kendal. I've seen you angry." He laughed and lightly punched her shoulder. "Why so worried? Your father's office is scripting the interview. I'm here only as a buffer. Hopefully, one you feel comfortable with."

"Olivia being there *will* take some of the pressure off," she said pensively. "Will you still get a personal interview with her?"

"Yes, Olivia and I will get together tomorrow afternoon. Stop worrying," he said. "I'll take good care of you."

Her stomach did a flip-flop. She looked out the window and once again scolded herself. The man made an innocent remark, one meant simply to calm her. And her thoughts had taken it to another level. She had to get a hold of herself before she said or did something really stupid. And maybe she should stop reading those silly fairy tales to Marcy. She certainly didn't want her growing up with silly notions about Prince Charming.

She needed to focus on something other than the current situation and tangled circumstances surrounding Frank's murder. Though her desire to have a baby was still intact, the urgency had diminished. That was no small wonder, given the recent added turbulence in her life.

They were silent for several long moments. It wasn't an uneasy silence, but a respectful one. They soon resumed with lighthearted talk that turned into a joke-telling contest.

"Listen to this one," Quincy said. "Late one night a mugger in a ski mask jumped into the path of a well-dressed man and stuck a gun in his ribs, yelling, 'Give me your money.' Indignant, the affluent man replied, 'You can't do this—I'm a United States congressman!' 'In that case,' replied the mugger, 'give me MY money.'"

They both laughed, and she chimed in with a few knock-knock jokes. She even talked a little about Eric's and her childhood. Occasionally, Quincy responded with a frown, a look of compassion, or a boisterous laugh—depending on the story. From time to time, he asked questions to clarify. But mostly, he simply listened.

It was the first time in years that Kendal could recall a man taking the time to really listen to her. It felt good to be heard, even in such a minor way.

By the time she had finished telling him about why she wanted a child, her throat was tight and stomach had begun to jump. She suddenly felt awkward and tried to change the subject. "Did you give any thought to my grandmother's riddle?"

"I've been praying about that," he said. "If I tell you what I believe it means, will you answer a question for me?"

"Will you print it?"

He reached over and gently clamped her nose between two fingers, but soon sobered. "Why do you dislike reporters so much?"

She immediately turned away, her heart pounding as though something was chasing her.

"Don't feel like you have to answer that, Kendal. I shouldn't have asked."

She didn't know why, but she wanted to tell him. His profession notwithstanding, she somehow knew she could trust Quincy Morgan. After several moments of struggling with an onslaught of emotions, she began. "Reporters are deceitful. I've never understood how people can become so animalistic when it comes to the private lives of others."

"I realize some papers aren't known for their accuracy," Quincy said. "They thrive more on scandal and rumor than fact. And I'll agree that some reporters are dangerous to the general public."

She stared at him, surprised to hear these words from a reporter.

"So how did you come to the conclusion that we're all heartless hooligans?"

Kendal suddenly felt warm and removed her jacket. "When I was ten, a local reporter came to the house to interview Nana. The air force had sent Dad to Germany then. He wasn't in politics yet, but I think party leaders had their eyes on him."

"Yeah, reporters tend to get word about things like that, sometimes even before the potential candidates."

"Anyway," she continued, "he seemed very nice. He walked around the house snapping pictures and talking to Nana about Dad's child-hood. While we were in the living room talking, Eric fell from a tree in the backyard and broke his arm. I didn't know he had hurt himself like that until much later."

He glanced towards her when she paused. Kendal couldn't meet his eyes. "What happened?"

"While Nana was out back with Eric, this—this reporter tricked me into getting into his car. I tried to get away. I remember being so scared. He told me I was adopted, and at first pretended to be my real father."

Quincy glanced at her with a degree of uncertainty and skepticism. "You didn't know about the adoption?"

She shook her head, swallowing hard. "I guess I was so stunned by the revelation I reacted too slowly to successfully get away from him. I tried, but…."

"What! You were actually abducted?"

She kept her eyes down, somewhat relieved that the details disturbed this particular reporter. "He held me out in a rural area for almost a week before I managed to get away. Thankfully, someone found me wandering down a road in Auburn. They called the author-ities."

"I've heard all kinds of rumors and notions about your childhood, but nothing like this."

She smiled sadly. "You weren't supposed to. With Senator Howard's help, Dad managed to keep my name out of the headlines."

"This is scandalous! How could a journalist in good conscience…?" He shook his head, obviously agitated, and gripped the steering wheel so tightly, his knuckles looked as if they would pop open. "Did you even know what it meant to be adopted?"

"Yeah, I knew," she said, moistening her lips.

"Kendal, I'm so sorry. It must've been horrible for you. Thank God, you got away safely."

Looking down, she forced a smile void of mirth. "I have never remembered anything about the confinement itself," she said dully. "At least nothing I can grasp—just vague shadows."

"Nothing at all?"

She shook her head. "I remember Dad's face when the police arrived with me at the hospital. I was so angry with him." She rotated her head to relieve the tension in her neck. "Sometimes I still am. I don't want to be, but the rage is just there…just below the surface. My emotions sometimes bounce from one extreme to another. One minute I want to talk to him for hours, and the next I want to lock him out of my life." Her voice trailed off.

He reached across the console and gently squeezed her hand. "It's understandable, Kendal. You were traumatized. What happened to the reporter?"

"I know he got fired. Last I heard, he died…not too long afterwards. I never really wanted to know any more details than that. Dad filed suit against the paper for Sumner's actions. The settlement paid my college tuition. The paper printed the story, but they agreed not to disclose my name. And the picture Sumner took of us appeared on the front page a year later, but it was attached to an article about Dad being named a party candidate."

He squeezed her hand again. The contact felt good, but she wouldn't meet his eyes. "Any lasting effects from the ordeal?"

"I had nightmares for years. Recently though, I've been getting little wisps of memory. It's odd."

"Not so odd. Look at what you're going through. The recent developments have probably reactivated a form of posttraumatic stress."

She took a deep breath. "You a closet psychoanalyst or something?"

"Nah," he said, snorting. "Just one semester. Enough to make me think I might have an edge. Tell me about your nightmare."

Kendal pressed the back of her head into the headrest and closed her eyes. "I'm running through wet grass and mud—gray-brown, soupy mud. Someone is chasing me, but I can't see his face. He's yelling, 'Run, Kendal, run for your life.' Then it starts to storm. The rain is coming down so hard it stings. When I slip and fall in the mud, it starts to harden around me. I can't move. That's when I wake up."

"That's pretty intense. But I don't understand."

Her stomach was in knots. "I don't, either. But I'm sure it has something to do with Jack Sumner."

"Jack Sumner?"

"Yeah, that's the reporter's name. I guess I'm a little scared to press for something any deeper than that. I'm not sure I want to remember the details."

"Why?"

"I don't want to know if something happened out there, Quincy…if he hurt me." Her voice was wobbly now. "But the flashes of memory are so pushy, so urgent."

"It's over, Kendal. You're fine," he said. "Sumner stole a precious part of your life—your security and trust. But the main thing to remember is that you're alive and well. There's nothing to be afraid of now."

She moved her head slightly forward. "But I'm not very safe right now, am I?"

They both fell silent for a time.

"The worst thing of all is that I lost Dad somewhere along the way. I used to be such a spoiled 'daddy's girl.' I felt different after everything was over. Dad said he regretted leaving us, but then just one year later, he threw himself full force into politics."

"You seem to resent that."

"I guess I do."

"I'm sure he had to deal with the circumstances in his own way. He had lost his father, his wife, and certainly went through hell thinking he had lost his little girl. None of that means that you lost *him*. He's called every day to check on you, right?"

"I know, Quincy. But he's never even broached the subject with me. And I was always afraid to." She shrugged. "I suppose I thought he would say more than I needed him to. Is that crazy?"

He shook his head. "Sometimes when children are traumatized as you were, something is arrested inside. Even after they've grown up, they cling to the child's perception in certain areas. That perception constantly wrestles with adult logic. You two just need some time alone…to reflect and talk things out. But you have to understand, that doesn't come easy to men."

"I wish I knew how to make that happen. I always get so angry."

"I can only imagine the tangled feelings you grew up with— wondering about biological family members—needing to belong."

Kendal gawked. His words were kind and sympathetic. How could he possibly understand the confusion and pain she had gone through? Until now, Sheila was the only person she had ever been able to talk to about it. And yet his eyes and voice told her he indeed understood.

The SUV suddenly jerked and sputtered, causing the car behind them to skid on the wet pavement as the driver braked. Quincy released her hand and swerved onto the next exit ramp. He let the vehicle coast onto a paved path that led into a remote area. There were no sign of houses, cars or people. She looked around wildly, trying to determine where they were. She hadn't been paying attention. Panicked, her heart began to gallop as she watched Quincy try and fail to restart the engine.

"What's wrong with it?"

"I don't know," he said. "I'll take a look under the hood in a second."

Since the ramp meandered down into a rural basin of thick forestry and undergrowth, the vehicle could continue moving without power. "Why don't you pull off the pavement?" she asked.

"Just in case we were followed by unwanted guests, I don't want to be seen from the highway."

A prickling sensation moved down her spine as he continued to struggle with the steering wheel. "Quincy."

"No power steering. The brakes aren't grabbing the way they should, either. If I can't find a way to safely stop, I want you to be ready to jump and roll."

Though the prospect of jumping from a moving vehicle was alarming, his instructions came as a great relief. A man abducting a woman wouldn't be trying to save her life.

"Okay," she said, unfastening her seatbelt and inching closer to the door.

But the road leveled off and Quincy was able to roll onto the grass beneath a tree and bring the SUV to a stop.

"Thank God," he said, dropping his head against the steering wheel.

She remained silent, but repeatedly patted her chest in an attempt to calm herself. Quincy unlatched the hood and got out. After a moment, she joined him.

"I suspect someone tampered with it when we stopped to eat, but I can't really tell. There's no telling what's all wrong with it." He closed the hood and turned to her. "We better get out of sight."

The trees were wet, thick and looked somewhat foreboding. No one would be able to see them from the highway, and that worried Kendal. Her knees buckled as they ran into the wooded area beyond the stretch of road. Her breath came in shallow puffs and her pulse throbbed as her mind reflected on where her feet might be stepping. "You think any wildlife is out here, Quincy?"

Surrounded by bushes and tall trees, Quincy moved about erratically with his cellphone. "I wouldn't think so. We need to keep moving though. There's a possibility this guy tampered with our transportation. We can't be too careful."

She gazed anxiously at the sky. The deep gray clouds had thickened into an angry mass. She looked back, still hearing him move about to and fro. "What are you doing?"

"I plan to call your brother if I can get some decent reception. Do you know where we are?"

Kendal glanced around, struggling to keep her legs from giving way. The distant rumble of thunder jangled her nerves. "Not exactly—somewhere off I-90."

Large drops of rain began to pelt their heads. Even though they were some distance into the woods, she could hear the thumping sound it made against the vehicle. In seconds, the drops became a downpour, thrusting Kendal into greater fear and confusion.

-ELEVEN-

Quincy grabbed Kendal's arm and pulled her back into a steady pace. Based on yesterday's phone threat, her stalker had now targeted him. The man was clearly watching her very closely. He hoped they weren't followed.

Keep us safe, Lord.

He kept one eye on Kendal as they moved through the wet foliage. The rain was cold and heavy. Clad only in jeans, sneakers and pullovers, neither of them was prepared to be outside in a chilly downpour. They were already soaked completely through.

Her stride was quick and her posture erect. For all the brave front she was putting up, he sensed she was scared out of her mind. "Do you know where we're going?" she asked, without looking back.

"I saw ballpark lights out in this direction. I figured we could at least get to a landmark where I can direct Eric."

She slowed. "You think he tampered with the car in broad daylight?"

"It's possible."

Kendal was tough. But despite the time that had elapsed between the childhood horror and now, he wondered if being stranded with a reporter conjured up the worst kind of panic. Anger grew as he thought of the injustice that had been dealt her, not only by Jack Sumner, but also by all the reporters like himself who saw her as a protected prima donna. And now some nut was triggering the rebirth of her worst nightmare.

He didn't want to question her further. But he had to know more about this Sumner character. He glanced at her shivering frame and let the simmering anger infuse his thoughts. What had that monster done to her, he wondered. He wanted to find out what the man's motive was.

Had he harmed her in the way she suspected? Even at twenty-nine, her subconscious had a reason for refusing to release her memory.

His hands balled into fists at his sides. *God, I can't imagine how to pray for her. She's obviously still in a prison of sorts. Please show me how to help her.*

He looked up just as she was folding her arms around herself for warmth. He had to do something, but he didn't want to frighten her by suggesting anything she might consider forward.

He looked around warily, his mind going a hundred miles an hour. The sound of raindrops hitting the foliage was almost deafening. He tried to shield her head with his hand, but gave up when he realized the move was futile. "There's something up ahead," he said, pointing to a metal roof above the top of the trees. "Looks like a warehouse of some kind."

"Maybe so." Her lips were trembling uncontrollably. She looked as though she would be sick if they didn't get inside pretty quickly.

"Kendal, we need to get you warm."

Still hugging herself, she stopped and gazed up at him. "How? We both left our jackets in the SUV."

He wrapped her in as casual an embrace as he could manage. "Let's walk slower…together. Our mutual body heat can help."

After another five hundred or so feet they moved into a semi-clearing. The brush wasn't clinging around them as it had been. A large red barn with a faded white X painted on double doors stood before them. It was obviously vacant and looked as if it hadn't been used in years.

At precisely same instant, they raced through the heavy rain towards the entrance. A loud clap of thunder sounded and she shrank against the door, tugging at it frantically, but it was locked.

The rain pounded against them with reinforced vigor. In her desperation, Kendal began to claw at the handle. Quincy quickly pulled out his pocketknife. "Wait, Kendal. Let me see what I can do."

He reached around her, enclosing her between his arms, and jabbed the knife into the lock. He cringed as the rain struck the metal roof with eerie precision. Suddenly, a lightening bolt danced nearby and another clap of thunder sounded just above them. Already encased between his arms, Kendal hysterically swung around and pressed herself into his chest.

He managed to force the doors open. With Kendal still clinging, he scanned the wide-open structure and spotted an orange steel ladder on wheels. It was the kind with a platform several steps from the floor. He squeezed her shoulders and gently urged her towards the steps. Her strong reaction to the storm was obviously deep-rooted. Who but God could say to what degree Sumner's actions had influenced her life?

After they sat down, he continued to hold her close. "I don't like thunderstorms," she said in a quavering voice.

He remained quiet, trying to steady himself for God's instruction. He sensed nothing. Perhaps he had allowed himself to get too close, too emotionally involved to perceive any direction.

"You must think I'm a real basket case."

"Nah. Old issues are simply resurfacing because of everything that's going on," he said, gently patting her shoulder. "But sometimes we have to pull the covers off things in order to be free of them."

"Quincy?"

"Yeah."

"Would you just talk to me about something else?"

"All right. What would you like me to talk about?"

"I don't know. Anything. Tell me what you think Nana's riddle meant?"

"Well, I know that balm is referred to in the Bible as a healing ointment. Your grandmother apparently felt you still needed to heal. You said she also mentioned being still, right?"

Nodding soberly, Kendal pulled away from his shoulder. She stood and began searching for a tissue in the pockets of her jeans. She finally found one and wiped her nose. Moments later, he stood and instinctively drew her back into his arms. She felt good there.

"My mother used to quote Psalms 46:10. 'Be still and know that I am God.' "

She turned slightly. "But how does one be still?"

"The Bible teaches that God's voice is still and small. See, He abides in the believer's heart and speaks to us from there."

She readily nodded in agreement. There was just enough light to see the tears in her eyes. She opened her mouth to speak, but no words came out. After a moment, she cleared her throat and tried again. "So He whispers?"

"In a sense. But if we have a lot of stuff going on in our minds, we can't hear Him. We're too busy. That's when we need to find a way to get still."

"What exactly would He whisper?"

"Words of instruction, of love and kinship. Words that heal, Kendal."

Though her shaking had lessened, he sensed an upsurge of shivering as she laid her head against his chest. He pulled her closer. "I'm not sure if I trust Him enough," she whimpered. "I mean, I want to, but I've been so angry."

"Maybe a little disillusioned," he whispered into the top of her wet hair. He closed his eyes, savoring the fragrant scent of her shampoo.

"I wish my relationship with Him was as intimate as yours seems to be."

He smiled. "I'm certainly not the grand authority on intimacy. But I believe the Father longs for that kind of closeness with His children. I cling to that belief in times of loneliness."

She straightened and looked up at him, and he wondered if she could even see him. He knew the answer when he felt her palm against his cheek. The touch charged his mind and body with an energy he had long since forgotten. He closed his eyes, fighting to remember everything he had told himself from the moment he laid eyes on her. Clearing the thickness from his throat, Quincy tried in vain to break his train of thought.

"Oh, Kendal," he said, lowering his head to hers. Before he could stop himself, Quincy brought his mouth down on hers.

He kissed her slowly, heavily, keenly aware all the while that it would no doubt prove a grave mistake. She stood there, unresponsive. Desperate now for a reaction, he grasped the back of her head and deepened the kiss. She trembled and her mouth softened. A tiny moan escaped her throat as she clung to him. The soft warmth of her seized him in a grip so powerful he trembled.

As they stood locked in an enchanted embrace, Quincy realized he couldn't let go of this now even if he wanted to. He had been struggling all day to keep from thinking about her this way. He reluctantly drew himself back. Just then, her trembling body incited another surge of yearning and he again brought his lips down to hers.

After several moments, he held her back and teasingly touched her nose with the tip of his finger. "May I ask you something personal?"

"As long as...."

"As long as I don't print it. I know, I know," he said with a grin. "Is there something going on between you and Hadley Jr.?"

"No, of course not. Why?"

"What about Dr. Peck? Were you in love with him?"

She stiffened, then shook her head. "You think I'm a real kook, don't you?"

"Why would I?"

"Well, I'm a single, fairly intelligent woman planning to be impregnated through artificial insemination. But I can't seem to fall in love. I refuse to marry without it, Quincy. Is that crazy?"

Her voice broke and she pulled away. He drew her back to his chest and smoothed back the hair from her face. "No, sweetie. I think it's perfect."

The shrill ring of his cellphone caused them to jump and break apart. He fumbled to pull it from his shirt pocket.

"Morgan."

"Quincy, where are you?"

"Eric. It's good to hear from you. We need your help!"

-TWELVE-

Quincy pored over the list of suggested questions the congressman's press secretary had faxed to his hotel. They were all pretty routine, but he saw an angle that could make Kendal come out smelling like the proverbial rose. He wondered what she would think when she awakened this morning to find him gone.

He smiled as his mind went back to yesterday's unexpected turn of events. His resolve to maintain professionalism was now history, and he had moved beyond Hadley's insinuation after Kendal told him there was nothing between them. Still, he couldn't help wondering why Hadley would imply such a thing. A wave of annoyance washed over him. Was it possible that Kendal had played Peck against Hadley and vice versa? If true, to what possible end?

Despite his obvious attraction, he had to remain clear-headed and unbiased regardless of what had happened yesterday. He hadn't meant to kiss her. Not yet. It was too soon, and the timing was wrong. He shouldn't have let his emotions become so unruly. Kendal was possibly a very skilled schemer, and he had no doubt played right into her hands. Could she be completely innocent of everything his reporter's mind was entertaining about her?

He inwardly shook himself. What was he thinking? The woman he had spent the day with yesterday couldn't possibly be that deceptive. His mind was simply dithering in a last ditch effort to stay above the influence of his growing affection. He knew that Kendal was innocent. Even so, by letting things get out of hand, he had possibly imparted an impression that he currently couldn't afford.

Lord, I didn't want this Seattle assignment, but I'm here, and I believe you sent me here. I've asked you to show me how to help Kendal. I can't help but believe her charm and innocence are real. But something is happening that I didn't expect. Please make your will plain to my mind.

He pushed the empty breakfast plate away just as the waiter approached. "May I bring you something else, sir?"

"Just the check, please."

He recalled the look on Eric's face when he conveyed his suspicion that the rental had been tampered with. His vehicle had been parked several places, but the only time he could determine it had been out of view long enough to allow such tampering was in Kendal's driveway, or during yesterday's lunch stop. According to the neighbors, the only unfamiliar car they had seen was a black Mercedes. This man had to be extremely determined and bold to tinker under the hood of a vehicle in the open. He obviously had no fear; and, based on Eric's analysis, he was a sadistic murderer.

Nobody deserved to be terrorized and executed. Especially not Kendal. Not now.

Lord, you know I don't want to hurt her. I've overstepped some boundaries here and don't know what to do next. Help me reason clearly and keep my thoughts about her pure. Becoming involved with her is the last thing either of us needs.

Quincy left a suitable tip and hurried to the front to pay the hostess. He was much too wound up, and needed to find a way to relax. "Could you tell me how to get to your fitness center?"

The hostess smiled. "Take the elevator to the lower level. Turn left and go down the hall. Go through the double glass doors. The center will be on your right."

"Thanks."

He needed to phone Beverly, an old friend at the *Baltimore Sun*. He was certain she could dig out some answers about this guy from Kendal's childhood. It was clear the very thought of him still haunted her. He wouldn't rest until he uncovered a few more facts that would help Eric as well.

After sweating out most of his tension in the hotel gym, Quincy headed for his room. His mind continued to replay the previous day. The whole scenario—the car breaking down, the thunderstorm, and even the way they had kept each other warm—seemed to have unfolded like a frivolous screenplay. Despite his misgivings, the instant

Kendal Boyd jumped into his arms at a clap of thunder, she had also jumped into his heart.

She was resilient, but there was still the essence of innocence and compassion in her manner. Her genuine way with Marcy, the way she came out of hiding and talked freely about her affection for her dad, her fixation on becoming pregnant, and even the way she resisted her brother were indicators of the depth of her compassion, as well as her loneliness; Quincy was well acquainted with loneliness.

He strained to remember what she had said just before he succumbed to his raging emotions. *I can't seem to fall in love.* What did that mean, he wondered.

By today's standards, her refusal to marry without love was, without a doubt, unusual. His ex-wife had moved into it without a second thought. Based on Kendal's determination to produce a child without marriage, however, told him that she felt she had no hope in the matter.

Quincy thought of Hadley's words and chuckled under his breath. Deep down, he had known the man had fed him a line. But he was just one of many journalists. The executive couldn't have known Quincy would eventually be considering Kendal in a different light. What had he hoped to accomplish by his subtle lie?

It amazed him how relieved he had been to hear she hadn't been in love with Peck. But if she didn't think she could fall in love, how could he possibly stand a chance with her? He hadn't just kissed Kendal yesterday. She had kissed him back, and with a depth of passion far beyond an empty gesture. Could she actually feel something for *him*?

He reached for his Bible and opened it to the book of Psalms. He hoped by reading the word he could put a cap on his runaway thoughts. After carefully reading several passages, one line suddenly stood out on the page. He read it several times.

In all thy ways acknowledge him, and he shall direct thy paths.

He looked at the tan colored hotel phone. *Direct thy paths.* With all his heart he believed God had directed him to Seattle. Although he had reluctantly accepted the assignment, the outcome wasn't a surprise to the Lord. For the first time since his release from jail, he knew it wouldn't be hard to love again. But he couldn't afford to rush into anything. He absolutely had to hear from God. He needed God's will in every situation of his life, particularly in regards to love.

His thoughts were vacillating and he needed sound advice. He reached for the phone, and, pausing only a second, dialed James Timmons, his friend and pastor.

Kendal's eyes fluttered open. She rolled over and smiled, wondering if she had dreamed it all. Memories of yesterday's events flooded her mind. She had never in her entire life felt the way she had in Quincy's arms. Even now she felt his comforting embrace. His kiss was more than she could have imagined. It had awakened something in her that both delighted and frightened her. She wondered if he had heard her heart hammering against his chest.

It was dark when Eric had picked the two of them up and brought them—still damp but contented—back to the house. She had showered and gone to bed while Eric and Quincy worked on getting the rental towed to the lab and replaced. She was so content she had fallen asleep almost immediately and had no idea what time they had returned.

She stretched lazily and threw back the covers. The aroma of bacon drifted up the stairs, making her mouth water. From the sound of it, the two men were playing catch with her kitchenware.

Still basking in the afterglow of yesterday, Kendal smiled and peered out her bedroom window. Her feeling of enchantment was suddenly smashed by a dose of grim reality. A man in an unfamiliar car was parked in her driveway. Apprehension returned full force. It was probably the agent assigned to her. After all, a murderer was after her. She turned from the window, longing to be comforted by one of Quincy's lively smiles.

After a quick shower, Kendal hurried down the stairs and entered the kitchen expectantly. Sheila and Marcy had temporarily moved in with her ex-mother-in-law, but she could at least enjoy the company of her guests. She tried not to think about Eric's warning about answering the phone, or the fact that she was in a virtual prison. She just had to deal with it until they found this killer.

"Smells wonderful," she said. "Quincy still sleeping?"

Eric was filling a glass with juice. "He'll be stopping by after he talks with Olivia Howard. He plans to go over the questions with you for the taping on Monday."

"Stopping by?" She tried to keep her tone free of emotion. "What do you mean?"

Eric leaned over the counter and stuffed a slice of bacon into his mouth. "We towed the rental to the crime lab last night," he said between crunches. "We picked up another vehicle, and he decided to stay at the hotel. Said something about expecting a fax."

Her heart sank. Emotions she was unaccustomed to feeling began to churn inside her. She slumped back in the chair and for a moment felt silly. "So somebody did tamper with it."

Eric nodded. "So I need you to be especially careful. The finger-prints were too smudged to be conclusive. Even those could have been from a mechanic at the car rental. Our perp probably wore gloves."

Kendal ate her eggs and toast in a haze of confusion and disap-pointment. She didn't want to pout like a child, or feel sorry for herself. But she wondered if Quincy had decided that this inexperienced woman wasn't worth the trouble. A sense of rejection swelled up in her chest, and she immediately shook herself free of it. She was being ridiculous. Quincy hadn't held or kissed her as if she was repulsive. She had to stop being so negative. Even if he wasn't the right man for her, at least she knew she could feel. She glanced up at her brother.

"Is that my guardian I see parked in the drive?"

"Yeah. I'm sure he doesn't appreciate being here on a Saturday morning." The doorbell rang just as Eric got up to refill his coffee cup. "I'll get it."

She had lost her appetite. Though her brother had proven to be a competent chef, the food had no taste. She forked through the eggs on her plate and held her breath, hoping it was Quincy at the door. Eric returned with a slight scowl on his face.

"It's just the mail."

She dropped the fork and reached for the bundle. "Good. I'm expecting a couple of invoices from…."

He handed her several envelopes, but kept back one. "I'll open this. There's no return address, and I want to intercept anything that might be harmful." He ripped open the envelope defiantly. "By the way, I want you to tell me a little more about Jed Mason. He left a message on your phone yesterday."

"Why?"

"I don't know. Said he was leaving the city and would call you again today. Because of the investigation, he had to leave his destination address with the FDA agent."

She tensed. She certainly didn't relish the idea of talking to Jed. "There's really nothing to tell other than that he didn't like me. Never has. But I can't see him making calls and sending threatening faxes."

Eric found nothing, and tossed an invoice onto the table. "But they fired him, Kendal. He could easily hold a grudge for that."

She sat rigid, eyeing her brother's intense expression. "Walt told me they had been thinking about it for some time. I have nothing to do with that."

"When did he say that?"

"The day I quit. We were in his office talking. Apparently, Jace had gathered some information from other employees about Jed's attitude toward me. Walt had requested the data for my annual review."

"Who's Jace?"

"Walt's assistant. He's nice. Been there about six months now."

"Still, Mason may ultimately blame you. He didn't get the boot until this incident with the FDA. And if he found out you were offered his job, he would have even more reason to dislike you."

She swallowed dryly. "Eric, are you saying Jed killed Frank?"

"We don't have any solid evidence against him," he said, avoiding her eyes. "Right now, we can't seem to locate him. I'm going to ask Quincy to call some of his contacts for information about several ideas I'm working on."

"Why?"

"Because Quincy's a reporter with all kinds of contacts and ways of getting information I can't."

"You're FBI."

"Unfortunately, I'm being watched rather intensely. Anything I do, especially on this case, will be closely scrutinized and possibly stalled. Dad's interference combined with my over-zealous behavior has my boss analyzing everything I do or suggest. I'm restricted to the task of keeping you safe, Kendal. Nothing more."

As the hours ticked away, Kendal made her way through the house, doing laundry and tidying up. Eric postponed his meeting and released the agent to go home just before noon.

"You could've gone to your meeting, Eric," she said, entering the dining room just as he got off the phone. "I'm not a baby."

"I know. But I saw your face when I introduced you to Sullivan. I know it would have been easier to have Sheila here with you. Besides, Vera will update me."

"Vera, huh?"

Eric smiled and looked away just as the doorbell sounded. Eric hurried to answer it, while she went into the living room.

She was finally beginning to accept the idea that Dr. Frank Peck was probably into a lot more illegal activity than the feds even knew about. She just wished Jed had removed him from her client load when she had asked him.

"Good afternoon."

The greeting made her heart leap. Quincy strode to the couch and cleared a place on the coffee table for his briefcase. Evidently, this was going to be all business, she thought. But then, what was she expecting? Desperately trying to bite back the rejection she felt, she let her eyes move from the briefcase to Quincy's face.

"Hi."

"I thought we would go over the questions I'll be asking you on the air," he said, taking a seat. "Ms. Howard agreed that you should be prepped."

"What?"

"I had to tell her your father's office scripted the questions. Just to make sure she would still participate in the interview."

"I see."

Quincy pulled several sheets of paper from a file. "Since the media has made a real festival of the FDA's findings, the company's stock has declined considerably. I'm sure Olivia wants to do whatever it takes to resuscitate their standing."

"Can she do that?"

His eyes held hers. "It might work. Are you ready for this?"

"A little scared."

He smiled and patted her hand. "It'll be okay. I'll be right there at your side."

"I was more than a little surprised to find you gone this morning."

His smile faded, and his eyes wandered. "I need to apologize for yesterday, Kendal. That never should've happened. I might have subconsciously taken advantage of the situation. I knew you were vulnerable. In any case, I want you to know I would never intentionally hurt you. Under the circumstances, I thought it best to move to the hotel."

The words stung, sending a battery of splintering sensations through her. Embarrassment and annoyance warmed her cheeks. "I wish you would stop with the amateur psychoanalysis of everything I do. Or, for that matter, what you think I'm thinking. Anyway, you were downstairs with my brother."

"I know. But I have to think of your reputation…what people will say, especially after we air. Besides, I don't want to make promises I can't keep. We both know I'll be leaving in a few days."

It had slipped her mind. She wanted to press him, but knew there was no real basis. Obviously, he was afraid she would become more of a problem than he could handle. She could feel him watching her.

"It *did* mean something, Kendal," he said, as if reading her mind. "I care about you, maybe more than is healthy for either of us right now. For both our sakes, I have to avoid even the appearance of indiscretion. Please say you understand."

She reluctantly nodded. "Of course."

He tapped the bottom of the papers against the table to even them out. "I *have* thought of a way I can help you, though. With my connections, I can locate more solid information about your birth parents."

She was oddly unmoved by his offer. She had to get control of her emotions and ride the discomfort out. "Eric mentioned he needed help on the case. Perhaps that would be a better use of your time."

Quincy leaned closer and touched her cheek with his fingers. "Kendal?" Her name had come in a throaty whisper. And with every ounce of dignity and resolve she could muster, she refused to turn away.

"You're right," she said, looking him in the eyes. "Yesterday should have never happened." She reached for the papers he was holding. "Maybe we had better go over these questions now."

-THIRTEEN-

"Why are you stalling on this, son?" Eric winced as Bill Andersen's voice blared through the speaker of Kent Cashion's phone. "The best thing we can do for her is get her out of town…to a safe house."

"She won't go, Bill. I've already tried. She's dead set on opening her flower shop this coming Saturday and she won't let anything stand in the way."

"You need to change her mind about that, Agent. It could very well cost you her life."

"I know."

"Where is she now?"

Eric glanced at his watch. Ten thirty-five. "Probably just finishing up on the taping of her public statement."

"Somebody on her?"

Cashion cleared his throat. "Yeah, we've got Claude Sullivan on her right now." He leaned back in his chair, placing his hands behind his head. "I've been chatting with Boyd here, Bill. He thinks we need to consider forcing this guy's hand. But if this is a murder suspect or even our serial…."

"That sounds a little premature," Bill interrupted. "Not to mention risky."

"I know, Bill," Eric said. "But we've got to do something. It's been long enough for him to have made a more aggressive move, but nothing. I really think we need to provoke him."

"It doesn't feel right. And it certainly doesn't fit the profile—not unless he's been trying to get to Kendal all along. And that's unlikely."

Eric's stomach tightened. "What do you mean?"

"What if he befriended Peck a while back just to get close to your sister?"

"That doesn't make sense. Kendal wasn't involved with Peck, and he was in the middle of a federal investigation."

"So you're certain this all ties in together?"

"Nah," Eric admitted. "I'm not certain of anything. I just want my sister well protected when we smoke this guy out into the open."

Bill cleared his throat. "I take it you have a plan."

"Based on the warning in that second call, he's pretty unstable. It almost sounds like he hates her and is in love with her at the same time. I think we can play on his jealousy."

"Do you realize forcing his hand like that could put your sister...."

"I know," Eric said, cutting him off. "But dragging this thing out is tearing her to shreds. Rather than playing his game, we need to make him play ours."

"You sound like a real agent now, Boyd," Cashion said. "Have you talked to Kendal about this plan of yours?"

"Not yet. I wanted to run it by you guys first."

"Do you plan to use the reporter?"

"Seeing that he has already concluded that the SUV driver is Kendal's companion, it's the only thing that makes sense. I just hope they both go for it."

Quincy watched curiously as Eric burst through the front door and rushed to the dining room. He followed him. The end of the cherry wood table was set up with a computer, fax and telephone ensemble. Wondering what had Eric all keyed up, Quincy cleared his throat and stepped closer to the table.

"Hey," Eric said, lifting his gaze from the phone. "How did the taping go this morning?"

Quincy eyed the strained look on his face. "She did well. After a few minutes of Olivia taking the lead, she flowed in rather smoothly."

"That's good," Eric said, toying with the buttons on Kendal's answering machine. "When will it be aired?"

Quincy stretched and suppressed a yawn. "Tomorrow night, and twice on Wednesday. Since you're home, I think I'll head on over to the hotel for a shower."

"You mind if I ride over with you?" Eric asked. "I have a couple of ideas I need to run by you. But first, I want you to listen to a taped message."

Quincy raised an eyebrow just as Eric punched the playback button on the machine. "Kendal, this is Jed Mason," the gravelly voice began. "I can't seem to get hold of you. I just want you to know…I don't appreciate you and Hadley pushing me out of my job the way you did. Maybe you don't know what you've gotten yourself into, but I suggest you watch your back."

The men heard a gasp behind them, and swung around to see Kendal's stricken face. They had not heard her come into the room. She moved closer to the chair at the end of the table and stared mutely at the phone.

Quincy's jaw muscles tightened. He desperately wanted to go to her, but he was determined to restrain any show of fondness or familiarity. He swallowed dryly and watched as Eric put a protective arm around his sister's shoulders.

"That sounded like a threat," Quincy said.

Eric nodded and stared at him over Kendal's head. He turned back to her then. "I need to call Cashion and see if he's heard it. In the meantime, we've come up with a plan I need to talk to both of you about."

Kendal looked wobbly. "Plan?"

"Jed's call may shed a whole different light on the case, but my superiors and I decided to force this guy's hand."

"What do you mean, *force his hand*?"

"He's already assuming you and Kendal are involved, so we want the two of you to reinforce this notion by posing as a couple. We need you to put on a show for him…make him jealous so he gets sloppy and shows himself."

Quincy couldn't believe what he was hearing. "But this could backfire. Why would you suggest placing your sister at risk like this?"

"We'll definitely tighten her surveillance."

Kendal pulled away from her brother. "No!"

Eric's face hardened. "What do you mean, *no*?"

"You have no right to ask Quincy to get any more involved than he already is. He came out here for a news story, nothing more."

Despite his own doubts about the plan, Kendal's words still hit Quincy hard. She didn't want him around. He wasn't sure why her refusal to go along felt so unpleasant, but it shouldn't have surprised him. After his apology for something he wasn't sure he regretted, she had been decidedly cool towards him.

But Eric was not to be deterred. "Kendal…."

"No, Eric."

He grasped his sister's hands. "Do you want to look over your shoulders for another twenty years? We need to do this…unless, of course, you agree to go to Spokane."

"I won't go, Eric."

"Then stop fighting and let me do my job. After all, you promised."

"But…."

"No buts. We found similarities between Frank's murder and the serial victims."

Tension had inched up from Quincy's arms and into his shoulders. He impulsively moved towards Kendal when she pulled away from Eric.

"A serial killer is after me?" Her voice quavered. "Why?"

Feeling deflated and helpless, Quincy just stood there, uncertain if he should try to comfort her.

"They need to make some other connections before they can draw any solid conclusions. Right now, they're leaning towards this being an entirely different case. Unfortunately, you seem to be the only living common denominator."

"That's not the same voice," she insisted, glancing timidly at Quincy.

A hint of anxiety flitted across Eric's face. "Sis, it probably sounded different because he's not trying to disguise it like before."

His sister was unmoved. "I don't believe the voice that threatened me was Jed's."

Eric bowed his head and shifted from one leg to the other. "Well, they can check that out. I'm sure they monitored the call. I need to check with Cashion to see if this changes any plans. In any event, I need you to stick around the house this afternoon." Turning to Quincy, he asked, "Can you hang around a bit?"

"Sure." Kendal looked at him. He shoved a hand into his pocket and began idly weaving a coin through his fingers.

"Eric, what are you going to do? Where are you going?"

Touching her brow lightly, Eric playfully smoothed the worry lines away. "I need to go back to the office for a little while. In the meantime, an agent is posted outside. If you go anywhere, give me a call on my cell."

"I'm sure Quincy has better things to do with his time. I don't need a babysitter. Besides, I plan to work at the shop."

Eric's eyes flashed impatiently. "Quincy had planned to shadow you for his article anyway, Kendal. And I wish you would put off working at the shop until tomorrow."

She planted her hands at her waist. "The opening is Saturday," she said combatively. "Besides, if I don't keep busy I'll…I need to act as if everything is normal." Her voice broke, betraying her feeble attempt at bravado. "C'mon, Eric. Sheila and I have things to do."

Sighing, Eric pressed one hand against his forehead. "Kendal, I can't just let you go traipsing off as if nothing is wrong."

Despite her spirited words, Quincy hadn't missed the fear in her eyes. She looked almost like a little lost princess who, in fairy tales, is rescued after some terrible ordeal. Quincy smiled when her eyes met his. He could almost understand her resolve. All she wanted was to reaffirm her independence and take back her own life. Because of her association with an unscrupulous physician, an unknown adversary was jeopardizing everything she had worked to accomplish. Thinking about Peck caused an upsurge of fury in him.

"I'll give you a call later," Eric said, bringing an end to Quincy's musing.

"Eric." Her voice was hoarse, her eyes like saucers. "I'm sorry. I know you're trying to help."

"We're going to get this guy, Sis. I promise. The connection between you, Frank and your former employer is obvious. We need to find a link between the three known serial victims. We won't know our next step until you have seen photos of the victims."

Quincy tensed. "She won't have to look at dead bodies, will she?"

"No, we'll get photos from their homes."

"Do you think the killer might've left messages for the other victims like he's doing with Kendal?" Quincy asked.

Eric raked his fingers over his hair. "They're going back over the evidence…rechecking their homes and phone records, along with the list Kendal gave me."

Quincy frowned. "List?"

"Of people she and Peck both knew. I'll have more information a little later, I hope. Right now, I'm heading back to the office. Will you two be all right?"

But Kendal did not hear her brother's question. Leaning against the back of a chair, she seemed to be in an entirely different world.

"Eric, have you given up the notion that this might have something to do with her search?"

"I'll admit something about that is still nagging at me—something my boss in Denver mentioned earlier. I still want you to help if you can, but her safety is top priority."

Looking over at Kendal, Quincy nodded reassuringly. "She'll be fine. I'll take care of her."

After the waitress had cleared the dishes, Special Agent Vera Mackey spoke up. "I like you a lot, Eric. I think you know that. I'm concerned that something has been eating at you since we found the link between Peck and the three serial victims. What is it?"

Eric's belly contracted into a tight ball and he let his upper body slump forward. "I'm worried about her, Vera. And I don't understand why it took so long to find such an obvious link between the murders. My God, they were all viciously stabbed with ice picks."

"It's not really an issue with me, but I suggest your unrest goes deeper than being worried about Kendal. I just hope you'll work it through with God."

"Thank you. I appreciate your concern." Eric smiled and took her hand in his. "I suppose a lot of it is ego. Men don't like feeling so helpless, so useless when it comes to protecting the women in their lives. These cases seem to intersect and revive repressed childhood memories. As you say, I need to work through it with God."

She pursed her lips. "By the way, how is it that an FBI agent like yourself isn't familiar with the chemical changes in a body exposed to the elements for three days?"

He shrugged sheepishly. "I guess my supervisor was right; I am too emotionally involved with this one. I'm not thinking all that straight. I know I have no right to ask, but I'm hoping you'll help me stay on track."

She nodded knowingly and squeezed his hand. "Peck's body was so bloated the wounds went unnoticed until the autopsy was performed. Besides, this one was different. The killer left the murder weapon beside the bodies of the other victims. It was still inside Peck."

"And you're certain it's the same perpetrator?"

"Yes. There are slight differences, but we're assuming Peck's murder was a last-minute thing. As you know, stabbings are generally personal."

"Peck knew his assailant."

-FOURTEEN-

Kendal peered through the curtain at Quincy, who was out front, casually chatting with Agent Sullivan. Sheila was yet again rearranging the potted plants. It had been two days since she and Quincy had begun performing for her stalker, and she was as confused as ever about her feelings.

She went back to her computer and started downloading her new bookkeeping software. Despite her busy schedule, her role-playing with Quincy had been unsettling. It was difficult to refrain from looking over her shoulder every few minutes.

At Eric's suggestion, Quincy had taken her to dinner Monday evening. Trying to calm her and keep up the pretense, he had talked a lot about his faith. They had spent most of yesterday in Bellevue picking up the fountain for the front display. Afterwards, they had walked hand in hand through the mall like a cozy couple. He had regularly drawn her closer, whispering in her ear. To an onlooker, he might have appeared to be wooing her.

Despite countless opportunities, Quincy hadn't tried to kiss her again. Though disappointed, she knew keeping his distance was necessary. She closed her eyes and rubbed her temples with trembling fingers, hoping to ward off a looming migraine.

"Kendal?"

She jumped reflexively and swung around to face Quincy. Coming closer, he said, "You are way too tense; turn back around." He grasped her shoulders gently but firmly. "Try not to worry. In times like these you've got to lean on your faith."

Obeying his direction, she turned around to face the computer.

The physical contact was restrained but sure. She shivered involuntarily when he leaned down and whispered, his voice misting her ear with warmth. "Close your eyes now and breathe deep. Slower…much slower. Relax. That's it."

His touch was so soothing and effective that, after a few seconds, she indeed relaxed. He placed his thumbs at the nape of her neck and skillfully kneaded upwards into her hairline. The sound of his voice was so mesmerizing she almost felt guilty for allowing this diversion. Without so much as a break in rhythm, Quincy moved back to her neck and shoulders. For several minutes, she delighted in the heavenly escape provided by his hands and voice. The panic she had felt for days just melted away.

"Where did you learn that?" she asked lazily, when he swung her around to face him.

"Just something I picked up along the way."

"It's great," she said, giving her shoulders a good roll. "Wish I could bottle it. Thanks."

He grinned and playfully clipped her nose between two fingers. "Any time."

Without warning, all the confused emotions she felt for him started to choke her. The dull ache in her throat returned and she closed her eyes to keep sudden tears from escaping. If anything, his arms had taught her that she needed to live. She needed more than she had allowed herself over the years, not only in respect to relationships with men, but also in respect to a relationship with God. She envied that.

Eric called her the religious one, but there was so much she didn't understand, so much she hadn't given herself to. She had never known anyone like Quincy—a man who wasn't ashamed to talk about his relationship with God. He spoke of Him as if He were an intimate friend.

It had been some time since she had spent time praying. She hadn't even prayed about how Quincy's appearance at her front door had impacted her. She hadn't allowed herself to admit to anyone—not Sheila, not even herself—that feelings for him were churning inside her. In light of the fact that she had met him just a week ago, the idea was absurd. Even though the unfamiliar feelings might have been initiated by the present horror, she had never responded so completely to a man. Why now? And why this one?

"You okay," he asked, touching her cheek.

"I'm fine. Thanks."

Had she responded to him presumptuously? Had God sent him into her life to teach her, or rip her apart at the seams? Whatever the case, she knew without a doubt that, more than FBI protection or even Quincy's arms, she needed God.

She also knew that she first had to admit that somewhere along the way she had picked up the old anger she had struggled with as a child. And although she loved her dad, she had never really forgiven him for being away when Jack Sumner walked into their home. It had made things even worse when he accepted the candidacy for state representative one year later. The campaigns, the endless trips—it was always something, always a secretary or hundreds of miles between them. In a weird sense, she had shut both him and God out of her life years ago.

She went through the motions all right, attending church and occasionally even praying.

She moistened her lips and looked up, surprised to see Quincy still watching her. "Quincy?"

He squatted down beside her, taking her hand in his. "Yes."

"I want what you have with God. I've been trying to quiet my mind and listen. But it's hard. Can you tell me how to do it?"

"I guess I just try to be straightforward and honest with him. Sort of…naked. Then I place myself in a posture of thanksgiving."

She pulled free, unwilling to allow the familiarity that had developed between them to engulf her. She realized, of course, that Quincy was only being honest with her when he said he couldn't make pledges. She had no real place in his life. He would be leaving on Sunday, and she would probably never see him again.

"Naked," she repeated. "Nana said something similar. I think her exact words were, pray wide open."

"Would you like to pray now?"

His question took her by surprise. "Now?"

He nodded.

Could she actually utter a prayer in front of this man? Out loud?

Kendal breathed a sigh of relief when Quincy, on his knees beside her, began voicing his petition.

"Father, thank you for my new friends here in Seattle. And thank you for protecting and guiding us even at times we don't hear you. You're aware of the predicament here, Lord. So Kendal and I approach you in agreement. Soothe away fears and anguish so she can see clearly. Help Eric and his team solve this case without anyone else getting hurt. And Lord, help Kendal learn to be still before you. Help her know that you can be trusted with every desire of her heart. Let her hear the whisper of your great love...the whisper of your favor. And if there is anything at all hindering that, show her. In the name of Jesus. Amen."

Kendal was stunned and at a loss for words. Quincy's voice, humility and very presence were a gentle rebuke to her. How could she expect to hear from God when she hadn't been open and honest?

"Thanks, Quincy."

She realized that it was hard not to wish things were more than an act between them. She longed for the strength of his arms around her again, not while playing a role but in reality. She had never felt such refuge as when Quincy had held her so close that she had actually felt his pulse pounding between them.

He lifted her chin. "You know, there's a difference between hearing and listening, Kendal."

Disconcerted but intrigued, she asked, "What do you mean?"

"I was at a place in my life once...too busy to listen. Everyone— my mother, editor, even that inner voice—kept telling me to slow down and pay attention."

Something about the way his voice trailed off told her he was haunted by something from his past. She could see the muscle in his jaw moving, and without conscious thought, touched his face with her fingertips. "What happened?"

"I heard it, but I didn't heed it. I kept pushing for what I thought was right. I got myself into a fix that cost me precious moments I can never get back."

Despite the simplicity of his words, the conviction in his manner was deep and compelling. She suddenly wanted to hold *him*. Apparently, she wasn't the only one with issues. "Was it right?"

He shook his body, as if to wake himself up. Then he smiled, brightening and actually dissolving the gloomy mood that had settled around them. "What?"

"The thing you pushed for," she reminded him. "Was it right?"

"I think so, but I still should've slowed down and listened."

Quincy made several calls on his cell while watching deliverymen set up another plant stand. Live plants were placed near the front window on large artificial boulders atop the running fountain. He saw the anxiety on Kendal's face magically turn into pure joy as she made her first arrangement using a new contraption that placed a small stuffed animal inside a balloon. She and Sheila were like two kids in a candy store. He suppressed the urge to laugh right along with them.

They had continued the charade for the benefit of Kendal's stalker, but he had to force himself to be more detached. It was one of the hardest things he had ever done. He had noticed a remoteness in her manner as well. She had been hurt by his apology. He knew he was giving mixed signals now, but he didn't know what else to do. He would be leaving her soon. Too soon.

He thought of the moment he had brought up his past. He hadn't meant to unleash his own ghosts, but they were a part of him now, and perhaps God had a way of using them to help Kendal. She had indeed responded. Hopefully, his sharing would help in navigating her own minefield.

Quincy held his cellphone close to his ear while Bev scolded him about the cost of researching unassigned work for people outside the *Sun*. Despite her testiness, she still treated him as though he had never left. He hoped she had come up with something more on Sumner. But he also needed to help Kendal locate information on her birth parents without letting Bev know what he was digging for.

"The microfilm's really smudged, Quince," Bev said. "But in all this chicken scratch, I can make out the names Stan Boyd, somebody Baylor, and...it looks like Senator Howard. This Sumner guy must have been on the edge. His penmanship is atrocious."

An acute awareness hit his gut the moment she uttered the names in the entry. It was the same sensation he experienced when he was close to a break in a story. "You sure those are reporter notes?"

"Yeah, they didn't have the laptops we have today. It seems the *Rose Creek Clarion* was ordered by the courts to hold on to them because of some kind of police investigation."

Quincy's stomach tightened. "Does it say what the investigation was about?"

"I'm still digging for that."

He tried to slow his breathing, hoping he didn't sound too eager. He didn't want to rouse Bev's curiosity about why he needed this information. "How did you get this so fast?"

"I have my ways," she said high-handedly. "And I'll expect a steak dinner within the month." She laughed. "Nah, I already had them from your initial inquiry. Just hadn't had a chance to go through them completely. I'll get back when I do. Oh, by the way, I'm still trying to get a list of employees from Senator Howard's office. You still need them?"

"Sure do."

"There was a fire a few years ago, so a lot of the records were destroyed. I'll try and go another route. But don't worry—if they exist, I'll find them."

"No problem. I'm more interested in the Sumner thing right now. I would really like to know the details of that investigation." He frowned, wondering if Sumner might have been blackmailing someone. "Thanks, Bev. If you do get the list, I want it, too."

"Talk to you soon, Quince."

He was very grateful for Beverly. She simply did what she did as a favor, and because she enjoyed digging for information in archival databases. She had thought of him as another of her sons who had gotten a raw deal from the top, and she had no qualms saying so to Max.

The door chime roused Quincy to full alertness. A man who looked familiar entered the shop, and he tried to pinpoint where he had seen him before. Agent Sullivan came to attention and approached the man with his hands in the 'halt' position. "I'm sorry, sir, the shop is not open for business."

"I wasn't looking to buy anything," he said, shrinking back a little. "I just wanted to say hello to Kendal."

Kendal's head jerked up at the mention of her name, and she hurried from behind the counter. "Jace!"

Quincy moved towards the back to give them a degree of privacy. However, he remained within earshot.

"Hi, Kendal," Jace said, waving like a timid child. "I saw your ads in the paper. They look great. Thought I'd drop in and see how you were coming along. A lot of the office staff have been talking about it."

Quincy peered from behind the curtain. He remembered now. Jace Tate was Hadley's assistant. He seemed a lot warmer today than he had when Quincy visited the office. Kendal was obviously enthused to see her former co-worker. "I'm glad you dropped by. Would you like a tour?"

"Nah," he said, anxiously eyeing the agent. "I was wondering if you needed any part-time help. Maybe a driver? I saw your van outside."

Quincy stepped out from behind the curtain when he noticed Sheila struggling with a helium tank. In an attempt to stop it from crashing to the floor, she dropped a box of balloons. The sound in the quiet shop was deafening, causing Jace to turn suddenly. It was then he spotted Quincy. He apparently hadn't noticed him earlier.

"Oh, Mr. Morgan. Nice to see you again."

Quincy planted a smile on his face and walked towards them. Purposefully placing an arm around Kendal's shoulder, he offered his free hand to Jace. "How are you?"

"I'm well, thank you." Judging by the look on Jace's face, he wasn't surprised to find Quincy there. "I saw the interview. It was really good. I was surprised Olivia agreed to be included."

Quincy grinned and drew Kendal closer. "You knew about that, huh?"

"There's very little that goes on at Howard-Hadley I don't know about, Mr. Morgan. Or used to, anyway."

"Perhaps Ms. Howard has decided to break some old habits." Quincy's cellphone rang, and he excused himself and went to the back near the sink.

"Quince, have you started on that piece yet?" Joe's anxious voice whined.

"What?" His boss's tone grated like sandpaper on his nerves.

"Just thought I'd check on the status of things." Although Quincy's irritation over being strong-armed into coming to Seattle had subsided, he was still peeved by Joe's bullying tactics. That kind of mentality had cost Quincy his passion, and Kendal her childhood.

"As you know, the taping went well. I don't really have anything else to tell you right now. I'll get home Sunday night and see you Monday."

"You in a hurry?" he asked. "I want to know if you have an angle on the *real* story."

He was suddenly distracted by the sound of the door chime. "Joe, I really can't talk to you about that now. Ken-I mean Miss Boyd hasn't really had a chance to discuss anything specific."

"What are you waiting for? This whole excursion is costing me a pretty penny, and I need a lot more than *you can't talk about it now.*"

The man had probably been looking over his budget. "You'll have it as soon as I write it, Joe. I really can't talk right now."

"That's not good enough, Morgan. I need you to nail the ice princess down. After all, we did her a favor."

Quincy's irritation rose as his tolerance for his boss plunged to a new low. "Ice princess or not, I will not be pushed on this. Now I know I work for you, but I have my ethics. You can either wait until I write the story or accept my resignation right now."

Joe laughed nervously. "Now don't go getting all uppity, Quince. You know how obsessive I can get on these things. I'll see you Monday morning."

"Yeah," he said, closing down the phone. The curtain was swinging when he turned. This prompted him to check the front corner where the desk was located. Just as he suspected, Kendal was working on her computer. He wondered how much of his conversation she had heard.

"Quincy?"

His head jerked up when he heard the distress in Sheila's tone out front. "Yes?"

"Can you come move this box to the corner for me? It's in the way."

"Sure," he said, looking at Kendal sideway as he passed through the curtain. After completing the task, Quincy brushed his hands and straightened.

"Thanks," Sheila said with a pat on his arm.

He gestured toward the back room with his head. "She okay?"

"Yeah. Just hired Jace to make deliveries. He'll work part-time starting Saturday."

Quincy frowned, and wondered why Tate would leave such a cushy job to become a delivery person. He didn't seem the type. He went back through the curtain. She was still working on the computer when he came up behind her. "Kendal?"

She turned, her mouth tight and her eyes ablaze with anger. "Yes?"

The hiss in her voice made him wince. He cleared his throat, hoping to ease into the discussion. "I didn't realize you were on such friendly terms with Mr. Hadley's assistant."

"Are you accustomed to knowing every last detail about your targets?"

Her words were singed with distrust and indictment, and they stung as surely as if they were hornets. Not the words themselves, but the implication that she actually believed he would betray her. He couldn't blame her. After all, who better than himself would know the destruction a reporter's account could bring. And clearly, her first encounter with one had been traumatic.

"I understand you hired him," he said, ignoring her biting tone.

"He was fired and needed a part-time job. I needed a driver."

"Why just part-time?"

"He's going back to school to get his degree," she said, turning her back. "Now if you don't mind…."

He grasped the back of the chair and swung it around. "You're mad about something I assume you heard me say on the phone. If you have a question, ask it. Don't treat me like an annoying insect flitting about your face."

She stood and carefully pushed her chair under the desk. "If I'm angry, it's only at myself for forgetting you're first and foremost a reporter." She tried to stalk past him, but he gripped her arm and gently but firmly pressed her against the wall near the phone.

"Stop it," he whispered, needing to see the familiar shine in her eyes. "I don't play those kinds of games. And despite your current impression or mood, I would never betray you."

Her eyes held his for a long moment before softening. His fingers touched her face, then gently lifted her chin. "I'm sorry. I'm behaving…."

Before she could finish, Quincy drew her into his arms and kissed her with more fervor than he had intended. He wouldn't give his mind the chance to warn him off. He didn't want to think about the ramifications of his recklessness. He simply wanted to hold her in his arms and consume her loveliness.

Even before he tightened his arms around her, Quincy knew it would be difficult to simply leave her behind.

He laughed aloud as he roamed all the upstairs rooms, making extra sure that Marcy's room was in order. He returned to Kendal's bedroom door and gently stroked the doorjamb. All those years of being forced to go to church hadn't served any good purposes, he thought. His pathetic mother had convinced him they needed to purge his father's tendencies for harming others.

He loved these old houses, he thought, looking around. Circumstances were lined up just the way there were supposed to. He was the chosen one. He laughed so hard he nearly strangled. After catching his breath, he inhaled again. Deeply. He could smell Kendal's perfume even out in the hallway. He looked at the clipboard he had left on her windowsill. He had brought it along to validate climbing her backyard fence and tampering with her breaker box. From all appearances, he was just the electrical meter reader. The roses in the side yard were perfectly situated to hide his entry after turning off the power. The cameras never even saw him. He had parked down on the corner the night before, and entered the house while they were downstairs watching television.

What would Kendal Diane Boyd think if she knew he had slept in her home last night—and even in little Marcy's room? He laughed again. None of them were aware that he had even turned off the alarm and unlatched her window prior to leaving this morning. He had easy access to her and everything that belonged to her. It took a little extra maneuvering to return things to normal, but he could come and go as he pleased.

The man they had watching the place was too busy reading his paper and talking on his cellphone to notice him sneak into the backyard. Before the FBI started interfering, she would leave her window cracked for him. Once he had almost fallen from the trellis. In her own little way, she was beckoning to him.

He smiled and strode into her room, sensing an awakening flame within him. He could tell he was reaching a point of losing control. The very thought of wrapping the rope around her throat and watching the life drain away seemed to feed some inner beast. But he had to maintain restraint for a while longer.

He lifted the framed picture from her dresser. Her likeness stood between her brother and father. She was an exquisite specimen, to say the least. Without spot or wrinkle. Her smile seemed to reach out to him. He pressed his lips to her face and held it there for several moments.

"How enchanting and appetizing you look, my sweet rose petal."

He placed the photograph back on the dresser and moved to her bed, touching the satin pajamas draped across the footboard. What would she think if she knew he had been watching her for weeks? How would she feel if she knew he had actually gone through her mail, as well as her computer? He knew her cell number, her e-mail address, even the other one—the free web mail account she had set up temporarily for the business. She was orderly and methodical, writing everything down in a notebook that he just happened to make a copy of using her copy machine.

He liked watching her. She tended her roses every other evening—spraying and clipping them. He sat down and bounced on the bed, then covered himself with her pajamas. Tears filled sinister eyes as he moved to the center and leaned back against the headboard. It was a shame something so beautiful had to die.

He shook himself, trying to beat back the recurring image of his dad's feet swinging from the rafters of their home. At eight, he was struck more by the fact that one of his dad's shoes had come off and landed on the windowsill. He was only a little boy and didn't quite know the meaning of death. The kids in school had been cruel. In the weeks following, his mother seemed to go a little crazy. He'd had to take care of her, as well as fend for himself. When he turned twelve, she insisted on their joining a local church. He had hated her for that.

Not until eight months ago, when she cleaned the attic, did his mother contribute significantly to his life. Not surprisingly, she had no idea of the good fortune she had bestowed. She was simply giving him a box of his father's personal effects.

He laughed again, twisting the shimmering sleeves around in his hand. Perhaps the same chamber in hell that imprisoned his father was also reserved for him.

His duty was clear. He was in the right place at the right time, and all the signs pointed to his calling to exact revenge. Her death would have purpose, he thought, hopping off the bed.

He straightened the covers and fluffed the pillows. "Live while you can, my love, because your time on earth is short."

-FIFTEEN-

Kendal closed her eyes and inhaled the incredibly blissful fragrances surrounding her. Several orders had come in overnight and she was busy with floral arrangements in the back. Opening day had finally arrived, and Jace was in and out delivering so many she had lost count.

Kendal and Sheila had both taken a class in flower arranging a year ago. They had gotten Mrs. Miller, a neighbor, to come over and sit with Nana and Marcy two nights a week for six weeks.

From the moment the doors opened, the shop had been humming with exciting and demanding activity. Still, Quincy's imminent departure eclipsed her exhilaration in their grand opening.

She would miss him terribly, and wondered what her brother had planned after he was gone. Thankfully, the stalker hadn't been heard from in days. Maybe he had given up trying to frighten her. In any case, she had secretly enjoyed the role-playing she and Quincy were still engaged in. Last night, he had taken her to a very elegant restaurant for dinner. Although Eric and Vera were at a nearby table, she had felt like a pampered queen on a desert island.

She snipped unwanted leaves from a bunch of greenery and let her mind wander over the morning. Lance had stopped in and taken countless photographs while Marcy followed him around chattering away. She admired the patience and devotion he had developed for the child.

Even though she still detested the way he had treated Sheila after Marcy was born, she could see a vast difference in his character. He had taken on some of the responsibility of caring for Marcy, even periodically chaperoning her class on field trips. She smiled, thinking how much he had matured. He had been completely professional when he approached her about a layout in his magazine. Sheila had finally gotten used to the idea of him marrying someone else. In fact, she and Jackson were spending all their free time together these days. She giggled, wondering how Sheila's new relationship was affecting Lance's mother. After all, Jackson had to pick her up over there.

As she took a container of roses from the cooler, her mind meandered back to Quincy. At least they had one more evening together. Half-listening to Sheila ring up another sale out front, Kendal put the finishing touches on a phoned-in request for an array of carnations, roses, and tiger lilies. As she placed the arrangement in the cooler out front to await pick-up, she noticed several customers looking over the houseplants.

Their advertisements had brought in quite a few potential buyers, most of them promising to return. Some admitted that her public statement had piqued their curiosity. Quincy's arranging the question so that she could plug Small Whispers had paid off.

Things were going better than they had hoped. Still, the tightness in the pit of her stomach was intensifying, she knew her discomfort wasn't entirely due to the threats, but also to Quincy's imminent departure.

"Look, Aunt Kem," Marcy said, shuffling towards her with something wrapped in paper. Kendal looked at her skeptically, remembering too well that the last time Marcy produced something wrapped in paper, it was a frog.

Sheila was helping another customer at the register; Eric and Vera were talking with Quincy near the small settee. She bent down to Marcy's level. "What is it, sweetie?"

"A cookie."

"Mmm. It sure looks good," she said, cautiously looking it over. "Where did you get it?"

The child looked at the remaining customers one by one. Her shoulders slumped with noticeable disappointment. "Don't see him no more."

Kendal's heart seemed to stall in her chest. As calmly as she could, she removed the paper-covered cookie from Marcy's hand. It looked all right, but she couldn't be sure.

"A man gave you this?"

She nodded, letting her protruding tongue jut out a bit more.

"A man you didn't know?"

Her eyes widened and both hands flew to her mouth, evidently remembering that she wasn't supposed to talk to or accept gifts from strangers. She folded her chubby arms across her face and rolled her eyes towards her mother. "Did bad."

"You just forgot, sweetheart. But try to remember to be really careful about strangers. Okay?"

Sheila strolled over, a scowl marring her normally cheery face. "Maybe it was a bad idea to bring her with us today. Lance's mother had a hair appointment and I…."

By now, Marcy was so distraught she began to howl. But Sheila's attention was drawn from her daughter by a customer needing help. Kendal scooped the bawling child up and hurried to the back. Seconds later, she was joined by Quincy, Eric and Vera.

Kendal carefully positioned Marcy on the tall stool beside the worktable and snatched a wet wipe from a box to clean her face and hands. "I'm sorry, Aunt Kem. Didn't mean to."

"I know, sweetie," Kendal whispered. "Everything is fine, but we'll have to toss the cookie. We don't know if it's safe. I'll buy you one a little later. Okay?"

Marcy nodded and looked around curiously at the audience she had attracted. For an instant, Kendal thought she might start wailing again. But the child suddenly flashed a smile as she peered past her. Kendal turned around and caught Quincy making faces and clawing his fingers behind her.

Kendal playfully glared at him and he promptly sprang toward her desk in the corner, inviting a chase. His exhibition had obviously been a tactic to distract Marcy. It had worked. With Kendal's help, Marcy climbed down from the stool and started running towards Quincy, giggling as unreservedly as Kendal had ever seen her.

"What was that all about, Sis?"

Kendal motioned towards the cookie on the worktable. "Some man gave her that. Did one of you see who it was?"

They looked at each other then back at her, shaking their heads. "Nah. So many people have come and gone today, I guess we weren't paying attention."

She was openly annoyed. "But isn't that why you're here, Eric? She could've been…."

Kendal stopped when she felt Quincy's hands squeezing her shoulders. "Marcy is fine. Let it go."

Eric placed the cookie into a bag and left to transport it to the lab. Quincy and Marcy wound up sitting outside the shop on the metal bench, watching the cars go pass. To avoid thinking about the worst scenarios, Kendal threw herself into finishing her orders—after convincing herself that she was probably worrying for nothing and behaving too emotionally. It was probably just an innocent gesture from a friendly customer, and they had no way of knowing who it was.

She forced a smile and snipped the stem of a rose beneath standing water. Her smile faded as the familiar anxiety once again gripped her. It had been almost two weeks since she had gotten the first call. Why wasn't he reacting to their little masquerade? Not that she wanted to hear from him. She simply wanted to get this whole thing over with so she could get back to normal.

Kendal took a break and went to her desk; she needed to think. Her elbow accidentally hit the keyboard when she sat down, the screensaver cleared and an open document appeared. She gaped at the large letters on the screen. It was a message…intended for her.

My sweet rose petal,

Congratulations on your grand opening. Beautiful beginnings for a beautiful woman. Your guards are doing a sloppy job. As you can see, I can get to you anytime I want. I could've very easily killed the brat, you know. She's very trusting, and I wouldn't have had any problem getting her to follow me. Remember that if you're thinking about letting someone else see this note. I'm watching. And I can get to you, or little Marcy, anytime I want. Would you want Marcy's disappearance on your conscience? It would be your fault if something happened to her. I'm certain that you will eventually come to me, my love. Incidentally, I wanted you to be aware that I know who both your birth parents are. I'll tell you all about them when we meet face to face. Come alone.

Kendal went cold, the note not only heightening her dread, but also fueling her anger. Her thoughts began to race dangerously. Whoever was doing this was obviously demented and audacious, a dangerous combination of behavior traits. She stood and peeked through the curtain, wondering who could've sent it. There was no possible way of getting a clear description from the child, nor did she want to frighten her with questions.

Vera noticed her almost immediately and nodded an acknowledgement. It took all of Kendal's resolve to not beckon to the agent, but she wasn't willing to risk the possibility that he was indeed watching. He had threatened to hurt Marcy.

She quickly checked the back room, feeling the sensation of eyes on her skin. She knew she should let Vera do her job, but she couldn't risk the possibility that he would follow through on his threat to hurt Marcy. She returned to her desk and hit the delete key. Then she hurried to the back door. As expected, it was locked. She moved to the bathroom to make sure the window was secure. It was. Her heart was pounding as the inner struggle of anger and dread continued to intensify. She looked from one corner of the back room to another. After making sure everything was secure, she moved back towards the worktable. Her vision began to blur as outrage tore through her.

For a few priceless days, she had felt free. And now he was threatening her sweet little Marcy. Her breath caught in her throat when she saw the child coming through the curtain. "Aunt Kem?"

"Yes, sweetie?" she said, wiping her face on the towel she'd thrown over her shoulder.

"I'm sleepy."

Kendal took her hand and helped her into the sleeping bag they had placed on the floor beside her desk. She hesitated as she sneaked another look at her computer screen. "Let's lie down over here together," Kendal said, holding the child close.

With her head on Kendal's arm, Marcy drifted off to sleep almost immediately. Kendal closed her eyes and tried to quiet her mind, but it was no use. The whole situation was beginning to wear away her confidence. Panic was rioting within her.

This man had obviously gotten much too close. But how? When?

Quincy leaned back against the metal bench, feeling a little alone without Marcy. It had been a big day for Kendal. He was looking forward to taking her to a quiet place tonight to celebrate. Maybe even see a movie…if Eric would approve. Perhaps they could talk about their future. A black Mercedes swung into the parking lot.

"Mr. Morgan?"

Quincy jumped reflexively. Walt Hadley Jr., dressed in a dark blue suit and a striking burgundy tie, was approaching him. He couldn't help wondering if the man had any casual attire in his closet. He stood and offered his hand. "Mr. Hadley, it's good seeing you again."

The dapper executive forced a smile and returned the reporter's firm handshake. "Likewise," he said, looking puzzled. "I assumed you would've returned to the East Coast by now."

"No, I thought I would hang around for a while longer," he said. "I see you heard about the opening."

He grinned, looking a little embarrassed. "It was hard to miss with the ads in all the papers. I think I'll go on in. Good seeing you again."

"Same here."

Quincy lifted an eyebrow as he watched the man, who could pass for a very competent politician, stroll through the front door of Small Whispers. He was almost certain Hadley had obviously been a little uncomfortable admitting he had only known about the opening through the papers.

After waiting several moments for Hadley to leave, Quincy decided to go inside. He immediately saw that Hadley was nowhere to be seen. Sheila was wiping down the counter. Catching his eye, she silently motioned toward the back.

Quincy stared hard at Sullivan, who had just recently relieved Vera. He hurried through the curtain, stopping just inside. Neither Kendal nor Walt could see him.

Marcy was asleep on floor to the right of Kendal's desk while Hadley was seated on a stool to her left, trapping her between them. "I thought you would do well in Jed's position, Kendal. I was disappointed when you didn't return any of my calls."

"I should have," she said apologetically. "As you can see, I've been a little preoccupied." She paused long enough to hit the key on her computer that shut it down. "And thanks for the flowers, but you really shouldn't have sent them."

"That was before I knew you would be surrounded by them."

Quincy frowned. He didn't know Hadley had sent her flowers. He told himself it didn't matter, yet it bothered him on some level. He was being rude and possessive by standing in the shadows eavesdropping, but clearly Sullivan assumed because Hadley was recognized, he had a carte blanche with Kendal.

"I wish I had heard about the shop from you rather than reading about it in the paper." He playfully twirled a lock of Kendal's hair between his fingers. Quincy felt his muscles tighten. "Then you go and hire a man I've fired. You should've asked me about *that* first. I think you owe me an explanation."

Kendal's dry chuckle alerted Quincy that her anger was gaining on her attempt at diplomacy. "*Owe* you? I owe you nothing, Walt. And why should I ask your permission to hire someone for my establishment?"

That's my girl, Quincy thought with a smile.

"I don't trust Jace, and I don't think you should, either. I don't want him around you."

Kendal looked down at Marcy and began stacking the papers she had been working on. "Jace is doing a fine job, and I'm grateful to have him. If you're concerned we might discuss Howard-Hadley business, I assure you, that's the last thing on our minds."

"No, of course not. It's just that I feel a little out of the loop here. I really went to bat for you in the investigation, Kendal."

Kendal cocked her head to the side. "Why is that, Walt? Why would you go to bat for someone you hardly know?"

"I'm very attracted to you, Kendal. I've had my eye on you for years. I never approached you because I thought you were involved with Frank."

She released an exasperated groan. "I appreciate any support you've given me, but other than friendship I'm not interested in a relationship. And today I'm really busy. Is there anything else I can help you with?"

"Don't be coy with me," he said, placing his hand at the back of her neck. "I think you know how I feel about you. And from that kiss in my office, I thought you felt the same way."

Quincy flexed his arms and was about to intervene when Kendal jerked away and stood up. The movement inadvertently forced Hadley to jump from the stool. "If I've given you the impression that there was something between us, I'm sorry."

Hadley's stance stiffened. "Is this the frigid little…."

Before he could complete his remark, Quincy rushed forward and lifted Hadley up by the knot of his tie and belt. "I think the agent out front will be able to help you find your way out. In the meantime, I suggest you not bother *this* lady any further. Do I make myself clear, Mr. Hadley?"

The man's eyes were bulging, but he managed to nod. Quincy released his grip and carefully placed Hadley's feet back on the floor.

Hadley turned a questioning eye on Kendal, grinning as he straightened his tie and faced Quincy. "So this is why you haven't left Seattle. Sorry, Morgan. Didn't mean to intrude."

Quincy's irritation slowly subsided as he watched Hadley move through the curtain. Kendal fell against him, badly shaken. "Its my fault, Quincy," she whispered. "I shouldn't have let him kiss me. Being scared and confused is no excuse for being reckless."

"We all make mistakes, especially when we're distressed. But I think Eric needs to know about this."

Kendal drew in a shaky breath. "You don't think…."

"I don't know. But you're right in the middle of something here, Kendal. Eric needs to be told exactly what transpired between you and Hadley in his office, as well as here today."

She tried to step back, but he tightened his hold. He could feel the fear racing through her like an electrical current. She looked up at him, and her eyes seemed to touch a place in him that staggered his mind. "Thanks for being here, Quincy."

It had taken all of his willpower to restrain himself, especially during the last few days of their play-acting. But presently, logic and good sense didn't stand a chance.

"My pleasure, beautiful."

Tossing caution aside, he tangled his fingers in her hair and brought his lips down on hers.

-SIXTEEN-

Quincy pushed through the revolving door of the hotel with his cell-phone pressed against his ear. Beverly answered on the third ring.

"Hi, Bev. Just wanted to check in before I get ready for dinner. You find anything else on Sumner?"

"Mr. Morgan!"

Quincy paused and looked towards the concierge's desk; a uniformed hotel employee was waving him over. He held up a finger to acknowledge the man's wave and then turned back to his call. He had missed part of what Beverly was saying.

"...wild and crazy. *The Clarion*'s information is pretty sketchy. A lot of it was obviously deleted from the records. I *did* manage to find a little something from another source, though. It's inconclusive, but it's from a Seattle paper."

"That's all right. I appreciate getting whatever you've dug up."

"Based on what I've learned from several sources, including a former *Clarion* employee, Sumner was an alcoholic. I guess that explains the odd scribbling in his notes."

"Maybe so."

"I assume since you have me looking for Howard's employee list, these two cases are related. I think the reason he scribbled Howard's and Boyd's names had to do with Stan Boyd's *then* future candidacy. Anyway, he was a copy editor at the paper for thirteen years. Then he snapped and insisted on being given a chance for a byline. He kidnapped a little girl on his first assignment. Thankfully, the child was found unharmed."

Quincy held his breath. "Does the article mention the child's name?"

His heart pounded as if he had run a marathon. He closed his eyes and took a deep breath. One of Kendal's greatest fears was that her abductor had molested her. His stomach was contracting spastically. *Lord, will she be able to handle it if he did?*

"Nope. This was almost twenty years ago. This article was hidden in the back of one of the larger papers. It just says she was ten years old. Sometimes papers tend to accommodate each other in personal matters."

"What do you mean?"

"Well, the *Clarion* printed very little on the abduction…probably because he was *their* employee and there was litigation involved. Small-town papers rarely oblige us with details in matters like this. I grew up in a town like that in Tennessee. If a family wanted to keep certain details out of the press, all they had to do was slip cash to the editor and he would oblige them. In spite of the status of the other paper, perhaps this article was treated in the same manner as a favor to the editors of *Rose Creek Clarion*."

"How long did Sumner keep the child?" Quincy asked, swallowing hard. "Did he…."

"Abuse her?" she asked. "Paper doesn't say whether he did, but he kept her way out in a rural community for five whole days. The city of Auburn, I think it said. The very fact that basic info is omitted tells us the family was prominent and wanted to protect the child's identity. I can only imagine what a drunk would do when his own family is away."

"What do you mean?"

"One of the articles stated that his wife and eight-year-old son, Jonathan, had moved out three weeks earlier. After the little girl was safely home with her family, the wife had a notion to go back."

"And?"

"It's the kicker in the entire piece, Quincy," she said, pausing. "Sumner strung himself up in his bedroom. Jonathan was the one who found him."

Quincy winced. "Poor kid. Thanks, Bev, I owe you."

He closed down his phone and went to the concierge desk. "Mr. Morgan. This letter arrived for you by courier."

"Thank you," he said, taking the plain white envelope, addressed only with his name. He immediately ripped it open, but at that moment, two men across the lobby got into a loud disagreement. Quincy looked for several seconds, then slid the envelope into the inside pocket of his jacket without reading it and hurried to the elevator. His thoughts once again moved to Kendal. He could hardly wait to see her later.

After a long shower and shave, Quincy dressed for dinner. When he pulled the jacket from the bed, the envelope he had placed inside tumbled to the floor. In his excitement about his evening out with Kendal, it had slipped his mind.

He took out a note typewritten on plain white paper.

"Get on a plane tonight, or I'll slit her throat before you wake up in the morning. Marcy's, too. I'll be watching to make certain you comply."

Quincy stood paralyzed. This guy was off the hook. He didn't want to give in to the outlandish demands of a terrorist, but neither did he want to provoke him into hurting Kendal or Marcy.

His face grew hot with rage. Frustration and helplessness engulfed him. He balled the envelope and sheet into a tight wad and tossed it onto the table near the window. Blood rushed to his head and before he knew it, he had hit the wall, leaving a dent in the thin construction. His throat felt raw, and he began pacing the small room.

Lord, what should I do? Help me think clearly.

Minutes later, Quincy pulled out his cellphone and dialed Eric. "Hey, buddy, we've got a problem."

An hour later, Quincy was standing with Eric at the airport check-in. He tried to keep his voice even. "Tell Kendal something serious came up, and I had to fly back East. I hate to leave her at a time like this."

Eric squeezed Quincy's shoulder and smiled. "I appreciate what you're doing, man. After she told me about Hadley's attraction, I think I can see why you're so suspicious of him. I can't believe you actually had to peel him off her. We had a long talk with Sullivan about his sloppiness. He just thought Hadley had been cleared."

"I couldn't quite figure out why he felt the need to stake his claim during an interview with a reporter. Unless he somehow knew I was staying in Kendal's house at the time. It's a real possibility he's working with Mason. Please keep her safe, Eric."

Eric nodded and peered around guardedly. "I'll check him out again. But you said he was surprised when you stepped in for Kendal. Surely, if he's the stalker he would have seen you two together by now. After all, we've been performing for a week. And don't worry about Kendal. I won't let her out of my sight."

Quincy felt like he was running out on the best thing that had happened to him in a long time. He looked at Eric closely. He had noticed something different about his mood the last couple of days. Maybe it was the pressure and stress of protecting his sister.

He looked briefly at the photo and background information Eric had given him on Jed Mason. "I'm glad you're giving me something to do. I don't know if I could leave otherwise. You think I'll be able to find him?"

Eric gestured toward the photo. "You should. I just wish the bureau would let me follow my instincts and go after him. Let me know as soon as your contacts find out anything else about Howard's employees. It's important."

Quincy frowned. "Why? I thought...."

"I know," Eric said, holding up a hand. "I have my reasons."

"Eric, you seem to be going in a hundred different directions. Don't get yourself in such a bind you can't keep Kendal safe."

"I won't," he promised, returning to the task at hand. "Mason has a brother and two sisters in Birmingham. It looks like his last call was made from his younger sister's home. All of the addresses are there. When you spot him, give me a call on my cell."

Quincy's eyes narrowed with contempt. "You sure you don't want me to break his neck?"

Eric flashed a hesitant smile. "Nah. Call me before you approach him. By then I might have a heads-up for you."

"Are you sure it's him?" Eric asked anxiously.

Quincy held his cellphone with one hand and the small pair of binoculars to his eyes with the other. "I'm sure."

The heavyset man had come out of the house and was sitting on the top step of the front porch. Several young children piled onto a school bus in front of the house. A woman, probably Mason's sister, came out and handed him a large glass of milk.

It was the same man, all right. The sound of tires grinding into the gravel prompted Quincy to crouch lower as the bus passed. Dust rose up above him. He held his breath until it was farther down the road.

"Eric, I want to move in. I just want to find out why he threatened her."

"Don't lose it now, Quincy. We can't afford to make a mess of things. It could be Kendal's life, as well as my career."

"I know, I know. I'll call you after I talk with him."

Mason stood and walked down the steps and into the garage, leaving the woman on the porch. Wiping the dust from his lips, Quincy looked down the gravel road to where he had parked his rental. He took a deep breath and scrambled through the barbed-wire fence and down the embankment into the front yard.

Loathing for the man surfaced instantly. He headed for the garage, determined to remain calm and focused. Hopefully, Mason would cooperate and tell him exactly what's going on with all the threats.

"Hello. May I help you?" the woman asked, rising from the porch swing. She shielded her eyes against the eastern sun as he moved closer to the whitewashed picket fence.

Quincy turned to face her. "I'm here to see Mr. Mason, ma'am. Jed Mason."

Walking toward the screen door, she turned and yelled, "Jed! There's somebody here to see you."

Mason walked out of the garage, wiping his hands on an oily rag. "Yeah? Who are you?"

Quincy was suddenly glad the woman had gone back inside. His face grew more heated with every step he took toward the man, but he managed to keep his resentment restrained.

"I'm Quincy Morgan, a friend of Eric and Kendal Boyd's. We've intercepted some of your calls. We need to talk."

Mason turned on his heels and without a word headed for the garage. Quincy wasn't sure whether Mason was of the mind to go for a weapon, but he followed him, anyway. "I have nothing to say to you," he said, opening the door to his car.

Quincy grabbed the door and slammed it shut. "You seem to have plenty to say to Kendal. I want to talk about that."

"Get off this property," Mason said, taking several steps forward.

Quincy clamped a heavy hand down on the man's shoulder, struggling to keep his temper in check. Mason winced as he tightened his grip. "We will talk, Mason, either now or when you wake up."

Several hours later, Quincy sat up in bed and answered his cellphone. Sleep had evaded him since he had left Seattle. "Morgan."

"Hey, it's Eric. Sorry about the hour, but I just now got your message."

Quincy saw that the lighted digital clock read 2:30 a.m. Immediately, his chest tightened. "She okay?"

"Not so good. She's not talking very much...to anyone. And she's especially not mentioning *your* name. I almost wish Jed had turned out to be our culprit. The message you left was kind of sketchy. I've checked Kendal's former client list from Howard Hadley. Everyone clears there."

"I'm just glad she is seriously being guarded," Quincy said.

"She hadn't been contacted for several days. If it hadn't been for the warning threats you and Amory received yesterday, I probably would've been worrying that they might consider pulling her surveillance. Incidentally, they don't want me to mention those threats to Kendal just yet."

Joe had contacted the FBI after receiving an anonymous e-mail the same day Quincy had received his note. The message had demanded he recall his reporter. If he didn't comply, he was warned, he would be responsible for the deaths of Kendal Boyd and little Marcy Dodd. He was thankful Joe had contacted the bureau, but he hadn't wanted him to know too much of what was going on. A thought suddenly occurred to him. "Hadley knows what paper I was from, Eric. I gave him a card. He could have very easily sent those warnings."

"I've been thinking about that," Eric said. "The e-mail was sent from a free account, registered with an obviously invented name. It was sent from the library just two miles from *Small Whispers*. Naturally, we're assuming the customer who gave Marcy the cookie is also the stalker."

"Eric, I don't want to lose her. I'm in love with her."

The long pause at the other end of the phone made Quincy anxious. He was hoping Eric wasn't opposed to the idea.

"I think I kind of figured that one out. Have you told her?"

"Not in so many words. With all that's going on, I didn't…." His words trailed off. He hadn't told her because he hadn't been sure of it himself. Not really. Not until he was forced to leave without telling her why.

"Based on the way she's shutting down, I'd say she has some pretty intense feelings for you, too. But I'm worried about her, Quincy. I mean, Kendal isn't as strong as she would have you believe."

Quincy's ears prickled. Although he had already seen some of Kendal's vulnerabilities, he asked, "What d'ya mean?"

"Kendal holds a lot of stuff inside. She craves affection more than anybody else I know, but she's sort of built a wall around herself."

"She told me about Sumner, Eric. Even agreed to let me look for a motive for his snatching her."

"I'm glad," Eric said, sounding relieved. "You're the first man I've seen her open up to so totally. Ever."

"Whether she would admit it or not, the fact that you and the congressman were my character references played a big part," Quincy said. "By the way, you think Sumner is the only reason for the wall?"

"Mostly. It's been hard for her to trust men. She's lived her life in continual pain. And I'm sure these threats remind her of Sumner."

Quincy squeezed his burning eyes shut and drew his free hand over his face. He let his mind go back to Joe's last call. The editor was going crazy with questions and had begged him to come back. Even Eric's superiors had demanded he return to Baltimore, not realizing he had already left for Alabama. Eric, who was the only person who knew exactly where he was and why, had placed his own career on the line. He had taken the opportunity of Quincy's warning to send him to Alabama to get more information out of Jed. Quincy would fly to Atlanta on an early-morning flight to visit with his aunt. "I just hope this is over very soon, and you don't lose your job."

"Did Mason have any usable ideas about this situation?"

Quincy watched as the minute digit on the clock change. "He's angry, Eric. What he's saying doesn't make a lot of sense. It very well might be resentment and revenge talking."

His mind went back to the gruff posture of the man he had talked with several hours ago. He didn't like him, primarily because of his antagonism towards Kendal. But his gut told him that Kendal had been right. Jed Mason hadn't sent those messages.

He smiled as Kendal's face suddenly floated before him. He had felt a sense of great relief when Eric suggested that she might have feelings for him, too. But she also probably thought him a scoundrel for disappearing without one word. Because of the warnings he and Joe had gotten, the bureau had even restricted him from phoning her.

"Mason's call to Kendal was nothing more than a warning to stay away from Hadley. He says Hadley just recently started making subtle suggestions that he and Kendal were a couple, especially if he thought another man might catch her eye."

"Apparently so," Eric said. "He's called and asked her out a couple of times. But she's declined each invite."

Eric's prompt addendum hadn't gone unnoticed. "Please don't let him near her when she's alone."

"I don't understand all this," Eric said. "He came out as clean as a whistle in our background check. He's never even gotten a parking ticket. He lives with his ailing father, who is still a bully to be reckoned with."

Quincy closed his burning eyes. "I haven't had a good feeling about Hadley since my interview with him in his office. And Mason says he saw Hadley and Peck in a scuffle about six or seven months ago. That was just after he had mentioned his concern to Hadley about Peck getting too cozy with her."

"Mason approached Hadley about this?"

"Yeah," Quincy said. "As soon as Kendal had talked to him about it."

"Why didn't they take him off her client roster?"

"Hadley told him to forget it, that it would be taken care of." Quincy leaned his head back against the headboard. "What's his father like?"

"Hadley Sr. is a very angry man," Eric said. "Used to keep company with Olivia, but now he can hardly stand to hear her name without growling an insult. He told me she cheated him."

"How?"

"Don't know; he wouldn't go into any details. Started mumbling about something else entirely. I don't know whether he's crazy or just pretending to be. Did Mason say why he hassled Kendal?"

"Sour grapes," Quincy answered. "Five years ago, his niece was up for the same job. He thought your dad's relationship with the Howards had influenced Kendal's win."

"Kind of petty, isn't it? He say anything about Hadley Sr.?"

"Yeah. He's always been heavy-handed and demanding towards his only son. But Jr. will do anything to please him—even steal the gold cap from a dead man's tooth," Quincy said. "Mason thinks the whole place is a cover for illegal activity, but he doesn't have anything substantial to prove it."

"Quincy, what's your gut feeling about Mason? Do you believe him?"

"I don't like him, Eric, but I believe he's telling the truth. He has nothing to lose now by lying."

"Based on what Mason says, I suppose Hadley Jr. could've been Peck's accomplice. But it doesn't make sense where Kendal is concerned. Why would he stalk and threaten her when he's pursuing her romantically?"

"Maybe he thinks she knows something that could land him in prison—something she doesn't know she knows. Perhaps his attempt to court her is a scheme to draw it out."

"Because of the way we gathered this information, I'll need to tread lightly, Quincy. Cashion is doing a lot of sweating over the manpower it's taking to work the case." Eric chuckled. "By the way, have you found anything else on Kendal's birth family?"

"No, but I did learn that a woman in Senator Howard's office left after getting pregnant. She was an aide—young, black and pretty. Uh, Eric, I don't—I mean…."

"Say it, Quincy. I realized when I asked you to do this that I might hear something I didn't want to."

"My source tells me your dad was rather friendly with this woman."

"Was he having an affair?"

"Is that why you've pursued this angle?"

"Maybe."

"I don't know. I've learned to dig until everything fits, man. Right now, I don't have anything that proves he was unfaithful to your mother, nor do I have anything that proves otherwise."

"If you don't mind, keep digging. I need to know if there is a connection between Dad and this woman. If this is Kendal's birth mother, then Dad could really be her biological father. That would open up a lot of possibilities."

"Would it be so bad?"

"He would be a fraud, Quincy. He not only would have cheated on my mother, but he put my sister through a living hell. And if that's the case, he's lied about other things. His actions could've placed her life in jeopardy. I don't think I could forgive him for that."

Quincy admired Eric's devotion to his sister, but was somehow aware that the sentiment went a lot deeper than what he actually said. Something was going on that Eric wasn't willing to share right now. His heart thumped as he visualized Kendal's smile. "Take good care of her, Eric."

"I promise," he said. "I'm sorry to ask for so many secret favors, but I can't tell them I've gone outside. I'm trusting you to get the information I can't get caught digging for."

"I understand."

Quincy hung up the phone and made a list of research questions for Bev. Later, while trying to get to sleep, he thought of Kendal and how tough she tried to be. He wanted her—needed her by his side.

Lord, fix my feelings for this woman in a place that pleases you. Right now I want her desperately. But if that doesn't fit into your plans for either of us, take this intense love I feel for her away. And Lord, please keep her safe.

-SEVENTEEN-

"You destroyed something of mine," his voice whined. "Now I'll have to destroy something of yours. Just make sure you come alone."

Kendal sprang upright in bed and stared into the darkness. Her hand was still gripping the phone. She had taken a sleeping aid and had finally gotten a couple hours sleep, but in her sluggishness, had forgotten and answered the phone. She slammed the receiver down, flicked on the bedside lamp and tried to calm herself. She had been foolish to make such a fuss about Eric's desire to reroute all her calls, but she hadn't wanted to feel so helpless and imprisoned. As if she didn't anyway.

The calls and messages were coming more frequently now. He had even started calling her cellphone. The caller ID always registered out of area, and she would answer in hopes that it was Quincy. Aware of her affection for Marcy, the stalker often included the child in his threats, even going as far as describing what she was wore to school. She was glad Eric decided to place an agent outside Lance's mother's home as well.

It amazed her that this guy wasn't afraid to leave messages. After all, he knew the FBI was recording them. He even taunted them on occasion, often reminding her that he was as close as her own breath and there was nothing her tattered fence of feds could do to stop him. He ended each call with the same two words: "Come alone."

Kendal mulled over why he was waiting to reveal where or when she was to come. How would he divulge the location? He obviously wouldn't broadcast it, knowing he would likely have to contend with a qualified law-enforcement team.

She hated this sick game, but she would do anything to prevent Marcy from being the victim of a psychopathic killer.

Kendal's thoughts turned to Quincy. She hated to admit it, but his sudden departure had thrown her into a depression so deep she had moped about for days. But she refused to be the first one to break the silence. She couldn't believe how rude he had been.

She couldn't understand why God would at last unlock her heart to a man, only to allow it to be ripped to shreds in a matter of days. What kind of urgent matter kept him from calling her? She wanted to ask her brother, but he was obviously too wrapped up in smoozing his superiors to talk to her.

A dull ache ate at her like a canker. She scolded herself for falling so hard for Quincy Morgan. *You knew he was going to leave,* she told herself fiercely. *One day earlier didn't change that. A phone call won't change it. Nothing will change it.*

She had no grounds for complaints. She had to accept the fact that Quincy had walked out of her life just as unexpectedly as he had walked in.

Kendal climbed out of bed, got down on her knees and began to pray. *Lord, Nana told me to be honest with you. Well, I'll be honest. I'm angry. I see all kinds of people with families who take them for granted. I see people who seemingly fall in love with a different person every week. Then you bring Quincy into my life, and for the first time, I can actually feel affection for a man. But now he's gone.*

You haven't protected me like you promised in the Bible. It's just like before…when I was a child and Sumner took me away. Dad couldn't protect me, either. What am I supposed to do? Keep blindly trusting in a God I can't see or hear? I'm angry. Do you hear?

And on that bitter note, she rose and got back into bed. Her mind kept shuffling through all the things that were happening.

After learning that all three stabbing victims had been linked in some way to Frank, Eric and his team reassessed their strategy and insisted that she and Sheila keep away from the shop until further notice. The only real staff left was Jace, who was busy making deliveries, while temps from a local agency attended to the daily operation of the shop. Each evening after work, Jace would drop off the receipts and sit and talk for a while. The situation was frustrating and extremely unnerving.

She hadn't been able to identify any of the victims as someone she remembered meeting, but Frank knew each of them. Victim one was a woman he had been dating; victim two, the postal delivery person; and victim three, a patient Frank had been distributing to.

Kendal glanced down at trembling hands. For the last couple of days she had felt like a caged turkey on the eve of Thanksgiving. Walt had called several times to invite her out, and she had been tempted to accept, but feared he would draw the wrong conclusion.

It was no use. She missed Quincy. She missed the lazy smile he flashed at odd moments; the look that told her he would protect her. She missed the tender kisses and the taste and smell of him. He made her feel alive and safe, and she longed to have his arms around her again, even if it was just to say good-bye.

Her bedroom door burst open, and she instantly jumped up and screamed. "Didn't mean to scare you, Sis. I heard the call…just got off the phone with Cashion. You okay?"

"I'm sorry," she said, her voice wavering. "I took a sleep aid and was so out of it…I just forgot. I don't even know what I said."

"It's okay. You didn't say anything wrong; we got it all on tape. I just don't want you any more upset than you already are."

She pushed back her escalating fear, warily glancing at the phone. "I should have let you re-route them."

"Don't worry about that now. We can use it. Just remember I'm right here, and I don't plan to leave until we get this guy."

"You have any idea where it came from?"

Her voice sounded squeaky in her own ears. Eric shook his head. "It was a cellphone. Based on the triangulation results, he was in this neighborhood when he called. He may have been driving past in a car. We'll check the camera recordings. Think you can keep him talking next time?"

"If I have to. But what will I say?"

"Anything. Ask him about the other people he killed, or what is it he wants from you…things like that. Make him think." Eric moved back towards the door. "He probably won't call back tonight. Try to get some sleep."

Kendal lay back, feeling more alone than she ever had. For the first time in a long time, she picked up her Bible from the nightstand and turned to Psalms ninety-one. Nana had called it 'the promise of protection' and had made her memorize it.

But a wave of irritation passed over her, and she slammed the Bible shut without reading even a verse. After turning off her lamp, silent tears turned into deep sobs. But despite her defiance, the memory of the Psalm cut through her foggy mind like a laser beam.

He will cover you with his feathers, and under his wings you will find refuge....

"Then where are you?" she whispered. "I don't want to be so angry, but I'm scared to totally trust that you'll keep me safe when you didn't before. I really do want the kind of relationship with you that Nana had—that Quincy seems to have. I know I keep jumping from one extreme to another. I need you to stabilize my mind and help me be still and hear your direction...to know without a doubt that you'll protect me from this maniac."

She closed her eyes and the scene with Walt at the shop came to mind. Recalling the intensity of the moment, she shuddered. Quincy had been terribly angry, but he hadn't even raised his voice when he lifted Walt up in the air. She remembered being very grateful that Marcy had not awakened.

Afterwards, she had clung to Quincy so desperately she could barely breathe. Then he had kissed her, causing her thoughts to turn to mush.

But he wasn't here now when she needed him most. Had he really abandoned her? Had he fooled her so completely?

Quincy lounged on his aunt's couch, feeling strange and restless to be in Atlanta. He knew Baltimore would never hold the same attraction for him as it had, and he had no intention of checking in with Joe. Not just yet, anyway.

He glanced around the living room and recalled the faith game his aunt had initiated the morning she left Baltimore. *What do you see yourself doing in two years, Quince? Reach for the stars.*

I have a job I'm proud of. I'm married to a beautiful Christian woman like you, and I'm bouncing a chubby son on my knee.

He stared at the phone on the lamp table. Call her, he urged himself. The feds only asked you to avoid contact for a few days. It's been almost a week. He closed his eyes. The last few days, he'd driven through the streets of Atlanta, half expecting to see her shrink back fearfully when he got too close to another car. He had tried to suppress the memory of her endearing bossiness and the sweetness of her kiss. He never wanted to yearn for the woman with a body built for dancing, but he did. She was beautiful, intelligent and eager to give of herself. And though stubborn, she wasn't obnoxious or overbearing.

Smiling expectantly, he picked up the phone and dialed Kendal's number. But in the middle of the first ring, he disconnected. He knew she was there. At that exact moment, his cellphone rang and he grabbed it, hoping.

"Morgan."

"Quince, my man. How are you?"

Quincy let out a disappointed sound and slid further down into the couch. "Hello, Max. I'm sort of in the middle of something right now. Can I call you back?"

"I've left several messages for you at home. You haven't returned any of my calls."

"I really don't think I would be interested in anything you have to say."

"Hold up, Quince. I know how you feel. And I'm sorry you got caught up in the rush of things, but my hands were tied by some of Senator Vincent's constituents. We were on the edge of a lot of legal tossing. I know that doesn't make you feel any better about me, but I couldn't risk it."

Quincy's muscles began to twitch. He appreciated the candor, but it was too much too late. "So you hand me over on a silver platter by not backing me? Max, if I had known your backbone was made of jelly, I never would've worked for the *Sun*."

"Listen, this paper has pulled plenty out of the hot seat. Your case just fell at an awkward time…that's all."

"What do you want, Max?"

"I wanted to give you a heads-up on a job opening. I know Joe can't pay you what you're worth, and I'm not stupid enough to think you would come back to me. It's in Seattle."

Quincy straightened as exhilaration clutched his gut. Was this God? "W-what?"

"I heard through the grapevine that you've been snagged up by a certain princess out there."

"Don't push me, Max."

"Hear me out, buddy. It's obvious you've lost the taste for print. I mentioned your name to a friend at an NBC affiliate. He needs a correspondent."

"Why would you do that?"

"I owe you, my man. I know that. And Beverly hasn't let me get a good night's sleep in eighteen months. You deserve better than you got." Max fell silent, but after a moment he cleared his throat and continued. "His name is Sidney Hayes. I hope you'll agree to talk to him."

-EIGHTEEN-

It was Saturday morning. The sun shone brightly through Kendal's bedroom window—as if all was right with her world. But she had very little motivation to get up, so she just lay there. Today marked one week since Quincy's departure. She and Sheila had spent most of the night talking and crying into the phone, mostly about him and the mystery surrounding his silence. She was sure his past had something to do with it. But what?

Kendal had asked Eric not to mention the threats against Marcy to Sheila, but to just keep an extra eye on her. "Come in," she said, after she heard a light knock at her door.

"Sis, I need to leave early this morning. Cashion has called a meeting, but we have a couple of rookies outside. Local PD has agreed to come through every ten minutes."

Kendal sat up. "You got a minute? I want to ask you something."

He strode over and sat on the edge of her bed, looking as innocent as he had all those years ago. "What's up?"

Her stomach knotted with uncertainty. "Will I ever see him again?"

Eric smiled. "See who?"

"Don't play with me, Eric Boyd. You know very well who I'm talking about."

"I'm sure you will, Sis," he said, chucking her chin.

She held his gaze. "Will you tell me about him?"

Eric crossed his arms over his chest. "What do you want to know?"

"He mentioned something to me about his past." She paused and moistened her lips. "He left before I had a chance to ask him about it."

"You sure you want to know?"

She nodded, willing back a pang of uneasiness and apprehension. "Yes."

"Quincy used to work as a political reporter for *The Baltimore Sun*. Right now, he's with a much smaller outfit."

"*The Hill Watcher.*"

"Yeah. He's always been the kind of reporter with heart, Sis. He didn't trick or con people, and he took care of his informants. He's the one who broke the story on Senator Vincent out of Nebraska a little over a year ago." Eric paused and shook his head. "The judge hadn't been impressed when Quincy withheld the name of his source. He charged him with contempt and threw him in jail."

Kendal gasped. "Contempt? What kind of judge would expect him to reveal his sources? That should be against the law."

"People in high places can twist the law sometimes, Sis. Dad and I believe they really did Quincy an injustice, especially when Senator Vincent was so obnoxiously arrogant about his dirty deeds. When Quincy was released three months later, he'd lost everything. His mother had died of cancer, his wife had divorced him, and the *Sun* no longer had a place for him."

Her indignation grew as she tried to cope with the pain Quincy must have felt. She dabbed at rebel tears with the edge of her bed sheet. "Was he even allowed to go to his mother's funeral?"

"Only with an escort. The papers had a field day with it, too—even the *Sun* ran an article. It was the silliest travesty ever perpetrated with taxpayer's money."

"That must have felt horrible, especially to be betrayed by your own paper. Poor Quincy."

Eric smiled. "I like him, too, Sis. The thing is…he didn't have to go through any of it. The informant he was protecting committed suicide, leaving a note that Quincy should divulge everything. That's one of the reasons Dad and I chose him."

Her whole body slumped as love stirred around inside her. She had been right. Quincy Morgan was a man of principle. It took some effort, but she finally got her voice to work. "What are the other reasons?"

"Huh?"

"You said Quincy's integrity was *one* of the reasons you and Dad chose him. What are the others?"

Eric stood up. "Just something between me and him. Nothing important."

"Was his informant a man or woman?"

"A woman," Eric said, pausing at the door. "Driven by grief, her husband came after Quincy. Shot him in the parking lot outside the newspaper building. Even though Quincy wouldn't press charges against him, the man was arrested for aggravated assault."

After her brother left, Kendal buried her head in her pillow and sobbed. She felt empty and lost. How was it possible that such a man existed? And why had the world been so ready to destroy him?

Her mind instantly latched onto the things the Lord had suffered in the place of mankind. Although Quincy's torment couldn't be compared to Christ's, she could certainly recognize some of the Lord's qualities in him. The Lord had died for people who were rejecting him. She thought of the way the crowd followed him and worshipped him. Then a few days later, the same crowd chanted for him to be crucified.

"Why do such animalistic and contradictory tendencies exist in man's nature?" she asked aloud. Then she realized that she had been just as fickle about her own faith. "Lord, forgive me."

Like a windblown feather, words floated haphazardly into her mind. *He knew what was in man.*

Her stomach seemed to do a somersault. The sun streamed through the billowing curtains in diagonal shafts of color—brighter than before. She held her breath as the familiar passage kept bouncing around in her mind.

She got her Bible from the nightstand and turned to the concordance. But it wasn't detailed enough to enable her to locate the specified passage. She couldn't remember where to find it. She knew it was in one of the gospels, but which one?

Feeling the urge of mission, she pulled on her robe and padded down the hall to Sheila's room. She hoped her friend had left her electronic Bible at home. She spotted it on the dresser as soon as she pushed open the door. After typing the passage into the device, John 2:25 came up. She reopened her Bible and read the whole chapter.

She read through the marriage in Cana, the casting of moneychangers from the temple, and then she came to it.

Now when He was in Jerusalem at the Passover, in the feast day, many believed in His name, when they saw the miracles which He did. But Jesus did not commit himself unto them, because He knew all men, and needed not that any should testify of man: for He knew what was in man.

Kendal slid onto Sheila's bedroom carpet and wrapped her arms around herself. The Lord had suffered the greatest of injustices. He had loved and suffered much for an inconsistent people—a people not much different from herself. She warmed, feeling the Lord's forgiveness in every fiber of her being.

In a much smaller way, Quincy had done what he believed was right and suffered for it. She understood now that that's what walking by faith was all about. Quincy's words came back to her: *Got myself into a fix that caused me to miss precious moments I can never get back.*

Did the moments referenced involve his ex-wife or his mother, she wondered. Kendal's muscles ached as she got up from the floor, clutching her Bible to her chest. What difference did it make? He was the kind of man who measured the moment with his heart.

She faltered at the door, feeling there was more for her in the passage. Perhaps that she should lean her whole self on God only—that she should rest the past on her faith in his love and not be frightened by flashes of memory?

Be not afraid of terror.

At last she knew what it meant to be still and listen. Kendal stood in the same spot for what seemed like hours, just in case He would speak something more to her heart. She had heard the references, not with her ears but with the rest of her. The encounter had been so wondrous, so commanding she had sensed the Lord's presence and delighted in the knowledge of his attention. She walked back to her room in awestruck silence.

Every cell in her body wanted to call Quincy to tell him what she had experienced. But should she? After all, she had no idea how he really felt about her. Sure, she knew he was attracted, but then so was Walt.

Quincy still couldn't believe Max had called him with a job prospect he could actually jump at.

Lord, is this your doing, or am I grabbing at straws to be near her? What exactly does this trip mean? Do I even have a chance at this position? If I do, should I take it?

Instinctively going into reporter mode, he once again combed their conversation for clues as to who or what had prompted his former editor to call with such a tempting—and timely—lead. Who could have told Max about Kendal? Bev? He shook his head. Never. Then Joe's face flashed into his mind.

But why would he, Lord? Joe has reminded me of my debt to him at every turn. Why would he contact my old boss?

Quincy sat on the bed and held his head between his palms, his heart aching at the thought of flying back to Seattle today and not being able to see Kendal. He would be only miles away and not be able to hold her. He tried not to think of her, but her face kept floating into his mind like a fragrance lingering in a room long after the wearer has gone.

He had drafted an article from notes made during their pretend romance. She had been open about her past, her dreams and her fears. Even so, he was surprised when she had actually suggested that he break the story of Sumner after the current danger had passed. She thought it would rid her of his ghost.

Much of his draft centered on the complex relationship between an overprotective father and a lonely daughter. He could incorporate Sumner's mischief while clarifying the congressman's obsession to protect his daughter's privacy. Thinking of Joe's eagerness to print a story on Kendal, he smiled. The congressman had already talked to him about holding off on printing anything about the threats—at least until after the perpetrator was caught.

He hoped the article would set the record straight about her true nature. In actuality, she was a warm and beautiful person longing for love and the joy of family. Despite already having the love of family, Sumner's act had distorted her perception.

Hardly a minute passed without his thoughts compulsively turning to her. He drank his morning coffee with her backyard garden in his mind. It was no use. She had penetrated his heart the instant he first saw her smile. But it was her innocence and genuine compassion he had fallen in love with. He groaned. Is it possible he had gotten in over his head?

"So much is going on, Lord. She must be scared out of her mind. Keep her safe."

He fingered at his cellphone. "I hate to see you go so soon," his aunt said, shuffling into his bedroom, "but you've been moping around like a sick puppy. You call her yet?"

Smiling, he turned to face her. "No."

She sat on the end of the bed. "What time is your flight?"

"This evening. I'm supposed to meet Sidney Hayes of NBC for breakfast tomorrow morning."

"Sunday?"

"I know, Auntie, but I think this is something I need to check out. I'll find a church to attend tomorrow afternoon." He smiled and touched her cheek. "If this is God's will, I'll have favor. If not, I'll come back and start over here in Atlanta."

"Do you love her?"

"Yes, I do. And I can only hope that my leaving so abruptly hasn't poisoned her heart against me."

"Surely she'll understand that you were ordered to leave. But you be careful, Son. That monster might still be watching her."

"I know. I don't plan to go near her. Anyway, she hasn't even tried to call me."

Grasping his hand, his aunt said, "Don't worry. God will work it out. I know it."

As soon as she left, Quincy dialed Eric's cell number. "Eric, just called to let you know I have a job interview in Seattle tomorrow morning. I'll be flying out this evening."

"Quincy?"

"Don't worry; Kendal won't even know I'm there. I'll stay in a hotel near your office."

Eric cleared his throat. "She finally asked about you—about your past and what happened to you."

Quincy's heart skipped a beat, and he could feel the tension in his fingertips. He should have told her about that. "You tell her?"

"Saw no reason not to. You okay with that?"

"Yeah, it's fine." He paused and willed his voice to remain steady. "How's she doing?"

"Pretty uptight after another call. This creep is weird. He keeps calling, but has made no move to approach or tell her what he wants."

"What did he say this time?"

" 'You destroyed something of mine. Now I have to destroy something of yours'," Eric replied. "I don't know. After hearing it for the umpteenth time, we thought maybe Peck had somehow hidden something here at the house. We've turned the place upside down, and there's nothing."

"What could the message possibly mean for Kendal?" Quincy asked. "What about gifts?"

"The only gift she still has from Peck is a necklace with a heart-shaped diamond cluster. She returned all the others. The necklace was still in its original packaging. We traced it to Emerald City Jewelers on Third."

"I see. What's she doing?"

"Bouncing around here polishing, buffing and stripping everything in sight. Temps are handling the business, so she's left with little to do. I try to stay out of her way when I'm here."

In a rare moment of levity, they both laughed.

"My contact has tapped dry on anything more on Senator Howard and your dad. Apparently most of the employee records were destroyed in that fire. Most of the information I've gotten so far has come through old articles and former employees."

"A fire, huh? How convenient."

"I do have a name for you—Stephanie Baylor. She was the assistant I mentioned yesterday," Quincy said. "There's something else, Eric. The name Baylor was scribbled, along with your dad's and Howard's, on notes written by Sumner. What do you make of that?"

Quincy understood Eric's momentary silence. "Thanks, man, I'll check it out."

-NINETEEN-

With less than her usual enthusiasm, Kendal closed her book-keeping program and completed another deposit slip. They were doing well, despite the fact that neither she nor Sheila had been at the shop. On those rare occasions when Jace couldn't bring the receipts, Eric stopped by after closing to collect them. She still placed the orders to their distributors and still did the bookkeeping and banking. At least it kept her mind occupied. She was beginning to get a lot of orders online, too. She was glad she had created that web mail account. Later, she would buy them a webpage.

She then opened a gateway to the Internet and clicked one of the sites on her favorites list. While it was coming up, she opened the manila file she looked through almost daily. Along with the birth certificate she had obtained from the hospital, she had received a package of non-identifying information from the state of Maryland. She idly flipped through the pages for the hundredth time.

Due to confidentiality restrictions, the records she needed could not be obtained. She knew the laws were set up to protect both parties in a closed adoption, but that didn't diminish her frustration that she didn't even find a name she could put into a search engine. Her only hope was that perhaps one of her birth parents was also looking for her. Quincy could probably cover a lot more ground than she could in the search.

Reacting to a sudden impulse, she dialed his number before she had a chance to change her mind. His recorder was on, but she hung up without leaving a message. She resolved not to shed another tear over Quincy.

She had all but given up on having a marriage, but some day perhaps she would still have a child.

Her mind went back to the frustrated call she had placed to her dad the night before. He had been shocked to learn of her plan to become pregnant, but she had given him a full dose of her wrath before giving him chance to speak. She had all but accused him of keeping things from her, of protecting her without thinking about what it might be doing to her. It should have been he doing what Quincy had offered to do.

She thought of the many times she had wondered what it would be like to know her biological dad. She shook her head. Biological or not, he couldn't possibly have loved her as much as Stan Boyd. Wouldn't her selfish desire to have a baby put the child in the same position? He wouldn't know *his* biological father. Could she do that to a child?

The ringing phone interrupted her troubled musings. She took a deep breath and answered. "Hello."

"Kendal, I'm glad I caught you."

She rolled her eyes and wished she had checked the caller ID. "Hello, Walt. Look, I'm really very busy."

"I know, I know. But I have some great news. I wish you would reconsider going out with me to celebrate. I promise I won't be a nuisance. I simply want to take you to a nice place for dinner and bring you home. You could probably stand to get out a little, right? How about it?"

"I can't, Walt."

"C'mon, Kendal," he whined. "Why not? Can you tell me that?"

"I just don't want to mislead you into thinking I want romance from you. I'm not up to it."

"Can't we just go out as friends?"

Kendal paused, feeling trapped by a sense of conscience. She was taking out her frustration on her dad, as well as on Walt. "If you're sure you understand it's just as friends…nothing more."

"How about Saturday night? I'll pick you up at seven."

"All right, Walt," she said in a flat voice. Kendal's heart sank the minute she caved in.

The phone rang again the instant she had hung up. And without thinking, snatched it up, hoping it was Quincy. "Hello?"

"Beautiful, sweet Kendal," the voice crooned. "I have it. I have something that belongs to you."

Her heart began to thump in her chest, the force of each beat almost taking her breath away. "What do you want?" she asked with more daring than she felt.

"I want you, my rose petal. And I shall have you. In fact, I'm certain you will come to me of your own free will."

Agent Sullivan came into the dining room and signaled her to keep him talking. Sullivan put a finger to his lips and strolled over to the table. The move somehow gave her the courage to continue.

"Why would I do a stupid thing like that?"

"Because, my sweet Delilah of Rose Creek, I have something of yours. I'm quite sure you would want him back. If you don't comply with my wishes to come alone, my next capture will be little Marcy."

And icy chill ran down her spine. He had said 'him'. Could he have done something horrible to Quincy? She hadn't heard from him.

Sullivan tapped her shoulder, snapping her back into her role. "Why should I believe you—a man who has killed four innocent people?"

"What?" he roared, his voice suddenly agitated. "What are you talking about? I've never killed anyone. Not yet."

"Oh? What about Frank Peck and those three women?"

"You're mistaken, Kendal." The voice she was accustomed to hearing was back. He laughed, and the sound made her skin crawl. "Your bodyguards aren't very bright, are they? It's only your life that's owed. Only yours. I'll take others until you come. Everything I do, sweet Kendal, is for a reason."

She could feel a scream fighting to break free from somewhere deep, but she willed herself to continue talking. "What possible reason could you have to do this? What have I done to you?"

"You destroyed my life. Now I must destroy yours, one person at a time, until you agree to come alone. But first, I want you to sweat a little. Then we'll have a little fun. Just you and me."

Her hands trembled so badly she nearly dropped the phone. Oddly enough, he sounded rather intelligent, perhaps not so unusual for psychos. His words and tone were menacing, but he spoke with precision. And the random way in which his pitch fluctuated told her he was adept at disguising his voice.

"I'm sorry," she said, unable to think clearly. "You haven't given me any reason to hand myself over to you."

"I'll give you two," he said with another cold cackle. "I have the full names of both your parents, as well as their medical histories."

Her heart leaped. "Who are they? Tell me."

"Your father was a coward, you know. The second reason is parked on M Street in Tacoma."

Before she could question her tormentor further, he hung up, leaving her numb and trembling.

"Your brother is on his way," said Sullivan, his hand resting lightly on her shoulder. "You did well. I think you had him on long enough to get a location."

Marcy wrapped her legs around Kendal's middle and squeezed her face between her palms. Kendal dropped onto the sofa and held the child as tightly as she could, fighting back overwhelming emotion.

"I missed you, Aunt Kem."

Sheila fluttered about, at one point bringing in a pot of tea and cookies. She invited Vera Mackey to join them, but the agent quietly declined. Kendal held the child back a bit and kissed her cheek. "I missed you, too, sweetie. I'm so glad to see your face."

Marcy wiggled out of her arms. "I go play in my room. My dolly missed me, too."

"No," Kendal said, startling everyone in the room. She looked nervously at Agent Mackey.

"It's okay, Kendal," the agent said. "The house is secure."

Kendal felt silly, but her nerves were on edge. "Okay, Marcy. Your mom and I will be right here talking."

She watched Marcy slowly ascend the stairs and then turned to see Sheila's worry-filled face. "Was the van wrecked?"

"No," Kendal said. "All the flowers had been delivered. They checked to be sure. But Jace was nowhere to be found. Eric is in the process of locating his physical address from their files. He used a post office box on the paperwork he filled out for me."

"Do you think this creep will hurt him?"

Kendal shuddered at the thought. "I hope not. He said he hadn't ever killed anyone, and that my life was all that was owed."

Sheila took Kendal's hand. "That's creepy."

"I know. But I don't want Jace hurt because of me. Eric thinks he forced Jace to drive to Tacoma. We didn't have any deliveries there. They're searching for any abandoned vehicles between the last delivery area and M Street where the van was parked."

"Jace is a man," Sheila said hopefully. "Maybe he can overpower him and get away."

Kendal shook her head ruefully. "Jace is competent and highly organized in an office setting, but I can't see him being very brave in a situation like this."

Sheila drew her friend into her arms. The display of affection unleashed the emotions Kendal had tried to keep at bay. They both sobbed into each other's shoulders. "Why is this happening to us, Kendal? Could it be God's will?"

"It's evil. God's not the doer of evil." She pulled away and stood. "I know that now. I've blamed him a long time for what Sumner did. But I had forgotten the power of evil."

"I know you're right; but it sure helps to hear it again."

"I'm just glad they let you and Marcy come back home."

"Me too. Eric said you did great on the phone by drawing more out of him. They needed all the manpower they could get to find Jace, so being in the same house makes it easier to protect us. They have someone inside with us, and someone outside, too. Have you heard from Quincy?"

Kendal crossed her arms and paced the length of the living room. "Not a word."

"Didn't you call him?"

"I tried, Sheila, but he wasn't there, and I didn't leave a message. I don't know. I might be feeling more for him than he does for me. I can't put myself out there like that. Men are such frogs sometimes."

"Quincy is far from being a frog. You know that. And from the way he looked at you, I know he cares about you." Sheila bit into a cookie. "He didn't like Walt or Jace getting too close to you. I could tell."

"Then why hasn't he called?"

Sheila paused. "I don't know; maybe something's gone wrong in his family."

"No, Quincy only has an aunt in Atlanta. He obviously doesn't care enough about me to call and let me know he's okay. And I don't intend to sit around here twiddling my thumbs. I have a date with Walt on Saturday night."

"Kendal! Why would you do such a crazy thing? You know he's a parasite. Does Eric know about this?"

"Not yet," Kendal said, boldly meeting Sheila's eyes. "At least Walt calls. At least he has told me how he feels about me, even if it *is* a line."

"That doesn't mean you should be irresponsible. Walt Hadley's a jerk." Sheila looked over at Vera Mackey, then leaned closer and whispered, "What are they going to do about poor Jace?"

"They traced the call. It came from a pay phone near where the van was parked. All we can do is pray and hope they find him alive."

"Gosh, goose. This is like a scene out of a horror movie."

The phone rang and Vera moved towards them. "Answer it," she said, her voice polite but decisive.

Kendal picked it up. "Hello."

"I see you found the van," the caller drawled. "I could have easily vandalized it, but I would've had to kill your driver to do it. Remember, Marcy is next. And if you want to see Jace alive again, you must come to me of your own free will. I'll let you know when and where."

"Where is Jace? Let me talk to him."

Kendal heard the phone bang against something, as if the caller had thrown it. After a few seconds, she heard whimpering in the background. *Talk to her, you sniveling puppy.*

Kendal covered her mouth with trembling hands as the sound of a man's scream rang out. Her tears flowed as images of her own abduction flashed across her mind. "Kendal, help me," Jace screamed. "He's going to kill me. He's crazy."

The high-pitched scream she heard next filled her with a mix of horror and primal terror. What was this animal doing to him?

"Jace!"

The phone line went dead.

Vera Mackey promptly dialed Eric, while the two shivering roommates clung to each other.

"Oh, God," Kendal cried, "please keep him safe."

-TWENTY-

Eric was driving from Olivia Howard's home to Hadley's. It was already after eight in the evening. His heart had settled into a steady but somewhat elevated beat after talking with the woman for almost an hour. Despite her composure and pleasant demeanor, he had come away convinced she was hiding something.

He hoped he could get more information from Hadley Jr., but he was doubtful he would. He parked in the circular drive and rang the doorbell. Fortunately, it was Junior who answered.

"Agent Boyd?"

Eric extended his hand and stepped into the foyer as soon as Hadley moved aside. "I'm sorry to trouble you, Mr. Hadley, but I was wondering if I could ask you a few questions concerning a former employee."

"Couldn't this wait until tomorrow, Agent?"

"No, I'm afraid not."

The executive was clearly not happy about this visit, but he nonetheless escorted Eric into a small study. He then moved briskly to the wet bar. "Can I offer you any refreshments? I realize you're on duty."

"No, thank you," Eric said. "I'd like to get right to the point of my visit, if you don't mind."

"Certainly," Hadley said, pouring himself a large drink. He then sat down in a chair facing the agent. "What can I do for you?"

"Lovely home."

"Thank you. It's my dad's. I plan to get my own, but recently he's been a little under the weather."

"When is the last time you saw Jace Tate?"

Leaning back in his seat, Hadley looked up at the ceiling. "I think it was last week. I saw him making deliveries for your sister. Why?"

"I understand you warned my sister to be careful around him. I need to know why?"

"Just a jealous impulse," he said, his upper lip noticeably twitching. "I take it she's told you about my advances. Well, it's difficult to accept other men so close to her. But I'm sure you can understand that. Why are we talking about Tate?"

"He's disappeared, Mr. Hadley. I would appreciate any information you could give me about him."

The man's face paled as he straightened and leaned forward in the chair. "Disappeared? When? Did he rob Kendal?"

"Tate was abducted this afternoon while making deliveries," Eric replied, feeling guarded. "We have his home address, but we don't have any other information on him."

"Have you searched his home?"

Eric fixed the man with what he hoped was an intimidating gaze. "Yes, we have, but it was unusually free of personal effects. We need to know if he has any family—someone we should notify. I understand you fired him before he started working for Kendal. What was the reason?"

Hadley took a large gulp of his drink and grimaced before answering. "He just wasn't working out. How is Kendal handling his disappearance? Should I go to her?"

Eric's gaze did not waver. "Kendal is doing well under the circumstances. Firing Tate seems rather rash for someone who was doing so well. I understand from Ms. Howard that he was a capable assistant."

Hadley abruptly stood. "Olivia really wouldn't know. Jace worked for me for nearly six months. I found him to be a little too inquisitive for our industry. I'll get any personal information that might be in his personnel file. I keep a set of diskettes of employee files here at the house."

Eric lifted a curious eyebrow and got to his feet. "That would be helpful. Thank you."

Later, at the field office, Eric printed out a copy of Tate's file from the floppy disk, which he then put into his briefcase to return to Hadley. He scanned the pages for next of kin and found a mother listed.

"Found something," he called to the other team members. "A mother lives over in Everett."

"How old is she?" asked Cashion, turning towards him.

"Sixty-three. Why?"

Cashion glanced at his watch, prompting Eric to look at his. "We need to get someone over there right away. She doesn't need to hear about this on the news."

"Sure thing."

Knock-knock-knock.

Quincy turned over on his back, hazily wondering if the dream about Kendal and his mother was taking another turn.

Knock. Knock. Knock.

He sprang up, certain now that the knock he heard was real. The clock read 2:32. "Yeah?"

"Quincy? It's Eric. Open up."

Had something happened? Quincy hurried to the door without turning on a light. "What's wrong? Is Kendal all right?"

"Kendal's fine," Eric said, walking to the table. "Do you mind if we turn on a light? I need to talk out some things with you."

Quincy held his breath. "What's happened?"

"Kendal got another call. Thankfully, we had already moved Sheila and Marcy back home. The call freaked her out so badly Sheila called the doctor. She's home, but she's medicated, Quincy."

Quincy's heart ached to go to her. "Why? Did he threaten Marcy again?"

"Yes, but this nut has abducted Jace and is apparently torturing him. He told her she would have to come to him on her own volition to prevent Jace's death, as well as Marcy's capture. He also told her he had the names of her birth parents."

Quincy's jaw dropped. "Eric, he seems to know a lot about her personal moves. Only those closest to her knew about her search."

"I know. We found the delivery van parked on M Street in Tacoma. I've been by his mother's house, but she's either not home or soundly sleeping. I'll go back first thing in the morning."

Realizing he was in his underwear, Quincy grabbed his jeans and pulled them on. "Who is this guy? Don't y'all have a profile on him yet?"

"Yeah, they believe he's a white male, twenty-five to thirty years old, average appearance, which would probably be why we keep missing him. We think he might be single and live alone. He's confident, clever and familiar with Kendal's daily activities. I hate to admit it, but he's probably staring us right in the face."

"So he might be shy around women?"

Eric nodded. "His need to taunt the bureau and drag this out indicates he's got issues with authority. He's obviously torturing poor Jace, who is probably in for a rough ride before it's all over."

"What about Hadley?"

Eric pulled a file from his briefcase. "I asked him why he was upset that Kendal hired Jace. He claims it was a jealous impulse."

"Jealous impulse? What is it about Kendal that invites these presumptuous men? And why is she the common denominator in all these occurrences?"

Eric placed the file on the table. "That's a good question, one we might need to take a closer look at. Right now, I have Mason warning Kendal about Hadley, Hadley warning her about Jace, four stabbing victims, Howard-Hadley's FDA investigation, and an unidentified psycho telling my sister the feds aren't very bright."

Quincy's brow furrowed deeply. "Have you come to any hard conclusions?"

"I'm missing something, Quincy. Kendal found the nerve to question him about killing four innocent people. He assured her he hadn't killed anyone—yet. The only life he wanted was hers."

Fear and anger knotted inside Quincy, and he began pacing aimlessly. "Using Jace and Marcy, he plans to lure her away from her protection. Eric, I can't leave again. I won't leave Seattle without her."

"Good. I think I would feel better if you were closer. After hearing Jace cry out in pain during that call, Kendal just lost it. I'm worried about her."

Quincy searched his mind for coherence—anything that would provide a clue. "This guy knows exactly how to manipulate her. Just like Hadley."

"What do you mean?"

"Remember when I walked in on him making a play? Marcy was sleeping on a pallet near her desk. I'm sure he noticed Kendal's restraint in the presence of the sleeping child. He used *that* to control her."

"Are you suggesting he's the villain just because he made a play for Kendal? Quincy, I need you to think without your feelings for Kendal coloring your view."

Quincy stopped pacing and looked at Eric defensively. "I didn't like it, Eric, but I can be impartial enough to give the man a fair shake."

"I don't think he's our man. He's got too much to lose," Eric said. "What do you think about Olivia? I know she's holding back."

Quincy frowned, surprised Eric would even suspect her. "She's a woman."

"But she has plenty of money. She can buy whatever she wants, even a death or an election."

"Nah. She was overly considerate of Kendal's reputation during the interview. Although she's prim, proper and subdued, she likes Kendal. I could tell." Quincy stopped suddenly and stared in horror at his friend. "What do you mean she can buy an election? Don't tell me that all this time you've been suspecting your dad."

Eric looked away. "Our profilers keep getting mixed signals from the stalker's movements and demands. It's almost like trying to chase down particles from a meteor shower. The cases come together then fly apart."

Quincy rubbed the bridge of his nose. "What's going on, Eric?"

"I found out something about the old case on Sumner. He was dead before he was hung, Quincy."

Quincy froze. "Then it couldn't be suicide."

"No. He was murdered. And because of pressure from Howard's office, the case was closed and never reopened."

"But your father was in Germany, right?"

"He was home thirty-two hours after Kendal's abduction. I'm thinking Sumner was blackmailing Dad."

Quincy nodded. "From the scraps of information I've been able to gather, blackmail was the conclusion I came to, as well. But what makes you suspect your dad?"

Eric leaned forward in the chair and held his head between his palms. "Things just never added up. I've been looking into this ever since I joined the bureau. Two years ago, my boss intercepted one of my inquiries and lit into me."

"This sounds a little...."

"I know, I know. And I feel terribly guilty for distrusting Dad. My boss could be right; I may be too close to this."

"You're doing all right, Eric. Don't beat yourself up."

"I've been trying to keep the cases separate, but something always comes up that raises a flag in my mind. I'm not sure why."

Quincy purposely directed the conversation elsewhere. "Is the agent from FDA still on this?"

"Nah, he finished his investigation and went back to D.C.," Eric said, fidgeting with a sheet from the file on Jace. "Why don't you tell me what makes you so suspicious of Hadley?"

Quincy stared at the carpet and bit into his lower lip. "Something Jace said the day Kendal gave him the job."

"What?"

"Jace had just lost his job with Hadley. He made a point of saying that nothing happened at Howard-Hadley he didn't know about."

"You're thinking Jace knows something Hadley wouldn't want to get out?"

"In a place steeped in controversy and secrets and with vast resources...I'd bet on it."

Quincy's reasoning intrigued Eric. "You might have a point. Hadley told me he fired Jace because he was too inquisitive for the industry."

Quincy sat on the end of the bed and faced Eric, his conscience goading him. "After Joe and I got those warnings, I considered Hadley a possible culprit because I lost it with him back there. The things Jed

Mason said confirmed my initial suspicions. I haven't been able to understand how Hadley became so obsessed by her all of a sudden. She had worked there for five years."

"He clued me in on his fixation when I spoke with him about Jace. Said the reason he warned Kendal about Jace was due to jealousy. With Mason's suggestions and your misgivings, maybe I have enough to justify looking a little deeper. Quincy, I really don't want to upset Kendal with our suspicions of...."

Quincy suddenly noticed a stricken look on Eric's face. "What is it?"

"Kendal is supposed to go to dinner with him Saturday night."

Sheila was getting last-minute instructions from Eric. "Don't worry. Just keep a close eye on her the next few days. Vera is right outside. She'll be in as soon as she sees me leave. Another agent will be outside at all times."

"But what...where...."

"I'm getting a late start this morning, Sheila. I needed to be back over to Jace's mother's earlier this morning. I just hope she hasn't seen any news yet."

"I see."

She hung her head. Eric could only imagine how frightened she was. He took her by the shoulders and gently drew her into a friendly embrace. "Everything will be fine."

"You think it's Hadley, don't you?"

He silently searched her face; she looked so scared. "What makes you say that?"

"Because for the last week, he's been pestering her to go out with him. I don't understand. If he's really infatuated with her, why would he threaten to kill her?"

"That's what I mean to find out."

Sheila gasped and covered her mouth. "They have a date...."

"I called and told him Kendal had been getting threats, and I couldn't allow her away from her surveillance at this time."

"What did he say?"

"He wasn't very happy, but understood. I'm glad you're back, Sheila, but I need you to give the agents a little room the next few days while I conduct a little experiment."

"What do you mean? You're not going to put Kendal in danger, are you?"

"Everything will be fine. If Hadley's our guy, he's not going to sit still for my restraint. I expect him to show his true colors very soon."

The thin woman answered the door wearing a robe, her hair in curlers. Her eyes were red-rimmed, and white wisps of hair strayed out of the curlers. Adjusting her glasses, she peered at them guardedly. "May I help you?"

"Mrs. Tate?"

"Yes."

"Special Agent Eric Boyd with the FBI." He gestured toward Sullivan, and they both held up their badges. "This is Special Agent Claude Sullivan. May we come in?"

Obviously surprised, she took both badges and carefully inspected them. After examining their faces closely, she stepped aside and let them pass. The morning paper was spread over the coffee table, and Eric was taken aback when she snatched the pages up and strode purposely towards an entrance to another room. "Sit down. I'll be back."

He and Sullivan eyed each other curiously. She returned a few moments later. "Y'all want a cup of tea?" she asked, sounding more chipper than she had a moment ago.

Though he could see the veins through her pale skin, she appeared to be fit and spry—even energetic. Sitting in a wing chair next to Sullivan, Eric noted her tendency to avoid eye contact as much as possible. She would look at them fleetingly, but she couldn't seem to manage a direct gaze. "No, thank you. We would like to talk to you about your son."

"I was wondering why I hadn't been called. My son is all I have left."

"Yes ma'am. I'm sorry, but it took some time to locate you. We came by last night pretty late, but we didn't get an answer."

"Once I take my night medicines, I'm pretty well knocked out till morning." She carefully lowered herself onto the couch and leaned forward, her hands in her lap. "I don't believe he's dead. I would be able to tell."

Sullivan looked at Eric quizzically. "How, ma'am? If you don't mind my asking."

"I knew it when my husband died." She put her head back and gazed up at the ceiling. "My J.C. was a smart man, and Jace is so much like him. He was just a boy when his daddy up and died. But he never shed a tear."

Eric exchanged glances with Sullivan. "Maybe he felt he had to be strong for you, ma'am."

She smiled. "He's a good boy, my Jace. He used to get so mad…me making him go to Sunday school and all."

Eric shifted slightly in his seat. "I can only imagine how difficult it was raising a boy alone."

"Yes, but my Jace got me through it. Worked at that drug company until they fired him." She shook her head. "He knows something, you know…something they don't want anybody else knowing about. They're all crooks."

Eric's eyebrows shot up. Had they hit the jackpot? "What makes you think that?"

She leaned forward and said confidingly. "He kept a file on them. That Mr. Hadley stopped by last night, too. My Jace brought files here on some of those little square computer things."

Sullivan smiled. "Diskettes?"

She nodded. "Yeah, that's it. Diskettes. Told me to keep them in case anything should happen. I guess they got him."

Eric could hardly believe his good fortune. He was now on the edge of his seat. "You said Mr. Hadley stopped by last night."

"Yeah. It was just after dark. I was surprised to see him drive up in that big fancy car. Jace had told me he was feeling poorly of late."

Eric studied the woman carefully. Her hand repeatedly went to the top button on her dress, as if she thought it had come loose. "Mrs. Tate, which Mr. Hadley stopped by?"

"The daddy," she said with certainty. "He told me he had given Jace something to keep for him and was here to pick it up. But I wouldn't let him trick me. My son had already told me to say I didn't know anything."

Sullivan spoke. "It's quite evident something is very wrong, ma'am. Would you feel comfortable letting us see the diskettes? We'll return them, of course."

"All right." The woman stood and walked slowly to the fireplace and removed the screen. "Jace told me after everything was over I could give them to the feds. Anything that will catch those crooks."

Eric jumped up and went to help her. "Let me get that for you, Mrs. Tate."

But she got down on all fours and reached up inside the chimney. After several moments of probing around, she brought out a diskette case and handed it to Eric.

He counted six labeled diskettes in clear plastic cases. He then handed them to Sullivan and bent to help the woman to her feet. He replaced the screen and returned to his seat.

Staring off into space, Mrs. Tate began to chuckle. "You know, even though Jace was a little boy, he could mimic his daddy's voice real good. It was almost like his daddy talked to him every night."

Eric smiled and shot a sidelong look at Sullivan. "Boys always try to emulate their fathers. Jace must have been close to him."

"Not really. Jace's daddy had a mean streak. He didn't like a lot of noise, and active boys are noisy."

Sullivan chuckled. "I'm a witness to that; I have three of my own."

-TWENTY-ONE-

Still in her bathrobe, Kendal strolled into the kitchen. She felt as if she had been asleep for an entire week. "I refuse to take any more of that dope, Sheila. It makes me sluggish and disoriented."

Sheila turned away from the coffeemaker, a slight smile on her lips. "I'm sure that's fine."

"What are you smiling about?"

"I think Jackson is about ready to pop the question."

Kendal studied her friend's face as though she had never seen it. Maybe she hadn't. She looked serene, yet excited. And her eyes had a sappy look—like the one she had after her first kiss.

"How do you know? You're not needlessly getting yourself all worked up, are you?"

"I don't know," she said, still smiling. "His reluctance to bring me home or even let me get out of the car once we get here. And he's so very attentive."

Kendal felt a tinge of envy. "I think that's wonderful, Sheila. How do you feel about him?"

She looked away. "I don't know. But I can honestly say I wish Lance and his fiancée well. It's worth a lot to have at least reached that point. I have to keep praying about me and Jackson."

Kendal smiled knowingly. Her friend had kept quiet about her feelings. Perhaps that was her way of being still. "I'm so glad you're not hurting anymore."

"I'm sure things will work out with Quincy. The two of you are meant for each other. Now sit down and let me fix you a gigantic breakfast burrito."

Just hearing his name set Kendal aflutter. She could see his face, his grin, his self-assured stride, and she could even smell his aftershave. But

a heaviness of spirit was creeping through her. "I've made up my mind to call him today, Sheila. It's been long enough."

A wide smile spread across Sheila's face. "That's it, girl. Fight for your man. Kick pride right in its slimy face."

"Pride?"

Chuckling, Sheila placed a fat burrito on Kendal's plate beside an orange slice. "You know, Eric got in really late last night. If I didn't know him better…I would say he was intoxicated. He made such a ruckus I almost came down and banged on the kitchen floor to make him shut up."

The two giggled, obviously pleased to find something to laugh about. "What do you have planned today? I'm hoping Eric will let me get out of this dungeon for a while."

Seeing the time, Sheila stood. "I'd better get Marcy up. Lance is picking her up in an hour. I'm glad Eric loosened the tight surveillance a bit. He's allowing Lance and his fiancée to take her on an all-day outing. Jackson and I have plans of our own."

"Ooh," Kendal crooned teasingly. "I guess I'll just have to live vicariously through your adventurous lifestyle."

Then Kendal casually pulled a newspaper from under the napkin holder. Jace's face was plastered on the front page. She read the caption beneath.

"Former Howard-Hadley Employee Feared Dead."

Her throat tightened. "Sheila, why didn't you tell me about this? This paper is three days old. And where did they get their information?"

"From me."

The two women turned to see Eric coming up from the basement. Hackles rising, Kendal rose slowly to her feet. "How could you? You could very well get him killed."

"It's just a tactic Quincy and I are using to force the perp to react. We talked to the editor Wednesday morning. I want to smoke this guy out. Hopefully, we can get Jace back alive."

Limp and confused, Kendal plopped back down. Her heart was beating wildly. "You talked to Quincy?"

Eric went over to the coffeemaker. "Quincy's been back since Sunday, Sis. He's been working with his contacts to help me piece some things together."

Kendal's eyes brimmed with tears and her lips trembled. "He's back?"

Sheila patted her friend's shoulders soothingly. "Sit down, Eric. I've got to go get Marcy up."

"No, I need to talk to both of you."

Eric sat and began toying with the wire-mesh napkin holder. "I know you haven't understood why Quincy left Seattle so abruptly, but he didn't have much of a choice. Both he and his editor in Baltimore received a warning the day of your opening. They were told that if Quincy didn't leave town immediately, his next target would be Marcy. It seems our little romantic charade back-fired. I'm sorry, Sis."

Kendal watched as alarm and gratitude quickly spread across Sheila's face. "He did *that* for Marcy?"

"He did it for all of you. Cashion insisted he break off all communication with you, Kendal. We couldn't take any chances with this guy so close. He seems to know too much about you."

"Any suspects?" Kendal asked softly.

"We do, but I don't really want to go into that just yet. I know you probably want to get out, but I need you to stick around the house today. With us trying to smoke him out, I'll feel a lot better if you stayed put."

"Smoke him out? Is this the experiment you mentioned, Eric?" Sheila asked.

"What experiment?" Kendal asked, suddenly paying closer attention.

"I'll be able to tell you more later."

Kendal now understood the reason for Quincy's action, but still felt confused and hurt by his continued silence. Certainly he could have found a way to let her know something. She wasn't a child. She would have understood. She rose on wobbly legs and took her plate to the sink, as she leaned forward to rinse the dish, a hand touched her arm.

She turned and fell into Quincy's arms, a mixture of relief, excitement and longing rising to the surface. Her voice quavered as she tried to coherently voice a fitting greeting.

He cupped her face between his palms and kissed her long and passionately. When he released her, he whispered, "I love you, Kendal, and I'm going to find a way to make this work."

Kendal felt his muscles ripple as he drew her closer. The ache of loneliness fell away, leaving her exposed and eager for his kiss—his touch. Almost certain she was dreaming, she whispered his name. "Quincy."

"I love you, sweetheart."

"I love you, too," she said. "I've missed you so much."

Suddenly feeling exposed, Kendal looked around only to find that Eric and Sheila had discreetly vanished.

Quincy smiled and touched her cheek with his fingertips, and then her lips. "You can't imagine how hard it was staying away from you."

She smiled, feeling warm and content just to be in his arms again. The shape of his jaw line tightened as he gathered her even closer. And then, his mouth was on hers in a kiss that made her forget everything else except their declarations of love.

God had brought him back to her, and she could only hope she wasn't throwing caution to the wind by loving him so much. He abruptly broke their embrace and looked into her eyes. "I'm lost in you, Kendal; you've gotten under my skin. If you have the slightest reservation about us, you'd better speak up now."

"No, Quincy. No reservations."

She couldn't tell whose heart was pounding harder—hers or his. He kissed her again, fiercely.

Four hours and a long conversation later, Quincy hammered the last nail into the lattice that Eric had promised Kendal he would repair.

The house was a combination of brick and wood. It was nice, despite its age. The unattached garage cast a shadow on the side yard, but the roses still thrived. A chain link fence surrounded the entire house, placing even more separation between the house and garage. He knew the fence was probably put in place to protect Marcy.

He climbed back down the ladder and promptly removed the florescent yellow rubber gloves, the only ones they could find to fit. He was returning the ladder to the garage when he saw Kendal coming around the rear corner of the house.

"It looks great, Quincy. You ready for lunch?"

"If you weren't on lock-down, I'd suggest we go out for lunch," he said, retrieving his ringing cellphone from his pocket. "Morgan."

"Quincy, this is Sidney Hayes. Sorry I didn't get back to you earlier. If you're still interested in the position, it's yours."

Quincy threw up his free hand and silently thanked God. "I, uh…yes, sir, I'm still interested. Yes."

"Good. As promised, we'll give you a relocation allowance and one month to get settled. Let's see. Today is May twenty-fourth. You're to report to my office on the first of July. We're going to have you very busy. I hope you don't mind working the holiday."

Scarcely able to breathe, Quincy closed his eyes and smiled. "Not at all, Mr. Hayes. Thank you very much."

As soon as he ended the call, Kendal threw herself into his arms, squealing, "You got it! Congratulations."

"Thank you, baby," he said, reluctantly releasing her. "Can I have a rain check on that lunch? I've got a lot of calls to make. If it's okay with you, I'll be in the basement."

"You go on. I'll gather some cuttings for the table."

Kendal put a final rose into the flower basket and removed her gloves. It had gotten warmer, she thought. She wiped her brow, pondering the ways of God in regard to her and Quincy. He had landed a local job. That would certainly make it easier on their new relationship. Certain God had answered her prayers, she was probably the happiest woman in the world.

"Thank you, Lord," she whispered.

She suddenly heard something toward the back of the house. Curious, she peered around the masses of rose bushes and saw Walt Jr. making his way toward her. Why had he come from the back?

"Hello, Kendal," he said. She clamped a hand to her mouth, realizing she hadn't called to cancel their plans.

"Walt?"

"Your brother told me you were getting threatening phone calls and would be unavailable this evening. Why didn't *you* tell me?"

"I'm sorry. I've just been a little overwhelmed by everything."

"You really are the martyr, aren't you?" he asked, not bothering to hide his annoyance. "How long have you been getting calls?"

She used her hand to protect her eyes from the glare of the afternoon sun. "Since the day I walked away from Howard-Hadley. Did you say Eric told you?"

"Yes, I always seem to hear things concerning you from other sources."

Although grateful, she wondered why Eric had called off her date without telling her. "You're right, of course. I should've been the one to call you. But with the threats and Jace missing, I've been under a lot of stress. I'm sure you can understand that."

He moved closer. "There's no excuse for rudeness, Kendal. I don't like being made a fool of."

Something undefined, but spelling danger, appeared in his facial expression. Wary and beginning to panic, she shrank back. With him so close, she couldn't think clearly. Why was he so angry? And where was her surveillance?

Unexpectedly, an indistinct recollection of something Eric had said sprang to her mind—and then vanished. Her heart beat furiously as she tried to refocus on Walt's face. He seemed faintly less manic now, but she wasn't fooled. She saw the pulse pounding madly in his neck. "Your brother told me you were under heavy surveillance. I decided to drive a rental in hopes of slipping by them. I see it worked."

"What do you mean?"

"I drove by first," he said. "I could barely see you for all the roses, but I did. I parked down the street and doubled back on foot through the neighbors' back yards. They never even saw me."

Her anger suddenly flared past the restraints of panic. "Have you lost your mind?" she asked. "This isn't a game. How dare you interfere!"

"I just wanted to see if…."

"Excuse me, Walt, but you seem to have forgotten that I agreed to go to dinner with you tonight as a friend. Nothing more. And I'm not trying to make a fool of you. If we're clear on the boundaries of such a relationship, I have no real reason to."

She drew back when he touched her face. Then despite her resistance, he took of her hands and brought them to his lips. "I want to marry you, Kendal."

Aghast, she tried to pull away, but his grip on her wrists tightened. She was now in a full-blown panic. Her eyes jerked toward the back corner of the house and she instinctively screamed.

Walt tightened his grip even more as he pressed her against the house. "I suggest you not make noise," he said. "I simply want to make you see the good sense in our union."

Quincy was in the basement on the phone and probably hadn't heard her scream. Think. She had to think. "I'm in love with another man, Walt."

His expression became darker, more menacing; his face became distorted with rage. "I just happen to know he's not around; I am."

Despite feeling weighed down, she yanked away from him and stood her ground. "You should leave now."

"Why? I've made my feelings clear to you, Kendal. You did, too—that day in my office." He seized her hands again, clamping his spindly fingers around her wrists.

"You must know that day in your office was obviously a mistake. I was upset."

He shoved her against the side of the house. "I'm not as sluggish as Frank Peck," he said, grinning. "I intend to have you as my wife."

Something was off, Kendal thought, her mind reeling. Two men connected to her employment had asked her to marry them in the last month. One was dead, and the other was obviously deluded, if not flat-out insane.

She frantically tried to look toward the street, but the roses, as well as the garage blocked her view. Eric's suggestion about cutting them back suddenly came to mind. Where was Sullivan or Vera? And the neighbors couldn't see them. The blood drained from Kendal's face as Walt pressed his body against hers, trapping her.

"Stop it, Walt!" she screamed, trying to push him away with her body.

He clamped his hand over her mouth and slammed her head against the brick of the house. "Shut up," he said through clenched teeth.

Twisting and kicking, she bit down hard on his palm. He struck her face with the back of his hand and slammed her head again the wall, causing stars to burst before her eyes. Terrified now, she shrank back against the wall. Her heart throbbed as memories of Sumner began to surface. She slumped against the disquieting premonition.

"You need to come with me," he said. "Someplace where we can talk alone. If the feds stop us, you'd better find a way to get past them."

"No, Walt."

Walt suddenly grabbed her by the neck with his free hand and kissed her hard. Her struggle only served to increase his brutality, and before long she tasted her own blood from where his teeth had cut her. Feeling numb, Kendal fought him with every ounce of her strength.

"You obviously need a good man." He taunted. "Once I tame you, we'll get along well together."

"Walt, you don't know what you're saying. You couldn't possibly be in love with me."

She finally managed to push him away. She dashed toward the front of the house, hoping to get Sullivan's attention. But he caught her and pulled her back to the back.

Heart pounding, Kendal shoved him towards the fence and rushed around the corner to the backyard. Just as she reached the back steps, he grabbed her wrist and yanked her to him. She screamed as they both fell to the ground. He straddled her, placing his thin hands around her throat and squeezing. "You're right. I'm not in love with you, but you belong to me. And if I can't have you, nobody can."

Scarcely able to breathe, Kendal managed to strike him several times in his face. He had just pinned her hands down again when his weight was abruptly lifted off her. She blindly scrambled to her feet, gasping for air. She regained her balance just in time to see Quincy slam his fist into Walt's face. Though Walt got in several blows, he was no match for Quincy's rage or size. Blood gushed from Walt's nose and mouth as he staggered toward Quincy again and again.

Kendal stood rigid with terror as Quincy slammed his fist into the man's face with the force of a sledgehammer. She pressed her back against the back door, nearly overcome with anguish and shock.

"Quincy." Her voice was unsteady, but strong. "Please, Quincy, stop."

Unable to remain upright, Kendal slid down the door onto the top step. Moments later, Eric and Sullivan rushed into the backyard. "Keep him away from me," Walt yelled, scrambling to his feet. "He's an animal. He should be in Baltimore. Why aren't you in Baltimore?"

Eric handcuffed Walt and read him his rights, even as he continued yelling. "Kendal, you can't have what belongs to me. It's mine. Do you hear?"

Quincy rushed to her the instant Sullivan released him, and gently lifted her into his arms. "I'm so sorry I wasn't out here. Are you okay?"

She nodded.

"Kendal!" Eric's voice was strained. "I'm sorry; we never imagined he would come from the back."

"I'm okay," she mumbled, pressing her face against Quincy's chest. She heard Eric speak to the other agent.

"Claude, process Hadley. I'll stay here and get their statements."

-TWENTY-TWO-

After getting statements from Kendal and Quincy, Eric left for the office. Kendal stood at the sink and overlooked the side yard and rear of the garage. She scarcely felt it when Quincy walked up and put a hand on her shoulder. Her head felt as if it would burst. She closed her eyes, trying to drown out the singsong timbre of Jack Sumner's voice.

Nobody loves you like I do. Not even God.

Kendal took a step toward the table and winced. She had hit her leg against the brick steps when she fell. Funny she could feel her leg and head, but the rest of her body was numb. Her mind felt like fuzz. Maybe it was the effect of the sedative Eric had insisted she take. She didn't like the way the drug made her feel, so heavy and lost. Quincy took her arm and urged her into a chair. She felt drained of words. There was really nothing left to say—nothing to ask. She felt so dead-ened inside it didn't matter.

"Kendal, do you need to go to the hospital?"

She shook her head. "I'm just tired."

With his hand on her elbow, he walked her up the stairs and into her room. She sat down on the bed. "I'll be right downstairs if you need anything."

"Is he the serial killer?"

He sat down beside her. "Eric suspects he is, but he's not certain." Quincy drew her close and rested his cheek on the top of her head. His nearness was comforting, but she could not let herself depend on that. "Kendal, is there anything I can do?"

He must feel helpless, she thought. Quincy, who always had the answer—Quincy, the doer and comforter, was stumped. She pulled away and curled into a ball on her side. "No."

He stood and covered her with the throw that was draped over the foot of her bed. "I'll let you rest, then."

Her eyelids scratched like sandpaper, but she couldn't sleep. Images crowded her mind, images she couldn't pin down.

I'm your real daddy, Kendal. You belong to me. Nobody loves you like I do. Not even God.

You belong to me. And if I can't have you, nobody can.

She suddenly felt icy cold. Hairs stirred in primal reflex, and she was tempted to call Quincy back to sit with her until she fell asleep. But that would be silly. She was just reacting to Walt's assault. It was hard to believe a man of his social standing had actually attacked her, had actually intended to force her to marry him. As she stared at the wall, her mind saw a superimposed image of Sumner with Walt.

You're a pretty little girl. You're my little girl. You've got to mind your daddy now. You can't have what belongs to me. It's mine. Do you hear?

Kendal closed her eyes, but the vision remained unchanged. Her tears spilled onto the bedding. Was she losing her mind?

Quincy sat at the kitchen table and stared at the basket of flowers he had retrieved from the side yard. What had Hadley meant by his remark? *You can't have what belongs to me. It's mine.*

Based on what Eric had told him about the call Kendal received during the night, Hadley's words were similar. He recalled Eric repeating them. *"You destroyed something of mine. Now I'll destroy something of yours."*

What could Kendal possibly have that belonged to Hadley? Something that he apparently felt was destroyed. Something was definitely off here. But what was it?

He recalled the haunted look in her eyes when she stood on the back steps. What was going through her head, he wondered. Sure she was in shock, but she was still too quiet for comfort. Quincy rubbed his jaw where Hadley had punched him, then rested his head in his palms.

"Lord."

He could go no further.

The afternoon stretched, but he was too shaken to think, too angry to pray, too spent to feel. He just sat.

Dusk had replaced the brightness of the day when the phone jarred him out of his stupor. He quickly grabbed it. "Yeah?"

"How is she, Quincy?"

Quincy released his breath when he heard Eric's voice. "Lethargic, quiet. She's lying down. Did you hear the words Hadley screamed at her?"

"Yeah, real similar to those of the caller."

"What's happening with him?"

"I think he'll plead insanity. Quincy, he's confessed to the serials, as well as Peck's murder. His dad was with him. Hadley Sr. doesn't seem as sick as everybody has suggested."

"Will his attorney get him out? I would hate to see him harassing her while out on bail. He has very little to lose now, Eric."

"Oddly, he refused to call his attorney. His dad slipped away and did it for him, but he hasn't arrived yet. I think everybody realizes it wouldn't be prudent to have him back out on the streets just yet."

"What will happen to him, Eric? I mean…about terrorizing Kendal. And what about Jace's abduction? What did he have to say about that?"

"He admits to murder, obviously a much more serious offense. But denies making those calls to Kendal or snatching Jace."

"Then why would he sneak around back and attack her outside her own home?"

"I don't know. But I have a feeling Hadley's entire story will change by tomorrow morning. Cashion thinks we have our man on all counts. But something's still nagging at me. And we still have to find Jace."

Quincy swallowed hard. "I hope it's not too late. I mean there *is* the possibility he's already dead."

"I know. Can you let Kendal know about Hadley's confession? I'm sure she'll feel a lot better knowing she can go back to living—to some degree, anyway."

"Yeah, I'll tell her."

Quincy hung up the phone, feeling numb and unexcited. He went upstairs and knocked softly on Kendal's door. The room was silent. He cracked the door and peered inside. Still sleeping. He didn't want to wake her. The news could wait. Feeling antsy, he went back downstairs and outside for a breath of fresh air.

Starting from the backyard, he strolled along the thin cement walkway that circled the entire house within the chain link fence. A five-piece wrought iron patio set stood underneath a large shade in the midst of a garden of roses. Roses of every color adorned the garden; a sparing volume in the back and front yards, but the side yard near the garage was nearly filled to capacity, including the lush yellow that climbed the lattice to her bedroom window. They were indeed beautiful, but after today Kendal would probably have no qualms about removing some of them. The lawn on the northeast side of the house had only trees.

As he strolled around the fenced-in area, he thought of her. She had been somber and quiet during Eric's questioning, simply answering without looking at either of them. Had today's occurrence triggered another episode of posttraumatic stress?

Lord, what do you want me to do?

When he returned to the house, he stood at the sink and could hear the water running upstairs. He put on the coffeepot and waited.

Kendal stepped out of the shower. Her bruised body ached. Her thoughts were murky. She dried herself and dressed in jeans and a loose white shirt, wondering what she should do next. After a few minutes, she went downstairs.

Quincy was leaning on the kitchen counter, a mug of coffee in his hands. She felt a rush of emotion the instant she noticed his drawn expression. He set the cup down and reached for her, but she didn't take his hand. His arms dropped to his side.

"Eric called. Hadley confessed to killing Peck and those three women."

She gasped amid another rush of memory. "Why, Quincy?"

"We don't know."

A serial killer, she thought, clasping her hands together. There was no sense of victory, no sweeping relief, no sorrow. She closed her eyes. "It's over, then." And that was how she felt. Like a closed book put back on the shelf.

He started towards her. "Kendal, there's something else—something that might give you a glimmer of hope in spite of all this."

She looked up, but her heart felt empty.

"I think I know your mother's name."

She stared at him. "What?"

"Her name is Stephanie Baylor. She was an aide in Senator Howard's office."

Kendal stared at him in stunned disbelief. "Where is she?"

"I don't know, sweetheart. She quit her job as soon as she found out she was pregnant. She was a good friend of your dad's. I couldn't find anything else on her."

"Dad?" Kendal moistened her lips. "Are you saying Dad is my biological father?"

Quincy held up his hands. "Whoa. I don't know that for sure, Kendal. I'm just telling you what I found. All I know is that your mother was never married."

"Stephanie Baylor." She wrapped her arms around herself and moved towards the stairwell. "Quincy, I feel as if I'm not completely here. A lot of strange things are rolling around in my head, and I need time to sort them all out."

He drew in a deep breath. "Okay. I'll get us…."

"Alone," she interrupted. She hoped he would understand what she needed and not make it harder than it was.

He leaned against the counter. "Kendal."

She couldn't look at him. "Would you mind leaving?"

If he cared at all, he would understand. He waited too long to answer.

"Please," she whispered.

"Fine." His voice was flat. "How long do you need?"

"I don't know." She unfolded her arms and went back upstairs without looking back.

-TWENTY-THREE-

"That was a wonderful sermon, Pastor Richards," Kendal said, extending her hand as she exited the door of the church. She was mildly surprised that he held it longer than usual.

"It's always an encouragement to hear that my efforts are not in vain, Kendal. I hope you'll be faithful in heeding God's direction."

Then he released her hand and casually took the hand of the next parishioner. Seated between Sheila and Eric, she had been perturbed and restless throughout the service. The pastor had spoken on the hunger of an empty soul, taking his text from Proverbs 30. The passage hit her closer when she read it from her New International Version of the Bible.

There are three things that are never satisfied, four that never say, 'enough!': the grave, the barren womb, land, which is never satisfied with water, and fire.

It had been a timely sermon, and in the wake of yesterday's events, revitalized her desire for real happiness. She had been surprised to glance over at Quincy during the service and find him watching her. He had sat across from them, and she had been acutely aware of his presence during the service.

There are three things that are never satisfied.

She closed her eyes, her thoughts jumping about like crickets in the night. Even after she had seen a therapist at fifteen, she hadn't become very well adjusted with life. And no matter how much Nana and Dad reassured her that Jack Sumner's words had nothing to do with truth, she had felt different, isolated. Clearly, her relationship with God had been infected with confused notions, unfulfilled expectations, elusive dreams and recurring nightmares.

Still very sore, she moved woodenly across the parking lot. Too troubled to sleep, she had tossed all night, afraid to see the images that pursued her. Jolted by the slamming of a car door, Kendal looked across the parking lot and saw Quincy shaking Eric's hand. Just as she decided to join them, he walked away. Her heart sank, but she walked calmly to the car and climbed in next to her brother.

Quincy got into his rental and turned a strained face on them before driving away. She had hurt him. But she wasn't sure anymore that she was the person he needed. She was a confused woman with issues, and very little trust in men.

"I want to sit with Aunt Kem," Marcy whined, already strapped into the back seat with her mother.

"No," Sheila said before Kendal could reach back. "There's no seat-belt for you."

"But I could share, Mum."

The humming sound Marcy made when addressing her mother amused Kendal. Her tendency to end many sounds with 'm' had always been musical to her ears.

Eric started the engine and touched her hand. "You okay?"

His query felt like a warm blanket over her chilled heart. She nodded, remembering how he had reacted many years ago to the Sumner incident. Despite his youth, he had come to her bedroom each night when she couldn't stop crying and sit with her until she fell asleep. Even then, he had felt responsible for some reason. Having him with her softened the feelings of separation. She hadn't remembered until now, but the event had changed her brother as much as it had changed her.

"Kendal? You have anything planned for tomorrow?"

"Tomorrow? Why?"

He snickered. "It's Memorial Day. Remember?"

"Oh. Well, I guess we can grill something if it doesn't rain."

"I invited Quincy to dinner this afternoon. That okay with you?"

She smiled tentatively. "Isn't it a little late to be asking?"

"I noticed you didn't even speak to him. Anything wrong?"

"What makes you think something's wrong? Can't you just—"

"Uh, uh, Eric," Sheila interrupted, slapping her forehead. "She's answering everything with questions. That means she's giving in to that old predisposition to chase away a perfectly good man."

Despite knowing how feeble it sounded, Kendal defended herself. "I just asked for some thinking space. That's all."

"Sis, I hope you're not being selfish here. Quincy has sacrificed a lot, in addition to doing us a big favor at a time he thought you were guilty."

Her jaw dropped. "He thought I was guilty?"

Jackson had picked up Sheila and Marcy for a Sunday outing, and Kendal was fussily tidying the living room in anticipation of their visitor. Olivia Howard had phoned during dinner to ask if she could drop by. Kendal hadn't seen the woman since the taping and couldn't imagine what she wanted.

"Everything looks fine," Quincy said, standing in the doorway. His gaze was direct but gently reassuring.

"I just don't want her thinking I live in a dump. She's from money, you know."

He started moving towards her, but she turned away. "Stop sweating; your home is beautiful."

She smiled gratefully. "Thanks."

"You doing okay?"

"Quincy, I'm sorry about yesterday. I hope I didn't hurt your feelings."

"I'm a big boy," he said. "Are you evading my question?"

She felt rattled and looked away. "I don't know. I've been thinking about everything. Dad, Walt, the murders, the threats. I know Walt is locked up, but I'm still worried about Marcy. I feel sort of numb, and I think something must've happened to me."

"Are the flashes of memory becoming clearer?"

"They frighten me. They're a little…disconcerting, and everything seems to trigger them."

"That's to be expected. Don't let the memories chase you. Turn around and confront them."

Suddenly, panic, seemingly always just a heartbeat away, surfaced, and she began to shake. "I don't want to know—I don't want to remember."

This time, she let him pull her into his arms. "It's all right to remember, sweetheart."

"It's all so strange. I feel like a wooden nickel."

"What?"

She pressed closer to him, seeking to draw strength from his strength. "I'm scared, Quincy."

He pulled back. "Of what?"

She turned away, feeling hot and cold at the same time. "All my life I've been saving myself for marriage. That's important to me." She swung back around to face him. "What if I'm not so innocent?"

She winced in pain when his fingers tightened on her shoulders, and he instantly released her.

"What is it?"

"I'm a little bruised from yesterday."

"I'm sorry. I forgot."

"Ms. Howard just pulled up, you two," Eric said, coming into the room.

Brushing imaginary lint off her red linen pantsuit, Kendal answered the door the moment the bell rang. "Hello, Olivia. Please come in," she said, standing aside. "I have a pot of coffee on. Or would you prefer tea?"

"Coffee would be lovely, dear."

Both men stood as Kendal led Howard-Hadley's largest shareholder into the living room and then to the sofa. "Hello, Ms. Howard," Quincy said. "I think you remember Agent Boyd."

"Oh, yes," she said, giving Eric a knowing look. "You look just like your father at this age. I noticed it the other evening when we talked."

"I don't know when I've looked through any of the old albums," Eric said, smiling. "I suppose I do resemble him a little."

Kendal smiled fondly at the likable fellow her brother had become. He could be sensitive and unassuming, and at the same time be strong and assertive. She left to fetch a tray of homemade cake slices, cookies and coffee.

When she reentered the living room, Quincy jumped up to help her. He winked as they deposited the contents onto the coffee table. "Cream or sugar?" she asked Olivia.

"Black is fine, my dear," she said, reaching for the cup. "I've heard a lot of good things about your Small Whispers. The name is intriguing. Where did you come by it?"

Kendal was warmed by her interest. "My grandmother," she said, as she took a seat beside her brother. "It's from the Bible."

"Oh?"

Handing her brother a cup, Kendal continued. "It characterizes the way God often speaks to believers."

When she looked into Olivia's faded blue eyes, they had widened. Then suddenly a smile broke out on her face, making her look like a younger version of Ethel Barrymore.

"Ah, yes, the passage from First Kings," she said, turning to place her cup on the end table beside her. "That's one of my favorites."

Kendal had just swallowed a sip of coffee. The woman's knowledge of scripture so surprised her that she strangled. Eric slapped her back lightly, all the while snickering along with Quincy.

"Please forgive me, Olivia. I just…."

"You didn't expect me to be a believer," Olivia said, a glint in her eye. "I know. My frozen face challenges that fact."

While the men were failing miserably at hiding their amusement, Kendal looked from one to the other and sighed. "I'm truly sorry about our manners."

"That's all right, dear," her guest said with a chuckle. "Let me get to the point of my visit. When I heard about Walt's assault on you, I was appalled. However, the company is prepared to take full responsibility for his actions."

Kendal sat forward. "What?"

"I'm so sorry that happened, Kendal. I am glad to see that you're indeed doing well. But you have every right to bring suit against us. After all, I'm aware that Walt Jr. was trying to convince you to take Jed's job." She turned to Eric. "I should have told you about this when you asked, Agent Boyd, but since Walt is in custody there's no longer any need to conceal it."

Eric, too, leaned forward. "How did you hear about this so quickly?"

"His father blames me. He was furious when he phoned last night. I *did* get him to agree to offer a settlement."

"I don't want to sue the company," Kendal said. "And why would Mr. Hadley blame you for Walt's actions?"

"Walt Sr. holds me responsible for his son's entire state of mind these days. Ever since he found a copy of my will and the partnership agreement, he's been behaving a little irrationally. They both have."

"I understand the company is to pass to a female heir only," Eric interjected. "I found a copy of your partnership agreement among some evidence we collected."

"So you've been trying to get me to admit to this all along," she said, smiling impishly.

"I was just trying to get to the truth, Ms. Howard. That's my job."

Olivia cleared her throat. "When my brother sold us the company, neither Walt nor I wanted to pay what he was asking. He reduced the price drastically, providing we agree to place that particular clause in our partnership agreement. We both saw the company's potential and agreed without thinking any more about it."

Kendal was curious. "But why would Senator Howard insist on a clause like that? He didn't have any children, and neither did you."

"I never thought about it until after his death. I think Walt agreed initially because he thought he and Clara would have more children. But it didn't work out that way. He only has the one son."

Kendal pressed further. "I hope I'm not being too inquisitive, but why didn't you change the clause after the Senator's death?"

"I found in some of my brother's papers that he had an illegitimate daughter on the East Coast," she said, glancing at Eric. "The company will eventually go to her."

"But that doesn't tell us why Mr. Hadley blames you for his son's bad choices," Quincy said. "I mean…he knew what was in the clause just as well as you, right?"

"We never intended to tell Walt Jr. Not for a while, anyway. But he learned of the agreement nearly a year ago. He's been a very determined and angry young man ever since…even openly opposing his father, which I had never seen him do."

"But I don't understand why he attacked me," Kendal said.

"I believe the man truly went mad when he realized the company would never be his. He even tried to blackmail *me*."

"With what?" Eric asked.

"He thought he had found something in my past to use as leverage to obtain my niece's name. Walt wanted to contact her. I couldn't allow that. Although I've kept track of her, I myself have never contacted her."

"So she knows nothing about all this?" Kendal asked.

"No, I'm afraid not," Olivia said. "I'm really sorry I didn't tell you about Walt's troubles before now. Perhaps I could have prevented those murders, and particularly the attack on Kendal."

Eric stood. "Things still aren't adding up for me, Ms. Howard. I need to find out why Hadley would murder four people. But that's not your problem. I appreciate your stopping by. I'm sure Dad will, too."

Kendal loudly cleared her throat, afraid she had missed her chance to ask the one question that had been bouncing through her mind since Quincy told her about Stephanie Baylor. "Olivia, I don't know if you're aware, but I'm adopted. I've been trying to obtain medical records of my birth parents."

The woman's face showed no surprise over the disclosure. She smiled. "But what have I to do with that?"

"I recently learned my mother worked in your brother's office. Apparently, most of the records were destroyed in a fire, and I was hoping you might have access to some of his personal files—something that might be able to help me locate her."

"I don't know if I can help you with that, Kendal. But I'll certainly have Suzanne go through the documents I do have." She reached out, grasped Kendal's hand and gently squeezed. "I'm really sorry about everything you're going through. And I truly hope they find Jace soon."

Kendal nodded and breathed in a shaky breath. She didn't mean to get emotional, but she couldn't seem to help it.

"There, there, child. Everything will be just fine. I wish there was something more I could do to help."

Eric walked over to the sofa. "If you could get us a current address on Stephanie Baylor, we would be in your debt. And anything else you can tell me about Walt Jr."

"Walt Jr. has been with the company since he graduated from the University of Washington. Until he learned of the partnership clause, he was doing a marvelous job."

"I understand his father owns forty-five percent of the stock," Eric said. "Is he still active in running the company?"

"He hasn't been very involved in the daily operations since he became ill. He's had a real bout with respiratory problems. Some days are worse than others."

"Do you have any idea why Hadley fired Jace Tate?"

"He mentioned Jace might be passing along confidential data to our competitors, but Walt Jr. has always been rather paranoid. Perhaps it was simply a matter of clashing personalities." She again turned to Kendal. "I thought it was kind of you to hire Jace."

Quincy stood up. "We're all very concerned about finding him, Olivia. Is there any light you can shed on his possible whereabouts?"

She shook her head. "Are you sure Walt had something to do with his disappearance?"

Eric shrugged. "To be honest, I'm not sure at all. But my superiors are very much convinced. I can understand their certainty. It's the only thing that makes sense."

The woman struggled to pull herself up. Kendal stood to help. "Let me give all this some thought. I'll call you soon."

Eric gave her a card with his cell number, and Quincy escorted her to her car. While he was gone, Eric turned to his sister.

"I'm sorry," she began. "I know I shouldn't have brought up…."

"It's okay, Sis. I had my suspicions about Olivia Howard, but after today, I don't think she could be mixed up in this. She's too blunt and forthright."

"I know," Kendal said, frowning. "But I sensed she was holding something back."

"Yeah, I've been feeling that for some time. I just don't know what to make of it."

-TWENTY-FOUR-

"You have anything to support this gut feeling of yours?" Bill Andersen asked. "All the evidence, as well as Hadley's confession, indicates the likelihood that he's also Kendal's stalker. Didn't you apprehend him in the act of assaulting her?"

Eric loosened his grip on the phone. "I know, Bill. But Cashion has already pulled the monitoring and part of her surveillance. I just want a little more time before he removes it entirely. We all appreciated Ms. Howard's explanation, but I still get the feeling she's holding back. I can't imagine what it would be."

"Let's go over what you have, including what you and your reporter friend collected when you flew him to Alabama."

Eric went silent for several long minutes. "You knew about that?"

"You didn't really think I wouldn't be keeping a close eye on you when you're so close to this case, did you?"

"I suppose I'll have to face...."

"Yes, you will. But tell me what you have so far."

"First of all, none of the calls Kendal got came from any of Hadley's phones. And he was out of town the week before her opening the shop."

"So he has an alibi. What dates?"

Eric flipped through his notebook. "He was the keynote speaker at a pharmaceutical symposium in Vancouver on May 2. He returned May 7."

"I see," Andersen said. "We've already talked to Jed Mason again. From what he told your friend, I think its quite possible he could've hired someone to terrorize her."

"I suppose it's possible. But Hadley doesn't strike me as a man who plays in a group—unless of course it's a short game."

"Like the game he allegedly played with Peck?"

"Yeah."

"Okay. So Hadley confessed to these killings. Exactly how is he connected to Peck's illegal activity?"

"I believe the FDA is reopening its investigation as we speak. A team is coming in to interview him later today."

"What about those tapes you got from the Tate woman? You find anything?"

"Just what Olivia Howard confirmed. Cashion has someone else weeding through them now."

After a long pause, Bill gave Eric a bit of hope. "You're in a lot of trouble, Boyd, but you're a good man to have on my team. I'm going to table any action until you're convinced your sister is out of danger. I'll talk with Cashion."

"Thanks, Bill. I really hope this is all over and I'm worrying about nothing. But until we find Tate, my gut will probably keep jumping."

Kendal gazed up at the gray clouds piled overhead. It would rain soon. Marcy tramped around the backyard with a paper cap on her head, a stick at her shoulder and a small plastic flag in her hand. "God bless America," she chanted. "God bless America."

"Hey, sweetie," Kendal called out. "Where did you get that get-up?"

"Attention!"

Kendal stood erect at the loud command. "Yes, ma'am."

Marcy smiled. "Aunt Kem, you love me?"

Kendal took the flag from the child's fingers. It waved stiffly in the breeze when she blew on it. "Indeed I do, my pretty. Now where is my afternoon hug?"

Marcy threw herself into Kendal's arms, causing her to lose her balance. They fell over into the grass and rolled around playfully. After some intense tickling, Marcy scrambled away. "I go back and play. Okay?"

Kendal saluted, picked up the flag and handed it to Marcy. "Okay. You're the guard of the manor. But don't go outside the gate."

Marcy returned the stick to her shoulder and strutted around the corner, singing to the top of her voice. "God bless America…."

Kendal glanced over at Sheila, who had fallen over onto the table with laughter. "What's so funny?"

She nodded towards the door. "Eric taught her that; she sang herself to sleep with it last night."

Kendal got up and dusted herself off. So, Marcy had finally warmed to Eric. "It's been nice having my little brother around, but he seems a little intense this morning."

"I noticed it, too," Sheila said, stoking the coals. "I'm sure it has something to do with Hadley." Just then Eric came out with the ribs. "Where's Quincy? I thought he would've been here by now."

Kendal looked at her watch. "I talked with him an hour ago. He was about to call his aunt."

"God bless America…."

Kendal turned toward Marcy. "You made it back, huh?"

"Look, Mum, I found me a present."

They all turned and stared at the gift-wrapped package beneath Marcy's arm. She was carrying it like a football. Sheila rushed over and pulled it away. After reading a small label, she frowned and turned to Eric. "It's for Kendal from…Jace's companion." She turned back to Marcy as Kendal and Eric drew closer. "Where did you get this, honey?"

Marcy looked up, her eyes widening. "Didn't go out the gate."

Kendal's heart rate quickened. Eric quickly scooped Marcy up and took the package from Sheila. "Okay, princess. How about showing Uncle Eric where you found that pretty present?"

Marcy pushed back a little, her eyes brimming with tears. Seeking to calm the child, Kendal said, "I'll go too, sweetie."

"Didn't go out the gate," she repeated, her lips quivering.

"We know, baby," Sheila said, stroking her arm. "Just show us where you found it."

Quincy pulled into the drive just as Marcy was pointing to a place on the walkway leading up to the front porch. Someone had obviously tossed it over the fence.

Quincy grinned doubtfully and scrutinized the group. "What did I do to deserve such a impressive reception?"

Eric put Marcy down and held up the package. With his free hand, he took out his cell and started dialing. "Y'all go on back to the grill. We'll be around in a minute."

Kendal felt her knees giving way. "Eric?"

"I'm just calling the team," he said, moving toward the front door. "Go on back. This little gift might be the glue we've been waiting for."

Everyone was stunned by the brazen confirmation that Hadley was either telling the truth or not working alone. Quincy rubbed between his eyes.

"Eric, where does all this leave us?"

"We know the person that's holding Jace is the same person who's after Kendal," Eric said. "He told her some time back that he hadn't killed anyone. Obviously, this has nothing, or very little, to do with Hadley. Despite my doubts, it's amazing how neatly things seemed to come together against him."

"Did you ever determine why Hadley killed Peck or the women?"

Eric shook his head. "I don't know, Quincy. He's as mute as a zombie. The judge has ordered a psychological evaluation before we can proceed with an indictment. I think that might have more to do with the FDA investigation, though."

Quincy scoured the front yard. He felt powerless. "It's unlikely a man as successful as Hadley would actually stab three women."

Eric shifted his weight nervously. "Quincy, there's something else you don't know. It wasn't just the way the bodies were arranged that led us to believe Frank Peck's murder was a part of the serial."

Quincy stared at him. "What do you mean?"

"This information hasn't been released to the public, for obvious reasons. Each victim was killed with an ice pick, which was left beneath each body."

Quincy was seized by a horrible thought. Kendal could have very well been the Hadley's next victim. "That's clearly premeditated," he whispered. "Are we sure this other person—the one who has Jace—is not the serial killer? I mean…."

Eric shook his head. "I know what you mean. It's been eating at me ever since we took Hadley into custody. It seems outrageous, but I'm actually praying Hadley is telling the truth and they are two different people. If this person isn't a real killer, I'll feel better. But this still leaves Kendal as a target. Even now I'm looking at the possibility that her history search might've unleashed…."

Quincy swallowed dryly. "Eric, you can't suspect your dad of any of this. He obviously loves Kendal very much."

"I know he does, but I can't shake the feeling that he knows something about Sumner's death. And Kendal is more upset about the possibility that he's her real dad than she's willing to admit."

"That's only natural. But it still doesn't tell me why you suspect him?"

"Think about it, Quincy. Could he afford to let Kendal's search uncover anything incriminating?"

Quincy stared at Eric in disbelief. "Eric, those are some pretty serious suppositions. Have you said anything about your misgivings to Kendal?"

"No, I can't do that. She's just now started to relax."

Quincy glanced at the package. "Yeah, I know. I just hope this new calling card doesn't push her over the edge. You have anything other than gut feeling and a set of odd circumstances to back up your suspicion about your dad?"

"Not really. I just know it all ties together somehow. I can't explain it. I can't even share my misgiving with anyone else. Dad hasn't been all that forthcoming with information."

Quincy leaned closer. "You know those flashes of memory she's been getting are becoming more lucid."

"I'm glad she's talking to you about it. You've given her an avenue of release. I'll always be grateful for that."

"She's afraid of a lot of things, Eric. Do you think Sumner hurt her?"

Eric's voice came out in a croak. "I don't know. It would shake her world if he did. Dad said the doctors didn't think so, but there are all kinds of things men like that can do."

"I know," Quincy said, not wanting to think about it.

Eric was composed by the time the team of agents arrived with several local officers. Quincy sat on the porch while they looked around the yard. Several minutes into the hunt, another vehicle pulled onto the wide gravel driveway. Eric rolled his eyes and groaned. "That's Cashion."

Obviously on the warpath, the barrel-chested man hurried toward the porch, gazing fiercely over the rim of his glasses. "All right, Boyd," he bellowed, "what are you trying to pull? I just got a call from *The Hill*." He stopped short and stared at Quincy. "Is this the boyfriend?"

Quincy stood and extended his hand. "Quincy Morgan, sir. How are you?"

Cashion gave up a quick shake. He turned to look at the group in the front yard and smiled. "Nice roses. My wife grows them, too. I'll get my gloves from the car and transfer the package to trace. I need names and prints of everyone who has touched it."

"Just my sister's roommate and her little girl—and me," Eric said, motioning toward the package in the chair.

As Cashion walked away, Eric confided, "I think he likes you."

"What did you do to get him so riled?"

"Called Dad."

Quincy was beyond surprise. "What?"

"Dad is a personal friend of the Attorney General," Eric said. "I convinced him to talk to him just this once. This doesn't change my suspicions. My primary obligation is to my sister. Besides, my career might already be up a creek."

"What did your dad say?"

"I tried to talk him out of it, but he's trying to get a flight out now." Eric glanced down at his shoes. "Quincy, I mentioned what we found out about Stephanie Baylor."

"How did he take it?"

"Didn't have a lot to say. He's planning to talk Kendal into going to Spokane to stay at the house."

"Might be a good idea. Kendal is important to me, and I'll do everything in my power to protect her. I just wish I could do more than just sit and be a sounding board."

"I don't doubt you will. But you've done so much to help us already." He shifted self-consciously. "This issue with Dad—it's one I haven't been able to discuss with anyone, especially Kendal."

"I know."

Eric's smile was shadowed by a recollection of grief. "You're not only my sister's leaning post, you've been mine, too. I've always felt a little responsible for what happened to her back then. If I hadn't climbed that tree…."

The young agent's sense of guilt surprised Quincy. "Eric," he said sternly. "You were a child. There's no way you should feel responsible for what Jack Sumner did."

"I know, and I also know she's an adult now. But as long as she can't remember exactly what happened to her, she's still vulnerable to things that we take for granted."

Quincy could feel the other man's anguish, and had finally got a hint to the reason behind his intense devotion to his sister. "Are you afraid of what she might remember?"

"A little. I really don't want to hurt Dad, but if he's involved, I'll haul him down just like I would a total stranger."

-TWENTY-FIVE-

Kendal's muscles ached as she descended the stairs to join the group huddled in the living room. Eric had promised to wait until she read Marcy her bedtime story before revealing the results of the lab's analysis of the gift-wrapped package.

The thick silence in the room unnerved her. She plopped down on the sofa next to Quincy and cocked an eye at a sniffling Sheila. "You catching a cold?"

"Uh...no," Sheila said, evasively. "Marcy asleep?"

Kendal kept her gaze on Sheila's face. "She was out before I even got to the second page."

Eric stopped making notes in a small pad. "She's had a big day."

The look on her brother's face made the small hairs on the back of her neck stir. Quincy drew her into the curve of his arm.

Sheila moved closer on the other side and threaded her arm through her friend's. Clearly, her brother hadn't waited for her return before announcing the lab's findings. It couldn't be any worse than what this creep had said to her on her cellphone earlier that morning. She hadn't told anyone about the call because he was still threatening to hurt Marcy.

"So what was in the box?"

"A small section of bloody scalp with hair still attached," he blurted out. "We did DNA testing, using strands from Tate's hairbrush. The lab is certain it's his scalp."

Kendal shrank against Quincy. Jace was dead.

"I won't leave Kendal again, Eric," Sheila blurted. "I don't...."

"You don't have to," Eric interrupted. "We realize it's better if the two of you stay together. But I want you both to move temporarily to Dad's place in Spokane."

Seeing Sheila so frightened incensed her, but she realized it might be a good way to get Marcy away. But he had promised that if she didn't comply with his wishes he would kill Jace and then come after Marcy. She couldn't leave, and she would not allow Eric to force her. She pulled away and got to her feet. Quincy moved to follow, but she waved him away and walked wearily to the mantle. "What does he want from me?"

"I'm sure we would have more answers if we knew who this was," Eric said. "Jace isn't dead, according to the note in the package."

Her heart quickened with hope. "Note? What note? What did it say?"

Eric looked sideways at Quincy, who rose and went to her. "It doesn't matter," Quincy said, taking her into his arms. "C'mon, why don't you just...."

She pushed him away and glared at her brother. "Tell me what was in the note."

Obviously resigned to telling her, he said, "If you want to see Jace alive, you're to come alone."

"Where?"

Quincy grabbed her arm, anxiety making him unusually rough. "Do you think I would let you go meet up with a sadistic psychopath?"

Kendal shook her head peevishly and stepped away. "We've got to do something," she shouted. "This is a man's life we're talking about. For now...."

"Sis, please. Dad is on a flight out of D.C. He'll be here within the hour. I'm sure he'll agree you should go to Spokane, or even to a federal safe house."

"I don't care what he agrees to," she said stubbornly. "This has gone on long enough. And why is he even involved?" Something fierce and unruly was building inside her. The sensation was frightening, but in that instant she decided to ride it to its end. She turned to Sheila. "I'm staying right here. But I want you and Marcy to go on. You shouldn't be in the middle of this."

Eric leveled one of his serious stares at her. "Sis, I know how you feel. But Dad has every right to be informed about what's going on with you. After all, he is your father."

"My father?" she snapped. "Dad has been immersed in politics our entire lives. And for the past few weeks I've been in a virtual prison. Where has he been?"

She cringed when Quincy squeezed her shoulder. "Kendal, your dad was advised to stay away. You know that; you're just upset."

She swung around to face him. "But nothing has happened, Quincy. Can't you see? I've got to do this. Jace is probably out of his mind with fear. I know how frightening that can be. And it's all my fault."

"But he didn't leave any directions. You wouldn't know where to go. Can't you see he's just toying with you?"

Quincy drew her close, and she reluctantly rested her head against his chest. "I'm just fed up with this waiting game."

"I know, sweetheart. But you've got to calm down. Don't let this push you into reacting rashly."

She pressed her head against the soft fabric of his shirt. "Jace was my responsibility. Now he's hurt. If I've done something that God— something I need to repent for, then I will. Jace shouldn't have to pay."

He drew back and gazed into her face. "Kendal, God isn't punishing you. He doesn't operate like that...."

Eric chimed in. "Sis, I'm sorry. It's me that's made a mess of things."

"Why would you say that?"

"I pushed this case on Cashion. I went about getting their attention the wrong way." He shrugged." Maybe I just wanted to make my mark, but that doesn't mean I was entirely wrong. It just means I went about doing what was right the wrong way."

What her brother said reminded Kendal of what Quincy had told her about his own situation. She softened when she saw the turmoil in his face. "Eric, I know you're trying to make me feel better. But this isn't your fault."

Their eyes locked. "This is one of the craziest cases I've been involved in. And me bulldozing my way in didn't help matters."

"What do you mean?"

"We've regularly accused Dad of twisting arms and manipulating the justice system, but I've done my share of riding on his influence. It took everything flying back into my face to realize my ego was placing your life in jeopardy, and I'm sorry about that."

The tension was so heavy in the room, Kendal could hardly breathe. Three pairs of eyes were watching her, waiting for her to either explode or fall apart. "That has very little to do with my decision to take control of my own life. You've all done your jobs—more than should have been expected. But I won't be able to live with myself if I let this monster continue to torture an innocent man."

Before anyone could comment further, Kendal strode decisively from the room.

Forty-five minutes later, Kendal heard her bedroom door open. Sheila tiptoed in, her eyes narrowed with suspicion. "I thought that martyr bit came on a little too strong."

"I'm not trying to be a martyr," Kendal whispered, tiptoeing towards the door. "I just want this over with. Is Dad here yet?"

"Yeah. You coming down?"

"No, I don't want to see him right now, Sheila. I need to get online." She opened the door a crack and listened intently. "What's going on down there?"

"Online?" Sheila asked, looking at her curiously. "You think he's sent another e-mail?"

Kendal came away from the door and plopped down on the bed, gazing at her friend's agitated face. "I don't know, but I want to check before Eric does."

"The FBI is tapped into your connection. Remember?"

Kendal shook her head. "That was before Walt was arrested." She looked down at her trembling hands, feeling guilty that she couldn't tell her friend that she had already received mail from him at the private web-mail account. "I've got to find a way to free Jace, Sheila."

"I know you're worried. So am I," Sheila said, joining her friend on the bed. "But you're really not responsible for what this nut does. It's too bad he uses a different server every time he sends you an e-mail. Eric said the FBI has identified the public places he uses. Most of them even have cameras, but each time, he wears a clever disguise. He's obviously pretty sharp."

Kendal waved impatiently and eased back to the door. "He'll slip up. Evil always does. But right now I need to get downstairs to the computer. Is the door to the dining room open?"

"Probably so. It's kind of nice seeing them all in the living room talking. So why are you so mad at your dad?"

Kendal purposely avoided the question. She didn't want to tell Sheila that he might be her biological father. Not yet, anyway. All these years, she thought, all these years without a single word about who her mother was, or why Tessa Boyd had even agreed to raise her. She couldn't help wondering what else her dear old dad had lied about.

But she couldn't think about that now. She had to find a way to help Jace. And Sheila was interfering with her game plan. Sheila scooted back on the bed, making herself comfortable. Kendal turned and shifted under her scrutiny. "What?"

"Do you realize this is the first time I've ever seen you in love?"

Now leaning against the door, unable to keep the smile she felt from emerging. "I know. I don't know if I deserve him. I mean, I thank God for him…for finally being able to feel. But there's something scary there, too." She stared at her friend. "What if he decides I'm not right for him? What if he disappears again?"

Sheila giggled. "Honey, he had no choice in that."

"I know. But it sure didn't feel very good not knowing why."

"There are uncertainties all around us, but we can't let them stop us from enjoying life. Besides, I don't think you have anything to worry about. He and your dad seem to be enjoying each other. Eric went to take a shower."

Kendal's brow knotted. "I wish I wasn't so abnormal, Sheila."

"What's normal? You just take on too much responsibility for things beyond your control. Your dad, me and Marcy, even poor Jace. You need to relax and allow the Lord to do what he wants in your life and ours."

"But I'm trying. Now that Quincy will be living in Seattle, I'm feeling obligated to be a certain way. Maybe he expect…."

"Quincy is a good man, Kendal. He's mature enough in the Lord to have no expectations of you. And he has nothing to do with your irritation towards your father or with the things that are happening now. If you mess this up, I'll never let you forget it."

"I really don't want to," Kendal said, fidgeting. "But I'll probably run him off before things get going good. I wish my faith was more steady. I vacillate so much the Lord probably doesn't know what to make of me. "

"Don't be so down on yourself. God doesn't waste his time. He brought Quincy into your life at this time for a reason."

Kendal lowered her eyes and went back to the bed. "Sheila, maybe something is really wrong with me. I feel like I might be going crazy. Quincy doesn't need a crazy woman."

"What are you talking about?"

"Jack Sumner. I've been having memory flashes...almost like on television. They're scary."

"That animal," Sheila said, springing up from the bed. "If he weren't already dead I'd wish he were."

Kendal giggled in spite of herself and moved to embrace Sheila. "Your friendship means a lot to me. Don't worry. I'm sure I'll be fine. And I was just spouting off about Dad. My emotions are just bouncing around." She looked hard at Sheila. "Seriously, if you want to go to Spokane, please feel free. I would feel better knowing that you and Marcy were safe."

"I'm staying right here with you," Sheila said. "I'll have Lance and his mother take Marcy for a while."

Kendal peered around anxiously, not wanting Marcy out of her sight. Hopefully, she could stop this psycho before he focused in on her again.

"Will you help me get downstairs without being seen?"

Sheila's eyes were filled with doubt. "I think you should let Eric take care of this Jace thing. But if you're determined to get on the computer...I've got to take clean linen to the basement for your dad. I'll go down the front and you go down through the kitchen. When I get to the dining room, I'll slide the door shut so you can slip in from the kitchen."

Her friend's cunning surprised Kendal. After a moment, she started laughing. "Sheila Marie Dodd, you're as sneaky as they come. You're really into this, aren't you?"

She smiled modestly. "I just want this over—just like you. And I intend to go with you if you plan to meet him."

Kendal stood. "Absolutely not. You have Marcy to think about."

"Kend...."

Kendal's hand flew up between them. "Sheila, I love you, too. But like the notes warned, I'm to do this alone."

Quincy admired the congressman's forthrightness. The instant they were alone, he had asked what Quincy's intentions were concerning his daughter. Obviously, Eric—or even Kendal herself—had informed him that they were a couple. He tried to quiet the pang of guilt he felt for having relayed information to his son that might create more division in the family.

Stan listened patiently as Quincy attempted to put his feelings into words. "I have to admit...I'm still not certain where this is all going, sir. But I am in love with your daughter. Naturally, I've been praying about it. I don't intend adding complications to her life; she's had enough of those."

"Prayer? That's good. I would suggest not making a move without it. I hope she's doing the same thing." He paused for several long seconds before continuing. "I assume from your comment that Kendal told you something of her past."

"I know about Jack Sumner."

"She must trust you."

"I hope so."

"Be patient with her, Quincy. She still has quite a way to go in the healing process. Even though I've been expecting her to remember everything, I've been worried about how it'll affect her attitude—her outlook."

Recalling Eric's suspicions, Quincy asked, "What do you mean?"

"Well, Kendal used to be a high-spirited little daddy's girl. She can still be high-spirited, but it is generally unleashed in anger. Jack Sumner's mischief turned an energetic child into a gloomy, angry one, full of misgivings and fear." He placed his feet up on the coffee table and leaned back. "Don't get me wrong. I'm glad to see her energy, but I hate that it took this ugly situation to get her going."

Quincy nodded understanding. At the edge of his focus, he saw Sheila coming down the stairs with a stack of linen. He turned and watched her pause at the foot of the stairs. She then pulled the dining room door closed and stepped just to the living room door. "Stan, I'll make up your bed downstairs. I know you must be tired after your flight."

Her kindness reminded Quincy of the first night he had stayed in their home. Stan turned his head slightly. "Thanks, Sheila. I just hope my snoring doesn't keep my son awake. I'm disappointed Kendal's already turned in. The last time we talked on the phone it got pretty heated."

Sheila, still in the hallway, chuckled lightly and continued toward the kitchen while Quincy turned back to Stan. "I think her agitation toward you might be my fault. I've been helping in her search for her birth parents."

Stan rested an arm on a cushion. "Nah, son, I don't blame you. Bless her heart. She's been stretched pretty tight since the FDA accused her in all this mess. She just didn't have anyone else to lash out at," Stan said. "Kendal's felt abandoned by me for years. Maybe you can help her fill that lack in her life. I hope the two of you will find great happiness together."

Quincy felt as if a great weight had lifted. "Thank you, sir. I'll do my best."

"I know she's frustrated and anxious to get on with the rest of her life. I want that for her more than she does, if that were possible."

Quincy liked the congressman very much, even more than he had before. Not just because he had given him and Kendra his blessing, but also because he wasn't forceful or demanding in his manner. He was almost tempted to warn him that Kendal knew about Stephanie Baylor, but thought better of it. He knew it wasn't easy to be on the receiving end of Kendal's wrath.

Eric returned and sat next to his dad on the couch, and Quincy at last relaxed. The Boyd men were both slumped down, their feet resting on the coffee table. In the face of the present danger, Eric had beaten himself up over suspecting his dad of foul play in the death of Jack Sumner, as well as cheating on his mother. But he still needed to confront the issue—something his sister also needed to do in regard to her own conflicts.

Stan Boyd checked the time. "It's only nine-thirty, but I'm still on eastern time. I really needed to talk to Kendal."

"This is one Memorial Day that will not be easily forgotten, Dad. She's had a rough day."

Stan took his feet off the table and leaned forward, clasping his hands. "Tell me about the abducted man. I know he works for her. Does she know him well?"

Eric rested an elbow on the arm of the couch. "I can't say she knows him all that well. As you know, Hadley fired him. He's been a great employee, even dropping things by the house."

Stan frowned. "I don't understand a young man taking such a big step down."

"Yeah. We believe there's a lot more to this than meets the eye. We're trying to determine the connection, if any, between the two cases. We think Jace was fired because he got caught snooping into what Hadley and Peck were involved in. I'm not sure I understand why Hadley, a confessed murderer, would let him live. But that's not the issue."

"It might be that Jace had been blackmailing them," Stan said. "I mean, if he knew about Hadley and Peck, what would stop him from purposely seeking out Kendal for a job…."

"I thought about that after he made a comment to Quincy about knowing everything that went on at Howard-Hadley," Eric said. "Apparently, there's been a lot of that going on. Ms. Howard mentioned that Hadley had attempted to blackmail her. But there was something missing in her logic."

"Olivia's a shrewd woman, but she's basically honest. If you like, I can talk to her and see if I can nudge her a little more."

"That might be helpful," Eric said. "Dad, can you clear up the mystery of Kendal and Stephanie Baylor?"

Uh, uh, Quincy said to himself.

"I know what you're asking, Son, but that's something I need to discuss with Kendal first."

"Fair enough."

Feeling like an intruder, Quincy stood and got his keys from his pocket. "I need to get back to the hotel and figure out how I can get my apartment packed up without my being there. I've already called the moving company."

An hour later, he was once again looking over notes he had made while shadowing with Kendal. He had left out a lot of things other reporters would have exploited. Kendal had liked his angle on the father-daughter piece and had given as much background as she could remember. He smiled as he remembered how her eyes would brighten when she told stories of their times together.

He paused and thought of her earlier outburst. In spite of her forceful protests to the contrary, it was clear she cherished Stan Boyd. And he, of course, adored her.

He put his notes into the file Joe had given him. Seeing the picture of Kendal and Eula Boyd brought a smile to his face. He would love to have known the lady who warmed everyone with her practical parables.

Closing the file, he wondered if it was too soon to ask Kendal to marry him. Perhaps he could even get her to take some time off and fly back with him. His aunt had already started in on him to bring her to Atlanta.

-TWENTY-SIX-

Kendal sensed the radiance of daybreak beckoning her awake. Recalling the words in the e-mail she had opened last night, she felt an unpleasant sensation in the pit of her stomach.

I will let this groveling insect exist until midnight Saturday unless you meet me at the intersection of Sanction Road and Mulberry Pass off 410. Saturday morning, ten sharp. If not, next package will be his skull.

Anguish ballooned as she thought of the area she had located on the map. It was isolated and densely wooded. Her biggest obstacle would be the federal surveillance. She had to find a way to sneak past the agents in broad daylight. She tried to think clearly. She still had four days to come up with a plan.

She straightened the comforter and grabbed her bag. She had a lot of arrangements to make at the shop. The temp would deliver them.

"Knock. Knock."

Her head snapped up. "Honey, it's Dad. May I come in?"

The grief she had been fighting rose dangerously close to the surface. "Yes, of course."

Dressed in a casual shirt and khaki trousers, Stan Boyd stepped into her room. His eyes were steady, his presence almost overwhelming, but his movements were hesitant.

"Hi, Dad," she murmured, instinctively moving into his arms. She felt horrible for the things she had said. He had chastised himself for years for not being with her and Eric while they were growing up. And she had gone and flung it at him as if he could turn back the hands of time. She had been agitated and annoyed when she called him. She knew she had to make things right. Still, she agonized over how to broach the subject of her mother.

Her father kissed her cheek and stepped back to study her face. "Still my girl?"

She smiled and bobbed her head up and down. He headed for the wing chair next to the window, then motioned for her to sit down. She sat on the foot of her bed facing him.

"Dad, I'm sorry. I was horrid. I should have called back by now and apologized." She could see his hand go up.

"You'd better let me go first. I know there's a lot going on in your life right now…some very serious things. The things you said in your outburst were strong, Kendal. I didn't realize you distrusted me that much."

"I didn't mean to let my emotions fly out like that. And I didn't mean most of the things I said. I just had to say them."

He smiled and lifted an eyebrow. "I think I understand."

"It's just that I feel so helpless. I want to be normal. I want to have a family of my own. I love you and Eric, but I feel as if I have no top or bottom to *me*. I don't know who I am, or what I could offer children." Kendal closed her eyes and tried to keep her emotions in check. "What's going on with this psycho aside, I don't even know how to relax and be happy. Ever since Walt walked into Eric's little trap— which he just happened to forget to mention—things I haven't thought about in years have resurfaced. I'm not sure what to make of them."

He smiled slightly. "That might be good, honey. Quincy said you told him about Sumner."

She nodded, without meeting his eyes. "I've been dreaming about him. I see another man there, too, Dad. But I wake up before I see his face."

"I like Quincy," Stan said, crossing his knees. "Tell me how *you* feel about him."

A wide grin appeared. "I feel so alive with him, Dad. I never knew it could be like this. The last few days though, I've felt numb—like the old me. It scares me a little. I don't want to go backwards."

"You have to stay hooked up to your source of strength, baby. That's the only way I've been able to make it."

"I'm not sure I know how. I feel like I'm vacillating in my faith walk."

"It's probably all the stress." He leaned forward and took her hand. "Eric has you well protected. Nobody can get to you."

She shook her head. "But I can't continue to live like this. And it's not just that. I'm scared to remember everything. I'm scared I might not want a future with Quincy if I remember."

He squeezed her hand. "Don't ever forget to factor God into these tight places, baby girl. I know Mama raised you to acknowledge him in everything. It's *time* to remember."

She nodded and managed a troubled smile. He hadn't called her that in a long time. It felt good.

"I'm right here, Kendal. But my arms aren't big enough to hold you right now. I can try. I *have* tried. But God wants you to trust him to hold you—to be with you through everything."

"I know."

"What about this baby business? You still want to do this?"

She answered without hesitation. "I don't think so. I wouldn't want to put a child through what I've been through—the wondering when you see a stranger that have your eyes, all of the why questions, feeling abandoned at the slightest unpleasant occasion. I need to listen for God's direction on a lot of things. But I feel like I'm at a real wall for some reason."

He stood up, still holding her hand. "I need to tell you about your birth mother."

Her sudden intake of breath prompted him to squeeze her hand again. His eyes had misted and she felt him shudder slightly. He was hurting.

He released her hand and stood by the window, his back to her. For a moment, he resembled the man she had known as a child—the man she had almost worshipped until that dreadful day she learned she was adopted. Despite the fact that she was once again wrestling with feelings of displacement, she wasn't certain she was ready to hear what he was about to tell her.

His hands shoved deep into his pockets, Stan Boyd's presence infused her room with an intense energy. She needed desperately to hear what he had to tell her, but she didn't want him to hurt. Despite her unease and perhaps in light of it, she could barely think straight. When he turned to face her, she took a deep breath. "I'm ready, Dad."

"Kendal, there's nothing I would like better than to say I was your biological father. But the truth is, I'm not. Eric tells me you've discovered her name. I love you, and despite bloodlines, you are my first born."

Her heart swelled with affection and gratitude. At age twenty-nine, she felt for the first time that she had heard precisely what she most needed to hear.

He smiled. "I suppose I felt a little threatened when I learned you were digging for information. I understand Eric's been digging a little, too. I think he believes I was unfaithful to Tessa."

Kendal stood and pressed her hand to her father's broad chest. "My need to know has nothing to do with my love and devotion for you. That will never change." Her breath quickened, realizing the truth in her words. "Do you know them…my birth parents?"

"Only your mother. I don't know anything about your father. Stephanie never told me. I never asked."

"I see."

"I visited the capitol regularly when I had the textile business, because Will…I mean Senator Howard had promised to help me with it, especially while I was still in the armed forces."

"How long had you known Senator Howard?"

"Will and I became friends when your grandfather died. He was very kind to your mother and me. He came into the general's office when I was trying to get a leave of absence to get a handle on the textile business. Will helped me find a manager and got his people to teach me things about the industry that Dad hadn't even told me."

"But why?"

"I don't really know. I guess that was just the kind of man he was. After a few years, he started asking me to consider entering politics. Your mother…Stephanie…we were just friends, Kendal. She was pretty much alone then, and very much aware that your mother and I couldn't have children. When she found out she wasn't going to make it after your birth, she had the senator witness her signature on documents granting us custody. She had an attorney draw up adoption papers right there in her hospital bed."

Kendal's knees would have buckled had her father not been there to hold her steady. "Why didn't you tell me earlier?" she whispered.

"I never thought it was necessary. When your mother got pregnant with Eric, we decided against ever telling you. After Sumner, I didn't have Tessa to help me think straight. I just didn't quite know how to talk to you about it. I know now that I should've stepped up and been a man about it."

"I wish you never would've had to. I mean…."

"I know what you mean, darling. And I can't tell you what it means to hear you say it. But in a world like this…our decision was an obvious mistake. We weren't thinking about politics at the time. We never wanted you to feel any different. We both loved you, Kendal. Then Jack Sumner walked into our lives." His face grew hard as he stared at the floor. "He was a devil from the pit of hell."

Her throat tightened as she watched her father's inner struggle play out on his face. All these years, he had tried to shield her from something that was an actual part of her. "I suppose I needed to know eventually."

"I know. But you were mine…mine and Tessa's. I raised the two of you alone for five years before Mama took over."

She purposely avoided the eyes filled with hurt and regret. "Then you had to go to Germany."

He nodded. Kendal pressed closer in her father's arms, releasing the hurt that had burned inside her for years. Her sobs were deep and uncontainable. He held her for a long time before she gently pulled away. "Thank you for coming to me."

"I'll be around a lot more after a few months."

She shot him a curious look. "What do you mean?"

"I've decided to retire, Kendal. I've already pulled my name from this year's ballot. They'll announce it in a few days."

"What?"

"I prayed about this a long time. I know it's too little too late, but you were right. I haven't been around for the two of you like I should have."

"Dad, I'll be thirty in December. Why…."

"I'm doing this for me, darling. I've missed too much. I'm ready to meddle and enjoy a lapful of grandchildren."

She grinned, her heart thumping with excitement. "Does Eric know?"

He shook his head. "I wanted you to be the first."

She hugged him again and kissed his cheek. "You sure you want to do this?"

He smiled and chucked her chin. "I am."

"I'm sorry, Dad, but it's after eight and I've got to get to the shop. You coming?"

"I have a meeting with Olivia this morning. Then I'm going to Spokane, and then back to Washington." He paused. "Does Eric realize you're going in today?"

She nodded. "An agent will be with me. Eric is more surprised that these are two different cases. He feels I'm in no real danger since this guy has stated his demands, especially since they have me caged in by agents."

"Yeah. There is one waiting for you downstairs," he said, moving toward the door. "Were you surprised about Hadley Jr.?"

"Yeah. I'll be glad when it's all over, though."

"Me, too." He smiled and tightened his arm around her shoulders. As she had done as a child, Kendal placed her ear to his heart. "I know you're safe, but I still hate leaving you. Eric thinks it's wise that I stay at a distance. You sure you and Sheila won't go to the house?"

She shook her head. "No. I think we'll be fine here. I know it'll be over real soon. Besides, we have responsibilities."

"I know," he said, nodding. "By the way, Quincy wanted me to tell you he'll come around to the shop later. He's out looking for an apartment. I'll drop you off, unless you want to ride with your security."

"Apartment, huh?"

"Yeah. I think he plans to leave Saturday. He's got a lot of packing to do back east, and he'll need an address before he leaves." He grinned and patted her shoulder. "He's quite taken with you."

Kendal entered the shop as Sheila was ringing up a sale; Quincy was just coming through the curtains from the back. Her heart leapt at the sight of him. "You find an apartment already?"

He grinned sheepishly and lifted her off the floor. "Hello, beautiful. I just thought you two needed some time alone."

He put her down when his cellphone rang, walking toward the back to take the call. Kendal started to follow him, but stopped abruptly when she heard him exclaim, "Sherry!"

Kendal went to the worktable and began getting what she needed from the shelves. Sheila had organized some of the phoned-in orders so she could get started. From the corner of her eye, she could see Quincy shifting his body and could hear some of what he was saying.

"Yes, I am. I had no idea you were still in touch with them."

Despite feeling a tad nosey, Kendal strained to hear his responses to the caller. She made a big show of being busy, going to the walk-in and selecting a variety of cut flowers.

"Thank you. I wish you well, too."

Ending the call, Quincy came over to where she was working, trapping her in the L of the worktable. When he tried to kiss her, she sidestepped his move and became rigid. "Quincy, I don't mean to sound…I mean…I won't play games with you."

"Come sit down," he said, leading her to a stool. "I'll tell you all about it."

A prickling sensation moved up her spine as she sat down. He pulled another stool over and sat facing her. "That was my ex-wife, Kendal. We were married for two years."

"Eric mentioned her. But I've been so wrapped up in what's going on, I guess I forgot."

"Yeah, he told me he did."

"How do you feel about her now?"

"I love *you*, Kendal. My marriage to Sherry was over long before I spent that time in jail."

"Quincy, I know things are moving rather fast. But I don't want you to feel locked into our relationship just because you're moving to Seattle. I mean…things *did* happen for us pretty quickly."

He lifted her chin and gently kissed her lips. "Be quiet."

"I'm just saying that I understand if you don't want to have a girl-friend right now."

Ignoring her half-hearted offer, he continued showering her face and chin with kisses. "We both have a lot on our minds right now," he said, checking the time. "I really do have an apartment lined up to look at." He kissed the tip of her nose. "I love you, and I have no desire to change my mind about anything."

The foreboding Eric had felt all morning moved back over him like a shadow. Jace had put several memorandums on the diskettes. Making sense of them was difficult because they were written in a way that suggested he had been in a great hurry when he wrote them.

He had apparently witnessed a confrontation between Hadley and Peck. Returning to the office late one evening, he had heard the two men arguing over Kendal. Recalling their notion of blackmail as a possible reason for Jace's abduction, Eric felt an uneasy energy shooting through him. The Jace file also contained the contract between Olivia Howard and Walt Hadley Sr., the two stockholders. It was all fairly standard except for the clause she had mentioned. Only female heirs could assume ownership of the company. An heir could marry a Hadley and vice versa, but ownership would transfer only to female heirs.

He went to talk with Cashion, but he wasn't in his office. Hal Dalton, a tall, well-built agent sporting a buzz cut and a deep tan, strolled towards him.

"Hey, Eric, you look as if you just lost your ball."

"I may have. You know where Cashion got off to?"

"I saw him talking to your dad downstairs."

"Dad?"

As if on cue, Cashion walked in, a grin on his face. "Come into my office," he said. "Your dad's on his way to Spokane. He told me to tell you he'll phone tonight."

"Thanks."

"It seems Ms. Howard admitted to the congressman that Jace Tate had attempted to blackmail Hadley."

"She led us to believe she wouldn't have known anything about that."

"Apparently, you were right about her holding something back."

"And she's beginning to forget what she's already told us."

"Your dad got the same feeling. But if Jace Tate really tried to blackmail Hadley, he isn't just an innocent victim, certainly not a random one. I'll need to talk with the FDA agent again. Any other thoughts?"

"Umm. Something's still not connecting for me," Eric said. "Even if Jace tried to blackmail Hadley, it doesn't tell us who is out there now torturing him."

"You're right, of course."

"I was wondering if we could try to bluff Ms. Howard into revealing her niece's name?"

"I can't really see where that's necessary, Eric. Hadley is in custody, after all. Besides, you don't want to violate the terms of a personal legal document unless absolutely essential."

-TWENTY-SEVEN-

Kendal was in her bedroom, tossing a few things into a sack, when Sheila poked her head in. "You riding with me?"

"Yeah, I'll be ready in a minute. Has Eric already left?"

"Yeah," Sheila answered, gazing curiously after her friend. "You okay?"

"I've been so stupid, Sheila. Things I should've seen since the beginning of all this are just now trickling into my head."

"Talking about your dad?"

"Quincy, too. I feel as if I've been trapped in the twilight zone or something."

Sheila came all the way in and slumped down into the chair. "That's one of life's mysteries—things that should be clear are not. But with Jace still out there with this madman, it's only natural to feel a little zoned out." She yawned and added, "You feel like driving? I want to take a nap on the way in."

"Sure. It's been a long time since I've been behind the wheel."

Sheila pushed up from the chair. "You sure this weirdo hasn't given any more directions? I mean, why did he say, 'Come alone.' What does that mean? Come where alone? It's as if he's suddenly dropped off the face of the earth."

Kendal dodged the question, not wanting to lie to her friend. "We have to remember we're dealing with an unstable person. He'll tell me when he's ready."

She felt terrible for keeping so much from them. But she didn't want to be responsible for anyone else getting hurt, especially her little Marcy. It would only change a bad situation into a worse one. Rather than put Marcy at risk, it would be better for her to go and try to reason with him. Still, she couldn't help wondering if it was wise to keep crucial information to herself.

She had prayed for guidance, but hadn't gotten any direction. In light of that, she had to move forward with her plan. After all, Jace's life depended on it. Perhaps God would somehow give her the wisdom and ability to get them both out of this alive. She had to believe that. She had to.

"I know you think the feds are taking too long on this, Kendal. To be honest, I can't stop thinking about what Jace might be going through out there. But you *will* tell me the moment you hear something, right?"

"Of course," Kendal said, brushing imaginary lint from the bed. She jumped when Sheila's hand touched her shoulder.

"You wouldn't do anything foolish like…."

"Let's go, Sheila," Kendal interrupted, already headed for the door. "You know I wouldn't go off half-baked."

As they were backing out of the driveway, Kendal rolled the window down to produce a breeze through the car. The wind whipped through her shoulder-length curls, tickling her ears. She approached a curve and veered left, tires rumbling on the rough pavement.

After pulling onto Rose Creek's main highway, Kendal checked the rearview mirror. The agent wasn't behind them. She frowned and glanced back over her right shoulder. A white SUV was coming up fast. "Sheila, is that car getting a little close?"

Sheila glanced back and blurted, "Who is this nut? And where is our agent?"

Suddenly, the SUV pulled up beside them on the two-lane highway. Kendal heard the growl of the powerful engine and eased the car to the right. The other vehicle remained at her side, the driver seemingly unconcerned about oncoming traffic. Fear tightened in her stomach, and she pressed down on the accelerator.

"Oh, God. I think it's him," she said, her grip tightening on the steering wheel. "Get my cell and dial Eric."

The SUV's dark windows prevented her from getting a clear glimpse of the driver. Gravel crunching under the right front tire, signaled that she was leaving the road. She quickly pulled the wheel left.

"Be careful!" Sheila cried, pressing the phone to her ear. "It's ringing."

"Help us, Lord."

By now, Sheila was bouncing frantically in her seat. "Eric, somebody's trying to run us off the road. He's in a white SUV. We haven't seen our agent since we left the house."

Kendal's heart hammered as she listened to Sheila's shrill responses.

"No, I can't see the plate. He's beside us."

Kendal wiped her sweaty palms on her shirt and took her foot off the gas just as the SUV pulled in front of them. The driver hit the brakes. They both screamed as Kendal slammed on the brakes. The screeching tires heightened her anxiety of an imminent collision. Miraculously, they came to an abrupt halt after slightly hitting the other vehicle's bumper.

Kendal sat perfectly still, unsure what she would do if the driver got out and came toward them. Suddenly, the SUV revved its engine and sped off.

"Eric's on his way."

Kendal was still shaking when they arrived at the shop.

"Are you two all right?" Eric asked. "I can stay a little while longer if you like." She leaned back in the chair at her desk and closed her eyes.

He had followed them to the shop from the site of their encounter with the SUV. "We're fine, Eric. Where was the agent you put on us?"

"Apparently this guy disabled his car while he was inside the house. In his anxiety, he lost your cell number and called in just before Sheila did. That SUV was reported stolen two days ago."

"My God," Kendal said. "When will this be over?"

Eric placed a hand on her shoulder. "Soon, Sis. Quincy's on his way over from the hotel. "I've got to get back."

"Go on," she said, glancing toward another agent standing just inside the back room of the shop. "We're fine."

After she finished inputting the week's transactions, she decided to check her web mail account. She looked around, even getting up to peer through the curtain. The agent was out front watching Sheila spritz the plants.

She felt a ripple of eerie fear pass over her the instant she saw his latest message. This one was from 'watcher' at a different web mail address. The opened message read, *WATCH ATTACHMENT.*

Kendal looked around before opening the attachment. It was a video, and it began with a bruised and battered Jace writhing on the floor in a pool of blood. The horrific image caused her chest to tighten, and her breathing to become labored. The door chime sounded at the precise moment the room faded out.

-TWENTY-EIGHT-

Quincy's lip twitched as he pressed a damp cloth to Kendal's forehead. He had put her on Marcy's sleeping bag in the space beside her desk. "Agent Thomas, you mind phoning her brother?"

"Sure thing," he said, quickly going to the front.

He shook his head in frustration. The video segment was monstrous. He couldn't understand why this guy was dragging things out the way he was. This should have been over when they arrested Hadley. Given Kendal's exhaustion, the video had to have been an overwhelming shock. *Oh, God, please help them protect her. And keep Jace safe, too.*

Kendal pushed unsteadily at the cloth and tried to sit up. "Lie still, baby. As soon as you feel steady, I'll take you home."

Sheila approached with a cup of water, and Kendal sat up and wrapped her hand around it. Quincy stiffened momentarily when Agent Thomas handed him his cell. He pressed the phone to his ear. "Eric?"

"How is she?"

He stroked her flushed cheek and got to his feet, moving to the front. "She's fine. Just blacked out for a few seconds."

"Thomas told me about the video. I'm worried about how much more of this she can take. After being harassed on the highway this morning, and now this, her nerves are probably shattered."

"This video is bad, man. I want to take Kendal to Atlanta for a few days. She can stay with my aunt until I get my Baltimore apartment packed up."

"If you think you can talk her into it, I'll talk with Cashion and get it set up. You were right about this guy. It looks like he's succeeding in making her feel responsible for all this."

"I'll do my best," Quincy said.

"I'm tied up for a little while. I've asked Thomas to stay with Sheila at the shop," Eric said. "Take Kendal home and don't let her out of your sight. I'll send another car to the house."

Quincy was surprised Eric wasn't rushing to the house himself. "Sure. What's keeping you?"

"The locals just called us in on a suicide. It's Walt Hadley Sr."

"What!"

"He shot himself while on the phone with Ms. Howard. She's taking it pretty hard."

Quincy sighed in exasperation as he moved through I-90 traffic. "I'm only talking about a few days…a week at the most, Kendal. It would do you good."

"I appreciate what you're trying to do, but you know I can't leave right now. Not until Jace is found. Maybe when all this is over."

Quincy reached across the console, took her hand and lifted it to his lips. "I love the way you put everybody before yourself, honey, but this guy is juggling your sanity. I wish you would at least think about it before totally rejecting the idea."

She shook her head adamantly. "I can't see how I can leave right now, Quincy."

He waited until they arrived at the house before telling her about the death of the senior Hadley. When he did, her face remained expressionless, as it had when she described in detail the morning's highway incident. His chest seized. This guy had confronted her twice in one day. Things were clearly escalating. His intent was clearly to torment her. What would be next?

He relaxed in the chair in the living room and watched her drift off on the couch. At his insistence, she had taken another sedative. The afternoon stretched, but he was too shaken to feel, too befuddled to think and too disillusioned to pray. How could he get her to safety before this animal gets to her?

When he heard the hushed sound of her easy breaths he rested his face in his palms. *Lord.* The sudden opening of the back door jarred him. He hurried into the kitchen to find Eric unloading his briefcase onto the table. He looked anxious. "How is she?"

"Sleeping."

"Did you ask her about flying out to Atlanta?"

"She won't budge, Eric," he said, shoving his hands into his pockets. "I don't think she realizes how much danger she's in. It's like she has been lulled into a sleep. She barely reacted to the news about Hadley Sr. Can't you find a way to force her to go to Atlanta?"

"I think you know by now that nobody can force Kendal to do anything she doesn't want to do. I'm more concerned about why she has an e-mail account we knew nothing about."

"What?"

"I guess it's my fault," Eric said. "I should have been more thorough in monitoring her web access."

Quincy watched Eric leave the kitchen. He had been so worried about Kendal that he hadn't thought about how the e-mail had arrived. He was placing two mugs of coffee on the table when Eric returned. "Eric, it's strange but I feel as if something's about to blow. Waiting is bad enough, but watching what it's doing to her is torture. I don't mind telling you…I'm more afraid than I've ever been."

Eric walked to the table. "I know. I've been trying to keep my mind on the facts, but there's still something here that's similar to the Sumner case."

Quincy shook his head. "I'm sorry, Eric, but I think you're way off track. Our main concern should be keeping Kendal away from this maniac *now*."

Eric remained quiet for a long while. "You're right, of course. But this gut feeling is more than what you termed 'my obsession.' I've been praying about it, but the nagging hasn't let up."

Quincy took a gulp of his coffee. "Let's talk about the matter at hand. What happened with Hadley?"

"Funny that you mentioned Kendal's lack of response. Hadley Jr. sat like a stone when we told him, too. It was as if he weren't even listening."

"It's a bad situation all around. Who do you think this other guy is?"

"My gut would say it was Sumner. But I know better," Eric said, turning his eyes toward the window. "Maybe I do need to see a shrink."

"How is Olivia?"

"She's holding her own. Dad talked with her earlier. She admitted that Jace tried to blackmail Hadley Jr."

Quincy rubbed his forehead in frustration. "Why didn't she just tell us that the other day? Maybe now that Hadley Sr. is dead and Jr. is imprisoned, she'll give you a little more information on this niece."

"If Jr. couldn't get the name out of her, I don't know how I would. I don't know anymore that it really matters."

"Why did she even have Hadley Jr. running her company, especially with her distrust of him so obvious."

"Guilt, I think. I guess after Jr. found out about the contract and questioned his dad, Hadley Sr. became hostile towards her. He apparently hadn't realized what he had done to his son. After the arrest, he lost it, too. He called Ms. Howard this afternoon, and while talking to her on the phone, blew his brains out with a .32."

Quincy had an unsettling thought. "Then the person behind this has nothing to gain, and much to lose, by releasing Jace alive. And that still doesn't tell us why he's after Kendal."

"Remember when I thought Kendal might know something she didn't know she knew?"

"But that was before Peck's body was found."

"I know. I checked the twenty-year-old timeline to see if there was a possibility Sumner could be Kendal's dad. As far as I could determine, he had never been out of the state of Washington. And based on what I could find on Stephanie, she had never visited."

"Which brings me to another question," Quincy said, suddenly sensing the certainty of something ominous. "What, besides the identification of her niece, could Jace have on Olivia?"

-TWENTY-NINE-

Kendal's cellphone rang early the next morning, jarring her awake. She answered it quickly, noticing that it was still dark outside.

"I changed my mind," he whined. "Just in case you're trying to set me up, I want you to meet me in two hours. Same place."

Startled, she willed herself into full alertness. "What?"

He chuckled. "I thought I would throw in a wrinkle or two. I enjoy toying with those federal clowns. Your brother really should find himself another profession. Eight o'clock sharp, or he dies. And remember, my next victim is Marcy." The line was disconnected before Kendal could say another word.

In her bathrobe and with her pulse racing, Kendal hurriedly prepared bacon and eggs and baked a canister of cinnamon rolls. She shook as she thought about what she had to do. More than anything in the world she wanted to marry and have a baby of her own; despite having found true love with Quincy, she had to go through with her plan. She knew she belonged to God, and he had given her the desire of her heart—one for which she had nearly lost hope. She was loved by, and in love with, the man of her dreams. And she trusted that He would keep her and Jace safe and help make this situation right.

Acutely aware that she would never be content knowing she had traded Jace and Marcy's life for her own happiness, she was determined to go through with her plan. She had to do something to save Jace. Although she felt foolish and wild with fear, she simply had to trust God for the outcome.

Kendal closed her eyes as agitation moved through her like a firestorm. *Lord, give me strength to do what I have to. I ask for your protection in this matter. I want to live. Give me ears to hear your voice and grace to obey.*

In a moment of hesitation, she glanced toward the door to the basement. Maybe if she gave Eric the messages he didn't know about, he would know what to do to save Jace. Still, her deception might cost her Marcy, and there had already been too much death.

The house filled with the comforting aromas of breakfast as she pulled the cinnamon rolls from the oven. Though she had planned the breakfast for tomorrow morning, she quickly set the table and went to the door to beckon Agent Sullivan inside. He followed her into the kitchen and sat down at the table where she served him a plate, coffee and juice.

"You didn't have to do this, Kendal. I could've grabbed a couple of donuts a little later."

"Donuts! It's a wonder you guys are still able to move after eating the poison you do." She forced a hearty-sounding laugh. "I'm going up and take a shower and dress. I'll be back. Eric should be up as soon as the aroma grabs his senses."

Feeling considerably deceptive, Kendal grabbed Sheila's keys from the tray behind the sofa and hurried back to her room.

She pulled off the robe she had worn over her jeans and shirt, and put on a pair of running shoes. Knowing Agent Sullivan would hear the front door, she widened the opening of her bedroom window, pulled on gardening gloves and carefully crawled out onto the lattice. Positioning each foot into the square-shaped sections, Kendal made her way down.

By the time she moved around through the gate and across the driveway to the car, her face had been pricked and scratched by thorns to the point of drawing blood. A sick feeling settled in her stomach, and the clammy heat under her skin produced a sticky perspiration. She took a deep, cleansing breath and gripped the steering wheel so hard her knuckles ached.

"Lord, please help me."

-THIRTY-

Something had jolted Quincy awake. What was it? The clock on the table showed it was eight o'clock.

He grabbed the ringing telephone. "Morgan."

"She's gone, Quincy. She duped Sullivan and went out through her bedroom window. That monster succeeded in luring her away."

Quincy shook himself, confused. "What? Gone where? When?"

"This morning," Eric said, his voice strained. "I found several messages we never knew about in the floor of her closet."

Quincy threw back the covers and scrambled out of bed. "You sure she wasn't just running to the store?"

"She took Sheila's car. Sheila believes she's been planning this for a couple of days now. She's offering herself in exchange for Jace and Marcy. He's been keeping her quiet by threatening to take Marcy next."

A sickening wave of terror engulfed him as his eyes went to the small box on the table by the window. He had planned to ask her to marry him today.

"Quincy, listen. I need you to come over to the house as soon as you can. Jackson's due in court and Sheila is coming apart. I've got to meet with the team."

Quincy quickly pulled on a pair of jeans and fumbled with the buttons of his shirt. In a haze so thick he couldn't think, he grabbed his keys and rushed through the door. His mind and was filled with her, making him numb and devoid of logic. *Lord, please.*

Ten minutes later, Sheila opened the front door and fell into his arms. Quincy carefully maneuvered them inside. "It's my fault, Quincy. I should've told you guys she got a message the other night," she said between sniffles. "I never thought she would do this."

He frowned. "The other night? Before the video at the shop?"

She gulped and nodded. "She didn't let me see it. I had no idea she had planned to sacrifice herself for Marcy." Sheila started to wail and once again collapsed against him. "Oh, God. I've killed my best friend."

Quincy took her by the shoulders and shook her gently. "Sheila, don't say that. Don't you dare say that. Is Marcy still with her dad?"

She nodded. "He'll keep her until this is over."

"I need you to print all the e-mails that are still there. Maybe there's something Eric missed. Go through her deleted files, too."

Sheila nodded and went to the dining room, probably thankful to have something to do. He wished he could cry as unabashedly as she did.

Lord, I need your help. My mind and will are running in too many directions. Help me slow down and hear.

His cellphone rang and sat on a lower step of the staircase. "Eric?"

"We can't get anything out of Hadley. Olivia has no ideas that could lead us to Kendal, but she did have some explosive revelations I'll tell you about later."

Anguish was building in every pore of Quincy's body. Frustrated, he slammed his fist into the wall. "What do we do now, Eric? How can we find her?"

"Look around her bedroom. Look good, and call me back if you find anything at all."

"What am I looking for?"

"A slip of paper, a pad she might've written on, anything."

New hope sprang up in his chest as he took the stairs two at a time. He walked down the hall and moved to the room decorated in blue and white. His eyes felt hot as cold fear coursed through him.

"Help us, God. Help us find her before it's too late."

Suddenly, a strange sensation fell over him and words seemed to pour through every fiber of his being. *Fear not. Trust me, and I'll give you more than you can ask or hope.*

Despite the pounding in his chest, Quincy breathed easier and continued to open and search through drawers. He looked through the closet and even went down the hall to the bathroom. There was nothing.

As he reentered her room, a gust of wind propelled the curtains into a light dance. His eyes instinctively moved to the open window and stared down into the side yard. She had shimmied down the side of the house using the old-fashioned trellis.

Quincy hurriedly went through the rest of the house, recalling her guarded manner yesterday. Soon he was back in the hallway. He sat down on the steps, holding his head in his hands. He had known she wouldn't be able to take the thought of Jace being tortured. Why hadn't he done something more to convince her to leave.

Who was he kidding? Kendal wouldn't have gone anywhere if she thought Marcy might be in danger.

The ringing of his cellphone interrupted his onrushing thoughts. "Eric?"

"Quincy, this is Bev. I got busy on some other matters and never got back with you. But I found something else on that Sumner matter."

Quincy stood up, irritation making his voice sound shrill. "Sumner?"

Something inside signaled him to be still and listen. After Bev hung up, he raced down the stairs and called to Sheila. She moved towards him, a hopeful look on her tear-stained face. "I've printed these," she said, handing him several sheets. "This one was in her 'keeper' file. It has his demands. I don't think Eric has seen it."

Quincy read through the printouts and headed to the basement. He nervously reached into Eric's drawer for his second handgun, and ran to the car while dialing Eric on his cell.

"I know who has her. Pick me up at the shop. I have the location where she was to meet him. We might need to get over to Mrs. Tate's."

"We're on our way."

Quincy skidded to a halt right next to Kendal's Sable and retrieved his briefcase from the back seat. He pulled out the dossier Joe had given him and flipped through the clippings. Joe wouldn't have known to pull the article Bev had found. The little girl was never named.

He remembered Eric's description of Mrs. Tate's proud assertion that Jace could imitate his father's voice. He jumped out and got into the Sable with Eric and Sullivan.

Kendal stood on the desolate road for ten minutes before the white SUV stopped in front of her. It was the same vehicle that had harassed her and Sheila on the highway. She frowned and glanced around as someone shoved open the passenger door.

Her heart leapt with delight. It was Jace. The back of his head was bandaged and his face bruised. Her throat constricted.

"Get in. Quick. He's watching."

Wary, she looked around, unable to move. Her throat was dry; her breathing difficult. She tried to think. Something wasn't right. "But...."

"Do you want him to kill us?" he asked in desperation. "Hurry. Get in."

She moved to the door but couldn't make herself get inside. Jace took hold of one of her wrists and pulled her in.

"Jace, are you all right? Did he hurt you much?"

"We've got to get back."

Her eyes jerked around as he reached over and pulled the door shut. "We can get away."

Kendal's heart froze the instant she saw the wide grin spread across Jace's face. "You're a beautiful person, Kendal. Inside and out. You risked your life to rescue me...somebody you hardly know. I was counting on that."

Her blood went cold. "Jace?"

"You're so gullible and spotless. I hate to destroy such virtue." He stroked her face and curls, a tremor in his voice. "Eye for an eye," he said, using the voice she remembered from the phone calls.

She jerked away and pushed open the car door. The jump wasn't difficult. The car was barely moving down the barren road. Just as she bounded toward a barbed wire fence, Jace grabbed her around the waist. "Stop that! Stop it now, or I'll hang you from the nearest tree."

He pulled her back and trapped her against the side of the car. She screamed, and then thrashed about when he clamped his fingers around her throat. "Your precious Mr. Morgan can't help you now," he said. "I intend to make you pay for everything I've missed in my life."

He started to laugh then, and Kendal felt something like a cold fist closing around her heart. She had fallen victim to her own naiveté, and been deceived by her benevolent inclinations. Her heart sank as she succumbed to the feeling of betrayal.

Jace held her hands behind her and pulled a roll of duct tape and twine from inside the vehicle. "Why?"

He grinned viciously and without turning her around, secured her hands with the twine. Then he jerked open the car door. She kicked out, hitting him in his shin.

He abruptly punched her jaw, and she fell screaming to her knees in the road. He kicked her in her side and stomach so hard she couldn't breathe. Then he grabbed and shoved her into the vehicle.

"Please don't."

Jace plastered a length of duct tape over her mouth and pulled a snub-nosed sidearm from the glove box. "I'll use it, Kendal."

The look in his eyes convinced her.

He held the revolver on her as he walked around to the driver's side and climbed in.

-THIRTY-ONE-

Kendal sneezed several times while sizing up the small room. Sunlight streamed through two grimy windows. The acrid smell of mold and mildew stung the back of her throat. She rolled over and winced in pain. Jace had removed the tape from her mouth, but her hands and ankles were still bound. Her muscles ached from lying in the same position too long.

She could tell by the dust and cobwebs covering everything that the house had been vacant for some time. Mildew covered the far wall, and the weeds waving outside the window nearly reached the top. Jace had apparently brought her to an old abandoned house. But why?

She glanced around. The sound of her pounding pulse was deafening in her ears. There was something familiar about the room.

"Am I going to die?" she whispered. "Speak to me, Lord. Make me hear you again."

Her mind tried to seize a hovering memory, but it slipped from her grasp. When it resurfaced, she lay still and closed her eyes, refusing for the first time to let fear steal her memories.

"You're my daddy's friend," she said to the blue-eyed man with white hair. She gasped as she realized who he was. Her father had taken several pictures with him.

"Yes, I am, sweetheart. C'mon, let's put your things back on. I won't let anything bad happen to you."

"Is Mr. Sumner really my daddy?"

"No, he's not. Mr. Sumner was trying to trick you. You must be careful from now on. Never trust strangers."

"Yes, sir. Is my daddy coming?"

"Yes. He'll be with you soon." The man smiled. *"When we get your shoes on, I want you to run as fast as you can now. Don't ever look back. Understand?"*

"Yes, sir."

"Promise me."

"I promise. I won't ever look back."

Jace toyed with the rope and moved quietly down the hall to his parents' old bedroom. He peered through the hole he had made in the door. She was awake. He pushed it open and strode inside.

"You're awake?"

She glared up at him. "What do *you* think? Jace, you need help. Let me…."

He laughed and pulled her into a sitting position. She quickly pushed herself away from him, and towards the headboard. "You've always had just the right amount of fire, Kendal Boyd."

"Why are you doing this?"

"For my father," he said, tossing the rope through an exposed beam. "I was a boy when he died."

"I didn't even know your father. What do I have to do with his death?"

Jace carefully worked the long rope into a hangman's noose and moved to sit next to her. "Maybe not. But he knew you."

He could smell her fear, and his adrenaline surged.

"What do you mean?"

"My father lost his job just because he wanted to gain something better for his family. His mistake was digging too deep into the life of a small-town hero. This hero later became a congressman." He laughed sardonically and gazed into her confused expression. "Let me start off by introducing myself. My given name is Jonathan Jace Sumner. My mother changed it to Tate after my father done himself in."

"Jack Sumner was your…."

Jace narrowed his eyes and nodded. "He hung himself right there, you know."

"Jace, I was a child. Your father kidnapped me. Why are you blaming me for what happened to him?"

"Because getting too close to you was his downfall. You see…the hero wasn't the only one who wanted to protect Princess Kendal. So did Senator Howard."

"What?"

"I wasn't lying about knowing who your parents were. I've got all the documentation right here. My dad spent months researching it."

"I don't believe you."

"Does Stephanie Baylor ring a bell with you?" he asked.

Her eyes widened.

"I see it does. How did you find out?"

"What difference does it make?" she snapped.

"What about your father's? Do you know his name?"

She shrugged. "I think I do. But I'm not sure."

"My daddy did. Not only did I find it in his notes, I found it on Walter Hadley Jr.'s computer. That's when he fired me."

"Why would he…."

"Senator Howard was married," he said, his eyes glistening. "He had an affair with Stephanie, who happened to be African American."

Kendal gasped. "So it's true. William Howard *was* my father?"

He laughed. "Stephanie Baylor only lasted a week after giving birth."

Tears rolled down Kendal's cheeks. He leaned closer and brushed them away.

"Please don't cry," he said, his voice breaking. "I can't stand it when you're sad."

"Dad lost the mothers of both his children in childbirth," she whispered.

"I planned to blackmail Olivia. Stan Boyd, too. But I found out she was already being blackmailed by Walt Jr." He shrugged. "Besides, getting fired changed my plans a little. I just want you to pay."

He moved closer and gripped her arm. "C'mon."

She struggled, but he gripped her jaw, pressing his fingers into her skin until she flinched. "Don't fight me, sweetheart."

Quincy was relieved when Eric told him Cashion had convinced the Rose Creek police to send a woman to stay with Sheila until the end of the day.

Apprehension raced through him as he read each printout aloud while Eric sped through the traffic towards Everett. "He had originally planned this whole thing for tomorrow morning," Quincy said. "I wonder what made him change his mind."

"Or how he got word to her," Sullivan added. "I think I'll call and check phone records. What's her cell number?"

"He likes taunting us," Eric said, before giving Sullivan the number. "Are you sure about Jace, Quincy? He seemed so...."

"I'm sure. That gut feeling you've been having is right. The two cases *are* connected. Do you know the intersection of Sanction Road and Mulberry Pass off 410?"

Eric glanced back. "I should've remembered that Sumner had a son when Mrs. Tate mentioned that her husband died when Jace was a boy. What threw me was her last name. She called her husband J.C."

Quincy spoke without looking up. "Jack Sumner's full name was Jack Cecil Sumner. Mrs. Tate changed their surname for obvious reasons."

"Quincy, would you read the one that tells where they would meet?"

" 'I will let this groveling insect exist until midnight Saturday unless you meet me at the intersection of Sanction Road and Mulberry Pass off 410. Saturday morning, ten sharp. If not, next package will be his skull.' "

"Got it," Sullivan yelled. "She got a call at six this morning from a pay phone in Auburn."

"That's where *Sumner* used to live," Eric said. "That intersection is a few miles north of there. Maybe we should bypass Mrs. Tate and call the sheriff out in Auburn."

"I'm on it," Sullivan said, already dialing.

Apprehension gnawed away at Quincy's confidence.

After what seemed like hours, Sullivan closed down his phone. "The sheriff will be waiting for us at the intersection."

-THIRTY-TWO-

Jace smiled and glanced around. He liked his old house. The trees were dense, the yard wild with grass and debris. They were far enough out of the city that nobody ever came around. He could actually keep her here for weeks and nobody would know.

Jace moved over to the bed and stared at her pretty, frightened face. What would it be like to kiss her?

He grabbed her collar and pinched her cheek hard enough for her to gasp. She began to struggle again. He pressed his thumb to the pulsating center of her throat. The fear made her pulse go wild, and it exhilarated him. He yanked her closer. Her breath was warm against his face.

"Please, don't," she gasped, trying to move away from him. "I think I'm hurt…inside. You kicked…."

He yanked her up from the bed. "You belong to me now. Not Peck, not Hadley, and not even Quincy Morgan. Do you hear me?"

She nodded her head in quick little jerks. He could feel her heart pumping like a scared rabbit, and tears brimmed on her lashes. He grabbed her by the hair and pressed his mouth hard against hers. He liked that flicker of fight that had come back into her eyes. She struggled frantically against him, but he held her fast. After a moment, he shoved her against the wall, and she screamed.

Her shrieks were maddening. The sounds reminded him of the moment his mother walked into the room and saw him standing beneath his hanging father.

Tremors passed through him in waves. He turned back and watched as she slid to the floor and, as best she could, being bound, curled into the fetal position.

Pain throbbed in Kendal's head and ribs. Her stomach churned, and she was having difficulty staying focused. She was thankful that Jace had left her legs unbound when she returned from a bathroom break, but had retied her wrists. She had to think—to figure out a way to get back to safety. Surely she could do it, now that she didn't have to worry about rescuing *him*.

Perhaps if he went to sleep, she could slip away. She pressed her back against a grimy wall in a room not much larger than a closet. *Lord, you've got to help me. Show me what to do now. I want to live.*

"Get up! It's time," he said. "I think you'll be more trouble than it's worth."

She swallowed hard. Her thoughts went to something Quincy had told her. *But we have to learn how to still ourselves in the midst of the storm.*

She took a deep breath and struggled to her feet, her trembling knees barely able to hold her up. If she was to find a way out of this mess she had to stay calm so that she could hear God's instructions. She took several deep breaths and looked straight into Jace's eyes.

"You don't have to do this, Jace. You don't have to be like your father."

"Yes, I do. You've got to die in the same way he did…in the same room. That's the only way I'll be free of him."

"I'm sorry about your father, Jace," she said, her voice quavering. "I'm sorry."

Without a word, Jace yanked her back towards the bedroom. She stumbled and fell to the floor near the living room. It was dusty and had very little furnishing.

Run.

Her heart quickened. She had heard it clearly?

Run now.

When Jace bent down to grab her again, she shoved him back with her feet and scrambled up. He stumbled backwards, hitting the wall. Her hands still bound, Kendal sprinted for the front door.

-THIRTY-THREE-

Quincy's heart raced with both apprehension and anticipation when he spotted Sheila's car parked at the intersection. Cashion apparently had pulled some pretty serious strings after Sullivan called in. A small army of sheriff's deputies was waiting for them. *Lord, please. I know you can save her.*

Quincy couldn't articulate any more than that. God knew his need. They followed behind several squad cars for about five miles down a muddy road. When they stopped along the road, Eric and Sullivan got out.

"The old shack is just over that next hill," a deputy said. "No one has lived there for years." They all started out. Quincy raced across open ground behind Eric and the others. His hand on the gun in his pocket was white-knuckled, and his temple throbbed with terror.

There were tracks leading up the soggy path. He heard a noise ahead and looked at Eric. A deputy spoke into his radio then continued up the trail. Jace Tate had better hope they found him first.

Those ahead of him were talking, but he couldn't hear any of it. He kept seeing Kendal's face from the night before. Her beautiful lovely face, whispering her affection.

Sweat collected in the hollow of his neck, and had plastered his clothes to his skin. For a few moments, all he could hear was his own blood ringing in his ears.

"Oh, God, please help us find her before he hurts her."

He jumped when he felt a hand clamp down on his shoulder. "Quincy, we see the SUV parked around back. We need you to stay here."

"No, Eric, I need to go to her. I know who her father is."

"Olivia told me," he said. "Right now, I need you to calm down and stay put. Otherwise, we're going to lose valuable time."

Forcefully recapturing his emotions, Quincy nodded and gestured toward the old house. "Hurry. Keep her safe."

Suddenly they heard gunfire in the wooded area behind the structure, and then a scream. All bets were off.

Kendal ran as fast as she could with bound wrists and an injured side, but Jace caught her. His jaw was rigid and his movements jerky as he slung her to the ground beneath an evergreen. After rolling her over, he emptied the contents of a burlap sack onto the ground beside them. She wanted to scream again, but she didn't have the strength. Her side felt as if it was on fire, and every other place on her body ached.

Once again, he bound her ankles with duct tape, as well as her mouth, heightening her dread. "No more noise," he spat. "No more."

He yanked her up and stood her against the trunk of another tree—one with an outstretched branch that he quickly tossed a rope over, securing it to the trunk. He disappeared for several seconds, and she tried to jump towards the wooded area. But she stumbled and tumbled back beneath the tree.

When he came back, he was holding a rusty five-gallon bucket. He grabbed her up by her collar and placed the noose around her neck. She started to struggle again.

"Mmmm mmm." She couldn't make him understand through her gag.

He laughed, lifting her and placing her feet onto the bucket he had turned down. "You better stop squirming now. When this pail falls, you're a goner."

Kendal closed her eyes and breathed as calmly as she could through her nose. She had to stay as still as she possibly could. But her breaths were coming too fast. Was she hyperventilating? She mustn't do that. She would fall and hang herself.

Oh, Lord, I need you. Forgive my double-mindedness. I choose to trust You now. If I have to die, please receive me into your glory. But if you don't mind…whisper once more to me on this side.

Suddenly, a calm washed over her and tears of relief streamed down her cheeks as she breathed in deeply and slowly exhaled. She had submitted herself to God's will. Fear was gone.

I am here. Do not fear.

Kendal felt herself slipping into a strange stupor, yet her legs did not buckle under her.

"You've got to mind your daddy now. Why don't you come on over here and sit on Daddy's lap?"

"No. You're not my daddy."

"Shut your mouth and do as I say. If you don't, I'll kill your daddy."

The noise she'd heard was someone else entering the house.

"C'mon, let's put your things back on. I won't let anything bad happen to you."

"Are you my daddy's friend?"

"Yes, I am."

Quincy's heart stopped when he saw the noose around her neck. *Oh, God, don't let that bucket tumble over.* Jace was busy attaching the other end of the rope to another tree. Rage blinding him to reason, Quincy raised Eric's handgun and aimed. Someone tackled him from the side and took the gun from his hands. He landed hard on the ground.

He watched in horror as Jace froze, having spotted movement. Suddenly, he fled up the slope into the thickness of trees. It took three deputies to restrain Quincy. Jace was getting away.

Quincy hollered, "Go after him! I won't follow."

After they rushed after Jace, Quincy ran to Kendal and carefully lifted her into his arms. He breathed deeply as relief flowed through him in waves. Eric hurried up and pulled the noose from around her neck.

"Thank God, she's all right," Eric said, as he continued to cut away his sister's bonds.

Quincy held her, pressing her protectively against his chest. She went limp. And though the gag had been taken away, she hadn't said a word. "Talk to me, baby. Please talk to me."

Did she even hear him? It must be shock or….

Eric pulled her from Quincy's arms and laid her on the ground. "Sis, I'm going to check you out. Make sure you're all right." Quincy watched as Eric gently poked and prodded over Kendal's body with the skill of a physician. When he touched her ribs, she moaned in pain.

Quincy winced. "What is it? What's wrong?"

Eric pulled up his sister's blouse to expose a mass of blue and purple bruises. "From the looks of her, he did a lot of hitting. Maybe even kicking."

Quincy groaned. "I'm taking her to a hospital."

They gently lifted her to her feet. She could hardly support herself. Quincy wanted to carry her, but the terrain was uneven. He bore as much of her weight beside him as he could.

"Sullivan, you got this?" Eric yelled behind him.

"Yeah, you go on and take care of your sister."

"She's holding her side with her free hand, Quincy. So I can't help you without hurting her."

"Walk in front of us in case I stumble with her."

Quincy paused a second and glanced back.

Fury had turned to cold rage, and was worse than anything he had ever experienced. If Jace Tate got near him now, he would crush him with his bare hands. The coldness of the thought terrified him.

When they reached the road, an ambulance was standing by. As the paramedics placed Kendal on the gurney, they heard a single gunshot.

-THIRTY-FOUR-

Kendal's heart filled with delight as Quincy carried her into the living room. His affectionate devotion humbled her.

"Wait right there," Sheila said, rushing upstairs. "I'll get a blanket."

The walls seemed to embrace her, and a rush of relief overflowed as she drank in the room. She was home.

She was thankful she only had to stay in the hospital for two days. "I can stand," she whispered to Quincy.

"I enjoy holding you," he said, brushing his lips against her cheek. "I don't ever want you away from me again."

As he placed her on the sofa, she playfully punched his chest with a loose fist. "And how do you suppose you'll manage that, Mr. Morgan?"

"Reach into my shirt pocket."

She smiled and glanced up into his face. "What?"

"There's a present for you in my pocket. I meant to give it to you a couple of days ago, but you managed to avoid me."

She chuckled lightly and complied, pulling out a small green velvet box. She held her breath, her heart dancing with anticipation.

"Open it."

With trembling hands, Kendal opened the box. A warm glow flowed through her as her eyes fell on the diamond. "Quincy, it's beautiful," she said, slipping it onto her finger.

"I'll say it is," Sheila said, coming in with a blanket in her arms.

"I love you, Kendal. And with all my heart I want to marry and take care of you the rest of my life."

She rested her head in the curve of his neck and breathed in the fresh scent of his aftershave. "I love you, too."

"So will you?"

Kendal glanced up at Sheila, whose eyes had become slits. She loved Quincy, and she wanted to be his wife, but were things happening too fast? She cleared her throat. "Quincy...."

"Here we go," Sheila interrupted, tossing the blanket onto the sofa and leaving the room.

Quincy gently covered Kendal with the blanket. "I want to marry you, Quincy. I just don't want you to get into something you'll later regret."

"I know this is right, Kendal. Don't you?"

She hesitated, lowering her gaze. "I believe it is. I think meeting you was the best thing that's ever happened to me. Now that I know who my birth parents were, I realize I don't need to replace what God gave me. I've been so busy thinking I missed something I assumed I was supposed to replace it."

Quincy smiled and nodded. "With a child."

"Yeah."

He squeezed her hand. "I think I understand that kind of desire. And maybe you were pursuing it for the wrong reason, but that doesn't mean the pursuit itself was wrong." He brought her fingers to his lips. She shivered as his lips touched her. "I would be honored if you would agree to have *my* baby. Of course, you'll have to marry me first."

She smiled, tears stinging her lids. "I would like that, Quincy."

"Thank God!"

They both jumped and turned at Sheila's noisy comment. After she turned to go into the kitchen, they both laughed.

"I'm so proud of you," Quincy whispered.

Her heart pounded as his arms gently enclosed her. Moments later, his mouth was on hers. She felt as if she was flying through the heavens on a cloud. When he drew away, he left her breathless.

"Tomorrow is the first of June. When would you like to jump the broom, my dear?"

She giggled, feeling like a child at Christmas. "As soon as possible," she whispered. "It is all over, right? I mean…."

Quincy smoothed the hair away from her face. "It's all over, baby. Your dad and Eric are making sure of that. They drove over to Olivia's, and should be back in a couple of hours." He stood and straightened. "Can I get you a glass of juice or tea?"

"Juice sounds good," she said, unable to stop looking at her ring. She lay back against the pillow and watched him walk towards the kitchen. She wished she could look at him like this the rest of her life.

It was hard to believe that Jace had chosen to go the way he assumed his father had—by taking his own life. Clearly, he had been unstable and had no real chance to stabilize without truly knowing the love and grace of God.

Two hours and a satisfying nap later, the living room filled with her friends and family. Her dad, Quincy, Eric, Olivia, Sheila and Jackson all sat around chatting and drinking coffee. She was still stretched out on the sofa, as Sheila and Quincy would let her do little more than go to the bathroom.

Stan handed Olivia a saucer with a slice of lemon pie. "I'm so glad this thing is over. I think my son was beginning to prepare a cell for *me*."

Jackson stood and pulled Sheila up with him. "All Kendal will have to do now is give a statement," Jackson said. "I don't think Hadley Jr. will be fit to stand trial any time soon."

Kendal gazed at them. They looked like two people with a secret plan. "Where are you going?"

"We're going out for a while," Sheila answered quickly. "I'll be back in time to help you into your pajamas."

They were out the door before she could ask any more questions.

Olivia placed her cup on the table and cleared her throat. "Kendal, there's something I'm a little curious about. How did you feel when you learned my brother was your biological father?"

Kendal glanced up at her father. He smiled warmly and nodded. "Maybe a little relieved," she admitted. "When I awakened in that room, I remembered a little of what happened twenty years ago. Perhaps it's the reason I closed it from my memory all these years."

Eric straightened. "What?"

Kendal looked into four faces, filled with anxiety, waiting for answers. With Sheila and Jackson gone, she saw no real need to keep quiet about what she had remembered back in Auburn.

She focused on Quincy. "Mr. Sumner didn't get a chance to hurt me," she said. "I remember he had undressed me, but somebody came in and stopped him. He told me to run as fast as I could. And made me promise to never look back."

"It wasn't that you *couldn't* remember," Quincy said, his face brightening. "You wouldn't remember. Your subconscious was simply obeying your rescuer. I wonder who he was?"

Stan got up and stood by the mantel. "I can take a guess."

Eric spoke next. "What? Who?"

"Senator Howard was the one who rescued me," Kendal said, glancing at Olivia. "When I left, Sumner was in a drunken stupor on the floor. The senator had punched him."

Quincy kissed her cheek. "Are you all right?"

She smiled. "I'm sorry, Olivia, but my brother has been looking for this answer for years. I'm very grateful to your brother for saving me from God knows what, but…" She let her words trail off.

"He must've been the one who hung Sumner," Eric said.

"But Kendal didn't see him do anything, did you, dear?" Olivia asked.

"No, I just ran like he told me," she admitted. "I remember him. I asked him if he was a friend of my daddy's. And he said, 'Yes'."

Kendal hadn't realized she was weeping until Quincy squeezed her hand. "Perhaps you've had enough for one day."

"I'm all right. Really."

"He's right, baby girl," Stan chimed in. "You need the rest."

"No, Dad. It's time you started talking to me like an adult. I want to know what you knew."

The older man swallowed hard and forced a chuckle. "Will was my friend. He and Olivia were always willing to help with anything that concerned you. They said it was because they had been so fond of Stephanie. The truth is…I guess I suspected all along. I didn't know for certain, and didn't really want to. I didn't feel they were a threat to my family, and reasoned that confronting Will might poison a perfectly good friendship."

"That's right," Eric said. "He helped with the lawsuit against the newspaper, didn't he?"

Stan gazed intently at his son. "As a matter of fact, he did. He handled the whole thing. I was too torn up."

"C'mon. I want you to rest up," Quincy whispered. "We're flying back east in a week, remember? Aunt Barbara will fuss over you like nobody's business."

Olivia cleared her throat once again. "They say confession is good for the soul. I must admit I've known about you before you were born,

Kendal. Sumner was blackmailing my brother. When he kidnapped you, Will flew in and vanished for several days. I wasn't aware he was the one who rescued you, and I don't know if I'm ready to accept the idea that he may have killed." The older woman lowered her head. "I suppose anything is possible. He *did* love you."

"Okay," Eric said. "I don't know what to do with all this. I suppose I need to discuss it with my supervisors, but I can't see muddying a man's name on pure conjecture. After all, if Kendal's memories are true, it was simply a matter of a man protecting his daughter. Right?"

"My brother's dead, Agent. If the truth must come out, then so be it. You go ahead and talk with the authorities. I'll be happy to help in any way I can."

"Thank you," Eric said, breathing a sigh of relief. "Now, when is this wedding Sheila was singing about?"

Quincy grinned. "If it's all right with the congressman, as soon as we can push it through. In about three weeks."

"It's fine with me. I think you all know I've decided to leave the Hill. I've placed my house in Spokane on the market and I plan to move back here to Seattle."

Olivia cleared her throat. "Kendal, I suppose you know by now that I've purchased all the Hadley shares. I'm handing them over to you. I know Will meant for you to have them all along."

"But I don't need...I mean, I have my own."

"I know, dear. But since your father is unemployed, perhaps you would consider giving him the job of running the company for you. And I want you and Quincy to know that my private jet is at your disposal as long as you need it."

Quincy grinned. "That's very generous."

Kendal frowned and looked around at each face. "What just happened here?"

Everybody laughed, and Quincy kissed her forehead. "I agree with your father," Olivia said. "You've had too much for one day. If you don't mind, I'll help you get to bed."

"I can...."

"This may be the last time I can say this with such authority—Kendal Diane," Stan said, "go to bed."

EPILOGUE

One year later

Quincy's hand gripped hers with firm intensity. "Take some deep breaths, baby. We're just about there."

Kendal looked across the room at her infant son as she prepared to deliver his twin. "Easy for you to say. You're not turning inside out to bring them into the world."

He brushed her cheek and forehead with a kiss that projected all his hope, his strength, and his love. "I'm with you in spirit, baby. Get ready, now. This is it."

The contraction started and grew. She stared into his eyes and squeezed down on the pain with everything in her. Then the pressure released.

"Hold it. Wait," the doctor cautioned.

She puffed frantically as people moved into position. Quincy's hand pressed between her shoulder blades, solid and reassuring. His other palm stroked her head. "You're so beautiful. You're doing great."

"Just a little push, Kendal," the doctor said. "Slowly."

Kendal did. The sensation of silent applause was unforgettable as Tessa Stephanie took her first breath and joined her brother, Stanley William.

Kendal stared at Quincy's face as he watched them aspirate her tiny nostrils, and then he cut the cord himself. Tears glistened in his eyes, making them appear a deeper shade of brown. He turned to her, his throat working soundlessly, then bent and kissed her softly. "We have twins, Kendal. A boy and a girl."

A nurse tucked the bundled babies into each of Kendal's arms. Her heart swelled, thankful that she had waited on God to have her children the way He willed.

"Thank you, Lord," she whispered, staring in turn at each child's face. She giggled, thrilled with every feature—the thick black hair and pinched caramel brown faces. Quincy took their son and smiled while she ran a finger along their daughter's cheek.

Quincy pressed his lips to her forehead, his thankful thoughts certain to match hers.

ABOUT THE AUTHOR

Annetta P. Lee grew up in Starkville, Mississippi on her grandparents' farm. She later moved to Oklahoma City, where she met and married her husband, Kenneth. She works as Editorial Assistant for Lifesprings Resources, the publishing branch of the International Pentecostal Holiness Church.

After graduating from The Institute of Children's Literature in 1997, Annetta obtained a life long dream of becoming a published novelist. She also finds great pleasure in serving her community and church as a lay-minister.

Ms. Lee has been a popular guest on numerous radio programs and has lectured at Mississippi State University, as well as to church groups and conferences.

"It is very gratifying," she says, "to channel the passion for writing through the eyes of my faith."

2007 Publication Schedule

January

Corporate Seduction
A.C. Arthur
ISBN-13: 978-1-58571-238-0
ISBN-10: 1-58571-238-8
$9.95

A Taste of Temptation
Reneé Alexis
ISBN-13: 978-1-58571-207-6
ISBN-10: 1-58571-207-8
$9.95

February

The Perfect Frame
Beverly Clark
ISBN-13: 978-1-58571-240-3
ISBN-10: 1-58571-240-X
$9.95

Ebony Angel
Deatri King-Bey
ISBN-13: 978-1-58571-239-7
ISBN-10: 1-58571-239-6
$9.95

March

Sweet Sensations
Gwendolyn Bolton
ISBN-13: 978-1-58571-206-9
ISBN-10: 1-58571-206-X
$9.95

Crush
Crystal Hubbard
ISBN-13: 978-1-58571-243-4
ISBN-10: 1-58571-243-4
$9.95

April

Secret Thunder
Annetta P. Lee
ISBN-13: 978-1-58571-204-5
ISBN-10: 1-58571-204-3
$9.95

Blood Seduction
J.M. Jeffries
ISBN-13: 978-1-58571-237-3
ISBN-10: 1-58571-237-X
$9.95

May

Lies Too Long
Pamela Ridley
ISBN-13: 978-1-58571-246-5
ISBN-10: 1-58571-246-9
$13.95

Two Sides to Every Story
Dyanne Davis
ISBN-13: 978-1-58571-248-9
ISBN-10: 1-58571-248-5
$9.95

June

One of These Days
Michele Sudler
ISBN-13: 978-1-58571-249-6
ISBN-10: 1-58571-249-3
$9.95

Who's That Lady?
Andrea Jackson
ISBN-13: 978-1-58571-190-1
ISBN-10: 1-58571-190-X
$9.95

2007 Publication Schedule (continued)

July

Heart of the Phoenix
A.C. Arthur
ISBN-13: 978-1-58571-242-7
ISBN-10: 1-58571-242-6
$9.95

Do Over
Celya Bowers
ISBN-13: 978-1-58571-241-0
ISBN-10: 1-58571-241-8
$9.95

It's Not Over Yet
J.J. Michael
ISBN-13: 978-1-58571-245-8
ISBN-10: 1-58571-245-0
$9.95

August

The Fires Within
Beverly Clark
ISBN-13: 978-1-58571-244-1
ISBN-10: 1-58571-244-2
$9.95

Stolen Kisses
Dominiqua Douglas
ISBN-13: 978-1-58571-247-2
ISBN-10: 1-58571-247-7
$9.95

September

Small Whispers
Annetta P. Lee
ISBN-13: 978-158571-251-9
ISBN-10: 1-58571-251-5
$6.99

Always You
Crystal Hubbard
ISBN-13: 978-158571-252-6
ISBN-10: 1-58571-252-3
$6.99

October

Not His Type
Chamein Canton
ISBN-13: 978-158571-253-3
ISBN-10: 1-58571-253-1
$6.99

Many Shades of Gray
Dyanne Davis
ISBN-13: 978-158571-254-0
ISBN-10: 1-58571-254-X
$6.99

November

When I'm With You
LaConnie Taylor-Jones
ISBN-13: 978-158571-250-2
ISBN-10: 1-58571-250-7
$6.99

The Mission
Pamela Leigh Starr
ISBN-13: 978-158571-255-7
ISBN-10: 1-58571-255-8
$6.99

December

One in A Million
Barbara Keaton
ISBN-13: 978-158571-257-1
ISBN-10: 1-58571-257-4
$6.99

The Foursome
Celya Bowers
ISBN-13: 978-158571-256-4
ISBN-10: 1-58571-256-6
$6.99

Other Genesis Press, Inc. Titles

A Dangerous Deception	J.M. Jeffries	$8.95
A Dangerous Love	J.M. Jeffries	$8.95
A Dangerous Obsession	J.M. Jeffries	$8.95
A Dangerous Woman	J.M. Jeffries	$9.95
A Dead Man Speaks	Lisa Jones Johnson	$12.95
A Drummer's Beat to Mend	Kei Swanson	$9.95
A Happy Life	Charlotte Harris	$9.95
A Heart's Awakening	Veronica Parker	$9.95
A Lark on the Wing	Phyliss Hamilton	$9.95
A Love of Her Own	Cheris F. Hodges	$9.95
A Love to Cherish	Beverly Clark	$8.95
A Lover's Legacy	Veronica Parker	$9.95
A Pefect Place to Pray	I.L. Goodwin	$12.95
A Risk of Rain	Dar Tomlinson	$8.95
A Twist of Fate	Beverly Clark	$8.95
A Will to Love	Angie Daniels	$9.95
Acquisitions	Kimberley White	$8.95
Across	Carol Payne	$12.95
After the Vows	Leslie Esdaile	$10.95
(Summer Anthology)	T.T. Henderson	
	Jacqueline Thomas	
Again My Love	Kayla Perrin	$10.95
Against the Wind	Gwynne Forster	$8.95
All I Ask	Barbara Keaton	$8.95
Ambrosia	T.T. Henderson	$8.95
An Unfinished Love Affair	Barbara Keaton	$8.95
And Then Came You	Dorothy Elizabeth Love	$8.95
Angel's Paradise	Janice Angelique	$9.95
At Last	Lisa G. Riley	$8.95
Best of Friends	Natalie Dunbar	$8.95
Between Tears	Pamela Ridley	$12.95
Beyond the Rapture	Beverly Clark	$9.95
Blaze	Barbara Keaton	$9.95

Other Genesis Press, Inc. Titles (continued)

Blood Lust	J. M. Jeffries	$9.95
Bodyguard	Andrea Jackson	$9.95
Boss of Me	Diana Nyad	$8.95
Bound by Love	Beverly Clark	$8.95
Breeze	Robin Hampton Allen	$10.95
Broken	Dar Tomlinson	$24.95
The Business of Love	Cheris Hodges	$9.95
By Design	Barbara Keaton	$8.95
Cajun Heat	Charlene Berry	$8.95
Careless Whispers	Rochelle Alers	$8.95
Cats & Other Tales	Marilyn Wagner	$8.95
Caught in a Trap	Andre Michelle	$8.95
Caught Up In the Rapture	Lisa G. Riley	$9.95
Cautious Heart	Cheris F Hodges	$8.95
Caught Up	Deatri King Bey	$12.95
Chances	Pamela Leigh Starr	$8.95
Cherish the Flame	Beverly Clark	$8.95
Class Reunion	Irma Jenkins/John Brown	$12.95
Code Name: Diva	J.M. Jeffries	$9.95
Conquering Dr. Wexler's Heart	Kimberley White	$9.95
Cricket's Serenade	Carolita Blythe	$12.95
Crossing Paths, Tempting Memories	Dorothy Elizabeth Love	$9.95
Cupid	Barbara Keaton	$9.95
Cypress Whisperings	Phyllis Hamilton	$8.95
Dark Embrace	Crystal Wilson Harris	$8.95
Dark Storm Rising	Chinelu Moore	$10.95
Daughter of the Wind	Joan Xian	$8.95
Deadly Sacrifice	Jack Kean	$22.95
Designer Passion	Dar Tomlinson	$8.95
Dreamtective	Liz Swados	$5.95
Ebony Butterfly II	Delilah Dawson	$14.95
Ebony Eyes	Kei Swanson	$9.95

Other Genesis Press, Inc. Titles (continued)

Echoes of Yesterday	Beverly Clark	$9.95
Eden's Garden	Elizabeth Rose	$8.95
Enchanted Desire	Wanda Y. Thomas	$9.95
Everlastin' Love	Gay G. Gunn	$8.95
Everlasting Moments	Dorothy Elizabeth Love	$8.95
Everything and More	Sinclair Lebeau	$8.95
Everything but Love	Natalie Dunbar	$8.95
Eve's Prescription	Edwina Martin Arnold	$8.95
Falling	Natalie Dunbar	$9.95
Fate	Pamela Leigh Starr	$8.95
Finding Isabella	A.J. Garrotto	$8.95
Forbidden Quest	Dar Tomlinson	$10.95
Forever Love	Wanda Thomas	$8.95
From the Ashes	Kathleen Suzanne	$8.95
	Jeanne Sumerix	
Gentle Yearning	Rochelle Alers	$10.95
Glory of Love	Sinclair LeBeau	$10.95
Go Gentle into that Good Night	Malcom Boyd	$12.95
Goldengroove	Mary Beth Craft	$16.95
Groove, Bang, and Jive	Steve Cannon	$8.99
Hand in Glove	Andrea Jackson	$9.95
Hard to Love	Kimberley White	$9.95
Hart & Soul	Angie Daniels	$8.95
Havana Sunrise	Kymberly Hunt	$9.95
Heartbeat	Stephanie Bedwell-Grime	$8.95
Hearts Remember	M. Loui Quezada	$8.95
Hidden Memories	Robin Allen	$10.95
Higher Ground	Leah Latimer	$19.95
Hitler, the War, and the Pope	Ronald Rychiak	$26.95
How to Write a Romance	Kathryn Falk	$18.95
I Married a Reclining Chair	Lisa M. Fuhs	$8.95
I'm Gonna Make You Love Me	Gwyneth Bolton	$9.95
Indigo After Dark Vol. I	Nia Dixon/Angelique	$10.95

Other Genesis Press, Inc. Titles (continued)

Other Genesis Press, Inc. Titles (continued)

Matters of Life and Death	Lesego Malepe, Ph.D.	$15.95
Meant to Be	Jeanne Sumerix	$8.95
Midnight Clear	Leslie Esdaile	$10.95
(Anthology)	Gwynne Forster	
	Carmen Green	
	Monica Jackson	
Midnight Magic	Gwynne Forster	$8.95
Midnight Peril	Vicki Andrews	$10.95
Misconceptions	Pamela Leigh Starr	$9.95
Misty Blue	Dyanne Davis	$9.95
Montgomery's Children	Richard Perry	$14.95
My Buffalo Soldier	Barbara B. K. Reeves	$8.95
Naked Soul	Gwynne Forster	$8.95
Next to Last Chance	Louisa Dixon	$24.95
Nights Over Egypt	Barbara Keaton	$9.95
No Apologies	Seressia Glass	$8.95
No Commitment Required	Seressia Glass	$8.95
No Ordinary Love	Angela Weaver	$9.95
No Regrets	Mildred E. Riley	$8.95
Notes When Summer Ends	Beverly Lauderdale	$12.95
Nowhere to Run	Gay G. Gunn	$10.95
O Bed! O Breakfast!	Rob Kuehnle	$14.95
Object of His Desire	A. C. Arthur	$8.95
Office Policy	A. C. Arthur	$9.95
Once in a Blue Moon	Dorianne Cole	$9.95
One Day at a Time	Bella McFarland	$8.95
Only You	Crystal Hubbard	$9.95
Outside Chance	Louisa Dixon	$24.95
Passion	T.T. Henderson	$10.95
Passion's Blood	Cherif Fortin	$22.95
Passion's Journey	Wanda Thomas	$8.95
Past Promises	Jahmel West	$8.95
Path of Fire	T.T. Henderson	$8.95

Other Genesis Press, Inc. Titles (continued)

Path of Thorns	Annetta P. Lee	$9.95
Peace Be Still	Colette Haywood	$12.95
Picture Perfect	Reon Carter	$8.95
Playing for Keeps	Stephanie Salinas	$8.95
Pride & Joi	Gay G. Gunn	$8.95
Promises to Keep	Alicia Wiggins	$8.95
Quiet Storm	Donna Hill	$10.95
Reckless Surrender	Rochelle Alers	$6.95
Red Polka Dot in a World of Plaid	Varian Johnson	$12.95
Rehoboth Road	Anita Ballard-Jones	$12.95
Reluctant Captive	Joyce Jackson	$8.95
Rendezvous with Fate	Jeanne Sumerix	$8.95
Revelations	Cheris F. Hodges	$8.95
Rise of the Phoenix	Kenneth Whetstone	$12.95
Rivers of the Soul	Leslie Esdaile	$8.95
Rock Star	Rosyln Hardy Holcomb	$9.95
Rocky Mountain Romance	Kathleen Suzanne	$8.95
Rooms of the Heart	Donna Hill	$8.95
Rough on Rats and Tough on Cats	Chris Parker	$12.95
Scent of Rain	Annetta P. Lee	$9.95
Second Chances at Love	Cheris Hodges	$9.95
Secret Library Vol. 1	Nina Sheridan	$18.95
Secret Library Vol. 2	Cassandra Colt	$8.95
Shades of Brown	Denise Becker	$8.95
Shades of Desire	Monica White	$8.95
Shadows in the Moonlight	Jeanne Sumerix	$8.95
Sin	Crystal Rhodes	$8.95
Sin and Surrender	J.M. Jeffries	$9.95
Sinful Intentions	Crystal Rhodes	$12.95
So Amazing	Sinclair LeBeau	$8.95
Somebody's Someone	Sinclair LeBeau	$8.95

Other Genesis Press, Inc. Titles (continued)

Someone to Love	Alicia Wiggins	$8.95
Song in the Park	Martin Brant	$15.95
Soul Eyes	Wayne L. Wilson	$12.95
Soul to Soul	Donna Hill	$8.95
Southern Comfort	J.M. Jeffries	$8.95
Still the Storm	Sharon Robinson	$8.95
Still Waters Run Deep	Leslie Esdaile	$8.95
Stories to Excite You	Anna Forrest/Divine	$14.95
Subtle Secrets	Wanda Y. Thomas	$8.95
Suddenly You	Crystal Hubbard	$9.95
Sweet Repercussions	Kimberley White	$9.95
Sweet Tomorrows	Kimberly White	$8.95
Taken by You	Dorothy Elizabeth Love	$9.95
Tattooed Tears	T. T. Henderson	$8.95
The Color Line	Lizzette Grayson Carter	$9.95
The Color of Trouble	Dyanne Davis	$8.95
The Disappearance of Allison Jones	Kayla Perrin	$5.95
The Honey Dipper's Legacy	Pannell-Allen	$14.95
The Joker's Love Tune	Sidney Rickman	$15.95
The Little Pretender	Barbara Cartland	$10.95
The Love We Had	Natalie Dunbar	$8.95
The Man Who Could Fly	Bob & Milana Beamon	$18.95
The Missing Link	Charlyne Dickerson	$8.95
The Price of Love	Sinclair LeBeau	$8.95
The Smoking Life	Ilene Barth	$29.95
The Words of the Pitcher	Kei Swanson	$8.95
Three Wishes	Seressia Glass	$8.95
Through the Fire	Seressia Glass	$9.95
Ties That Bind	Kathleen Suzanne	$8.95
Tiger Woods	Libby Hughes	$5.95
Time is of the Essence	Angie Daniels	$9.95
Timeless Devotion	Bella McFarland	$9.95
Tomorrow's Promise	Leslie Esdaile	$8.95

Order Form

Mail to: Genesis Press, Inc.
P.O. Box 101
Columbus, MS 39703

Name _____

Address _____

City/State _____ Zip _____

Telephone _____

Ship to (if different from above)

Name _____

Address _____

City/State _____ Zip _____

Telephone _____

Credit Card Information

Credit Card # _____ ☐ Visa   ☐ Mastercard

Expiration Date (mm/yy) _____ ☐ AmEx   ☐ Discover

Qty.	Author	Title	Price	Total

Use this order form, or call 1-888-INDIGO-1	
Total for books	_____
Shipping and handling: $5 first two books, $1 each additional book	
Total S & H	_____
Total amount enclosed	_____

Mississippi residents add 7% sales tax